THE LAST DROP OF BLOOD

J. STEPHEN FUNK

authorHOUSE®

AuthorHouse™
1663 Liberty Drive
Bloomington, IN 47403
www.authorhouse.com
Phone: 1 (800) 839-8640

Published by AuthorHouse   12/03/2015

ISBN: 978-1-5049-2352-1 (sc)
ISBN: 978-1-5049-2353-8 (e)

DEDICATION

I dedicate whatever there is good in this book to my wife and children and their families. It would be easy for my wife, Shelley, and my children, Alan and Debbie, to think that I only have room in my heart for the grandkids, Noah, Tommy, Rachel and Isabel. In fact, I am filled with admiration and love for them all and for my daughter-in-law, Michelle. I'm grateful to them for all that they do and the fine people they all are.

JSF

Acknowledgements

I am grateful to my astute and talented daughter, Debbie, and my devoted and diligent wife, Shelley for their huge contributions of time and effort in the editing of "The Last Drop of Blood." I can't imagine it would've been publishable without their help.

JSF

Chapter One

Of course Herb Fletcher worried. He checked in at 11:30 p.m. that night at the Maternity nursing station on the fourth floor of Woodside Hospital on the north side of Seattle. Nurse Lois Hillibrand, a warm and friendly, grey haired, middle-aged woman brought him in. Myra, his small but innocently attractive, seventeen year-old wife wasn't feeling pain anymore, but she still bled fifteen days after childbirth. Myra lay there, dark and weak like an exhausted angel. Where was the funny, cute, happy-go-lucky sweetheart he took as his wife? A big, African-American teddy bear, himself inexperienced with health crises, Herb didn't know how to cope emotionally with his young bride's weakness and decline. In spite of all the doctor's efforts and his assurances, the bleeding continued.

Herb trusted and relied on Dr. Richardson, the eminent Kevin Richardson, tall and white-haired, dapper and dignified in a sparkling white shirt and gray pinstripe suit. Even the wrinkles in his face said age and wisdom, a serious and responsible man. Herb never doubted a word from his mouth.

Once, he looked Herb right in the eye. "Herb," he said, "don't worry. I'll tell you what I told your wife. It's not unusual for there to be a little tissue tear in a rough delivery. If it was worse, I would have gone back in, but it's safer not to when there's no emergency. Baby Melissa was big for such a little mama. The coagulant will eventually allow the tears to heal, and the bleeding will stop. I could re-operate and maybe find a bleeder, but that would be a damaging strain on Myra and an expense you guys don't need. Okay?"

Herb couldn't argue with Dr. Richardson. Everyone said he was the top OB/GYN on the north side, and the nurses worshipped him. Herb told Myra how lucky she was that Richardson was her doc.

Herb took Myra's small hands in his and kissed her again. She looked up at him, so sad, weak and depressed. "I want to go home, Herb. My arms are aching to hold Melissa. I see her so rarely. I'm not getting any better here. If I'm going to die, I want to die at home."

Herb's face showed his shock. "No, Myra, don't say that. You're not going to die. You've got the best doc in town."

"If you say so. I'm not getting any better, Herb. I like Dr. Richardson, but he doesn't know everything. Maybe we could get a referral for another doctor."

"Myra, you and I aren't as smart as he is. If some other doc said Richardson was wrong, I wouldn't believe it. I'd still believe in Richardson."

She didn't have the energy to argue anymore, and nurse Hillibrand gently took Herb's elbow and walked him out the door. She knew how important it was for Myra to spend time with Herb, but his visits put such a physical strain on her. He went out carrying the weight of his unspoken fears, resisting the anxiety of possibly caring for Melissa by himself. He strained to convince himself he was confident. Otherwise, he couldn't convince Myra. After he stepped out of the lobby elevator, he unconsciously stopped at the newspaper kiosk and picked up the December 17, 1963 *Seattle PI*, dropping a dime in the slot. He headed across the dimly lit parking lot, past Dr. Richardson's bright, new, red Corvette on the way to his tired, old Ford pickup and drove off into the starless night.

Hillibrand didn't want her husband to get Myra overtired. She thought his visit would lift Myra's spirits, but the nurse remained anxious. Silently, Hillibrand promised she'd care for Myra as if she were her own daughter. She washed Myra and fed her and wouldn't let her take a step to the bathroom without holding her steady. Hillibrand cared for all her patients, but there was something about Myra that particularly tugged at her. Lois

Hillibrand was a tall, straight woman with a ramrod spine and a firmly fixed, worried look. She knew how to cope with the demands of the dictatorial doctors and didn't regard them as the demigods other nurses did. Patient welfare came before the doctors' pride. Herb knew how much she cared and placed all his trust in her and Dr. Richardson. He didn't understand why Myra was so skeptical.

That evening, nurse Hillibrand became alarmed. Myra Fletcher's bleeding had markedly increased though it was over two weeks past the childbirth. Lois never forgot her feelings for the innocent, trusting, little thing. Hillibrand could see so much of herself as a young mother 25 years ago in Myra. Dr. Richardson, a medical and community powerhouse, kept Myra in the hospital all this time, still bleeding slowly, controlling it with Pitocin coagulant. Hillibrand heard Dr. Richardson assuring the anxious husband, Herb. "It will be fine. It will gradually taper off, and she'll be breastfeeding Melissa at home. You can relax." Hillibrand couldn't imagine why he didn't do a D&C, but her tongue was quiet. Despite her concerns, she knew her place.

But then someone called in the Quality Control Chairman, Dr. Elliott Karel. When Charge Nurse, Sue Steinman asked who called, Hillibrand swore it wasn't her. Despite her concerns, she'd never go beyond her authority and stick out her neck.

When Karel met with Richardson, Hillibrand couldn't hear the conversation except some yelling after which, Richardson stormed out. He must have swallowed another downer, because he came back smiling and relaxed, checked Myra and went back out after saying, "I'm going to be unavailable for a while." That ended up being 45 minutes.

Hillibrand's helper, a young student nurse, Nelda Fox, wondered where Richardson went when he was medicated. Lois wasn't about to comment to Nelda about Richardson's apparent drug use, not knowing who Nelda might pass that information on to. When Nelda asked, "Is that common?" Hillibrand said, "You'll learn not to see what you aren't meant to see."

Nelda almost seemed a light skinned Myra, small, pretty, intense and a little nervous. Hillibrand understood how dependent on her Nelda was, and training Nelda included more than the nursing procedures by the book. Lois began to sense there was more to Nelda than was apparent and suspected Nelda was the one who called Dr. Karel.

Richardson's little break in his office meant he'd have to stay late. That night, when he finally appeared to be totally exhausted and medicated, he lay down in the doctor's lounge, probably useless in the event of any emergency. It was the worst possible night for him to dose himself up.

Hillibrand helped Myra on the way to the bathroom. The bleeding increased by the time she helped Myra struggle out of the bathroom. Blood trailed across the floor on her way back to bed. Myra looked directly into Hillibrand's eyes. She couldn't tell how much of what she saw in Myra's look was fear and how much was pain. Myra could only manage a weak, "I'm sorry," apologizing for making extra work. Hillibrand felt the anger rising in her, having to carry Dr. Richardson's and the hospital's guilt for the shoddy treatment, even while doing her best. She quickly checked Myra's pulse, which was elevated and thready and her blood pressure which had declined. Respiration was still normal, but she saw an emergency coming. Hillibrand called Dr. Richardson in the doctor's lounge. Never mind that he had done 5 deliveries that day, Myra's life was on the line, and Hillibrand needed him stat!

She could tell from his phone manner, he was still under the influence of the self-prescribed meds, sounding calm, relaxed and content. Nothing worried him when he had his meds in him, Quaaludes, Hillibrand guessed. "Okay, up the dosage. Write it on my pad, and order another pint of blood."

"Doctor, I can't do that. I could go to jail for writing a prescription."

"Don't be such a worrier, I'll back you up, but I'll tell you what. Bring my pad and I'll initial a few scripts for you, and then you won't have to bother me again tonight. I have to get some sleep or I'm going to end up on your ward." He sounded as if he were on the verge of laughing at his little joke.

Hillibrand grabbed up the pad and ran full tilt to the staircase, up two flights, then down the hallway to the doctor's lounge. She knocked loudly, and Richardson opened the door a crack with his hand held out. There was a happy, sleepy smile on his still handsome face, and his mop of white hair was disheveled and carefree. He signed one sheet after another, giving Hillibrand free reign to prescribe whatever she wanted for whomever she wanted. This was insanely, irresponsibly careless, but that wasn't her worry right then. She had to save Myra's life, because nobody else would. Richardson's last words as she was rushing away were, "That will do it. Don't call me again unless it's absolutely urgent."

As soon as Hillibrand got back to her, panting hard and with her heart pumping furiously, Myra asked, "Is it going to be okay? Why isn't Doctor Richardson here?"

Hillibrand just looked, but Nelda felt obligated to say something. "Don't worry, Myra, we're taking care of it."

Myra laid her head down either from trust or sheer exhaustion. Hillibrand sent Nelda to the pharmacy with the prescription for an increase in the Pitocin and another pint of AB positive. The head pharmacist immediately called Hillibrand, asking "What's this? You're writing prescriptions?"

"Dr. Richardson is very tired and has to get some sleep. He had me write it for him, and he signed it. It's a valid prescription. You can call him at the doctor's lounge if you need confirmation."

Hillibrand knew he wouldn't have the nerve to call Richardson. In just a few minutes, Nelda ran back into the ward, and the two of them immediately went to work. First they injected the coagulant meds and then the blood. They could see Myra's vitals go back to normal and the flow of blood gradually lessen. Finally, they were able to get her and the room cleaned up, free of the fear she would die in front of them while they changed the bloody sheets and mopped the floor. They made the room look like a normal, ordinary ward, not the scene of a medical breakdown. Dr. Richardson would be pleased, but at that moment they didn't care much about his opinion. The crisis forced Hillibrand to consider the consequences if Myra died later. She set out to back up her actions in case Richardson might need a scapegoat.

She charted in detail everything that had occurred. Before going out the door, she told Nelda to watch the patient carefully. Nelda was nervous with the burden of caring for a patient who only a few minutes before had been at risk for immediate death. With her focus on the patient, she didn't see Lois smuggle the chart out of the room. With remarkable and fortunate prescience, Hillibrand slipped into the copy room, heart pounding, made her copies and got back out, with no one the wiser. She feared what might be coming and refused to be anyone's sucker. She was sure Dr. Richardson was the type to look for someone else to blame if his incompetence killed the patient. He was not above altering the record that would prove his failures and forcing the staff to cover for one of its most prominent and powerful members. Hillibrand, however, wouldn't put anything past any of them. Doctors rewrote charts at Woodside when the history wasn't pretty. This time, she hid a copy to protect the truth.

It wasn't as though she only had one patient to worry about. In the slow, dark of the late night with no visitors, and the doctors at the north end of Lake Washington sleeping, she could expect mostly to rest on her shift. Not this time. Mrs. Zoeller's gastro-intestinal reflux was acting up again, and she wasn't sleeping. The antacids worked for her until they didn't. Laura Branson belonged in a psych ward. She shuddered and cried that night, in fear of something she couldn't identify and complained of some sort of pain she couldn't describe. Hillibrand's duties were getting hectic, and she worried about her own problematic blood sugar level. She was too busy to check it, because she put her patients first.

Hillibrand wore down as the end of her shift neared and hoped Glenn Yee, next up, would get there early. Lois plunked herself down in a corner chair, feeling the last hours of her shift eating into her store of energy. Myra Fletcher was now sleeping, if rather fitfully. The last BP was down but not dangerously. Hillibrand felt as though she were abandoning Myra, when she left before Glenn arrived. Charge Nurse, Sue Steinman, knowing her diabetic condition, told her, "Go, I'll see you're covered till Glenn gets here. You're past your limit. Don't worry."

Hillibrand doubted how much Sue could do if the bleeding got worse and Emergency was too busy to help. She doubted Nelda, only a student, could cope with such a crisis. Hillibrand, down to her last reserves of energy, said a little prayer in her mind for Myra as she folded herself into her heavy parka and headed out to her car in the cold, northwest night. She could only console herself with having gone almost nose to nose with Nelda to protect Myra.

"You monitor Myra, even between vitals checks: breathing, complexion. If you even see her getting pale check her BP. Don't you dare let her go sour. Call the ER or call a code if you have to."

* * * * * *

Nelda felt nearly in a panic. This was responsibility she'd never had to bear and wasn't sure she was ready. She sat by Myra, watching her intently. Myra asked for help, and when she helped Myra to the bathroom again, Myra slipped and gasped in pain. Nelda saw a little spurt of blood as she helped Myra back to bed. The call to Dr. Richardson went unanswered. She waited five frightful minutes and called again. No response. That left the unthinkable. Sue Steinman had once chewed her up one side and down the other for calling a code when, supposedly, she didn't need to.

"When the attending is there, you call him if there's a problem. The ER people have their own issues to deal with."

"ER, nurse speaking."

"This is Nelda Fox in 417. I've got a patient with serious bleeding. Young woman, Myra Fletcher. I can't reach the attending, Dr. Richardson, and this is a real emergency. The pulse is up and the BP and respirations are down and I don't know anything I can do."

"I'd like to help you, but we've got our hands full down here."

Nelda didn't know what to do and struggled with the new crisis. "This is life and death! We need emergency help here right now! We need a pint of blood, stat, AB positive."

"Okay, if I can't get the attending, I'll send someone there. What room you said?"

"417, now please. Right now!" Then Nelda heard the dial tone. Myra's BP dropped to 68/42, and her pallor showed it. Respiration dropped to seven per minute and became shallow. She injected another 30 ccs of Pitocin regardless of the prescription. She had no idea of anything else she could do. She just knew she didn't dare chart it. Then came a call. It was the ER. "Nurse Selvage at ER. We couldn't get the attending. What did you say was the blood type?"

"It's AB positive. Please. Hurry!" The BP and respiration continued to decline, almost to nothing and the pulse became weak and racing; Myra was going gray and her lips blue. Nelda fought back tears. She remembered when she saw a patient die before her, but not a young girl dying from simple neglect. She charted Myra's minimal signs of life, as best she could, until there wasn't another drop of blood, and she couldn't get any BP or pulse at all. Nelda gave a try at artificial respiration, but it was an idle gesture.

When Dr. Rosen and the med tech from ER burst in with the crash cart, the blood, the oxygen mask and tank, the injectables and the defib, Nelda, with heart pounding, shrank back away and looked over their shoulders. They jumped into action with Rosen in his ER cap and mask pumping feverishly on Myra's chest, the tech doing the injections and blood and then attaching electrodes. Despite the apparent ineffectiveness of their labors, they stuck with it. Finally, Rosen had to face it. The epinephrine, heart compression, oxygen and defibrillator had all failed. Myra, really just a child, was gone, her face a gray mask and her lips a ghastly blue.

When Rosen took off the mask and pushed back the cap, Nelda looked pleadingly into his blank face. She supposed he was satisfied he did all he could for half an hour. Perhaps his stoicism in the face of death was a defense mechanism. Do your job, whatever the result. You go back to the ER. There was no one for him to console, no one to whom he could apologize. Nelda suddenly realized her stomach had been clenched the whole time, and her gut was angry. For several minutes she concentrated on releasing the muscles. She couldn't unclench her mind and surrendered to a burst of grief, tears flowing freely in the bathroom until she gathered herself and could be a professional again.

A fill-in nurse finally arrived to take over, and Nelda stood down. It turned out a fender bender on the freeway jammed up Glenn Yee and kept him from getting there. As the perfectly calm Dr. Rosen and the tech walked out with the crash cart, Nelda wondered who was going to call Herb Fletcher. "Doctor, Mr. Fletcher might walk in here at almost any time; will you call him? I can't do it. He can't come here and see the empty bed."

Rosen smiled, perfectly placid. "Sure, no problem, Fox. Do it all the time."

Rather than call Herb Fletcher, Rosen went to the doctor's lounge and woke the dozing Richardson. He grabbed him by the collar to get his attention.

"The Fletcher girl has died. You better get her husband on the line before someone else does. I looked at the chart, and I can't believe you let her bleed day after day and didn't do a D&C. She bled out, and I couldn't do a damn thing. If there's an autopsy, I don't think that's going to be real healthy for you. If you're smart, you'll get Fletcher on the line and explain to him what an autopsy is. If you work it right, he might refuse it." Richardson's dull eyes told Rosen he wasn't getting through. Slowly Richardson fought his way through the Quaaludes, processed what Rosen had said and made the call to Herb Fletcher.

He sadly and gently gave the awful news to Herb Fletcher. He tried not to put too much blame on the nurses. "I'm not sure what Fox, the student nurse did. When Hillibrand went home, she left her in a tight spot. I'm sure Fox did the best she could, but something happened, and the bleeding got bad. You have the right to demand an autopsy. I can't promise what they'll do. Usually they can fix the body up enough for the funeral, but you don't want to know what they do in an autopsy. Your choice."

* * * * * *

Nurse Steinman reminded Nelda she needed another three months before she'd be off probationary status. On top of that, she said, "I'm keeping you with Lois Hillibrand, because you still need the guidance of an old pro." The assignment to Hillibrand had proven wonderful for Nelda, and she knew everything Nelda wanted to know. Nelda wanted to be as much like Hillibrand as possible. Hillibrand told her to be careful what she said. Even Hillibrand didn't have the courage to stand up to the establishment and its "conspiracy of silence." Those on the inside could see the medical malpractice, but if they knew what was good for them, they kept quiet. A nurse, or even a doctor who told the patient's family a doctor made a medical error, wouldn't last long in the medical community. Nelda was shocked that medical professionals would tolerate such thinking and was overwhelmed by the death of Fletcher.

Nelda didn't expect much help from her mother back in Iowa, and she didn't get much. Her reaction was right in line with what Lois had said.

"You keep your mouth shut. The girl is gone. You can't do anything for her. You can fight the hospital if you want, and then you'll come back home and be a dollar an hour babysitter again. You'll never meet successful people, the kind who can help you, maybe not have a family of your own, and all of your hard work in Washington will be wasted. If this Hillibrand doesn't want to stick her neck out, you don't either. You just stay away from it."

"Mom, I can't just pretend it didn't happen; Richardson will do it again, and the hospital will let him. Young girls will die."

"Fine, Nelda, I'll get your room ready for you, because you're soon going to be coming back home."

Nelda had a strange, dissociated feeling, like drowning in a dream, a vague, free floating fear she didn't understand. She felt like she was going crazy.

* * * * * *

The door plate said Elliott Karel, Director of Quality Control. Rosen dropped the charts on Dr. Karel's crowded desk with little comment. "I think you need to look at this, and you might want to talk to Richardson before this blows up. I believe I warned you about his Quaaludes."

Karel knew Richardson all too well and wasn't anxious to confront him no matter what Rosen said. And he knew Rosen would never rock the boat. He had just dropped the mess on Karel's desk and left. It was going to come down to either facing off with Richardson and all his rich friends and political influence or burying it. How nice if he could just tell Richardson to go somewhere that doesn't mind drug addicted doctors and carelessness. Karel's assignment included keeping the hospital running no matter how incompetent the staff. He knew very well the staff didn't worry about what would be nice for him. He hated the cover-up part of his job. He wanted to go the most prudent route and deal honestly with malpractice, but he gave up on that long ago. Confronting Richardson wasn't an option. Richardson would win any face-off and run Karel out of town. He'd seen that kind of battle played out before and remembered what happened to Dr. Martens.

CHAPTER TWO

Dr. Richardson didn't think he could face Karel without the Quaaludes. The only question was 150 mg or 300. He feared a real food fight and knew he could lose control if Karel came down on him. He decided 300 would keep the stress level down where it ought to be, but he'd be too close to the edge of total incoherence, so he settled on 150. The mustachioed, pudgy, balding Karel gave him a big smile and a firm handshake and calmly looked him right in the eye, so Richardson thought maybe he wouldn't have to get tough. "Well, Kevin, pretty bad result, real shame, young girl. So what happened?"

That was a milder response than Richardson was anticipating. At first, he sat up close to Karel's institutional grey desk, leaning forward aggressively, and now, less tense, he sat back in the hard chair, showing a friendly little smile. Karel too, had a buddy-buddy side, ready for a showdown, but was able to tone it down to meet Richardson on pleasanter turf.

"Don't know, Elliott, looks like that young nurse, Fox, didn't really monitor her. She should have been more careful when Myra went to the bathroom. Then again, maybe Hillibrand shouldn't have gone home. I don't think she'd let the girl have that accident in the bathroom. Everything was under control when Hillibrand left, it seemed. Maybe it's just bad luck. Yee didn't get there on time, and Hillibrand went home. Sometimes people die, and there just isn't anybody you can blame."

Gently, almost off hand, Karel asked, "Where were you, Kevin?"

Richardson restrained the instinctive snarl starting from his belly. "I was right where I was supposed to be. I told Hillibrand to call me if there was any problem. She had called me earlier, and I responded right away. That young Nelda Fox girl should have recognized how serious the condition was and called me, and I would've come just as fast. If she had, it wouldn't have ended up being necessary to call the code."

"She says she did call you."

"It's not so surprising she'd try to cover herself if she knew she was at fault for letting the Fletcher girl hurt herself."

"Did you talk to the husband?"

"Yeah, I called him as soon as I heard."

"Did you ask him if he agreed to an autopsy?"

"Yeah, I asked him. He said no."

"The problem I'm having, Kevin, is that Hillibrand and Fox seem pretty firm. I haven't talked to Rosen yet, but you need to know this has the potential to blow up. I need you to talk to Rosen, and maybe you can get this resolved. You have a pretty good grasp of what's important around here. I want you to get the hospital out of this, not just yourself. If you can do it within, say two weeks, I won't have to draw up the report. I'd rather sign off on your report."

Karel continued. "I have these chart notes, but I haven't really looked at them closely yet. Sounds like Hillibrand is putting the blame on you, and I doubt there's anything the young girl, Fox, can say that will help you. Too bad Fletcher refused the autopsy. It might have got you off the hook. Here, you study the records and see if there aren't any mistakes. Figure something out."

Karel finally took a breath and waited for Richardson to say something. Customarily, the staff papered over anything that could spoil the reputation of the hospital or doctors. Richardson understood Karel was giving him the chore. The bile rose in his throat as he contemplated having to clean up his own mess. Dealing with Hillibrand wasn't going to be a picnic. She was experienced, sharp and tough. He kept his mouth shut, picked up the chart notes and left. He went to the copy room, back to records to drop off the originals and then to his office at the North Seattle Professional Building. He told Maxine, his energetic assistant, to punch the copies and put them in binders. Then he called Cora, his wife, at home.

"We have to talk. I told you about my patient that died, Myra Fletcher. I've got a problem with the medical charts and the nurses. I'm not sure what to do."

"Kevin, you keep getting yourself into messes, and then you come to me to find a way out. It's those Quaaludes. I told you to get off them. My dad could handle his liquor, and you can't handle those damned Quaalude pills. You had a chance to get off them. You had to come to me about that Mickens girl, and then you didn't know what to do about Martens. I have a position in the community, and that means something. I'm not going to stand by and let you wreck it. You come home right now, and we'll deal with it."

He expected a response like that. She had the clear-eyed amorality and nerves of a career criminal, and Richardson depended on her. He could talk to her about things he couldn't tell anyone else. She had the backbone he didn't. When he got back to the palatial Montlake home, Louisa, the maid, had left for the day. He showed Cora the chart notes. She caught on quickly as he explained, and she called her dad, Dr. Jerry Alden, MD. He'd retired years ago, a big white-haired man, slow moving, ponderous and oozing authority. Alden quit medicine when he faced his own problems with malpractice. He never talked about how he maneuvered out of them. When he arrived, Cora sat him down on the couch with a Scotch in his hand and the copied records in his lap. He saw this, except for the medical records, as a replay of Mickens. The Mickens girl threatened Richardson, and Dr. Alden told him what to do and how to do it, and it worked out. She'd never trouble him again.

After looking at the records, Dr. Alden saw what Kevin needed to change to make himself appear innocent. It wasn't enough that the patient slipped on the way back from the bathroom without anyone's fault. The husband could still target Kevin for a malpractice claim. He shouldn't have allowed a bleeding problem to last fifteen days. Myra's slip may have exacerbated the bleeding. Alden wasn't willing to waste his time explaining to his son-in-law why he was guilty of malpractice. You shouldn't have to worry that nurses and doctors won't stand behind you, and he counted on their silence, but now, here and there, you'd find a nurse or a doctor who would undermine everybody. They called it "conscience." Alden felt his blood boil with anger at the medical community, but he blasted it out at Kevin, a fool who had more respect in the hospital community than he deserved.

"What can I expect from you? I told you to get off the Quaaludes, and I thought you were listening. It's just one thing after another. You slid by with Mickens, and now you have another mess to get out of. You're going to have to tell me everybody who knows about this problem and everybody involved in this Myra girl's death. Anybody who can testify against you is a threat. You know what to do about threats. If you listen to me, I can get you out of this, but you have to get off the damn Quaaludes. You hear me?" Richardson stared at him with a blank face.

I can hear him. It's easy for him to say, but he wouldn't *like the result if I didn't have my Quaaludes to keep me from killing him.*

They sat in the Richardsons' expansive living room with its oriental rugs and French impressionist art. Alden quizzed him closely about all the people who knew about his drug problem, all the people who could destroy his career, anyone who had knowledge of the Fletcher file. The sky had long since gone dark, and it was past dinner time when Alden finally heard enough. He felt exhausted but no more than Kevin. He knew they weren't finished.

"Okay, the hospital staff probably aren't going to blow the whistle on you, but I worry about this Hillibrand. She sounds tough. The young girl, Fox, won't be a problem if Hillibrand isn't. Karel and Rosen, no problem.

The head nurse, Steinman, she's had plenty of opportunities to blow the whistle. If she hasn't yet, she won't. I'd worry about your drug supplier up in Canada. And then there's Martens. You've put him in a spot by getting your Quaaludes in his name. If this blows up, it will probably come out that the Quaaludes were going to you, not Martens."

Alden laid it out as he had before with Mickens. Cora adamantly insisted Kevin had to follow her dad's plan as he had learned before. If Hillibrand didn't do exactly what Kevin told her, she'd pay the price. Richardson decided, when he went to the office the next day, he would have the chart note copies with him and write out how the nurses were going to change them. That was step one. Alden told him what step two had to be, and this time he quickly agreed. He didn't waste his energy arguing as he had with Mickens. He killed her because he had to, and it hurt to think about it. If there were no other reason for the Quaaludes, that would be enough. When Kevin finally promised to obey orders, Dr. Alden shook his hand pleasantly, finished his Scotch, put down the glass and went out the door with a big smile, as if he hadn't just ordered Kevin to do a terrible, unforgivable thing.

"Cora, how can I do that again? You know what I went through after Mickens. Are you going to put me through that again?"

"Kevin, my dad is right. You're gutless. You said you'd do it, and it worked out fine with her. You fought me on that. You knew I was right, and I'm right again. You can't face the messes you, yourself create. You do what Dad told you or I give up on you. My dad told me a long time ago you were a weakling. Now I can see he was right. I should have dumped you when you had that affair. You picked a real bimbo. She got what she deserved, trying to blackmail you."

* * * * * *

Richardson sat in his big desk chair bitterly pondering his problems. He officed on the fourth floor of The North Seattle Professional Building, conveniently located across the street from Woodside Hospital. When a patient was in crisis, he could get to her bedside in ten minutes. His personality and willingness to drop everything gave patients confidence and, at one time, vaulted him over some veteran OB/GYN docs. Richardson didn't find it easy to stay at the top with the issues confronting him in recent years. He twisted a paperclip while contemplating when he could take his next "lude." He didn't really need it now, but he sometimes acknowledged his addiction back in the depths of his mind. A former colleague, Dr. Martens, once tried to face him up to his vice. Richardson didn't put up with it, and that's why Martens was a former colleague, gone from the state of Washington. Richardson didn't know or care where he went. He refused to think about Martens.

Richardson had tried measuring and scheduling his use of Quaaludes but failed. There were a few times his temper blew and a few times he suffered confusion, like the time he crossed the Lake Washington Bridge, headed for downtown Seattle and found himself asleep in the parking lot next to Sick Stadium, the old Seattle Rainiers ballpark in Rainier Valley. He knew something had to be done, but that would mean letting go of what he had and where he was in his profession, and Cora wouldn't permit it. He didn't have that option. He refused to drop the practice and, even temporarily, enroll himself in a treatment center. Whatever else he did, he wouldn't argue it out with Cora, and certainly not her imperious dad. He didn't have it in him. Anybody who wanted to take a serious run at Alden was asking for more trouble than he imagined. What Richardson lacked in courage, Cora made up in her stern will, inherited from her dad.

Richardson went to work on the charts. The Quality Control Committee meeting had to be held within two weeks, so he didn't have time to sit around and ponder. After he spent two hours minutely dissecting the charts, he had a rough draft of Hillibrand's and Fox's rewrites. His redraft didn't really nail Hillibrand but slid a share of the blame off to the student nurse, Nelda Fox. And yet, he allowed for a certain amount of understanding and tolerance of the younger nurse. Alden had warned him, he needed to soften the blow against the nurses or provoke too much of a firestorm. Richardson put the draft into final form and headed back across the street. He pulled Hillibrand aside. "Lois, I need to talk to you.

Can we go over to the Cavalier? I'd like to buy you a dinner, and it'll give us a chance to talk. Okay?"

Hillibrand suspected what he wanted and was wary of going somewhere alone with him, but she'd dealt with Woodside doctors before, when they needed a little butt protection after a screw-up. She'd "corrected" records before and sometimes got favors, i.e., money or a dinner in return. Most of the nurses would have fainted flat out on the floor if Dr. Richardson invited them to dinner, but his motive was obviously not romance. She didn't happily look forward to this dinner meeting, but she couldn't refuse him. Hillibrand prepared to look out for herself as he knew she would. Planning a forgery had to be away from the hospital, away from witnesses. Still, Richardson contemplated how he could outwit the wily nurse.

Hillibrand was careful. "That's kind of a long drive. Can we meet in Northgate? I need to take my insulin by seven."

He offered to give her the injection at his office, but she didn't trust him to put a needle in her arm. He reluctantly agreed to go to Northgate despite the additional impact of a fifteen-minute drive there and back on his schedule.

He smiled his warm and professional smile. "I know a great place near Northgate. You'll like it: Rix."

The restaurant would have been impossibly pricey for Hillibrand, but why not take a nice meal with Richardson paying. "Sure, thank you. That would be nice." She'd never been there before but found it quickly. She ignored the valet at the canopied entrance and saw Richardson's red Corvette in the landscaped parking lot when she arrived. Hillibrand didn't ordinarily frequent restaurants with thick carpets, white linen tablecloths, a mammoth wine rack and waiters who pull your chair out, but Richardson seemed much at ease, obviously adequately medicated. And then the maître'd addressed him as Dr. Richardson, so Hillibrand knew he was a regular customer and quickly took to the experience. She calmly waited to see what Richardson had in his attaché case. Hillibrand appreciated that, with consideration for her insulin schedule, he told the waiter they had to be out by 6:30. Then, when the waiter virtually knelt and kissed his ring, she guessed he must have made a reputation as a big tipper.

Hillibrand declined a glass of Pinot Noir. After they each ordered the fillet with potatoes au gratin and the Caesar salad, he pulled out the medical records and his notes.

"You left at 3 AM. This is what you wrote for that last half hour before you left. That needs a little correcting. Then Fox took over, and her notes aren't good up until Rosen came in. Those are the parts I'm worried about. We just have to make a few changes, and our problem goes away. You have to talk to Nelda."

"What problem do I have?"

"Lois, we've worked well together long enough that I think we have a certain amount of regard for each other. I know you wouldn't want to hurt me any more than I'd want to hurt you. I've got some corrections to the charts, which would say essentially, the same thing but not make it look like I was derelict. Don't make this you against me. I never lose."

"Could I see what you're proposing?"

"Sure." He pulled out his notes, and she went through the few pages.

"Doctor, this is quite a rewrite. I can't say I like what it does to me and Nelda. Neither one of us would be very secure in our jobs if this goes to the committee. You have to put back in there that the patient slipped without Nelda's fault. She described how it happened in the original, and it has to stay that way, right?"

"Sure, fine, put that back in. I understand how you feel, and I guarantee you'll come to no harm as a result of this. Dr. Karel is on my side; I'll talk to him, and he'll take care of both of us. You can verify with him it will all be okay. Quality Control will be as much on your side as it is on mine."

"And Nelda?"

"I'll see she's protected too. You know I can do it."

"I know the hospital staff is going to kiss your boots, but Nelda might never get a nursing license and, come to think of it, the State Health Department could put me through the wringer with these changes, too."

"There's nothing terrible here, and anyway, they'll never see these chart notes. Who's going to complain to them?"

"Herb Fletcher or his lawyer."

"All he'll know is she had a bleeding problem, and Dr. Rosen did all he could. End of story. How about this, Lois? Write out the changes and hang onto them until you make up your mind. And I need to get back my notes when you're finished making your rewrite from them. Take this to Nelda. Tell her what I said. Get her to make the rewrite. You'll both have a friend forever, trust me on that. Also, before I forget, give me back the blank prescriptions I signed for you. Don't copy anything. That wouldn't make me happy or look good for either of us."

Hillibrand, not knowing what else she could do, scrupulously followed Richardson's proposed changes, and on the blank charts he handed her, laboriously completed the rewrite of her offending notes before the entrées arrived. He immediately picked up his own handwritten draft of Hillibrand's rewrite so she'd never have a chance to use it as proof he coerced changes to the chart notes. But he had to trust Hillibrand to get Fox to sign her rewrite and return it. He was uneasy, but in his mind, had to live with it. He figured his tactics would satisfy Cora and get him out of trouble.

Hillibrand promised to return the blank prescriptions and, when she got home, and after taking the insulin injection, retrieved the blank prescriptions, not sure what to do with them. The next morning, first thing, away from prying eyes, she went to a copy service near Bothell to make copies of the blank prescription forms and another copy of the original draft chart notes. Back at Woodside, when Nelda arrived, Hillibrand dragged her aside, told her about the nice dinner at Rix and how popular

Richardson was. She showed her Richardson's rewrite of Nelda's chart notes. At first Nelda was afraid, but Hillibrand explained how they would protect themselves. Nelda, evidently, wasn't used to resisting people in authority or doing her own thinking. She had been scared out of her wits when she made the anonymous call about Richardson's care of Myra but got by with that one. It would never get pinned on her.

She told Hillibrand about the strange, undefined fear she was feeling since Myra Fletcher's death. Hillibrand instantly knew what it was.

"It's a panic attack. You feel guilty. You didn't do anything wrong, Nelda, there's nothing for you to feel guilty about. Cut it out, right now. I think I had a feeling like that the first time I lost a patient. It goes away if you make it go away."

Hillibrand promised she would assure Richardson she'd made no copies of his notes. Nelda gave up her lunch hour in order to write out her portion of the chart notes exactly as Richardson directed. She made the copies and gave Hillibrand the originals in an envelope with Richardson's name on it. When he called, Fox, heart pumping, swore she hadn't made any copies, and he said, "You better not have." Without Hillibrand she wouldn't have dared challenge any doctor, especially Richardson. She would have been too terrified, and even now, her ragged anxieties weren't far below the surface.

Hillibrand walked into Dr. Elliott Karel's Quality Control office and started to describe her meeting with Dr. Richardson. He stopped her right away. "I don't care what you and Dr. Richardson work out between you. If you can agree on an accurate set of chart notes, I'm not going to question it. I'm satisfied you and Nelda Fox did a good job, and you aren't going to be blamed for your efforts to deal with an emergency. I know you had to get an insulin shot and couldn't wait for Glenn Yee to get there. No one can expect more from Fox than what she gave. So, as far as I'm concerned, the two of you are in the clear. If you keep quiet the problem goes away."

Hillibrand returned the altered chart notes and the blank prescription forms to Richardson at his office. By 10:00 AM. he called and thanked her. "Doctor, I've talked to Nelda, and the whole thing is done, nothing to worry about from us." She didn't tell him she copied everything in case she needed some leverage. She was an old hand at Woodside and knew too much about Richardson to trust his promises.

On her lunch hour that day, she took the envelope of copies back to the copy service and made another set of copies. She liked Nelda and decided she needed protection too. Back at the hospital she gave a sealed envelope with the copies inside to Nelda and wrote her own name on it. "Don't you open that until I tell you. That's yours and my security against Dr. Richardson selling us down the river. If he tries it, you save these for the last possible moment, and get a lawyer if that happens. I'm not going to let Richardson dump either of us in the crapper to get himself off if it ever comes to that. Got it?"

"I'm not sure I get it, but I'm not going to take the blame for his mistakes. If you've got something there to cover me I'm hanging onto it."

Hillibrand and Nelda had a bond between them, a common determination to survive the doctor's blunder and not pay the penalty if the "conspiracy of silence" should ever collapse. Nelda didn't know what the conspiracy was. She never before experienced the system covering up malpractice, but she was starting to learn. Hillibrand suspected Nelda wouldn't like what she was learning about the medical profession. Hillibrand's memory went back to the Mickens girl who seemed to be so cozy with Richardson and then died mysteriously.

If something happens to me, am I going to be
forgotten the way the Mickens girl was?

CHAPTER THREE

Herb Fletcher, in the depths of his impossible grief, suffered a duty he couldn't ignore. He felt compelled against his will to let Myra's mother back in Louisiana, Nadine LeDoux, know what had happened. Someone had to force on her the knowledge that her daughter, her beautiful, kind-hearted daughter, a new mother, was dead. He hated having to tell Mrs. LeDoux Myra was gone forever.

He couldn't muster the courage to tell her this terrible news. He was sure he'd break down even as he knew his duty. His mind was so locked in a spasm of love for Myra and the baby, Melissa, that putting words together and saying them to Myra's mother was an emotional impossibility. He needed help.

It wasn't easy, but he went back to the hospital and back to Maternity. When he saw the young nurse, Nelda Fox, he instantly knew what he was going to do and say. He and Nelda came together, crying on each other's shoulder. Herb gave her a slip with the phone number and begged her to tell Mrs. Le Doux what happened. At the same time Nelda cringed at the duty he asked her to assume, she also felt proud and gratified he trusted her to do it. He'd seen the bond between Nelda, baby Melissa and Myra. Nelda agreed to suspend her grief long enough to make the call Herb couldn't. "Thank you, Nelda. Say whatever you feel. Just tell her how sorry I am. She trusted me with her daughter."

Herb, after exhausting all his tears and energy, collapsed on the lounge chair in the waiting area as Nelda made the call. She gripped his hands briefly and disappeared with the phone number. She went back to the nursing office to get approval from Charge Nurse, Steinman, who gave the okay. Nelda called Mrs. LeDoux, who reacted with a sudden explosion of horror, just as Nelda expected. After one scream, she struggled for breath, but Mrs. LeDoux got a grip on her emotions and finally told Nelda how gratified Myra had been for her care.

"My daughter was in such fear. She wasn't sure her doctor cared about her, but she completely trusted her nurses. God bless you, Nelda. Ask Herb to call me when he's up to it. I can't talk any more right now, but I'll need to help him with the arrangements. I know he's as devastated as I am."

* * * * *

Joe Gold enjoyed the Saturday breakfast with his dad, Ed and stepmother, Marie. It was a nice reward for fighting through another high-pressure week at the Gold Law Firm. He helped his pregnancy-enhanced wife, Sandra, into the Caddy, and they were off to his dad's beautifully landscaped, grand, brick home in Seattle on the shores of Lake Washington, halfway between Madison Park and Leschi, near the Boeing mansion. Gretchen, the African-American maid, a valued part of the family, welcomed Sandra at the door with a big hug and a smile. Joe's brother, Mike, and Mike's wife, Diana, didn't come to every Saturday breakfast anymore. Ed and Mike touched base regularly at the office and both brought work home. They had great days when the two brothers and their dad went for their Saturday runs along the shore and up the Leschi hill. Those days were gone, but the family's memories and love weren't.

Everybody doted on Sandra, bearing Ed's long awaited first grandchild. The family valued her more precious than the crown jewels. Ed's second wife, Marie, couldn't have been prouder if Sandra were her flesh and blood and so fluffed up a pillow on the sunroom banquette for her, lest she suffer the most minor discomfort. Marie seated Sandra with gentle care. "Please don't fuss over me." Sandra loved the fuss more than she felt the embarrassment, and everybody got the joke.

Ed Gold, a big, solid presence, once managing partner of the powerhouse Carpenter Gold Law Firm, primarily focused on insurance defense, sold out his interest in the firm in order to establish the family firm. Ed Gold, "Dad" to the boys, achieved his dream of bringing his sons together in one firm. He now dreamed someday his grandchildren would run the firm.

Gretchen served breakfast in the atrium projecting out across the green expanse of lawn, into the varicolored garden and towards the lake. The family never tired of the sailboats chasing each other in the morning breeze. As usual, Gretchen laid out a buffet breakfast including bagels, French toast, pancakes, omelets, juice, fruit and coffee. Sandra and Marie always tried to help Gretchen put their usual epic breakfast together. Gretchen grumbled she could do it herself and, especially, she didn't need the pregnant Sandra doing her work. She didn't like to admit it, but she appreciated the extra hands, and the women all enjoyed the chit chat.

Ed led a handsome and accomplished family. He was born with athletic genes, still fit in his sixties, hiding his years. His late wife, the mother of the two boys, died when she was still a pretty woman, struck down by a brain tumor in her forties. Marie, gray and softening in her sixties, beloved by Joe and brother Mike, was smart enough to honor the first wife's memory, her portrait gracing the mantel.

Joe, like his younger brother, now in his mid-thirties, was a darkly, handsome, young man with wavy black hair. They both inherited their dad's legal aptitude and athletic skills. Mike starred in basketball in high school but couldn't get off the bench after making the team at Washington. Joe, outgrowing football, had taken off 25 pounds since his human battering ram, all-state days as a fullback.

Sandra, a somber, dark-haired beauty and tall, reflected the difficult marriage that ended with the death of her first husband, Marco Perini. She met Joe when the Gold firm represented Marco in a famous, multimillion dollar suit against a title company. The company's negligence and fraud had destroyed Marco's successful resort business, and the Gold family firm,

Mike especially, ferreted out the truth. Joe helped the grieving Sandra through the tough times, and eventually they discovered they were in love.

Ed sat with Joe in the library after the breakfast. He led the family law firm but no longer actively pursued the litigation that was their stock in trade. He needed to discuss the Fletcher case. "I have to get this out. Maybe you've noticed how upset Gretchen is. Her young niece died at Woodside Hospital. Gretchen knew I was on the board, but I didn't know what she was getting at when she started telling me. She says her sister in Louisiana wants me to investigate. I'll tell you the short of what she told me and what I've picked up at the hospital. Her niece, Myra Fletcher, was a patient there, a seventeen-year-old girl, and she bled to death lying in the hospital, fifteen days after giving birth. The doctor, Kevin Richardson, supposedly on Quaaludes, neglected her, and it sounds like it was clear fault, but the hospital emergency personnel might also be at fault. It's hard to say."

"Richardson's a big wheel, and I think the staff is covering for him. That's what they do with malpractice. You may have heard, lawyers call it the 'conspiracy of silence.' It's a pretty disgusting thing. Pretty much the whole staff thinks their first duty is to the profession, not the patients. I hear the doctor made the nurses change the chart notes to make it seem the whole thing was just bad luck. First you have to find the truth, and that isn't easy. Then you have to find a doctor to testify as an expert for the plaintiff, and that isn't easy either. One of the nurses talked to Gretchen when she visited, and she talked to me."

"Maybe I shouldn't have listened to her. I can't get involved because I'm on the board. I'm not sure if I can have you help her because we're partners in the Gold Law Firm. If I have a conflict, maybe that's a conflict affecting the whole firm. Gretchen looked to me to help the husband and the new baby. I always hated the doctors' cover-ups, and this is a chance to do something about it. I would feel like a real slug if I just passed the buck and told Gretchen I have a conflict. What do I do?"

Joe's dad wanted his help, and however busy he was, he'd never turn him down. Maybe it was his turn to take on a major case. Younger brother, Mike, had cashed in his big case already. Mike won the $47 million, title

THE LAST DROP OF BLOOD

company case, a success that helped build the firm, and Joe could see another front page case coming. He instantly wanted in, even if it meant he had to drop the idea of taking on a bigger role in handling the firm's major business clients. Hearing his dad talk about the "conspiracy," he wanted the achievement of beating it, an achievement that would mean something.

"Dad, let me take a look at the conflict issue and if we can handle it. Can I talk to the family? Is there a surviving husband? If I had a choice I'd rather do a major malpractice case than routine office business. I really fed off the adrenaline when Mike was doing the Marco Perini case. That's what I want to do now. We've got the right staff, so even with you out of it, I think we have the business clients under control. Even with the business taking off like it is."

Joe's remarks pleased Ed. "Yeah, there's a husband. I don't know if there's anything there or if we can do it. But assuming we take it, we could handle the business clients without you. I'd really like to see you take on a case like this. It's your turn. We may have to find someone to give a little help with the paralegal work. But other than that, I don't see a problem. If you sue the hospital it's going to be Brosius and McCallum on the other side. Larry McCallum has the reputation of a really tough trial lawyer. I bet my old partner, Mark Zale would represent the hospital and he's a smart guy."

"Of course, Gretchen will have to tell the husband to call you. We can't ethically call him. First things first. Dig out a copy of the Canons of Ethics and look at the conflicts provisions. We don't say anything until we're sure there's no ethical problem. We don't jump into the swimming pool till we know there's water in it."

Joe added, "And you're a belt and suspenders type of a guy, aren't you?"

Ed laughed. It was his favorite little aphorism. It's what he said when looking for a way to avoid taking an unnecessary risk. A belt isn't enough if you can wear suspenders too.

* * * * *

Herb Fletcher scheduled the funeral at the first AME Church in Seattle. Gretchen asked Ed for an advance so she could bring her sister up from Louisiana for Myra Fletcher's funeral. He was embarrassed. As much as Gretchen had become part of his family, he knew so little about hers.

Ed refused her request for an advance and instead said, "I was intending to give you a bonus for all the good work you've done for the family, so this is the time for that. You don't need an advance, you have the money coming. Just tell me how much you need to bring your sister up here. And by the way, how much is the funeral going to cost?"

Gretchen broke down in tears and threw her arms around Ed. He was caught by surprise, while Gretchen apologized for her behavior. He wouldn't let her go until she'd stopped shuddering in grief and gratitude.

* * * * * *

When they got to the church, they first saw the young nurse, Nelda Fox, holding on to little Melissa with all the love that welled up from inside her. She was an emotional girl who couldn't bear the idea of the infant forever deprived of her mother. Gretchen whispered to Joe who they were. He expected to talk to Nelda soon.

Nelda stood next to Herb. She supposed that the old, black AME church must never have seen so many white attendees at a funeral. Nelda met the full Gold family and Herb Fletcher's two elderly, Jewish employers. They grabbed onto Herb, who couldn't put one foot in front of the other without help that day. In spite of his grief and misery, he was a dignified presence. Nelda knew his strength and character that justified Myra's steadfast love up until her last moments of life. Nelda tenderly held baby Melissa until Myra's mother sat down and could hold her. The reverend marveled at Myra's sweetness and how she couldn't stop helping anyone who needed a hand, especially when it involved small children. Then her cousin talked about how bright she was to zip through school so fast and with the grades she had and all her public service. Nelda's heart broke all over again.

Why couldn't I have saved her?

Following the funeral, Myra's mother, Mrs. LeDoux, stayed a couple days at the Gold home, grateful for the chance to rest up before returning to Louisiana. Gretchen waited on her and saw that the baby was comfortable while Herb's bosses allowed him a few peaceful days to himself. The family told Joe to put the case on the back burner while Mrs. LeDoux was there. Distraught and depressed, over those few days, she turned angry and smoldering. She craved justice for her daughter and the baby and urged Herb and Joe to get on with it when Herb was ready. While Joe studied the Canons of Ethics, Mrs. LeDoux saw him light up too. Joe had to dig into the ton of work before he could justify a suit, but as soon as Mrs. LeDoux headed for the Sea-Tac Airport he started his investigation. Nelda and Hillibrand, the two nurses, told him to count on them. They didn't have to. He saw it in their hearts.

* * * * * *

As Joe reviewed the Canons of Ethics, he still pumped adrenaline due to the major malpractice case he expected to take on. He had self-confidence despite the huge responsibility and never passed up a sensible challenge. After a few days, when Mrs. LeDoux was gone, he would get the information he needed out of Gretchen. He hoped she was satisfied with him on the case rather than Mike, the hero of Sandra's $47-million case a couple years earlier.

Joe didn't face a real human challenge when he represented insurance companies. He planned to sit down with Herb, Nelda and Hillibrand, real people he could care about. He understood the difference in relationship with plaintiffs and insurance claims reps. He expected to call the shots for the client, even though he was never famous for tact and understanding. He was confident he could make the switch from defense of negligence to proving negligence. He owed it to Herb and the baby and especially to Gretchen, and his mind was clear. It was time to jump into the deep end. No matter what Dad said, even the most careful plaintiffs' attorney couldn't know if there was any water there until he jumped.

Chapter Four

The hospital's monthly board meeting preceded the Quality Control Committee meeting. Before the meeting, Elliott Karel called Rosen and Richardson and told them not to worry. The Fletcher thing wasn't going to come up until after the quality control meeting. No one told Ed Gold or Dr. Kelly Halloran, another board member. Karel made a big mistake, not clearing it with Halloran. Every large organization has someone who regards himself as its unofficial conscience, and Halloran was it at Woodside. He thought he had a duty at every meeting to demonstrate his knowledge, attention to detail and diligence. Once he'd wanted to know what happened to the extra quarters when the candy machine malfunctioned. More to the point, he almost unraveled one of Richardson's secrets when Woodside sent Dr. Martens bye-bye. The tall, freckle-faced redhead wanted to step on it every time he smelled a rat. Now somebody had spilled the Fletcher death to him, and as far as Halloran was concerned, if it wasn't under "New Business," he was putting it there.

Franklin Tobin, the tanned, wavy-haired, suave and urbane chairman of the board and CEO tried to run a taut ship, but there was no tactful or professional way to shut off Halloran. Almost from the first moment Tobin opened up new business, Halloran wanted to know why the death in Maternity wasn't on the agenda. Karel politely explained that the procedure was to first get a report from the Quality Control Committee. "That's what they're there for." The board, a long time ago, decided there had to be a professional review before they examined any potential malpractice issue. Without the professional review, there wouldn't be adequate information.

That was obvious. The board wasn't equipped to do a professional review, and it really wasn't the board's function, as far as they were concerned.

The argument didn't impress Halloran in the least. "It happened a week ago. If we made a mistake a week ago, how do we know it won't happen again this week? That's crazy. If we need to change something or fire someone in order to not get patients killed, let's do it now. Things tend to get swept under the rug. I never did find out what happened to Dr. Martens after he had a hassle with one of our top docs. Come to think of it, that was Maternity too."

Chairman Tobin had finally heard enough. "Doctor, that isn't New Business till I put it on the agenda. From now on, how about if you save your speeches for Good and Welfare?"

"This isn't a fraternal organization, and Good and Welfare isn't on the agenda. Our responsibility to patients is always on the agenda, even if it isn't on these pieces of paper you send us before our meetings."

Tobin's patience was wearing thin. "Then take it up with the committee. The rest of us need to talk about the financing for the new East Wing. Is that okay?"

"Yes, Mr. Tobin, of course, but I want those two nurses off Maternity until we hear from the committee – is that okay? And shouldn't the doctor step down until this has been reviewed?"

Before either Karel or Richardson could even twitch, Tobin had answered "Richardson is the doctor, and he can decide for himself whether he needs to step down until we hear from quality control. As to the nurses, I'll okay a short break for them." And he pointed at the Charge Nurse, Sue Steinman, saying, "See to it."

It was that simple. Tobin wanted to bring in someone to replace Hillibrand and Fox, who would then get whatever temp and fill-in work that could be dredged up for them. Tobin assumed nothing could be done about Richardson, as if there was no possible error by the exalted surgeon, only the ground level women carrying out the orders, who needed their jobs for survival. Halloran knew the "conspiracy of silence" was in operation and he was fuming.

Ed Gold saw it happen but didn't dare say a word. The Gold Law Firm hadn't evaluated whether Ed or the firm had a conflict. He would have said, "This is unfair and unprofessional" but didn't know if that would get him in trouble. Ed was not a rash or impetuous person, but he was getting angry that Hillibrand and Fox were taking the blame for what they had not done, and Richardson's responsibility hadn't even been touched. When Ed got angry, he also became extra cautious, one of the character traits that kept him on the board these many years. No one ever questioned his competence as the legal conscience of the board, and he wouldn't blow it now. If there was a line you couldn't cross, Ed didn't want to get close to it.

As the meeting turned somnolent and dragged on through the treasurer's report and one from personnel, Ed looked wistfully at his slow moving watch. Finally the meeting collapsed of its own weight and Tobin called for the motion to adjourn.

As Tobin walked down the hallway, a figure stepped out of the shadows and grabbed him by the tie, jerking him forward.

"What the hell are you doing, Karel? Let go of me, dammit."

"Do you realize what Halloran just did? Rosen and I had the Fletcher thing handled, and now he's blown that all to hell. Those nurses will run to a lawyer, and I can't begin to guess what happens then. You do something about it, or there's going to be trouble."

"Don't panic, Karel, it's not a big deal. There will be a committee meeting and report, and it will be fine. Go home, and don't ever lay your hands on me again. I don't like it."

Karel silently vowed someday he was going to do something from his quality control position to punish Halloran, the big-mouthed Irishman.

* * * * * *

When Ed got home from the board meeting, he wearily plopped himself down in his leather easy chair. Marie saw the same sour look on his face she'd come to associate with Ed's feelings about LBJ, "the cowboy president." He didn't think much more of LBJ than he did of "the bomber," Barry Goldwater.

When Marie saw that face she asked, "What did the president do today?"

"It wasn't the president this time. I get so steamed whenever some doctor commits malpractice at the hospital. You just know they're going to give it the 'conspiracy of silence' treatment. They'll go 'tut tut' and pretend they feel so bad about the poor patient. I've tried to ease into it before, but it's never done any good. They can always find a doc who'll conclude the mistake was just a misfortune, and the treatment was within the standard of care, so it wasn't negligent. Anyone who wants to pursue the case seriously has to find an expert out of state."

"Can plaintiffs get around that?"

"Not really, the defense will point out how desperate the plaintiff was. He couldn't find anyone in Washington to support his 'phony' claim. If I could ever blow a hole in the local silence, the patients would benefit from it. I thought I could count on the redhead this time."

"Halloran? What did he do? You like him, remember? He's a maverick."

Sour turned to sneer.

"I suppose he meant well. Here's what happened. Halloran wanted the board to talk about the death of Gretchen's niece even though it hadn't been through the Quality Control Committee yet."

"That doesn't sound so terrible."

"It was for the two nurses involved in the Fletcher death. His bringing it up meant somebody had to pay the price, so the nurses got suspended until quality control is done, and Kevin Richardson walked away as if he were a bystander. The nurses are scapegoats even if they didn't do anything wrong. I just know the staff will bury it."

Marie was persuaded. "You're right. That doesn't sound fair. The women need lawyers, and the hospital has to do something about the doctor. Can't you do something?"

"You know Joe's looking at filing a lawsuit for Herb Fletcher, but we have a conflict if we represent him and the nurses. Those women need an expert in employment law, and that isn't us. So we need to find someone and make a referral right away if we can."

* * * * * *

When Saturday morning arrived, so did Joe and Sandra. Dad grabbed him before breakfast. This was a first, a conference in the den before they ate. Joe knew this must be something pretty serious. Ed laid out what happened in the board meeting, and he and Joe were in full agreement. It wasn't fair, and something had to be done.

Joe was ready to go. "First of all, there's no conflict barring us from representing Mr. Fletcher. I've done the research, and I'll see if I can find attorneys for the nurses."

Around the breakfast table, the family agreed the firm had to offer its help to Herb Fletcher. They weren't going to trust Rosen, the Emergency Room doc, Tobin, the chairman or Karel, the Quality Control Director. All the hospital staff were more on Richardson's side than the patient's. Maybe Halloran would be the plaintiffs' Trojan horse. Nobody doubted that Fletcher's case would be damaged if they sat by and watched the hospital staff send Fox and Hillibrand down the river. Ed was still concerned about potential conflicts and wanted an explanation.

"What about my board membership at the hospital? Do I have to resign? Can't they object to the firm representing Herb Fletcher with me on the board?"

Joe pulled out his memorandum and explained what his ethics research established. "Dad, you aren't the attorney for the hospital. Being on the board isn't the same as being their lawyer. They can't object to our representing Fletcher if you recuse yourself from any board action on the death case and from anything we do on the law end of it, too."

After breakfast, Joe went into the kitchen where Gretchen had to deal with the pile of cups, glasses, dishes, pots, pans, silver and leftovers that always resulted from the Saturday morning breakfast banquets. She was about to warn him not to touch anything because it was her job, but he put his hand to her lips.

"Don't say it. I know you don't need my help. I just wanted to tell you we're talking about taking on your niece's case if Mr. Fletcher wants us. We know he can't afford the costs so the Gold Law Firm will front them. I don't even have to ask Dad about that. I'll just do it for my Gretchen, just like Dad would."

Joe was overwhelmed by the big bear hug and Gretchen's tears of thanks. She was always like that whenever someone did something she appreciated. It just came out.

"Thank you, Joe. You're too sweet. I don't know how Herb can support my little niece's baby by himself. He's a hard worker, and he's getting ahead, but he hasn't earned a lot yet. My sister, Nadine, doesn't have the money, and I don't think Herb's mom down in Louisiana has the wherewithal either. I don't know, Joe, I just don't know."

"Gretchen, Herb sounds like the kind of guy who'll move himself up, and your sister won't have to finance him and the baby. I'll see what we can do to help."

"I'm not giving up. Nadine says he's a good guy, but those hospital people don't care much. I'm grateful if you can keep them from wrecking the case before it even gets going. I'll call Nadine to have Herb talk to you as soon as I finish with the mess you hungry people left."

In less than a half-hour, Herb Fletcher was calling, barely able to talk through his grief, asking if he could come in Monday morning. "Darn right, but how about noon?" Herb said he could be there. Joe felt a sense of crossing a line. He'd been waiting for a case he could feel good about. He could feel the load piling up on his shoulders and hoped he was up to it.

As he started to walk out of the kitchen after getting off the phone, Gretchen said, "Hang on, Joe, there's another problem. What's going to happen to the nurses when they're the bull's-eye for the defense? Their jobs are going to be gone. You know that, right?"

"I'll find an employment attorney for them, and maybe he can solve it."

"I hope so. These hospital people will have reasons to fire them, and nobody will hire them. The hospital will use them, abuse them and dump them in the trash. And I hope you can find somebody who gives a rat's ass to look after them before it's too late. I appreciate your wanting to help Herb, and he'll need help from the nurses. You can't treat them as if they are simply furniture in your case."

"I know."

"If they aren't getting helped, you can't expect them to help you. I'm sure when Herb sees you, he's going to want to hear what you're doing for the girls, too."

"You're right, Gretchen. I'll find somebody who's got a heart for this kind of stuff. You understand, the lawyer who represents Herb can't represent the nurses, right?"

On the way home, Joe explained to Sandra he was already beginning to feel the heavy burden of representing Gretchen's family. She wasn't a stranger who just walked in off the street, and the family cared about her

THE LAST DROP OF BLOOD

in a more personal way than pure business. He was a competitor and liked a challenge, but this was a bigger challenge than he'd ever faced in the practice. Everybody said you had to do a perfect job to win a plaintiff's medical malpractice case. Of course, there's the "conspiracy of silence" but there's also the need to find a powerful expert and convince 12 jurors that a "godlike" doctor can make a mistake. There were plenty of stories of juries skunking experienced lawyers in good cases.

Sandra listened politely, though she was more focused on her burden of pregnancy and how her body was changing. She hadn't mentioned to her OB/GYN, Dr. Pederson, the occasional blurred vision or headaches. She didn't want to be a complainer, assuming this was what comes with pregnancy. She would rather contemplate the joys of raising another brilliant and talented Gold son.

CHAPTER FIVE

On Monday, Joe put aside all the business matters he was working on, including immediately, the important Northwest Coffee zoning application for a new factory. He'd been working on it for months, and it was hard to walk away from now. But, he determinedly made that choice. He turned it over to Mike, so that afternoon Joe took him down to the large brick Northwest office south of historical Pioneer Square and brought with him the files on several new stores. As far as Joe was concerned, he was out of it. He regretted having to tell Sandra he was walking away from a client that was someday going to be a mammoth international business. She dreamed someday he'd be a big mover and shaker in the business world, but he didn't.

Before Joe went to work on the Fletcher case, he had to satisfy Dad on the conflict of interest question. It turned out his dad appreciated Joe's conflicts memo and was satisfied ethics wasn't going to be an issue as long as he kept out of the case. Herb Fletcher came in at noon to see Joe as promised. With all his strength and dignity, he was still a sad and weary looking young African-American. His shoulders slumped, and nobody could doubt his sweet young wife's death had crushed him. It still showed all over. Joe liked him from the start and, from the first, was grateful he brought nurses, Lois Hillibrand and Nelda Fox with him. They could give him some answers Herb couldn't. The three of them sat close up, leaning forward, tension in their eyes, probably their first time in a lawyer's office, at least for Nelda and Herb.

"Mrs. Hillibrand and Miss Fox are in a tight spot. Helping my case is pretty risky for them. Dr. Richardson made them prepare phony chart notes covering up what really happened. They want the truth to come out, but they don't want to lose their careers. Can you help them too?"

Joe was impressed that the young man could worry about the nurses with what fate had dealt him! But then, Joe started thinking. Maybe this wasn't such a good idea. He wondered if meeting with a plaintiff's attorney could blow the insurance coverage the women had through the hospital. The insurance company expected the nurses to defend the claim, not help the plaintiff. Joe explained they could be liable for the loss. For a moment, Herb was embarrassed and apologetic. He didn't realize the jeopardy for them. Then he had the answer.

"Wait a minute. You mean if I make a claim against them, they could be liable? Hell, I'm not going to do that."

He looked at Joe. "Why would I make a claim against them? They didn't do anything wrong, and if they did, the hospital would be liable for it anyway, wouldn't it? If I don't make a claim against them personally, they don't have anything to lose by cooperating with you, do they?"

Joe didn't quite agree. "I'd be willing to answer that question, but I'm your attorney. I can't give them independent advice they can rely on. They should consult an attorney of their own. If they go ahead, they're risking the possibility I could be giving them advice that helps you and hurts them."

That took Herb aback, and the grin faded. Joe turned to Nelda and Hillibrand. "Sorry, you need an attorney of your own."

Joe had in mind that maybe no hospital would ever hire them again. They'd be out of work with nowhere to go, but he couldn't say that in front of the nurses. That was advice contrary to Herb's claim and interest. Until his client gave the okay to Joe, some other attorney would have to give them that warning.

Nelda was adamant. "I'm not going to do anything that would hurt Herb and Melissa no matter what they do, and I'll do anything I can to help them. Lois and I owe that to them. One way or another, I'll come out of this okay. I'm not going to worry about me."

Hillibrand smiled at Nelda's earnest fervor. "I'm not worried either. I'm trusting Joe and you can too, Nelda. They can't punish us for telling the truth, and if they do, we can sue them.." Joe, also smiling, refrained from nodding his head. He hadn't given them that advice. Hillibrand figured it out on her own.

Hillibrand pushed her chair forward and leaned in closer to Joe's desk. The fidgety, young, dark-haired Nelda sat next to her, listening intently. Hillibrand was ready to tell her story and launched into the horror of the night Myra bled to death in her hospital bed. She finally ended with Richardson forcing the nurses to change the records.

"He put no blame on himself and pretty much blackjacked me into going along with it, so I wrote out the story the way he wanted it. Anyway, I copied the original chart notes before they got changed. And I copied a bunch of blank prescriptions he signed and gave to me because he was too lazy and drugged up to pay much attention to the patient. I didn't tell him I made copies, so he doesn't know we have a little ammunition to hit back if we have to."

Nelda added, "I rewrote my notes too, and I still have our copies, so I'm hoping I'm covered. We're looking for other hospitals to work at just in case they fire us when Herb files suit and we bring out the truth about what happened that night. But I don't know if there's any that would really hire us. I hate the thought that we could be their punching bags if we don't abandon Herb and the baby."

Hillibrand continued. "The Quality Control Director, Dr. Karel, promised he'd protect me and Nelda, but now we barely have any job at all. We're sort of in the position of having to prove we aren't responsible for Myra Fletcher's death. We feel so bad for the baby. Melissa is such a cutie, and as you can see, Herb needs a lot of help to raise her. Richardson is so unstable you don't know what he'll do next. He's on pills, Quaaludes, we believe. He really shouldn't be treating patients, and yet he's still the biggest wheel in OB/GYN at Woodside. I don't know if you ever heard of the 'conspiracy of silence?'"

"Sure I've heard of it. Dad told me. Doctors and hospitals hate malpractice claims worse than anything, and if one of them makes a mistake everybody else covers up. The patient suffers, but the doctor and the hospital go on as if nothing happened. The horrible thing would be if the truth came out and malpractice rates went up. That's the way they look at it. It's really hard to find a doctor who will testify that another doctor made a mistake. Juries have never heard of anything like that, and they think a doctor is some kind of god. I wish we could destroy that conspiracy."

"Well, Joe, that's what we're looking at here. We're never going to be safe while that conspiracy continues. We need for you to help us or find someone to help us if you can't."

"Mrs. Hillibrand, I understand that, but you are here primarily because you want to help Herb. I can't take on your cases, but I'll find someone. Before I do that, I'd like you to work out a statement for the two of you to sign and bring to your lawyer, not me. If the hospital's lawyer tries to manipulate your words, you don't have to go along with it. I'll give you some names of lawyers. Does that sound okay?"

Joe was learning to be as cautious as his dad. After two hours, Joe was all wrung out, but he still had to dictate Herb's long statement about Myra and her short life. Joe figured he'd get more from Myra's mom, Mrs. LeDoux, from Myra's family and friends, doctors and teachers. Herb promised to get him more info. When the three left, Joe drafted up what Lois and Nelda said about Myra's death and Richardson's peculiar behavior. The statement was based on the actual medical records, not the forgeries the two nurses were coerced into. Next, he looked into employment law specialists and wrote down the names of three lawyers who were competent plaintiffs' attorneys in the area. He had his paralegal, Jodi, send the names to Hillibrand and Nelda along with Joe's note.

"I think any of these guys could help you. They're really on the plaintiff's side, so they'll help you better than lawyers who are used to defending employers. Mr. Meach might be the best because you need someone with knowledge in the medical area. He'll probably say you have a wrongful discharge case if you're fired, or it could be a constructive discharge. If they fire you wrongfully in this situation, I think they're liable. If they make it so uncomfortable you have to quit, that's a constructive discharge, and they're still liable."

That Friday, Hillibrand called Joe from the office of Harry Meach, "We've just met with Mr. Meach, and he said what you thought he'd say. We've gone over the statements you prepared. He says they're okay, and we can sign them, but he wants to talk to you also. We signed a fee agreement, but that isn't enough. Before he's going to do any substantial work, he wants to know if you can guarantee there's going to be some money coming his way. I'll let you discuss that with him. Nelda and I don't have much."

Joe saw trouble on the horizon. The nurses' credibility would be completely gone if their attorney's fees depended on the outcome of Herb's case against Richardson and the hospital. He'd have to set Meach straight. He had a good reputation as an employment law specialist, but if he started taking ethical shortcuts, he could wreck a good case. Joe explained the credibility question to Hillibrand. She was adamant, she did not want her lawyer to wreck her credibility and Herb's case. Shortly thereafter, Meach called and apologized for the "misunderstanding." He would charge the nurses at his regular hourly rate and trust them to pay in time. He understood he wasn't going to get a piece of the plaintiff's case. A bullet dodged.

In a couple days, he met with Meach who agreed they would pool their information resources. The central point that the clients agreed on was that however the cases came out, the hospital couldn't continue covering up for negligent doctors. They were sure Myra wasn't the first and wouldn't be the last killed by hospital secrecy.

It would have been easy for Joe to get at odds with Meach. The man was so unlike his dad, all rough edges and a cranky streak in him, a true curmudgeon. But once past the fee issue, he was a man with a taste for chewing up defendants. He liked to win, and Joe figured Meach's experience on his side, would help.

Jodi Hedlund, a crafty and precise, devoted warrior had come over to the Gold Law Firm from the old Carpenter Gold Firm when the Gold family split off and now was the chief of the paralegal staff. She could have filled her days with supervisory duties, but she needed the nitty-gritty of litigation. Her contribution, which most people would call mundane and routine, was her forte and pride, an ability to organize and tame the worst monster lawsuit and clarify the medical records for the lawyers.

When Herb came back, he brought a yellow legal pad full of his notes about Myra and their life together, with her awards and certificates for outstanding schoolwork and her contribution to community activities. Red Cross and the YWCA had given her letters of appreciation, and her high school principal thanked her for mentoring younger students. She'd been straight A in high school and graduated a year early. Herb also brought the picture with her wearing the sash and crown as "Senior Ball Queen, 1963." Mrs. LeDoux sent a box of photos and memorabilia along with her own notes and names of doctors, teachers and schools. That Nelda had been a National Merit Scholar was the biggest nugget.

Lois and Nelda filled their yellow legal pads with their observations about Richardson's care of Myra and some other incidents raising questions about his ability to take care of patients. It took Meach's assistant a full day to type it all up and then another half day to organize it in a coherent fashion. When she turned the whole stack over to Meach, including the yellow legal pads, the memorabilia and artifacts and her own magnum opus distilled from the mélange, she sat down, leaned back and heaved a sigh of relief. He gave her a half day off in gratitude and called to meet with Joe. He gave him the originals to use in court and they set out lines of authority that wouldn't endanger coverage. Joe thanked him for the huge contribution but still had to anticipate anything that could go wrong. He mentally cringed. It wasn't going to get easier. They agreed the nurses' employment cases would have to wait for the resolution of the malpractice claim. That trial would dig up all the information Meach would struggle to root out in an employment case. They hoped a good pursuit of the malpractice case would make a trial of any employment case unnecessary. Having Meach on board might scare the hospital off from abusing the nurses.

* * * * * *

A few days later, Karel, unaware of the incubating malpractice case, began his quality control investigation by meeting with Richardson and Rosen. Richardson refused to let the nurses off the hook, because he needed to have control of them. He feared what they might say if they were free to say it. Karel finally concluded that the best result was to absolve Hillibrand and Fox of blame and report to the board that nobody could have expected the rapid increase in bleeding Myra suffered after Hillibrand left. Ed Gold, wary about confidentiality, refused to show his sons the report the Quality Control Committee submitted to the board. The report emphasized that there was an Emergency Room crisis that delayed the response to Myra's emergency, but it only lasted a few minutes. Karel's report said nothing about Richardson's downers or the nurse's attempts to get his attention.

Later that day, without disclosing the content of the confidential report, CEO, Franklin Tobin, tried to explain to the nurses what happened: "Karel wasn't out to get you; he just thought it appropriate to exonerate Richardson. You still have your jobs in the hospital, maybe at another department, and you'll get your lost pay as long as you don't make trouble. As far as Karel is concerned, Richardson is free of fault too. When you testify, if you have anything more to say, I expect you to be loyal."

Afterward, Hillibrand called Joe to tell him how she felt about Tobin. She was still steamed. Even with her income restored, she knew it would be temporary, and there was still an inference of blame, especially for Nelda. Hillibrand had too much pride to swallow Tobin's dictates.

"I should be loyal? Try to tell that to Herb Fletcher. He's lost his wife. We aren't going to let Richardson get away with a whitewash."

"Far from it. I'm representing Herb, and with your help we aren't going to let Richardson slide by, and we won't let him have a good night's sleep until the truth comes out. We don't know how many careless doctors Karel has covered for. It's time for that to come to an end. My dad can't be personally involved because he's on the hospital's board, so from now on we'll talk to Harry Meach about your job and the hospital. Anything concerning Herb's suit should be discussed with me. If Dad gets involved, that's trouble."

But there were more troubles coming than Joe could have predicted.

CHAPTER SIX

Cora Richardson picked up her mother's orb and scepter when the elderly Margaret Alden abdicated as the queen of the Northwest charity empire. People wondered if the mom descended from John Alden of Mayflower fame but nobody asked, so Cora didn't need to magnify her pedigree. Her Women's League leadership and social sway gave her authority to say who would be on this committee or that, who was invited for bridge and who was ignored when planning major events.

When Richardson met his future wife, Cora, at a hospital fund raising event, she was already a busy young lady on the social scene. Cora's hair was blond, her waist slim, breasts worthy of comment and with the face of an angel. Though she wasn't the most experienced woman in the Women's League, the more experienced people, nevertheless, went to her for advice. When they met, Richardson loved her sexual urge, concealed from other men, but generously expressed to him. He would never forget the first time he drove her home when, after a tangle in the back seat, he was barely able to walk her to the door. Everything about her was powerful, her personality, intelligence and her need to dominate.

Cora, fit when they met, still used the custom-built gym four times each week and it showed. She wasn't small, but she didn't carry an extra ounce. Richardson wished he could match her, but that would take an inner strength he couldn't muster. She was still an attractive woman, still smarter than most men she would ever meet and judicious in her bestowal of the favors still craved by her husband. It wasn't lost on Richardson that now, her sexual desire coincided with her need of a quo to match her quid, something in return for every sexual favor. Everything was calculated and weighed. She measured and directed her charm and applied it so smoothly nobody seemed to mind, that in every social setting, she set the program. The Women's League was an extension of her will, and she didn't have to claim the credit for its fundraising successes. *The Seattle Times* and *PI* reporters knew to come to her, and she modestly passed out the thanks "to all those who helped me so much." People didn't think of Richardson that way. He felt like a tail on her kite, floating along behind her.

He cared little for his wife's charitable bent, but she compelled him to contribute, along with the good society folk of Seattle, to the praise heaped on her. So he endured the charity publicity and promotional articles and photos alongside his wife. Cora's community and professional zeal usually augmented the economic strength and glory of the staff and the institution of Woodside Hospital. Richardson took on all the patients he could competently handle and, regrettably, more. Cora's community prominence benefited the hospital, but her domineering presence was a heavy price to pay. Richardson seemed to glory at the attention his wife brought him, and the people who met him socially imagined him a responsible, competent, able, happy and successful surgeon. They didn't know the demons and weakness within.

His "old friend," the bushy-haired, stubby Dr. Leo Cooper startled Richardson when he saw him at the Christmas Charity Ball held at the Olympic, Seattle's grandest hotel. It was really the only place that could comfortably hold such a huge and magnificent event in downtown Seattle. Cooper had a big smile and slapped Richardson on the back. He held out his hand for Richardson to shake as if they were merely professional friends. He cornered Richardson and forced him to take his hand. With a smile fixed on his face, Richardson quickly dragged Cooper into a quiet alcove away from the bar and the flashbulbs. "What the hell are you doing here, Leo? I told you to stay the hell away from me. We both could go to jail if anyone makes the connection. Please Leo, go."

Himself still smiling, Cooper said, "Hey, aren't I your good buddy? Nobody in Seattle knows who I am. Even if people knew me and knew that we had both taught at the University of British Columbia together for one quarter, why would that mean anything to them?"

"I don't know, but it still isn't worth it. Didn't I pay you enough money to stay the hell away from me? If you want to keep getting that money, why don't you stay up there in Vancouver?"

Cooper still smiled. "Kevin, you're wonderful. You always expect everything to go your way. You'll be just fine if you keep calm and don't get me pissed. Need another 'lude?' Tell you what, my wife and I are going to enjoy a nice evening here. I'm going to forget that I know you for tonight, and you try that, too. But don't forget you've got nowhere else to go for what you need."

Cooper walked away. Richardson was sometimes able to cover up his inner turmoil, the stomach cramps, rapid pulse and elevated BP. He presented a smiling face without giving an outward sign of his anxiety. When Cora found him, it was time to come to the head table, pick up the microphone and introduce the honors and awards recipients and receive the adoration of the cream of Seattle society. Richardson noticed Cora's friends, the Kirkendahls, were missing. He wondered briefly how the prominent Linda had offended Cora. Somewhere down at the end of the table, the Mayor waited for people to remember him. In the star-studded crowd, Richardson kept in mind all the important people he had to recognize, even an elected public official. Cora kept him around for these ceremonial duties. Time to perform. It was like he was another person, smile, controlled breathing, commanding voice. He sighed with relief after he turned over the mike to the Mayor.

As the evening wore down, Richardson bore in mind how important Cooper was to him and how much he hated that. It was another problem for Cora and Alden to solve when the time was right. Before he left, Richardson took Cooper aside and told him he needed another bottle of insulin and another of chloroform. Cooper's eyebrows raised, but before he could say anything, Richardson stopped him. "Don't ask, Leo. Just get me what I need and we'll be fine." Cooper shook his head and smiled, as if to say, I just can't figure this guy out, but Richardson knew he'd receive the

anonymous meds he needed, confident his "friend" wouldn't dare expose his illicit life. Cooper would send the meds to him from Vancouver by UPS addressed in the name of Dr. Martens. By now Cooper and Richardson owned each other. He hated having to do whatever Cora planned for him, not seeing any good end to it, but sometimes even a bad choice is the best there is.

Richardson tried to forgive himself because he was only doing what she demanded. When she found the receipt from Rix for two dinners, she was suspicious. A few years ago, she "innocently" inquired about restaurants in Redmond and asked him if he knew of any good ones. Richardson mentioned Rix but said he hadn't been there lately. When Cora confronted the head waiter with Kevin's photograph, at first the man tried to deny he even recognized him. That's when Cora had him. The whole story came out, and soon Richardson had to admit his affair with Laura Mickens. Following a shouting confrontation, Dr. Alden laid down the demand, and with a planning assist from him, Richardson overcame the poor girl. First it was chloroform and then the overdose injection of insulin under her toenail, causing a catastrophic hypoglycemic reaction. Every day, he played the whole thing over in his mind despite every effort not to. The coroner's office could find no explanation and no basis for a hearing. Richardson's affair went unremarked, and Cora warned he better not do anything like that again, obeyed fearfully by the intimidated Kevin Richardson. Eventually the nightmares stopped and the "ludes" helped him through the day. Even so, a couple times he'd sat in the bathtub with a knife in his hands.

CHAPTER SEVEN

It seemed to the hospital staff that Richardson was continuing as if there had been no questionable death, no Quality Control Committee meeting and no potential malpractice claim. The medication helped, and the tolerance of hospital staff helped even more.

Even the hyper-nosy Dr. Kelly Halloran didn't throw him off when he was in his chemical euphoria.

"Hey Kevin, how's it going? I need to consult with you on something. Gonna be in your office this afternoon?"

Halloran caught him in the doctor's lounge after lunch, and Kelly seemed so cheerful and relaxed Richardson didn't turn him down. Intellectually, Richardson knew he should be wary, but Halloran had been so nonthreatening, and Richardson was medicated. When Halloran got to Richardson's office at The North Seattle Professional Building that afternoon he was right on time at 4 p.m. He dropped his briefcase and hung up his raincoat and umbrella. They were dripping, but so were a couple others. That's the Northwest in winter. Maxine, the secretary, saw her duty and wiped up the little puddle before it could ruin the parquet.

Richardson said nothing and just smiled his Quaalude smile as Halloran sat down. Halloran looked around the woodsy office that seemed more like a man's den than a medical office and admitted to himself, the man had style.

"What's this consultation all about, Kelly?"

"Well, it's not exactly a consultation. I've noticed your stress, Kevin. You're up and down. I worry and thought maybe if I talked to you a little, I might help you. People on the staff think you're moody. They're afraid of you. They think they've done something wrong when you get angry. They think you're overworked when you're tired. I know it's the Quaaludes, and you can't keep it a secret forever. You need to deal with it."

"Nonsense, Kelly. I don't need you to worry about me. This business involves stress. I can't imagine what kind of doctor you'd be if you didn't stress over the health of your patients. They count on you. I've been caring for people thirty years now, and you want to talk to me about my stress in the practice? That's it? You deal with it your way, and I'll deal with it mine. I've taken some prescribed meds and was under control. You're making a problem where there isn't one."

Halloran was still smiling. "I was talking to an old friend, Abel Sunderland, up in Bellingham. He runs a nice facility up there where people can get the pressure off and come back healthier. You need that. You can't tell me you don't need some help. Everyone at Woodside can see it."

"You're talking about the drug rehab hospital in Bellingham. You think I'm a druggie?"

"No, no, Kevin. That's not it at all. It's just a good place for the rest and you can cut down on the usage." Halloran's smile was fading despite his best efforts. Yet Richardson hadn't blown up as Halloran had feared he might. Must have been the drugs. Halloran stood up, smiled back in full force, shook Richardson's hand and said, as he was putting on his raincoat, "Can I set up an appointment for you to meet with Abel? It couldn't hurt."

"Thanks, Kelly, I don't need it. Just be careful not to tell anybody else this little theory you have about me, okay?" Amazingly, the smile still hadn't left his face.

As he left, Richardson wondered why he hadn't told Halloran to go to hell. Oh, well. He sat up for a moment, got his own umbrella and raincoat and checked that Halloran had gone. He walked through the rain, across the street to the hospital, umbrella held over his head, and arriving there, found Nelda Fox in Emergency, helping out until the full review of the Fletcher death. She had just finished injecting a patient. Richardson pondered that if he weren't careful he could be that patient.

He whispered, "Come up to the third floor in Maternity, and meet me in Mrs. Walters' room as soon as you finish with this patient. That's 437." Mrs. Walters was in a single, had been sedated earlier that day and was still half out. They could have a private conversation there they couldn't have many other places in the hospital.

When Nelda walked in, wondering what Richardson wanted, he handed her the Fletcher chart and was pointing to a blank spot. "Here on the 17th. There's a nice big blank area you can write in. I need for you to fill it in. You were there when I told Myra Fletcher I could do a quick surgery and maybe stop the bleeding. I'm sure you remember I told her it was her choice. She said she didn't want to. I need for you to write that down just in case her husband wants to sue."

Nelda was angry but controlled. She wasn't present at any such conversation. She felt more pressure than when she gave in on the record from the night when Myra died and refused to cave this time. She needed a lawyer then, and she needed lawyer Meach now. She couldn't completely rely on Hillibrand, wanted to be her own person, and this was the time to start. She did enough for Richardson and regretted it, yet he wanted more. Nelda had talked to doctors and knew the D&C surgery was a clear call. Richardson should have done it. Now he was just treating her like a tool. And she wasn't going to take it.

"No, Doctor, I wasn't there for that. Don't you remember? Must've been somebody else."

He was still pointing. "Just take care of this for me, okay? I had that conversation with her. You can trust me." Dr. Richardson started suggesting the language she should use, but she stopped him.

She was biting her lip, torn, trembling, between duty and fear. "No, it didn't happen in front of me."

When she walked out, head held high, even the Quaaludes weren't enough to control Richardson's anger. She could have backed him up. He got her out of trouble. She kept her job. She still had a salary. She could have written two lines, and there'd be no potential malpractice claim. Both nurses now became his enemies. He decided he had to deal with Hillibrand. Then Fox wouldn't be a problem anymore. Hillibrand gave her more backbone than he liked. He didn't know if a medical malpractice case was coming, but he knew it was possible and wanted the record to show he offered a D&C to Myra Fletcher. No one could say he hadn't had the conversation, but it would have been nice to be able to prove he had. It didn't yet occur to him, now Nelda could testify he tried to get her to alter the records again, to add something he couldn't otherwise prove.

* * * * * *

Harry Meach was an old war horse of plaintiffs' litigation. He'd partnered in the Harper firm which once commanded a large suite on the 12th floor of the Dexter Horton building just a few blocks from the courthouse in Seattle. The firm had dwindled away as partners retired, and he was the last man standing. He was wily and had a keen eye for the dollar. Plaintiff's lawyers knew he'd often find a way to turn an obvious loser into money for his client. Meach on your side was a good luck charm. Besides, he knew employment law inside out.

Hillibrand and Nelda took to the crusty, cranky, potbellied, bespectacled old man readily because Joe had sent them there with encouraging praise. He didn't look like much, but he was intense and had made quite a name for himself. Nelda was angry because of Richardson's renewed attempts to involve her in his lies. She told Meach she wasn't about to change the record again to bail Richardson out for not doing a D&C. Richardson's pressure might be enough to get Nelda fired or for a constructive discharge if the hospital supported it. Meach appraised Hillibrand and Nelda earnestly across his desk as he explained the law.

He'd written a law review article years before on Washington's "at will" employment law, wrongful termination and constructive discharge cases.

He explained to the nurses that every employee in Washington, in the absence of a contract, is an "at will" employee, who can quit at his or her convenience or be fired at the convenience of the employer. Neither has to give the other an explanation for quitting or firing. That's what "at will" means. But it's a "wrongful discharge" if the employer fires her for some discriminatory or illegal reason.

He explained that if a nurse in a hospital was fired for telling the truth about falsification of hospital records, that would be a good case in court. If the nurse voluntarily changed the records she'd be at fault, but if she were coerced by a doctor on staff, supported by Quality Control, that's still a good case for her.

"Now, 'constructive discharge' is a little trickier. It's a judgment call. Say the employer, every day, tells you 'I really hate your hairstyle.' Would that be so intolerable you'd have to quit? I don't know the answer to that one. If the employer had every other employee pointing a finger at you and yelling dirty words, that would sound like a good ground for you to quit. I'm guessing that could be a 'constructive discharge' just like requiring a nurse to falsify records. In other words, imposing some intolerable condition is just another way of firing an employee. You can treat that as a discharge and file your case. On the other hand, if you leave voluntarily, not under compulsion, your pay stops.

"Now Fletcher has this case pending against the hospital and the doctor. There's no way I'm going to file suit until that's resolved. It would just complicate everything and impact your credibility. It may be the current case will resolve everything you need and there's no reason for me to file suit. If you have any questions, or Joe Gold has any questions, either of you can just call any time. Unless you say otherwise, I'll assume you have no secrets from him. When you're done with this lawsuit, let me know and we'll talk. Keep in mind the potential for a really good case. When it's time, I want to be your lawyer. We'll just sit tight with it for now."

Right then, they were grateful Joe had sent them to Meach. Nothing could be more obvious than what was good for Herb would be wonderful for them, and they both felt deeply they owed him their best. "If you want your salary to continue, don't do anything without checking with me. Most of all, what I mean is don't quit or provoke a fight or get hostile." They would not see Meach again before Herb's suit against Richardson and the hospital was resolved, but they were grateful for his sage advice.

CHAPTER EIGHT

After Halloran's obvious effort to get him out of the hospital, Richardson knew he had to be smarter. He was afraid to do anything to Halloran, because it would be obvious to everybody, and they'd all turn on him. People liked Halloran. But, if he was forced to it, he would stop at nothing. Still, he had to play the game. When Rosen and Karel and Halloran roped him into a meeting without really stating a reason, he popped a Quaalude in preparation.

Halloran took a laid back approach to him. "We're just going to do some strategizing about the Fletcher case."

He always figured Tobin was the manipulator, and maybe he'd finally gotten Halloran onto the team. What would be their next move? Richardson figured to just listen. If they were planning a banquet, he wasn't going to be on the menu.

They met in the lounge, Rosen still in his scrubs, the others in their suits, white shirts open and ties askew after a long day.

"Okay, here's the deal," Karel said, "We need to clean this up right away. Steinman is going to send Hillibrand and that student nurse to work in the psych ward. It's going to be a cut in pay, and they aren't going to like working for Harriet Swett. She's the charge nurse over there, bit of a bitch if you don't know. Sooner or later they'll quit, and you can come back, Kevin. You need to be gone for a while. Too many people see you as a problem. You get too wired up and push people around. The committee gave you a pass so you could reassure everyone. Take a damned vacation, and calm yourself down. We can't make this nice unless we all work together. Next time you come before the board, we want to convince everyone chemicals had nothing to do with it. I mean everyone." He was looking at Halloran.

Halloran sat with his arms folded. "This wasn't my idea. I'd want everyone involved in that whole mess on the carpet before the board. I want to solve these things in-house. I've heard enough not to rely completely on the committee, but I know I'm just one member of the team." Referring to Karel, he told Richardson, "Just do what Elliott said, and I'm okay with that. I see trouble coming sooner or later anyway, but let's all use some sense on this. We can't really think this is going to go on forever."

Despite the "lude," Richardson felt the pressure and came back at an elevated decibel level. "I suspect you'd all like to be rid of me, wouldn't you? It would make it easier for everyone. But then when you have a problem, everyone will remember what happened to me. If we make it easier for people to sue doctors, we'll all pay the cost in higher malpractice insurance rates. So, you want to get rid of me?"

That stopped Halloran for a brief second. He had to decide whether he wanted to give the honest answer or the diplomatic one. It was a question he'd wrestled with for some time. Go to war with Richardson and get rid of the incompetents or accept the current reality? Tough question.

"No, of course not. What we want to do is to help you save your career. That's all your friends here at the hospital want to do. All of us here at Woodside are a team working together. If we wanted to harm you, we could team up with the lawyers. We wouldn't need this meeting."

Karel knew what Halloran was really thinking. He would have liked to have it out with the troublemaker right then, but it seemed like he was going to play ball, and a confrontation with him wouldn't have forwarded the goal anyway. He looked at Richardson who would rather be back in his dreamy chemical world where he didn't have to think. Karel hoped he would follow the common sense advice for once, despite his show of anger.

With his effective, most devious self, Richardson feigned charm. "Thanks boys, I know you mean well. I'm not going to give you any trouble. I keep hearing from some of you what a wreck I am. I think I just might take a vacation when I can get some time. I'm not in the least worried about those two nurses. You've seen the medical charts, there's no problem for me." That was the best Richardson could do.

Karel needed to play some politics. "Kevin, we know how the charts got that way, and the nurses could cause you some real problems if they decide to. This Fletcher thing has to go away, so we all have to work together. If we don't, it hurts the hospital and all of us. I'm not going to be the one who brings it up, but you can bet someone is going to someday if we aren't smart. It would help if you could take some time off."

Richardson tried to end it. "What are you people trying to accomplish? I don't get it. What do you think is going to be the result of all your efforts?" The anger was seeping through.

Rosen decided it was up to him. "Listen Kevin, just admit you're in a bind. I suppose Nelda Fox would disappear without Lois, but then there's Lois. She's got more guts than all of us, and the two of them together could really hurt you. If we allow it, this thing could damage the hospital too. There's too much downside if we can't smooth this over for you, and we all need the hospital to maintain our good reputation. We're doing what we can to discourage the girls. We hope they go away, but you have your own problem. We can't solve it. Notify your malpractice carrier, and just take a break until this all blows over. And then when you come back, you're all cleaned up, and everybody forgets you were accused of doing anything wrong."

Richardson restrained a snarl. "I'll think about it. Just don't try to push me around. I can push back, you know."

Halloran hadn't forgotten that a couple years earlier, something had driven Dr. Eric Martens away, and the outcome of that face-off with Richardson reminded him that in a fight with Richardson, second best was not a good place to be. Drugs or no drugs, Richardson could maneuver in the bureaucratic swamp of Woodside Hospital.

"Nobody's going to push you around, Kevin, we're just giving you a little advice. Think of the welfare of the hospital."

Richardson forced a disarming smile. "Okay, guys, I know you mean well."

* * * * * *

Richardson couldn't wait any longer. It was time to do what Jerry Alden had told him. He'd have to do some scouting around in Hillibrand's neighborhood to see if it would work. When he played it out in his mind, his hands were sweating, and he felt his stomach muscles tightening up. He felt the same fear when Dr. Alden told him what to do about Mickens.

Was this the answer to everything? Could I go through that again?

When he got the insulin and drove around Hillibrand's woodsy neighborhood in an old Chevy he knew it could work. Despite a soul sadness, he told Cora he would leave early that Saturday morning. He told her that would be the day, and he could do it without anyone knowing. His golf foursome wasn't playing till 10 a.m. The firetruck red Corvette was in the shop, and he was driving the anonymous, plain-Jane, gray, "rent-a-wreck" Chevy that day. He decided there was a ticking coming from the Corvette engine. The mechanic at the dealership couldn't hear it but promised he'd take the car out on the road and track it down. They knew a satisfied Richardson might send some of his rich buddies their way and didn't question anything he said. That was a neat way for him to get the anonymous loaner no one would associate with him. His leather bag with the meds was on the seat next to him. Cora said she was glad she referred him to her dad again. It was a "perfect" plan, and though she was his wife, she was his alibi, an unimpeachable community leader, he told himself. It didn't lessen the pain.

Richardson found Hillibrand's house in the forest, down a gravelly road between the little towns of Redmond and Fall City. He had mapped out the route beforehand. When she stepped out of the door that morning, he'd be ready. There were just a few small, old houses, cabins really, so he would park between two ponderous fir trees and out of sight. Richardson was tense, every muscle ready to snap. He didn't dare take a Quaalude. Mellow wasn't what he wanted. He had to be alert. He quickly checked the two neighboring houses as best he could. They probably wouldn't spot the "rent-a-wreck," and if someone spotted the tall man dressed in dark clothes lurking behind the Hillibrand house, his white hair and face were covered. She'd have her back turned the other way when she came out. He'd have her muffled and drugged before she could make a sound.

Richardson kept telling himself his place in the profession and Cora's in the community were more important than anyone's life and couldn't be threatened. A scientist, he could analyze himself and recognized what he was becoming. He coolly concluded the only treatment that would satisfy him was complete security, but it was a security that demanded too much. He'd gotten past the suicide ideation and nightmares once. Could he do it again and survive? And what about the Quaaludes? When Hillibrand was gone, he liked to think he'd be much safer. The young trainee, Nelda Fox wouldn't likely have the guts to challenge a doctor, but could he chance it? Chancing it wasn't security. It was that simple. He sat waiting and wondered about himself.

Can I do this? Will I ever go back to normal? What is normal?

With his Vancouver contact, he had no problem getting the meds he needed over the border and to his office. He didn't need Martens. His connection worked for the Quaaludes and now had supplied the chloroform and insulin. Nobody at the hospital would have any record or knowledge of the origin of his supplies. Richardson focused on his current challenge. The key was getting the chloroform over her nose and mouth and holding it on firmly until Hillibrand was helpless and then do the injection. She would squirm. He knew there was a risk she could wriggle free enough so she couldn't be injected. He simply didn't know what he'd do if she got loose. He decided he would summon up whatever strength he needed.

Richardson made himself familiar with the minimal, rutted country lane leading to the Hillibrand home. He pulled into the turnoff and parked the car, as he planned, between the biggest of the ancient trees, out of sight from the road and the other moss encrusted homes down the lane. He hadn't seen a sign of any neighbors at home, yet he could feel his blood pressure rising and his stomach muscles tensing again. He knew he had to get control of his muscles for them to work. He had to have both strength and coordination, and without his nerves under control, he would have neither.

* * * * *

Lois Hillibrand, getting ready for work, pulled out her insulin kit. The bottle was empty, so she got out a new one. As usual, she didn't plan to inject until after breakfast. She grabbed a quick bowl of oatmeal and was ready to toss the banana peel into the waste can under the sink when she noticed it was full. She sighed with annoyance, pulled out the paper sack stuffed with rubbish and headed out the back door. The bright, sunshine cut through the dark, ugly cloud she'd been living under since the death of Myra Fletcher. She didn't like being a depressed person and lifted her head to a new, brighter day.

Before she got to the garbage cans came the horror. She felt strong hands grabbing her from behind and was helpless to resist the chloroform rag jammed against her face, no matter how much she tried to scream, kick, flail and squirm and was soon senseless. She didn't know it when she was injected with a hypodermic full of insulin, then another. Richardson left her where she was, an apparent victim of a self-administered insulin overdose. He administered some more chloroform with the rag and dropped her onto the pathway. He was suffering from a feeling he remembered, a feeling he suffered when Mickens died. His heart pumped furiously, and he hated the feeling. It was almost like guilt.

The backdoor was still open, and he had to go in. He didn't have to look for the insulin kit waiting to be seen right on the counter. He didn't think of drawing some insulin into the hypodermic and didn't have time to waste. His heart was still pounding, and he realized he was hyperventilating. Richardson left the works on the counter as if Hillibrand had just used it. He ran through the rooms till he found her little office and her file cabinet. He rifled through it until he found what he was looking for, the telltale medical records of Myra Fletcher's death. With his handkerchief he wiped the file cabinet clean as he could and was off with her copy of the records. He was satisfied he'd got the offending records, left no fingerprints, no footprints, no evidence of any kind and was gone, as if he'd never been there. If anyone had seen the nondescript loaner car and the big man in the raincoat and baseball cap, they still couldn't have picked him out of a lineup.

Busting the traffic laws on his way to town, Richardson was right there at the Wellbroke Country Club when his golf gang got together that day, and he had a pretty bad round. He convinced himself he didn't need his Quaaludes. He tried to tell himself he was at peace, done with Hillibrand, and whether he had to deal with Fox would depend on her. He had his ideas. There was little satisfaction at having killed Hillibrand as he thought about Fox and the loose end she might be. Jerry Alden and Cora wouldn't let him rely on Fox's weakness and fear. His own weakness and fear were increasing with every effort to remedy them. When he wasn't drugged, his rage could arise without warning or provocation, even when he was at his calmest. He controlled it and even then the "ludes" would eventually wear off. Feeling the stress rise, he apologized to the guys for his early departure, and couldn't have a second drink. After he left, his group discussed the Richardson problem. What was wrong with him? They wouldn't find out till it made headlines.

CHAPTER NINE

Nurse Harriet Swett needed someone to come in and cover at the psych ward when Hillibrand didn't show up and didn't answer her phone. As far as Swett was concerned, Hillibrand was just a body doing a little time at the ward and was easy to replace. Hillibrand and Nelda knew they'd been exiled to a nothing job and understood the reason. They agreed they'd take it until they were ready to file the lawsuit. Swett didn't particularly care whether Hillibrand or any other space filler came in for the low skill job. Swett called Hillibrand to find out if she should plan around her, but there was no answer. Nelda volunteered to go out to check on Hillibrand after her duty ended that day.

When Nelda got to Hillibrand's house, no one responded to the knock on the door. She couldn't see anyone through the windows and went around to the back. There, she saw Hillibrand next to the path, curled up, gray and dead, collapsed to her knees. The back door was open, so Nelda ran in and called the police. When they arrived, they questioned her as if she were a suspect. Nelda knew a strange face in the suburbs east of Seattle after an unexplained death was grounds for suspicion. Yet they went easy on her as she sat shuddering under a blanket they provided. They were a couple decent sheriff's deputies, hovering over her for a little while after they saw they could do nothing for Hillibrand. Nelda could barely talk. Hillibrand had been her only backbone, and now she felt crushed, adrift again in a dream world of all the fears she had felt, and she couldn't find her way out. Every instinct in her said Richardson was responsible for the death, and somewhere would be the proof. She struggled with the unimaginable and intolerable fact that she'd face life at the hospital without Lois Hillibrand.

The coroner's truck came out, and one of the men was a Dr. Hsu, a precise and fussy little man. He took particular interest in the insulin kit which Lois apparently hadn't used that day. The insulin bottle in the kit was full and didn't appear to have been injected, and the hypodermic was clean and appeared dry. He was looking forward to checking Hillibrand's blood sugar level and calling her internist whose name was on a card inside the kit. When he called, the doctor promised to provide a complete chart to the coroner's office. Nelda tried to tell the young deputy coroner about the intrigue surrounding the suspicious death of Myra Fletcher, but that wasn't within his purview. "Don't tell me, tell the police."

After reviewing the chart and checking the lab work the next day, Dr. Hsu called the coroner. "This is very suspicious. Well, maybe more than suspicious. The lady was quite hypoglycemic. Somebody injected her with a very severe overdose of insulin, but I doubt it was her, and it sure wasn't from her kit. I haven't asked the police yet what they found, but this is looking like a puzzle. Maybe we do an inquest?"

Larry Barnes, the grey, veteran coroner rolled his eyes and held the phone away from him. "If I have to, I suppose."

Looking at the file, the coroner saw that the lead detective was Leland Tracy, formerly known as R. Leland Tracy. He'd gone to court to drop the "R" because, even though the "R" stood for Raymond, not Richard, the guys were calling him Dick Tracy. He was tired of it and hoped dropping the "R" would end the nuisance. When Barnes got Tracy on the line, he summed up Hsu's theory that Hillibrand had been murdered with an insulin shot. Hsu figured that since the bottle in the kitchen hadn't been used, somebody must have injected her and taken their insulin away from the scene. Hsu mentioned the suspicion of Dr. Richardson suggested by a young nurse who'd been at the scene. Barnes pondered an inquest which would be necessary to get a finding that a crime had been committed.

Tracy responded. "That's a good theory that Hsu is pursuing, but before he goes any further, let me bring you up to date on what we found in our search of the 'so-called crime scene.' I understand Hsu found an unused insulin bottle, but in that paper bag Hillibrand dropped, there was a used insulin bottle completely drained. If Hillibrand didn't inject herself with the bottle in the kitchen, it's pretty hard to say she couldn't have used the one in the garbage. Besides, she could have gotten a little hypoglycemic and disoriented and injected herself twice, or maybe she committed suicide. I suspect Hsu might have been a little over-influenced by the nurse lady. Let me know if Hsu has another theory, okay?"

When King County Coroner Charles Barnes told Hsu what the detective had said, the eager-beaver deputy was reluctant to simply label this death by accident and let it go at that. The scene just didn't look right. The clean needle still hadn't been explained.

"And who ever heard of suicide by insulin or taking two doses because of disorientation?"

At Hsu's insistence, Barnes called up Tracy again and said, "My deputy isn't really satisfied. The needle didn't seem to have been used. Will you guys follow up with neighbors, associates, friends, and all that? And there was a young nurse, Nelda Fox, who works at Woodside. She has a theory that a Doctor Kevin Richardson might be involved."

Wearily, Tracy said, "All right, Charles, we'll look for any little whisper of foul play. If we come up with something your office couldn't find, we'll let you know. That clean needle is a little funny. Let's think about that."

Tracy liked a challenge, and this was an interesting one. He took a detective and cruised the neighborhood but turned up nothing. The next thing was to call in Nelda. She made a staunch case for the motive of Doctor Richardson but had nothing to connect Richardson to the death. The clean hypo was suspicious, but there was nobody to charge. He had to settle for telling Nelda to call if anything else turned up. He tried to call Richardson then went to the doctor's office. After making him wait an hour, Richardson, a tall, well put-together, white-haired man, met with him for two minutes. He showed no surprise at the young nurse's accusation. The hospital had disciplined her for negligence in connection with a death she tried to blame on him. He had no information about "poor Lois's" death and was home at the reported time of it. "You can call my wife; she's the President of The Women's League, you know."

It turned out, not surprisingly, Mrs. Richardson remembered that day very well. Her husband was home doing handyman jobs in the early morning and went golfing after that. If there'd been a crime, Tracy still had no one to charge with it. When Nelda called, he reported how little he'd found. She didn't conceal her creeping fear of Richardson, was convinced he committed a crime and believed he would target her next. Tracy didn't think it was his job to calm her fears. He was in law enforcement, not psychiatry. Nelda saw it was up to her.

If he won't do anything I guess I have to. But how?

Chapter Ten

Now Joe had the Fletcher case. He was firm and committed and ready to go, but in the Gold firm anything as serious as that was important to all the partners. They had sent out to the deli, and got loaves of rye, 12-grain and French bread, cold cuts, bottles of pop and fresh fruit to polish it off. The firm officed two levels up from the old Carpenter Gold office which had slimmed down a bit as the Golds were now flourishing. They enjoyed the view from the conference room, the same as it had been at Carpenter Gold. Joe looked out over Puget Sound, while the rest of the partners sprawled along the 9 foot leather couch, and above them was the Picasso liberated from Carpenter Gold when they left. Only Ed was missing, excluded by the limitations of his ethical conflict.

The remaining partners, Joe, Mike, and Mike's wife, the lovely Diana, batted ideas back and forth on a Friday afternoon. Everyone else had gone home, most of them early. As a general rule, by Friday afternoon, the law practice drained all the office staff, so there weren't many left then. The Gold partners had too much on their plate and not just the sandwiches which would be their dinner that night. Joe figured he'd be hearing about it from Sandra when he got home. They decided to meet, pretty much at the last minute, and Sandra was probably making Joe's dinner when the phone calls went out.

Joe voiced his frustration. "We damn well know Richardson killed Hillibrand, but there are only so many ways you can connect somebody to a crime. Everybody agrees there was a motive. She gave Nelda a copy of the incriminating medical records, but somehow Hillibrand's copies

67

disappeared from her house. Funny how that happened. Only problem, we can't prove Richardson was ever there. The police canvassed the neighborhood, and nobody saw his red Corvette, which would stand out like a sore thumb. They looked for fingerprints and found nothing. We can't even prove for sure there was a murder. It's a bare theoretical possibility Lois might have injected herself, but that little accident, if that's what it was, was just too convenient."

"Anyway, I talked to the investigating officer. By the way, he hates it when people refer to him as Dick Tracy. He's got nothing to take to the prosecutor except that the hypo appeared not to have been used. Tracy says that's not enough. Theoretically, it could have been cleaned. The coroner isn't going to do an inquest, because there isn't enough to even justify that. I guess I can forget about the police proving that case for us. Tracy said he'll give us everything he's got that he can provide, and if we find something to connect with Richardson, we give it to him."

Diana shrugged. "Sounds like a good deal to me. Better than nothing."

It was Mike's turn. "As long as we watch it, we might get some information from Dad, but we can't forget the ethical issue. He has to leave the witnesses and the detective stuff to us. Someday down the line, they're going to be questioning us about how much help he gave us in handling the case, and I'd like to be able to say on oath, we did it on our own. He knows what goes on in the staff at Woodside and we don't yet."

Diana turned toward Joe and added, "If this Nelda is believed, you may be able to prove the board and staff routinely cover up for negligent doctors. Richardson's alteration of hospital records may not be a one-time thing. She claims he asked her to make another alteration. He wanted her to falsely write in that he made a suggestion to Myra for a D&C. So, Nelda, by herself can testify to a request for more than one forgery. That's an unfair and deceptive business practice right there and brings into play the Consumer Protection Act, treble damages and reasonable attorney fees. And besides, that would be such a black eye for the hospital, I don't see how they could let a case like that go to trial." She laughed. "Their Quality Control Committee is a joke, it's a quality prevention committee, but with Hillibrand gone, we need medical witnesses to back up Nelda. Let's not kid ourselves. We can't count on her to win the case for us all by herself."

Joe stood up to end the meeting and had the last word. "Mike, I might be asking you to help me out on this one if I get jammed up. This is going to be a big case like Perini."

As the others stood up, Joe had another thought. "You know, I remember Dad mentioning a doctor that disappeared, fellow named Martens. I'm going to call him about that."

They all sat back down as Joe called his dad. Gretchen answered the phone and got Ed on the line. "Dad, we're talking about witnesses, and I remember your saying something about a doctor who disappeared. You said there were some rumors about Richardson forcing him out. Was that something we need to follow-up on?"

"Well, I'm not sure how much I can say ethically. I'll just tell you there's a doctor at Woodside named Kelly Halloran. Some time back, a Dr. Eric Martens disappeared, and the story was he had some info about Richardson. Halloran reminded me, we never found out what happened to Martens, where he went or why he left. The rumor was he had some kind of a run-in with Richardson about his drugs. There's nothing I can tell you for sure. What you do is up to you, Joe."

Joe relayed what his dad had said and added his own conclusion. "Somebody should talk to Halloran and see what he knows. Maybe there's something there. Maybe there's a secret about Richardson, and if we turn over that rock, Halloran might talk off the record, and we'll find out something we can use. Maybe he'll even testify."

Nobody was joking as they walked out the door. It was a heavy load Joe carried and not just legally. Diana gave Joe a sisterly pat on the back, and Mike gave a brotherly slug on the shoulder. They were with him. Ed's and the firm's reputation and Herb Fletcher's case were at risk, and no one wanted to talk about what a dangerous guy Richardson was. Richardson had to know Nelda was the crucial witness.

Two people dead. Would Nelda be next?

CHAPTER ELEVEN

That night, Joe and Sandra strolled their way to the library in the 50-year-old Magnolia mansion they had finally moved into. The restoration had taken months, but it was worth it. The apartment overlooking Puget Sound had been nice, but it was just an apartment, and with the baby coming, clearly inadequate. From a certain point of view, the mansion made no sense, a drafty old 5,000-square-foot relic, five bedrooms, library, office, dining room, living room, kitchen, ballroom for Chrissake, and a laundry room. Here they were, just the two of them and one little one on the way, in this monster museum piece.

With all that was against the house, there was one fact of compelling logic that led to their purchase. "I love it," Sandra had said, and Joe was helpless to resist. Joe had met Sandra while Mike was representing her first husband, Marco, in a major lawsuit. Sandra and Marco's marriage was a mess. After all Sandra had to endure with Marco and then the scene of his murder, the litigation and the threat of loss of all she and Marco had built together, Joe couldn't find it in him to resist something so important to her. The baby and the magnificent house would help restore all that was optimistic in her.

She'd recovered sight of that long missing light of joy, and Joe was seeing it, too. This big house would soon be ariot with running little feet and the kind of laughter Joe remembered from his own wild, preteen years with his brother. Dad's gift of shares in the Harbor Building and then hitting it big with the settlement annuity from the huge Perini case ended their money worries forever. The new mansion didn't even make a dent. Money wasn't the problem.

Something was still missing for Sandra, and Joe didn't get it. Marco Perini had been a business whirlwind, and that's what she expected with Joe. But Joe was bitten by the trial lawyer bug and wanted to help the little guy, not the insurance companies he'd represented at Carpenter Gold. He and his brother, now together in The Gold Law Firm, agreed on that. As happy as Sandra was, she still held back. The library had a big picture window overlooking Elliott Bay. They sat on the puffy antique loveseat enjoying the view. Joe was patting Sandra's tummy, the current residence of the expected infant. Joe's contented smile was a dream come true for Sandra after her years of failure to conceive with Marco.

"I can't tell you how happy I am, Sandra. Boy or girl, doesn't matter. I've got my career, and I've got my wife, and my baby is on the way. I don't know what more I need."

"I love it all too, Joe, and I'm really happy. You rescued me. But I wonder about one thing. You once told me Mike said he felt like a comic book hero when he was a little boy. He said he wanted to grow up and be Batman. I think he still has that mentality, and you're starting to get it, too. But, you know what? It's more like you're following in your younger brother's footsteps. If he's Batman, you're Robin. Litigation is great for someone who wants to live in a comic book world. A comic book life's a little messy, if you ask me."

"I suppose, if you want to look at it that way, but I think it's what I was born for. It feels really good devoting ourselves to righting wrongs, when you don't have to worry about money. The firm's a goldmine. I'm lucky to have the ability to do good things for good people and make money at it. Some of the great men in the community are just crooks in suits, and I can make them step up. Maybe you think litigating is just getting your hands dirty, but the way I look at it, we're cleaning up the community. The hospital is burying its mistakes, and unless someone does something about it, they'll keep doing it. Myra is just the latest victim, and there'll be more."

"You shouldn't be just a trial lawyer. I'm glad you're enjoying your fantasy world, but your firm has real business clients. I think you have a great business sense, and you shouldn't waste it. Joe, there's another thing that you haven't talked about. Aren't you afraid of Richardson? Maybe I'm just nervous because I'm pregnant, but the idea of sitting home alone, just me and the baby scares me. Isn't there something you can do about that? I know what you guys have been talking about. You think he's a murderer, don't you?"

Joe was not smiling. "I'll have to think about that. I don't want you having to worry about him. After all, you're not his target. Nelda is the one who has to worry. We'll do whatever we have to do to keep you both safe."

When their maid, gray-haired, old Mrs. Davidson, brought scones, mugs and a ceramic coffee pot to the library, he just stared, his mind somewhere else. He had to get Sandra's silly anxiety out of his head in order to think clearly about the main burden he'd assumed and the real fear issues he couldn't evaluate. Richardson's mind was beyond the world of his experience. When he came to bed at 1 a.m. Sandra was asleep, and he was careful not to wake her. She needed her rest.

The next morning was Saturday. Sandra, at first, was as cheerful as usual, and the fears of the night before had, at least for her, disappeared. She smiled. "Okay, Joe, I'm happy. This is your Family Saturday, but it's mine too. I get to see Marie and Gretchen and especially my sister."

With Sandra more cheerful, Joe felt a little weight ease, and he grinned. "I bet Diana wishes she were pregnant."

"No, I think she enjoys being a lawyer, and then she's going to have to take a break from that one day, and she'll be a terrific mom. Knowing her, one day she'll say she'd like to have a baby, and a week later she'll deliver. Then the day after that, she'll be back to her normal size and shape and cute and not a grumpy blimp like me. Look what you did to me. I'm an ocean liner. I need a tugboat to get me around the house. Or maybe I'm a dirigible. I need a ground crew, and Diana is still the baby gazelle. If someone came after me I'd be helpless."

Here was the pessimism again. Joe pretended to laugh off Sandra's pregnancy blues as if they were piffle, helped her down the long stairs and seated her carefully in the Cadillac. Maybe Diana and Marie could talk to her and get her back the optimism she had before she started to worry about Richardson. Joe hoped the stress was just a temporary result of pregnancy and curable. Then there was still that fear thing in the back of his own mind. And how could he deal with it? All through the happy day at his dad's home there was still one thought gnawing like a worm in the back of his skull.

Could it be real? Did he have to fear for Sandra's safety?

Chapter Twelve

When Joe first met Halloran at his busy office, the doctor sat him down in an idle examining room with charts on the wall, a gurney and an EKG. He seemed tentative and cautious talking to him. They agreed the board needed to know what was going on with Quality Control and especially what happened with the Fletcher girl. Halloran wanted to make it clear, if Joe was calling for help suing the hospital, Halloran wanted no part of that. "Mr. Gold, I still have some loyalty to the hospital, even though it needs a lot of help and needs to get its act straightened out."

"I'm not expecting your help on the lawsuit. And I'm not blaming you for getting the two nurses suspended, but I admit I was pretty stunned that Richardson got off clean."

"Honestly, so was I. You know, I wanted him to be looked at before he could use his staff privileges again. I guess they figured his patients shouldn't be deprived of their doctor. But in my opinion, they're better off with someone who's less a big wheel and more a physician."

"But I came here to talk about Eric Martens. I hear you were wondering about him too. There was something about him disappearing after some kind of a hassle with a doctor. Was that Dr. Richardson?"

"Yes, Eric was a friend of mine. I think your dad knew him, too."

"Perhaps. I hear these stories, and I'm wondering if it bears on the secrecy at Woodside. If we lift the lid on that one, maybe this whole policy of covering up for doctors who shouldn't even be practicing goes away. I think you and I can agree that the best thing for Woodside would be a reputation for honesty and more care about the patients. You're on the board and nobody can say you're disloyal if you're promoting honesty."

Joe could see Halloran weighing his words. "Well, in a way you might be right, but I have to be careful what I say. Don't think just because I'm doing the right thing, no one's going to try and nail me. Even if they won't say so, everyone suspects Richardson for what happened to Hillibrand. But if anyone bucks the system, I guarantee you, one way or the other, the system will buck back. The only way I, as a member of the board, am able to do anything is quietly and around the back door. I'd like to think I'm too smart to get my ass in the wringer. I can answer questions for you, and I can point the direction to go, but I'm not going to do it if it's going to end my career. Don't count on me being a witness and getting on oath. Let's talk about this, just you and I together, keep it away from the board, and you can do your own little investigation. What do you think?"

"Sure, Doctor, that would be good. But I can't guarantee you somewhere down the road, no one is going to subpoena you to testify. If the truth comes out, I don't think anyone is going to want to go to jail for perjury, and you may have to be the first one to blow the whistle. So it could come down to truth or consequences. Still want to talk to me?"

Halloran shrugged. It wasn't obvious what the gesture meant. "Okay, that's fair. Well, let's say, just hypothetically, maybe a few years ago, Martens and Richardson had some kind of side business together. All I heard was it was something involving a drug distributorship. Most drug companies deal direct with hospitals and pharmacies, but this might have been an agency with an office in Vancouver, B.C. that took care of shipping and record keeping. Supposedly, it was real cost effective for the companies, and maybe it was good for the pharmacies and hospitals, too. Maybe you can find the records to verify this."

"One day, Martens just popped into my office about 5:30. He was down the hall from me, so sometimes we'd go have a drink at the end of the day. This day, he came in, and he was real wired up, pale and shaky. He told me this Canadian company's records were screwed up, and Richardson told him that if the B.C. Province audited them, they'd lose their business and then maybe their medical licenses, too. Eric said he'd been suspicious about Richardson, because sometimes he seemed spaced out, like he was on something. He asked him, but Richardson insisted he wasn't on anything. Truthfully, they both were a little out of it at times. I don't want to testify, you understand, but there were rumors about Quaaludes, and I might guess there was some reason for the rumors."

"Of course, Kelly, I get it. Just idle chit chat." Joe knew it was anything but chit chat.

"And then, supposedly, something went wrong, and as far as Martens knew, the whole thing ended. Then there was some trouble, and Martens was suspected of doing something underhanded, I don't know what. I ran into him in the lobby of the North Seattle Professional Building, and he was real upset, and he couldn't talk. All he could tell me was that Richardson was putting some kind of pressure on him, and he had to leave. The next day I went up to his office, and the staff was closing it. His patients all over town were looking for a new OB/GYN doc and getting their charts back. Finally all that was left was his name on the door, and then that was gone, and I never saw the guy again."

"Did you do anything more?"

"Not really. I just innocently asked Richardson, one day, if he knew what happened to Martens. He pretended they were casual acquaintances and told me he didn't know anything. I asked around the hospital, and nobody knew anything except somebody said the name of the drug company Martens was involved in was Americanada Ltd. Oddly, a doctor named Cooper in Vancouver B.C. was the local rep. I called up the company, and I think it was Cooper that I talked to, and he said he didn't know where Martens had gone, and he couldn't give me any other information. He did tell me he could get me really good prices on drugs if I got a state permit."

"I was going to call up the British Columbia Medical Association to see what I could find out about Americanada Ltd., and then I never got around to it. A couple people wondered about Richardson being doped up, and supposedly he told someone he once was taking prescribed meds, and he'd stopped. But he still has his problems. You can see him getting all wound up, then he goes to the bathroom and comes back all calm and sleepy."

"Didn't get around to it? You mean you chickened out, right? You weren't going to take on Richardson."

Halloran looked away and smiled sheepishly, silently confessing, despite his reputation as a hell raiser, his prudence or perhaps, true timidity.

When Joe called the state's health department, after no more than the usual bureaucratic runaround, he found that Eric Martens was no longer in Washington and didn't have an active Washington license to practice medicine. Joe called the Seattle Police for Detective Tracy who was not in. He was about to head off to the gym for a noon basketball game when Tracy called back.

"What have you got, Mr. Gold?"

Joe laid out what Halloran had told him and put it to Tracy. "I suggest getting in touch with every other state medical society and finding out where the hell Martens is. I've got to believe he can tell us something about Richardson no one else knows. Can you make those calls?"

Tracy didn't answer right away. "You've got a pretty good sized law firm. I bet you've got some $2 an hour girl there who could make those calls. You're making pretty good progress, but what you're talking about is a manpower drain I'd like to avoid if I can. Can you do it?"

"All right, I'll find somebody for that, but the day is going to come when I ask for something in return. I don't mind doing work that helps our clients and the Seattle PD, but I'm going to need a favor from you someday."

"You've got it, Gold."

At noon, before he headed to the gym, Joe stopped by Jodi Hedlund's desk and gave her the task of locating Martens.

"Track this guy down. He's a doctor somewhere in the U.S.A and I need to know where."

He carefully spelled out Eric Martens for her and said, "We've already eliminated Washington State."

Then Joe took off for the noon-hour basketball tussle at The Washington Athletic Club, followed by a quick gut burger at the chrome and vinyl downstairs café. He got back to the office, wondering whether there had been any progress in locating Martens. According to Jodi, a girl on the office staff had found Martens after only 20 calls. It was 1:30 in Seattle, so 2:30 in Aurora, Colorado. When Joe called, a receptionist in the Quality Assurance Department of the University of Colorado Hospital stalled him. Finally he got through. The only way to talk to Martens was to get his trust. The only way to do that was to explain who he was, why he was calling and lay out the history. He wasn't sure Martens would listen that long. Joe explained what happened to Myra Fletcher and then the suspicious insulin overdose death of Lois Hillibrand. Joe was only halfway through when Martens said, "I can't really talk right now. Is there a number I could call tonight?"

Joe feared this could be a brushoff, but after dinner the call came. Joe laid out the picture Halloran had given him, and Martens was ready to fill in the rest. "I can tell you this stuff because I'm not that afraid of Richardson as long as I'm here in Aurora, but I'm not looking to be the front man in a fight with him. I'm willing to give you the background so you can develop your evidence on Richardson. Okay? I just don't want to stick my neck out and be a witness."

This was an annoying echo of Halloran. Joe would let him think he could skate. "Sure, that's okay."

Now Martens was ready to spill. "This is strictly confidential. It didn't come from me. Okay? I'm pretty sure Richardson got his drugs from

Americanada Ltd. in Vancouver B.C. I believe he and the guy up there were partners, and so Richardson was able to get whatever drugs he needed shipped from Canada to the North Seattle Professional Building with my name on them. But they weren't delivered to me. They were picked up by Richardson. His buddy forged the records, so if the Province ever investigated, it would be me who was in their sights, not Richardson. Taking that risk was Richardson's price for my peace and safety. My wife was really scared of him, you know."

"I finally got the guts and told Richardson he had to cut this drug business off or I'd report him. He blew up and threatened he'd report me for drug dealing. I knew who would win a battle like that at Woodside, so I got out and looked elsewhere. I found myself a nice quality control job here in Aurora, Colorado. What a load off my shoulders when I got out of there. Kevin was a scary guy. See, I'm not going to take him on. Do what you can, just don't ask me to testify."

"So you won't sign an affidavit and testify in a case in King County where we've had at least one person die because of Richardson's carelessness and a nurse's death where he's a suspect?"

"I'm afraid not. If I were still there I don't know, but by the way, you mentioned the death of a nurse. Was it by insulin?"

"Yeah, how did you guess that?"

"A girl who worked for Richardson died of an unexplained cause when I was there. I don't remember her name. There was some talk she was his girlfriend. There was an autopsy and the best guess was a stroke, mostly by history, but I wonder whether they ever checked for hypoglycemia, which is what you'd find if she'd been injected with insulin. They found her in her apartment's yard. She seemed in a daze, and then she just collapsed and never regained consciousness. Like everyone else, the first thing I thought when I heard the story was stroke, but if she died of an insulin overdose that would be a hell of a coincidence."

"Wow, I'd better mention that to the police. Do you know when that was? Can you try to remember the girl's name?"

"I can't help you with any of that. I just don't remember. All I recall is that it was at Woodside and it was, I think, 1961. Since there was an autopsy, you could probably get more info from the medical examiner, I guess you call that the coroner in Washington."

When Joe called Detective Tracy, he was more than a little bit interested, agreed the ball was now in his court and said, "Thanks, Gold, you can count on me returning the favor one day."

"Thanks, Detective, I'll remember that. Just tell me what you find. You know, everyone is afraid of Richardson."

"Watch your step, Gold. I don't want you playing cop, got it? I'm not sure what you're getting into."

What the hell am I getting into? If Sandra heard what I just heard, she'd be scared out of her mind. Maybe I should be.

Chapter Thirteen

The Gold family took advantage of a rare, sunny but cold winter day in early 1964 at the family residence on the parklike, green shore of Lake Washington. Breakfast, that Saturday, was served in the atrium, though there were no sailboats playing in their view. Gretchen wouldn't have complained about hauling the food all that distance anyway, but Marie insisted on buffet style. "You big, strong boys can help out a little here." She wouldn't let Sandra carry a thing.

Sandra was going to be carrying the baby for at least another three months. Despite her proud grin, she still sometimes let it slip how she felt about Joe "just" being a trial lawyer. It seemed odd, a litigator's wife who apparently didn't think much of the profession. But until the baby -- Lana if a girl or Lance if a boy -- was born, Joe feared tangling with her hormones. He didn't think of himself as "just" a trial lawyer. He knew who he was and where he was going. Ripping the mask off the medical ethics at Woodside was a far step ahead of "just" being a trial lawyer as far as Joe was concerned. Still, the family didn't want to stress Sandra over her odd attitude. Breakfast was the usual relaxed, placid and extended food orgy, but they never strayed far from law.

Joe's mind rarely went elsewhere. He looked forward to fighting it out with Brosius and MacCallum, who certainly would be appearing for Richardson and with whoever appeared for the hospital. Dad expected it would be someone from the Carpenter Zale firm, formerly Carpenter Gold. The Gold family had split off from them in a policy dispute. The Golds wanted to represent plaintiffs, and the firm insisted on representing only insurance companies. Now the Golds were on the opposite side of the fence, friendly enemies.

After breakfast, sitting relaxed in the booklined den, Ed warned Joe, "If you have to try this case against Mark Zale, he'll be a toughie, but I think you can handle him, and I know you can handle MacCallum. He sometimes gets a little over-aggressive, and I think that hurts him in court."

Joe didn't fear trying the case against the tougher litigator, Zale, if it came to that. He remembered Zale didn't lose often. But Dad said, "Don't worry so soon, might not be Zale, but anyway, if it's Zale he'll represent the hospital, not the doctor. Besides, neither of the defense lawyers can change the facts, and you're no slouch either." Joe appreciated the verbal pat on the back, and beating Zale would make his reputation the way the Perini case had made Mike's. However, losing the case would, regrettably, make his reputation too.

Mike focused on investigation, and his most interesting issue at this point was still proving the connection between Richardson and the mysterious Hillibrand death. The death of Myra Fletcher was connected with Richardson and may, arguably, have led to the need for Hillibrand's death, but courts don't allow cases to go to the jury on speculation. Even proof that Richardson killed Hillibrand wouldn't prove that any negligence of his caused the death of Myra. But, it could raise the inference that he considered Hillibrand a dangerous witness.

Joe wondered about the idea of another death being connected to Richardson. "Dad, Martens told me there were rumors about a girl dying suspiciously, and she might've had an affair with Richardson. There's this Detective Tracy of the Seattle PD who told me he's going to follow up on that. I wonder if Nelda might've heard some talk around the hospital about Richardson having an affair." Joe planned to call Nelda later that day. He thought out loud. "We're ready to file, Dad. You're probably going to hear about it at the hospital if you go to the next board meeting"

"I damn well am going." He didn't want to say more. Mike added, "Joe, one of us needs to touch base with Tracy pretty soon." Ed held his tongue. Every time the Fletcher case came up in conversation, Ed struggled to keep himself out of the loop as much as he could despite his natural inclination.

* * * * * *

In the kitchen, Sandra, leaning back in a chair to support her bulging belly ranted to Marie. Gretchen was listening with a bland look on her face but wondering what was wrong with that lady.

"I try to explain to Joe, he could be a business leader instead of just another courthouse lawyer, and he gets mad. I don't know why. He just doesn't take it well. I always thought he was looking for more. I kind of miss that go-getter business attitude that Marco had. Don't get me wrong, I'm grateful that Joe came along and saved me after Marco was killed, but I did love Marco's ambition."

Marie laughed. "You don't think Joe's ambitious? His ambition is to help people who need help. You sound as if it's a disgrace to be in the best firm of trial lawyers in town. Pretty soon, the whole town will know Joe's a great lawyer. Sandra, this pregnancy is getting to be too much for you. You should be proud. Cut that stuff out. Don't you get it? Just watch. Sandra, whatever the doctor has you on, it's making you nuts. Joe is the right guy for Herb's case, and you can tell it's damned important to him. Don't get on him. He doesn't need that."

"I don't want him to drop the Fletcher case. It's after that I'm talking about."

"I'm done. You keep it up and see what it gets you. I don't think it will go so well."

Gretchen busied herself with the dishes in the sink as if she hadn't heard a bit of it.

Later that night when Joe called, Nelda said, "If you can, get a picture of the girl that died and take it to a place called Rix in the Northgate area, they might recognize her. Lois told me that when she went there with Richardson, they seemed to know him pretty well.

* * * * * *

On Monday, Joe did talk to Tracy, suggesting that he get a picture of the woman who died, show it around at Rix and the hospital and see if people could put Richardson together with the woman. "And I understand there was no cause of death determined for certain. Maybe she wasn't tested for hypoglycemia. It would be quite a coincidence, if two women close to Richardson died of hypoglycemia due to an insulin overdose, particularly if one of them wasn't diabetic. Can you get the coroner to re-examine her? There's a doctor at the University of Colorado Hospital in Aurora, Colorado you might want to talk to. He used to be at Woodside. His name is Martens. He's in quality control there. They call it 'quality assurance.' He can tell you a lot about Richardson and drugs. There's a doctor at Woodside who seems to have a bit of a rebellious streak in him. His name is Halloran, might give you information nobody else there will. You should talk to him, too. You interested?"

"Damn right. I appreciate all those suggestions, and I will take them into account. Give me the names and phone numbers of anybody you think has information." Joe gave him the info on Nelda, Halloran and Martens, and Tracy told him he'd track down the identification of the mystery woman supposedly involved with Richardson. Two days later Tracy, now his good buddy, called him back. "I've done some work on those leads you gave me, and I've got something for you."

Joe had filed the case and went to work on the Requests for Production and subpoenas for hospital records. When Tracy called back, Joe set aside the discovery requests and subpoenas he was working on. He walked to the Seattle Public Safety Building as fast as he could. He sat on the edge of a hardback wood chair in the detectives' waiting room until Tracy stuck his head out and said, "Come on back." When they got back to Tracy's shoebox of an office, he sat Joe down in another hardback chair and handed over a couple pictures of an attractive young woman.

"This is Laura Mickens, the woman Richardson was taking to Rix and who died of unknown causes. She was a patient of his. Then she became a part-time office tech, basically a fetching and carrying specialist. After a while there, she separated from her husband, Milo Mickens. Cutesy name. And I think I have trouble with my name."

Tracy smiled at Mickens' alliterative name.

"Anyway, Milo raised hell when he found out Laura's doctor, then boss, was seeing her socially. By "socially," I mean, it looked to Milo like they were sleeping together. Milo was still trying to get her back home, but he thought she was under the influence of something. He thought it was booze, but it sounds more like downers. The coroner should have talked to him."

Joe reacted instantly. "Ludes?"

"Possibly. I'm just spitballin' here. She was a healthy young woman, but one day she was lying in the front yard and the emergency medics couldn't revive her. I got some pictures of her from Milo, and I had a couple pictures of Richardson. So I go out to Rix, and the bartender and hostess tag them. They were a hot item, gobbling each other up in the bar right in front of whoever was there. You should have heard what Milo said. 'If Richardson turns up dead, I did it.' Seriously. So next thing, I have to get a court order to dig Laura up. Milo will sign his affidavit in a New York minute. Hsu at the coroner's office will re-examine and see if he can find what killed her, now that we have this suspicion about insulin. So that's it."

"Quite a mouthful, detective. The other end of it is to talk to Martens. I think he can help you with the drug source."

"Thank you, Gold. I know you're doing it for a client, but I've been waiting a while to pull the plug on some of these fatheads who do what the hell they want in our hospitals, and then they cover it up."

"That's exactly how I feel about it."

Joe arrived back at his office. He and Mike took a coffee break. It was rare for them to have time to sit and relax together during the business day. Joe laid out the progress he'd been making in investigating the case, and he could see Mike's interest perk up when he told the story of the unfortunate Laura Mickens.

Steam was practically coming from Mike's ears. "This guy's a real SOB. We've got to nail him."

Joe took the longer view. "Yes, we want to get him, but even more than that, there's this system of covering up for negligent docs. You have to wonder how much malpractice there is out there that no one knows about except the doctors and nurses. They complain about their malpractice coverage, but how much would they be paying if all the malpractice were caught?" He passed a copy of his recently filed complaint against Richardson and the hospital and the proposed discovery for comment.

"Looks good. I'm glad you're on it."

As they walked out Joe was thinking about what kind of medical practice would be treating his pregnant wife.

Chapter Fourteen

Tracy carefully avoided overstating the case. He brought his affidavit laying out the findings of his original investigation of the death of Laura Mickens to the prosecutor. When she died, there was no reason than to suspect insulin, but then came the highly suspicious death of Hillibrand from an apparent insulin overdose and the connection of Richardson to both cases. Milo Mickens signed the consent to the exhumation and his affidavit attesting to his suspicion of Richardson. Dr. Hsu backed up Tracy with his own affidavit attesting that he hadn't looked for hypoglycemia as part of the original autopsy, because there was no reason to suspect insulin and that the recent death of Lois Hillibrand raised a concern for Hsu. He stated hypoglycemia would suggest that Ms. Mickens had received insulin though she wasn't a diabetic.

The documents satisfied the fossilized Judge Camorra, and he signed the order for exhumation and reopening the coroner's exam. This time, Hsu knew what he was looking for. If the blood-sugar level was below normal, Laura Mickens probably was injected, and what appeared to be a stroke was not. She wandered out of her garden apartment into oblivion at age 35. Within a week after the exhumation, Hsu called Tracy. "I'm sorry. It was too long ago, dammit. There's decomposition and chemical changes, and I just can't give you a result you can take to court. I can't make a finding with 'reasonable medical certainty."

When Tracy called Milo Mickens, he had to hold the phone away from his ear. Three whole years' worth of anguish exploded out of the phone at the detective. "Hell, he did it. You know it and I know it, and we still can't prove it?"

The lab results discouraged Joe, and as far as the coroner was concerned, there was no basis to claim a murder by anyone. Two inconclusive cases didn't equal one conclusive case. Was there a way to connect Richardson to the two deaths beyond speculation? Did Martens have the answer? And then, if you have a convincing case that Richardson killed Hillibrand and Mickens, it still came down to Nelda. She wasn't a very impressive little thing until you talked to her and looked in her eyes. Emotionally, she was a basket case but still was set firmly on the path for justice. It wasn't enough to be relieved of the blame for the death of Myra Fletcher. Joe wanted Richardson and the staff who covered for him to pay a price. When the jury saw Nelda and got to know her, Joe hoped, they would understand.

Am I kidding myself? Can I really trust her that much?

Before they got too far down the road, he would have to take it up with the rest of the Gold Law Firm brain trust. Hillibrand's sister called and wanted to sue Richardson. Joe had to tell her, if someday a case could be proved, she'd have to talk to another lawyer. He explained his conflict of interest and never heard from her again. He hated putting her off.

The next Saturday was a Family Saturday for the Golds, and Mike and Diana were there. After breakfast, all the Golds got together in the den. Joe laid out the disappointment of the coroner's inability to establish a cause of death for the Mickens girl. Ed sat mute, but Mike thought further conversation with Martens might be productive. "Joe, you need to get the Americanada, Ltd. records. They might turn up something interesting. What if Martens will testify all the shipments of drugs in his name were really shipments to Richardson? Richardson's credibility will go down the drain if you can prove he was a drug user and dealer and if we can show insulin deliveries he can't explain. CEO, Tobin and Quality Control Director Karel may have a little difficulty covering for him when their own fannies are hanging out in the wind."

Diana pointed out all the discovery Joe drafted was for people within the hospital, and all the records were hospital records. "You need to broaden your discovery. Get the names of all the people who worked in Richardson's office in the last ten years and all the healthcare practitioners he dealt with, even his own healthcare providers. It might be interesting to find out what he's been treated for and if Quaaludes were prescribed."

"Okay, those are all good ideas. I'll follow up on that, but it won't be a huge surprise if he lies about getting drug counseling or treatment. He's not going to tell us that."

Diana smiled. "Hey, like your dad always says, you've got to be a belt and suspenders kind of guy. If one trail peters out, you try all the rest of them till you find the right one. You're going to get that guy. One way or another you're going to."

Joe liked hearing that from Diana. It wasn't just a pat on the back and encouragement. That wasn't her style. It was legal advice from someone very young but very bright.

* * * * * *

On the following Monday morning, Joe went to work on expanding the discovery and meanwhile put in a call to Harry Meach. Finally about 4:30, Meach returned Joe's call. He'd been in court but had been thinking about Nelda. "I haven't been able to reach her. After Hillibrand died, Nelda's hours got cut down even more. She has no friends at Woodside. Even more, she's afraid of Richardson. She's sure he killed Hillibrand and that she's next."

"Harry, Hillibrand wasn't the first."

"What? What do you mean? He killed someone else?"

"There was a woman he was involved with, and after her husband raised a stink, she died under suspicious circumstances. The police looked at it, but they couldn't prove a thing."

"So, what good does it do, if you can't prove anything?"

"We've got some ideas. Nelda is in the middle of it for us, so we're going to be talking to her. Richardson might come after her and she needs protection. She's got terrible anxiety problems. We'll work with you if you need us. You don't have to take Richardson head on the way I do. Your battle is just a battle with the hospital administration and will probably come from a nice, simple, wrongful discharge. We're taking on a battle with the old 'conspiracy of silence' and we need to destroy it to win. I think we've got the case to do it with."

"Joe, I'll stick with you, but I don't envy you your job."

CHAPTER FIFTEEN

As Nelda's hours dwindled, nurse Swett didn't pretend to be tactful about it. She just said, "There are only so many hours we need, and I'm not giving extra hours to someone without much experience."

Under instructions from Mr. Meach, Nelda jotted down everything, but she felt depressed, living hand to mouth before her hours were cut, and so she asked lawyer Meach for help.

"They're cutting my hours down to almost nothing. By the time Joe tries the suit, it will be completely nothing. I can't go to work for another hospital, because they'll ask for references from Woodside. Even if I get hired, I'll be scared stiff that Richardson will find me, and I'll be dead just like Lois."

When she hung up the phone, Nelda felt worse than ever. Sometimes, asking for trouble doesn't get you anything except trouble. Meach didn't have much to offer other than encouragement. "This will be over someday, and you're going to be successful in court. I can't guarantee it, but I strongly feel it. We've won weaker cases. Just hang in there, Nelda. I know it isn't easy when you feel yourself detached from the world."

Nelda looked down at the street from her third-floor "nothing" apartment on 21st Ave. It wasn't raining in Seattle, but it's a safe bet that if it isn't raining on a February afternoon, it's at least threatening to. She planned on going to the store to get some milk and bread but couldn't decide whether to wear her warm wool jacket or her lighter raincoat. The Safeway was only three blocks away, but the raincoat was too light for the low 40s. If she took the wool coat and the rain started, she'd be drenched, and the wool would take a couple days to dry.

She recognized her inability to make a simple decision was a result of the anxiety and depression she was suffering. Her "psych" training was coming in handy. She understood depressed people sometimes can't make simple decisions and as a result can't function. They sit in their third-floor apartments without milk and bread, though they still have a few dollars left in the bank. They can't quit their hopeless, meager nursing jobs and go somewhere they aren't a targeted enemy of the powers that be. Nelda had only so much backbone. Hillibrand gave her courage to stand up to Dr. Richardson and the staff at Woodside, and now she was gone.

It persisted in her mind that Richardson killed Hillibrand, and it was only a matter of time before he'd kill her. She was telling herself this was her test. Meach understood and recognized she was in fear and didn't know how to handle it. He nodded his head when they met across the aircraft-carrier size desk in his high energy, busy office high in the Norton Building, but he still had nothing to offer. His head nods weren't a solution. He was known as a very capable trial attorney, but she'd never get to court unless she got a grip. Now she needed time to get a grip. She looked at the wool jacket and the raincoat and sat there, inert.

She sat until finally, she reached a point. She was not going to let anxiety and depression or Richardson kill her. She pulled out her suitcase and started stuffing it. She knew where she was going. First it was to Safeway for some baloney, mustard and bread to make a sandwich for the train and then it was to somewhere Richardson or anyone else wouldn't find her until she was ready to be found. She looked emotional stress in the eye and took it on. First she dropped off the rent check and boom, was out the door wearing a heavy sweater and the raincoat. Joe Gold's crucial witness prepared to disappear for a while. Even Nelda didn't know for how long.

After a long, dull train ride, she made it back to the Des Moines suburb and her mother's little home down a quiet street. Now they sat on the old, blue, chenille-covered couch Mr. and Mrs. Fox had carried from home to home for over thirty years. Marion Fox told Nelda, for about the tenth time, "I'm glad to have you back home again, Nelda, but you've got responsibilities. You have to call your lawyer. You told me yourself, he's a good lawyer, and he said you have a good case. He needs to know where you are. And what about the lawyer for that poor man who lost his wife?"

"I'll call my lawyer, Mom. I'm so scared. I told you, Dr. Richardson can't know where I am. He killed Lois, and he won't feel safe as long as I'm alive. I can testify against him."

"Nelda, you can't spend the rest of your life hiding out. You're sitting here watching soap operas all day long. It's not a life."

"I don't know what to do, Mom. Even if I can get a job in a hospital, Richardson will be able to track me down. Can't you see? Anybody would be scared! Anyone who hired me would want to check my references. As soon as they contact Woodside I'm exposed."

"I know you're scared, and I don't blame you, but you can't just run away. You have to be tough to get along in this world. Remember what I went through when your dad got sick? Get on the phone and call your lawyer. Maybe call Mr. Fletcher. He's depending on your testimony to win the case for his baby. You owe him."

Helpless to resist, Nelda burst into tears. She felt as though she were being pulled apart. There was no safe haven, even with her own mom. She crawled across the couch and buried her head in her mom's lap. She was tough, and Nelda wasn't.

"Nelda, can I call Mr. Meach for you? You don't have to do it. Is that okay?"

"Okay. I don't know what he could do. I told him they were going to make it hard for me. All he said was to "hang in there." He said when we got to court there would be a day of reckoning, but I don't have a job now. All I know is nursing."

Marion Fox figured it was 11 AM. in Seattle, so when she got Harry Meach's phone number from Nelda, she could call. The conversation didn't resolve the problem. At least Meach said he wouldn't disclose Nelda's location unless the judge ordered it. He said not to give the address to him until then. But, he asked that Nelda call at least once a week to keep in touch. As a last thought, he suggested calling Herb Fletcher just like Mom had said. Nelda had his number in her purse and dialed it. There was no answer, but that evening she tried again. "Hello, Fletcher residence."

"Herb, this is Nelda Fox."

"Oh, thank God, Nelda. Thanks for calling. My lawyers have been very nervous. They were telling me that if I couldn't find you, I don't have a case. Meach told me you called today, but where are you?"

"Herb, I'm really nervous about telling anyone where I am. I know Richardson would find a way to kill me if he could find me. But I promise I'll keep in touch, and I'll be there when you need me."

"I believe you. I wouldn't want to tell where I was if I were you either."

"Herb, how is Melissa? Is she okay? How are you taking care of her?"

"I'm still working my construction job, and I'm getting community help from the church for the baby. She's doing okay. She never really got to know Myra, so as long as the church women provide the daycare, I'm okay. She's a happy baby, so I guess I'm lucky in that way, at least."

"She's so sweet. I wish I could see her. I'd like to be back in Seattle, but, you know, I can't."

"I'm not so sure about that. We have some buildings, some nice ones that have empty space. If I talk to my bosses, maybe I could get a spot for you. There are some apartments you'd like. I could pay for the space when I settle the case, and I know my bosses are really on my side. If I talk nice to them, maybe I could get an apartment for you, and we could keep it quiet, and nobody would know you're in town. Maybe we could get you some work at the company, in the office where no one will see you, and that would carry you at least until the case is over, and maybe by then Richardson will be taken care of."

"I don't know. Could I call you back in a couple days, and maybe you could tell me then if your bosses will do it?"

"Sure. Call me the same time day after tomorrow. I know how important you are to my case, and I guess you know that, too. But it's more than that, Nelda. I really appreciated how you looked after Myra, and I know you really care about the baby, too. Thanks for that."

She hoped he didn't hear her crying as she said something that sounded like goodbye. She couldn't leave him in fear that she'd disappear.

I really care about them, but enough to risk my life? Yes, that much.

Chapter Sixteen

Her trust in Fletcher gave Nelda enough courage to head back down the road to western Washington. With trepidation she faced up to the risk that Dr. Richardson would be hunting her. Herb offered to hide her and find work for her. Living under her mom's roof had its upside but also an irksome downside. Mom still radiated love and concern, but she didn't treat her as an adult and she told her not to be a "frightened little parakeet." She meant it to sting and it did. Whenever Nelda went out the door, she had this feeling of being adrift in a world that didn't belong to her. She looked for a word to describe it and came up with agoraphobia. Whatever it was, she had to beat it.

Her mom still didn't seem to understand what a lawsuit would do to Nelda's safety. The hospital and Richardson, when he was sued, would have the right to demand that both Nelda and Herb's attorneys identify their clients and witnesses. That meant giving their addresses to Richardson's and the hospital's lawyers. Doing that would expose them and imperil Nelda. She took a chance and called Joe Gold. He was well aware of the risk to her and had thought about the answer.

"When you come back, I'll move right away to conceal your location and where you work. Ordinarily, all parties and witnesses have to be disclosed, but Detective Tracy is working with me. I located this fellow, Dr. Eric Martens, who had to get out of here because of Richardson. I can't get an affidavit from Martens, but I can get one from the detective plus something else on Richardson. I doubt they've got enough to charge

Richardson, but at least there's enough so I don't think we'll have to say where you are."

Joe didn't want to say that the "something else" was another possible homicide by Richardson.

"Joe, you sure I'll be safe?"

"I can't swear to that." Joe needed her as his witness, but he didn't have it in him to give her assurances beyond what he knew he could deliver."

Herb Fletcher's bosses, David and Saul Epstein, turned out to be nice, old guys who liked him and would back him up. He'd given them the full story of Myra Fletcher and how Nelda fitted into that story. Just as Herb told her, they were willing to go to unusual lengths to help him. That meant a job for her and a little hidey-hole of an apartment in White Center. It was a short drive away from the Epstein's business, Costello Construction, on Harbor Island. The company had gotten its name from the previous owner, a Mr. Costello. The Epstein boys liked the name and liked to tell everybody that they were "just a couple sons of old Ireland."

Costello Construction's office wasn't impressive. The Epstein brothers weren't into frills and fancy. The office, no better than meat and potatoes, contained well-worn Steelcase file cabinets of various colors and sizes and a potpourri of second-hand desks, chairs and tables. Binders and files were piled one on top of another, harum scarum. Mrs. Berliner, a frantic lady, tried to juggle assignments of personnel, construction schedules and office paper far beyond her capacity. David and Saul Epstein smiled benignly at her plight and somehow she got the job done. If the customers had looked behind the curtain they would have been appalled.

Herb braved the traffic from Lake City west to I-5, then south to Harbor Island every weekday morning. The Harbor Island industrial area was at the south end of Elliott Bay an arm of Puget Sound, exactly the right spot for the utilitarian Costello Construction.

Alvin Costello brought the Epstein boys into management when his health failed. Twenty years later, the Epstein boys needed one of their supervisors to move up, and Herb Fletcher was the most likely. At first they were dubious about giving the job to a very young, black man, but he instinctively saw everything around him needing to be done without being told. He found the best way to get a job done, regardless how it might have been done before he took over. He had self-confidence, intelligence and ambition, and the company prospered from his supervision. David and Saul agreed, giving him the rank and the clipboard was the smartest thing they'd ever done.

They faced a dilemma when Myra Fletcher couldn't come home from the hospital. David and Saul Epstein felt compelled to warn Herb, "We feel for you with your wife's health and having a baby, but we can't leave our supervisors out there without guidance. We're getting too old." But when Myra died, they comforted him and let him know they'd stick with him even if he couldn't get into work for a while. They told him "Just try your best."

When he came back, they were glad they'd stuck with him, and when he told them of Nelda's needs, they sympathized. After everyone else went home on a Friday afternoon, David Epstein brought out a bottle of Old Granddad and a couple Styrofoam cups, and he and Saul plunked themselves onto their desk chairs and discussed what to do. Saul took the cup away from his lips and said, "Herb needs this girl to win his case, and we could use her in the office if she's any good. I say we give her a try. What do you think?"

"Sure, Saul, we'll find something for her to do here. I can never find a damn thing when I need it. If she can't do anything else, at least she could clean up our filing mess. We still have those empty apartments out in White Center. Who knows how long they'll sit? Nobody seems to want them, so it's no loss if we put her there." The bottle and what little there was left in it was stuck back in the filing cabinet. If they couldn't find anything else, at least the boys knew where the whiskey was.

At first they assigned Nelda to simply provide Mrs. Berliner another pair of hands, but within a week, she felt emboldened to ask Herb if she could make some suggestions. He laughed. "Come on Nelda, you've been here a week. What do you suggest after one week on the job?"

She told him, and he stopped laughing and immediately went to tell the Epstein boys what she said. They sat her down in the "main office," really just another bunch of tables and file cabinets. They could sit in the office and watch Mrs. Berliner frantically herding cats all day long. They, like Herb, recognized that the massive disorganization, though an amusing habit, had its risks, hazards and expense. Just because you'd always done it a certain, haphazard way, and change is always uncomfortable, that's no excuse for eternal inefficiency.

Nelda worked in organized offices on her way to a nursing degree and had some ideas. "Look, if you have uniform size cabinets and file folders to fit, alphabetize the files, put the phone number and address on page one and put each file back immediately when you use it, Mrs. Berliner won't have to spend so much time scrambling around. Each desk should have a file holder, so no one has to rummage through the mail, design manuals, pro formas, bids, inventories and whatnot to look for them. If you'd let me spend a little money, really very little, I could streamline things for you."

The Epstein boys took a few days but finally came to grips with reality. "Okay, Nelda, we've decided to give it a shot. Just don't break us, all right?" The lady from Seattle Office Supply worked with Nelda while Mrs. Berliner grumped about the interference with her routine. David and Saul didn't like to spend money, but they liked how the office was coming together. David said "Thanks Nelda, we really should've done something like this a long time ago."

Nelda's big reward was Herb's smile and how it made her feel, a wonder that it could bring her back to earth. When she got to work, his smile was the best thing in her day. The more time she spent with him the less the racial difference seemed to mean. Here he was, a widower for such a short time, and yet, there was an undeniable mutual support far beyond the needs imposed on them by Myra Fletcher's death. She tried to force it out of her mind while Herb raved about how much easier it was for him to keep track of the jobs and customers.

They didn't have to wait for answers to their questions. Bidding a job was easier for David and Saul because material costs were quickly at hand. She couldn't let Herb know what his smile was doing to her. It would be awful to take advantage of his loss to satisfy her own need for a man in her life. There was no one else, and she wanted no one else. One day she realized that the more she thought about Herb, the less she suffered from anxiety and what she was now certain was "agoraphobia."

And yet Nelda never lost sight of her goals. It was all about justice for Herb and the baby, not romance, and she still wanted her career back. Richardson had to be out of medicine and off the streets, and she had to be able to feel safe. These goals meant dismantling the "conspiracy of silence" at Woodside Hospital. Now that she had a place to live and work and some security, the "frightened little parakeet" wasn't so frightened anymore, at least for now. Tomorrow was coming.

CHAPTER SEVENTEEN

After a long day at the office, Richardson arrived home to discover the ever faithful housekeeper, Louisa, alone in the kitchen and Cora nowhere to be seen. "Where's Cora?"

"The missus said to tell you she was going to the gym for her workout, but by now she's at her Children's Society meeting, and she said I should get you dinner. I was going to make a pork steak, and you could have potatoes or rice. I have a very nice orange glaze recipe for the meat if that sounds good to you."

Richardson barely had the patience to answer. "Sure, Louisa. That's fine."

"For dessert, I picked up some profiteroles at the bakery. Is that okay?"

"Whatever. Fine."

* * * * * *

Cora could have worked out at the exercise room in the house, but she liked to put on a show for the guys at the gym. She strutted her grace and beauty and enjoyed the flattery and flirting at the gym. At 51, she could easily pass for 35. Her vanity was at the center of her existence, and everyone knew she was ego driven, including her husband, Kevin. Fuming, he went into his home office. It was moments like this that spiked his need for the "ludes." He had come to terms with it to a degree. He understood his wife's life journey was her own course, and he only paddled along in her wake.

Cora insisted their son, named Alden, his mother's maiden name, would go to The Lennox Academy and then to her dad's alma mater, Yale. Richardson had really lost his son from the day the boy started playing cadet, and regarded his dad as an enlisted man. Cora didn't miss the boy, who after all, was just for appearances. Richardson was sure he, himself, was just for appearances. She used him as a prop for social and formal occasions, and then moved on to more important things, while his chemicals kept the rage in check. She somehow compelled him to stay with her, though he could barely tolerate the emptiness of his home life. Breaking things was no solution, and his career was his only refuge, and lately, not a soothing one. A strong man away from her, Richardson couldn't fathom his weakness in her presence.

He tried to explain himself to a high-priced, so-called, "advanced" psychiatrist, but the four-eyed chrome-dome was in his own never-never land of theory and deaf to Richardson, the best source of what was in his own head. He'd tried to explain to the genius that Cora was his link to the society world. Richardson needed the approval of the rich and powerful in order to feel any strength of his own. Cora and her God-awful, wealthy family kept him subservient. Sitting at the head table when she so directed, introducing the Governor, telling the hospital president who to place at Quality Control. Not real power but the simulation of power. He needed whatever it was.

When Cora, without him, went about her society life with the fashionable ladies, that was an implicit insult to him. She could go anywhere she wanted as if single and seemingly independent, a declaration that made her the household head. He was constantly alert to challenges for supremacy in the hospital and in society in ways she, with her lineage of power, never was. He had to take what she gave to maintain what sanity he had. There was never a doubt who was supreme at home, but Cora followed whatever her dad, the exalted Dr. Jerry Alden, said. More than once, Richardson's crucial life decisions were made by Dr. Alden.

Without the Quaaludes, Richardson's nerves were at the constant risk of snapping and destroying all that he had in his career. He submerged the overbearing shame he felt at what he had to do when there were threats to his position. The threats were now appearing more frequently. He recognized that every step forward was a further step into self-loathing. Every time something nasty came up, Cora would push him into it with some remark like, "You know what you have to do, whether you have the guts or not. You don't expect me to bail you out, do you?" And every time he did, it was one more failure she held over his head. She knew he was close to the edge but didn't imagine, as she was pushing him closer, he could drag her down with him.

Chapter Eighteen

Mark Zale had been through it with Franklin Tobin before and was aware of Richardson's position at Woodside. After the Gold family left Carpenter Gold, Zale became the top dog at the newly titled Carpenter Zale. The firm was retained by Hospital Provider Insurance to represent Woodside under its Errors and Omissions policy. The insurance company was not the client, Woodside was. He followed their directions, but if Woodside refused to settle on terms acceptable to Hosp-Pro, there were some risks they faced under the terms of the policy. It was a tough position for insurance counsel when the insured was irrational. The attorney faced duties both to the insurance company and to the client that could come into conflict. He had to consider his ethical duties too, as he talked to the hospital's head by phone about his taking on the Fletcher case.

"You have to understand, Frank, I know you're relying on Dr. Richardson and Dr. Karel to establish that Richardson's performance was within the standard of care. If there's no breach by Richardson, then you're clean. And I can usually find some suitably impressive expert to support him. Between you and me, Richardson should be in jail, not working in a hospital. If the police solve the Hillibrand case, that could be the end of the civil case. And just so you know, I'm not going to be putting witnesses on the stand to commit perjury even if Richardson's lawyer does. I know a little about medical ethics, but I'm not going to do anything I personally think is unethical or which the bar says is unethical. Hosp-Pro and Woodside can't make me do that. If that's what you're looking for, you need another law firm."

"Thank you for your honesty, Mark. You don't have to worry about that. We don't want an unethical lawyer anyway. But you do have to understand, Woodside is like a body dependent on the function of all its parts. The doctors have to know the hospital will back them up if they're in trouble. Doctors are human and they make mistakes. They need to know they can trust us, and if they don't, we're finished. There are other hospitals."

"Look, Frank, let's do this. I have to report honestly to Hosp-Pro what I see and what I think. I'm not the decision-maker, you know. They don't have any decisions to make until we've got the discovery done. There won't be any offers of settlement for a while, so what I'll do is tell them the case has these obvious weaknesses, but we'll see what the plaintiff can prove. I hope you heard me. There are some things I'm not going to do."

"Fine, Mark, but Fox has taken off, and I don't know where she is or what she's going to say if she shows up."

"If she shows up, why don't you settle her claim, if any, and hope she won't be too angry at you."

"You're seriously telling me that I can give her money not to testify about Richardson?"

"No, that's not what I'm saying at all. I'm not advising you to bribe her. You can settle her claim, and maybe she'll have some gratitude and be a little softer on you. But you can't bargain for it. Get a good labor lawyer."

"That's a good suggestion. Can you give me some names?"

"Don't worry about it now. When you need them, I'll find some names for you. Meanwhile, if Ed Gold is still on the board, you've got to isolate him from anything involving the lawsuit. I'm sure he'd like to sit there and listen to it all. Tell him he has to recuse himself. I don't think you can kick him off the board, but maybe you can persuade him to resign. He's got too much contact, and Halloran might get him to Martens.

"I understand, I'll talk to him. How do you know anything about Martens?"

"Remember, Frank, Carpenter Gold had to look at Richardson more than once before. I know why Martens left Seattle"

* * * * *

The next day, Mark Zale welcomed Brad Hultgren, the new rep for Hosp-Pro. Zale stepped up when they brought in the complaint. Back in history, Hultgren might have wanted one of the Golds to handle the case, but they'd gone over to the enemy, and Mark Zale was nobody's pushover. In fact, the story was that Zale had pushed the whole Gold family out of Carpenter Gold, and that's why it was now Carpenter Zale. Hultgren wheeled in a banker's box of Myra Fletcher records and plunked himself on the couch in the redecorated corner office of Carpenter Zale.

"Love what you did with Ed Gold's old office. You should have kept the Picasso when you shoved him out."

"Thanks for the interior decoration tips, Brad. Spoils of war, you know. I didn't shove him out though. He wanted his family in a plaintiffs firm, and now he's got one upstairs. I think he's just working for the fun of it. The guy loves hanging out with his family. Got to admit, they're a nice bunch. I'd love to beat them someday."

"Interesting. So now you get to litigate against your ex-partner and his firm. Did you tell Tobin they have to get him off the board? Gold can't sue Woodside and still be on the Woodside Hospital Board of Directors."

"I've already told him. It's not that simple, Brad. Woodside and the Gold firm could both isolate him from this suit, and he could remain on the board for other unrelated matters. The rules of ethics allow for that."

Hulgren's eyebrows lifted. "Really? But I think that that's our starting point at least. I like the idea of haggling after we lay down the law to Gold. That's the position of Hosp-Pro."

"Gotcha, Brad. That's okay. But let's go on from there. I have a problem with Richardson. He's a loose cannon. I don't think Woodside is very smart standing behind him. That's my advice to the hospital. I'd like to separate us from him if it's possible"

"Well, you've got a point. Hosp-Pro is going to either get an agreement from Richardson's Errors and Omissions carrier to indemnify us, or we could threaten to cross-claim against Richardson. His screw-up can cost us money."

"We shouldn't do that, Brad. A cross claim by the hospital against its staff doctor wouldn't look too good in a malpractice trial to a jury. It would sound like an admission of liability."

Hultgren nervously brushed back his hair. "Don't I know it. We could threaten them, though. If they want to keep the rates down, they need a little risk management. If the Golds win their lawsuit, there's going to be a lot of patients aware of how the doctors cover up negligence and a lot of potential lawsuits. Stuff they might have got away with in the past isn't going to happen anymore. I suspect Halloran isn't going to go along with it. There'll be more nurses like Hillibrand and Fox. But listen, this is confidential. You can't even tell my boss I said that, okay?"

Zale understood. "Still, we have a case we might win. Halloran can't beat us, and Gold can't beat us. With Hillibrand gone, this very young Nelda Fox is their whole case. She's got to be scared stiff. If she doesn't run away, still I might be able to get her to say what I need. But let's hope Richardson leaves her alone. Getting caught at witness intimidation isn't going to be good for the hospital or the case, so I hope someone warns him against that stuff. I can see what's been going on at Woodside, and it's easier defending their cases when they have some credibility. I can't make Fox look bad, but maybe her isolation with Hillibrand gone makes her 'flexible."

"So you need to either convince nurse Fox she's vulnerable or convince the Golds of that. I don't think she can stand normal litigation pressure. She's just a kid."

"Forget normal litigation pressure, Brad, I'm afraid Richardson what he could do to her. I'm glad he isn't my client. We need to stay arm's length from him. I'm tempted to have Tobin spread the word that Richardson's contagious. If they think covering up for bad doctors was the good old days, those days are either over or they're going to be over someday soon. Get too close to Richardson and go to jail. That Karel guy, whether he knows it or not, is on the hot seat. Quality Control. Hah! I hope Tobin understands."

Zale leaned forward, fixing his eyes directly on Hultgren. "We never had this conversation."

"What conversation?"

* * * * * *

As soon as the Hosp-Pro representative was gone, Zale got Ed Gold on the phone. "It looks like you and I are going to be on opposite sides of the Myra Fletcher case."

"Not me, I don't have a side. It's The Gold Law Firm. You have the hospital or the doctor?"

"I've got Woodside."

"That's what I figured. What are you going to do about that toxic doctor?"

"He's not my problem. He'll get his own lawyer."

"What are you going to say about all that covering up the hospital staff did for him?"

"Your firm is going to have to prove it happened"

Ed smiled. He enjoyed being an innocent bystander, as if he didn't care what happened.

"Mark, seriously, watch out. Don't get any of that on your hands. If there's perjury involved, it could be dangerous for you personally."

"You don't need to worry about me, Ed. I know you mean well, but you can be sure I wouldn't allow any perjury. I hope you know me better than that."

"Mark, I know you're smarter than that, but it's insidious. There are some people at Woodside who use some pretty bad judgment, and I don't think they're going to get smart just because you tell them to."

"Thank you for that, Ed, but if your firm does its job and I do mine, we'll get this case in front of the jury and they can decide who's telling the truth and who isn't."

"Well, you can tell your people my firm is going to be watching them. Anyway, my son, Joe, is going to be handling the case, and I'll be recusing myself."

"That's good, I was instructed you aren't to come to the hospital or act as a board member while this is pending. You'll be getting a letter, but I wanted to give you a heads up."

"Nope, though I'm recusing myself from anything related to this case, I'm still on the board, doing my job as a board member. I'm reading the Canons of Ethics, and I'm following the rules. Whoever wants me off the board is asking for a fight. I think I have some friends there. I've done a good job for the hospital over the years."

He put down the phone with a little smile of satisfaction, knowing his position and confident how a fight would come out.

Chapter Nineteen

Herb Fletcher struggled with the traffic on I-90, but finally made it to the Gold Law Firm office. He'd wanted to get in to see Joe though buried in work. Joe called to get him into the Gold office regardless of how busy he was. This was important. The girl answering the phone sounded remarkably familiar, maybe like Nelda, but Joe convinced himself it was his imagination. He promised to make the conference as short as possible. The Epsteins gave Herb their permission to leave the office for the morning. When he arrived, Jodi sent him straight back. Joe's eyebrows lifted when he saw him. He'd graduated from jeans and a sweatshirt to neatly pressed slacks, white shirt and tie. A smile appeared on his face, a welcome addition. "What's the deal, Herb? You're looking a little spiffier and a little more upbeat."

"Like I told you, Joe, new job. Now I'm the manager and don't have time to do the sweat work. Now my tools are clipboard and car phone."

"If you're getting more money too, congratulations are in order."

"Thank you. And you know, I'm a little upbeat because Nelda's back in town, and I think she's going to stay." Just then, Jodi came in and put a cup of coffee in front of each of them along with the creamer and sugar. Herb leaned back in the nice, comfy desk chair.

"She says she's going to work with us to beat Richardson. She really can't stand the guy's guts. I think she's more upset about him than I am. She's been hiding out, and she's still hiding, but at least now it's in the Seattle area, and she's going to be able to participate in the case."

"Don't tell me where she is. I know she's scared, and if I don't know where she is I can't tell Richardson's lawyer. We're going to try to get a court order to protect her." He had something else to say but restrained the impulse for the moment. Joe put down his coffee cup and handed over to Herb a thick document that needed some explaining. "These are Interrogatories and Request for Production of Documents. The Interrogatories are a set of questions we're required to answer. The Request for Production of Documents sets forth papers they think you have and they're entitled to see. This is standard operating procedure in lawsuits, and you'll see we've got just 20 days to respond. It's not unusual for it to take more than 20 days, and if I have a decent reason, I'm pretty sure Richardson's lawyer would give us more time. That's just the kind of courtesy lawyers give each other because they know, if they don't give the courtesy, they won't get it from the other side when they need it. I'll be looking these over to see if there's anything they're asking for they aren't entitled to."

"Richardson's attorney, you'll see, is Larry MacCallum of Brosius and McCallum. All they want to know about you is everything, work history, marriage history, access to all medical records of you, the baby and Myra. They want you to ID everybody you know and everybody related to you. Also, they want us to identify everyone who has any information relevant to the subject matter of the lawsuit. I think that means, basically, everyone in Maternity, management, records and, this is key, anything you know about Nelda."

"There's no way I'm going to sell out Nelda. She's running for her life, and she put it all on the line for Myra. I'll lose the case before I sell her out. She meant a lot to Myra so she means a lot to me."

Joe took a long sip of coffee then went on. "I was going to tell you about the motion I'm working on. I've got a call in to Larry MacCallum, but I'm not assuming he'll do the right thing. I also have calls in to Dr. Martens, to the coroner and to Dick Tracy."

Herb grinned. He knew the story of the long-suffering Seattle detective who had to bear the jokes about his name.

"So, they'll help you keep Nelda protected?"

"I hope so. I told her I couldn't promise, but I think Judge Camorra understands. He's the one who issued the order for exhuming the Mickens girl. I'll try to take it to him but that's not a sure thing."

Herb held up his copy of the discovery. "And what about the rest of this mess, Joe? Christ, it's 46 pages."

"I marked off the ones I can answer without your help. There's still plenty for you to do, but we've got 20 days and whatever MacCallum gives us voluntarily. Even if MacCallum says no, and I don't think he will, the judge will give us some more time if we answer what we can."

"I'll tell Nelda. She'll feel better."

Joe was interested. "Do you see her?"

"I can answer that question if you want, but I'm not sure you really want."

Herb finished his coffee and stood up. "What the hell, I know you'll keep it secret. I see her often. That's all I'm going to say. Joe saw a conspiratorial "cat that ate the canary" kind of smile on Herb's face and thought he knew what it meant. But if Herb was telling him there was a romance between the quiet little white nurse and the supposedly grieving black widower, he feared a backlash. Even without race issues, she was a witness and he was a plaintiff who'd lost his beloved wife. It would be hard to discuss. After Herb left, Joe sat quietly with his chin propped up in the palm of his hand, trying to come to grips with questions he couldn't ask. After he refilled his coffee cup, the phone rang. It was Mike.

"I just saw Herb leave. How's it going?"

"I'm not sure what I just learned. I'm a little troubled and I can't believe it, but it seems like he's got some contact going on with Nelda. He says he sees her regularly. That's secret, by the way."

"That doesn't necessarily mean romance, does it?"

Joe understood that. "No. Of course it doesn't, but it could be, and I can't ask." He still wondered. "I was talking to Herb about the interrogatories we got from Richardson's attorney. You know, Larry MacCallum is appearing for him."

"And he's going to insist we identify Nelda's location, right?"

"Right, I'm going to call MacCallum, and if he doesn't accept that Nelda's going to be protected I'll file a motion. I gotta call now. I'll talk to you later."

When he called, MacCallum was in a puckish mood. "Looks like you're headed for some newsprint just like your brother. Bet you can't wait, Joe."

"Larry, I've got a client who lost his 17-year-old wife, and there are some other suspicious deaths too. I hate to be a killjoy, but it just isn't that funny."

"My goodness. This isn't your style."

"It is this time, so listen. My key witness, as you well know, is Nelda Fox. She's afraid Richardson is going to come for her the way he got Hillibrand. I can't give you her location. And there's a lot of your discovery which would lead to her location, so I'm going to have to ask you to give me some leeway on this discovery."

"How am I supposed to prepare a defense when your key witness is hiding out? I don't know what the hell she's afraid of. You sound like you think you can prove Richardson killed Hillibrand. Can you?"

"I can't prove that right now, but Fox is entitled to be protected. She has a justified fear, but it isn't a problem. I'll get her here for the deposition when the time comes, so you'll be able to ask her everything you need except for the part that would expose her to danger."

"That's not good enough. I need to investigate her. That means talking to friends, relatives, neighbors, people she works with. There's no way I can do that without getting her location. Answer the 'rogs', Joe."

"Can't do it."

"If you don't, I'll have to file a motion."

"Don't bother. You'll be getting my motion by the end of the week."

"Well, thanks for calling, Joe. It's been a little slice of heaven."

"Larry, we'll be okay. I'm not trying to be a pain just for the fun of it. I have to fight the discovery."

"Okay, Joe. I was just kidding, but Kevin has his back against the wall, so I can't be your best buddy in this case."

"I know. We'll have a drink when it's over."

Joe knew he had to move, and so he started roughing out the affidavits on a yellow legal pad, Herb, Nelda, Tracy, Martens. There were the earlier affidavits by the coroner and Dr. Hsu, and they wouldn't have to be redone. By the time he finished for the day, he had eight scribbled pages to start with. There would be more. He picked up the Dictaphone input mike and started in as the Dictabelt rotated. He got it right on the first go round because editing would be a time consuming ordeal for Jodi.

When he finished, he got Herb at Costello Construction. "I need you to sign an affidavit. MacCallum is going to be tough. He wants Nelda's location, and I'm getting the Motion to Quash some of his interrogatories ready."

"Squash?"

"No, Herb, it's quash. That means prevent. It's a law term. That's how we're going to protect Nelda. We're going to ask the court for some help. To save a little time, I'm having Jodi bring it to you. If it's okay, sign it and give it back to her right away. Don't waste any time. You have to sign it before a notary or otherwise, bring it here and I'll go through it with you. If you have any questions, call me right away. If you want to protect her, this is a rush"

"Okay, got it."

He gave the affidavit to Jodi along with a quick set of directions to Costello Construction. She looked at the travel directions she had to follow, with a look of utter distaste, then shrugged. "Okay, I get the rest of the afternoon off." Joe laughed. "Oh well, you'll earn it."

After she took off, Joe started thinking about the Costello receptionist that Herb saw every day. He called Herb back and said, "Next time you get a chance to talk to Nelda, make sure to tell her, wherever she is, not to talk to anyone on the phone who could be connected with the case and recognize her voice. Can you just imagine if she answered the phone at a place of business and it was Richardson calling?" There was silence for a moment, then, "When I talk to her, I'll let her know you said that."

CHAPTER TWENTY

Med-West Insurance directed Richardson to go in for a conference with their attorney, Larry MacCallum, an enthusiastically aggressive insurance defense specialist. He was born with a lust for competition. As a high school kid, his grit and determination made him a powerhouse basketball forward and football fullback on the Franklin High School teams despite his moderate size and speed. Losing at anything made him angry. No one could claim he didn't try hard enough. As an attorney, his greatest asset was his instinct for the jugular even when he exercised prudence, which he sometimes didn't. He got caught once implying Judge Abelson was ignoring the law. Abelson said "You're about 1-inch from a line you better not cross, young man. I suggest you figure that out." McCallum backed off fast.

On the other hand, the insurance reps occasionally, wondered why he recommended some money for an injured kid. It didn't seem like him, but he always had a reason. A doctor accused of malpractice never wanted to say, "Okay, the plaintiff's lawyers are right." Even when they were. If he saw a loss coming, MacCallum tried to work out a deal if he could. When Med-West didn't take his advice, they wished they had and soon got the point.

Richardson went up the ancient caged elevator to MacCallum's office high in the historic Smith Tower near Pioneer Square. The secretary ushered him to the oddly modern, corner office in the old building, where MacCallum put him through the whole story of the death of Myra Fletcher. MacCallum listened with attentive ears and watched Richardson with skeptical eyes. He cross-examined Richardson gently, calmly and on the points the plaintiff's attorney would hit. He carefully avoided inflicting the kind of pain and stress Richardson would face on the witness stand and pointed that out to him. MacCallum was used to soothing the fragile ego of physicians who were not accustomed to a searching cross-examination. Richardson held up well when they went over Myra's records and, MacCallum felt 90% convinced he was going to war. Richardson didn't give him his whole story, nothing of the suspicious deaths MacCallum would hear about soon.

Then came Joe Gold's promised motion to conceal the location of Nelda Fox. He sent affidavits showing that Richardson demanded Hillibrand's and Fox's entries into Myra Fletcher's records be changed. Joe attached photocopies Fox said were handwritten drafts by Richardson she and Hillibrand were required to copy into the Fletcher charts. She said that she and Hillibrand kept copies of Richardson's writing. On top of that was an affidavit by a handwriting expert, together with his curriculum vita establishing his qualifications. He attested the writings were indeed made by Richardson. Next came the affidavit of a Seattle police detective named Tracy and one by the coroner, who stated Richardson was a "person of interest" in the murder of Hillibrand, that he had evidence she went to dinner with him two nights before her death then changed the records as he directed, and that her copies of Richardson's draft changes couldn't be found in her home.

Joe summarized a supposed scenario that cast suspicion on Richardson. He carefully did not assert his scenario had been proven, only that there was justifiable reason for concern that Richardson was dangerous. He referenced an aura of fear at Woodside that had a Dr. Martens leaving because of that fear. Joe argued the defendants' rights to discovery could still be honored reasonably without disclosing Nelda's location. When MacCallum received the motion and affidavits, he immediately notified Richardson to come in, "dammit." He got there at 9:30 the next morning, noticing MacCallum was not the smiling, cordial and welcoming comrade-in-arms he'd been.

Gruffly, he directed, "Sit down, Kevin. Cup of coffee?" Richardson was wary. He didn't know what MacCallum would do if he got the full story. He understood confidentiality but feared MacCallum would throw him out if he knew all he'd actually done. So he didn't give MacCallum more information than he needed. MacCallum's nice guy demeanor had changed, seeing the dark side depicted by what Joe Gold had presented. Still, he restrained his natural aggressiveness.

"Kevin, let's look at this motion. Thick pile of stuff. Let me show you what this young Gold fellow sent over. Were you aware we were going to be facing claims like this? You didn't say anything to me."

He laid it all out on the conference room table for Richardson to see while he walked him through it. Finally, after two hours of it, with Richardson saying "bullshit" and "crap" and "nobody will believe that," MacCallum, unsmiling, still suspicious said, "Well that's about it, Kevin. What do you want me to do? You keep telling me it's crap and bullshit, and you don't give me anything that disproves it. What do I do?"

Richardson sounded startled. "You don't know what to do? What is there to do but fight? Prove it's a phony game. People sue doctors all the time, and the cases get thrown out of court. They have to prove it, and all you have here is suspicions. They can't take that to court, can they?"

MacCallum saw the start of a sort of a snarl or a sneer disfiguring Richardson's mouth. It looked like Richardson's anger was taking control of him. MacCallum didn't know it, but the early-morning Quaalude was wearing off. MacCallum was on the verge of seeing the kind of behavior that Fox had described. MacCallum, having seen the motion, confronted the insurance defense lawyer's eternal dilemma. It was similar to that of the criminal defense attorney. The plaintiff's lawyer had it easy. If liability was dubious, he didn't take the case. If liability looked good, he was a hero fighting for justice. MacCallum took what Med-West brought in whether he liked it or not. It came with the territory.

"Kevin, look, you have to recognize, that if we defend this in court, you're going to be cross-examined on what you know about these deaths. Whatever you say can be used to investigate and maybe even support a criminal charge against you. If you refuse to testify in front of the jury on the civil case, in my opinion, a civil jury might infer, on a 'more probable than not' basis, that you committed a crime to conceal evidence. It probably wouldn't be enough to convict you in a criminal case, but it might be enough to establish you had a consciousness of guilt. It wouldn't be a very big leap for a jury to decide you committed a civil wrong, at least negligent contribution to the death of Myra."

"It's strictly the discretion of the trial judge to decide whether this stuff can come in. You know what you're going to be asked, but I don't know what you're going to say. You may have to testify. Before you do that, I have to advise you to consult with a criminal defense attorney. I have a conflict of interest because the insurance company is paying me. It's not my job to keep you out of jail."

"You're kidding me. There's something wrong here. You think you can't represent both me and Med-West? I have to win the civil case too, you know." Richardson's voice was getting louder and louder, and he feared what he'd do next. He got up and walked out, leaving MacCallum to figure out what was going through the guy's mind.

Was he coming back? When? Was he capable of doing what the plaintiff said?

Richardson walked down the hall to the restroom, took out his little bottle of Quaaludes, popped one in his mouth and washed it down. When he got back to the conference room, MacCallum wasn't there. Richardson went down the hall to his office and found him at his desk and on the phone. MacCallum pointed at a side chair, and Richardson, now calm and relaxed, sat down.

When MacCallum got off the phone, he said, "So, what's it going to be? You need to see a criminal defense attorney? You got some foolproof defense? Maybe you were performing an operation with a half-dozen witnesses at the time of each of the deaths? If you haven't got something like that, don't you see how these deaths would look to jurors?"

"A couple women I know have some sort of a mishap which I had absolutely nothing to do with, and I'm supposed to explain them? Hell, the coroner didn't. I wasn't even there when those things happened. Screw it. We're defending, and I don't need to talk to anybody else."

"Okay, Kevin, what about those records changes?"

"Easy, those nurses tried to cover up their negligence by claiming I was negligent. I told them they'd be in trouble if they didn't correct those messed up records that they made. Let's just call it their little mistakes. Then quality control and the board reviewed it and I'm okay, and the women are out. I had nothing to be upset about. It's crazy to think that I'd have a reason to be angry, when the hospital administration had already vindicated me."

"Sounds good, Kevin, but what about the drugs? You're taking pills aren't you? Were you taking anything that night the Fletcher girl died? People have said you're on something."

"There have been a few times I've taken pills or drunk coffee to keep on top of my game. That night I was drinking coffee to keep myself going during the break. People will tell you I'm pretty intense sometimes. I know what I need, and sometimes I'll take a tranquilizer. That day I'd done 5 deliveries including a couple tough ones I'd done for a couple other docs who needed my help. They weren't sure they could do them. I was pretty tired that night, so I had to drink some coffee. Any time I'm in the hospital, I have to be on top of my game, because somebody might need me at any time. Those nurses knew where I was, and they could've called me. They just didn't. So, Mr. MacCallum, I'm resisting that motion. It makes me mad. Nelda Fox is a little psycho to be worrying about me, and I expect you to investigate her the way you would investigate any lying witness on the other side."

"Okay, I will be resisting it. I've warned you about the risks. Med-West will pay me to defend you. I have to tell them what it looks like and what the other side is saying, but I'll go to the wall if you and they are up for it."

"There you go, Mr. MacCallum, let's do it."

* * * * * *

For the rest of the morning, MacCallum drafted the affidavits with Richardson's assistance, not only Richardson's own affidavit but also affidavits for CEO Tobin, Quality Control Director Karel, Charge Nurse Steinman and ER doctor, Rosen. Richardson had been blunt about getting the signatures.

"Don't call them. When they're ready for signature, I'll take them to the business office, and they'll sign them in front of our secretary. She's a notary. These people are allergic to lawyers. They'll sign if I explain the need to them. If they have to talk to you, they may take them to their own lawyers and then who knows what will happen."

That made MacCallum wonder. What was Richardson going to do to get the signatures MacCallum couldn't get? He supposed that was one of the questions you don't ask. MacCallum started to have images of the captain of the Titanic and how he felt as he sailed through the North Atlantic. With his best efforts, there could still be more icebergs out there than he could maneuver around. Captain, hell, MacCallum was beginning to feel as if he was the first mate and Richardson was the captain.

Notwithstanding his reservations, MacCallum's memorandum of law and Richardson's handmade affidavits signed by the hospital's witnesses provided as much support as you could hope for in resisting the plaintiff's motion. Not to be negative, but MacCallum had a strong sense that the motion would be granted. It was a matter of the judge's discretion, and no judge would be comfortable fully exposing the young nurse to an unknown hazard. The downside was too far down. MacCallum wondered if Gold held back something for his rebuttal argument. He was young, but he'd been weaned on tort litigation by Ed Gold, his dad, a master.

It took Richardson exactly one day to get the draft affidavits back to MacCallum, complete with signatures. MacCallum timely gave Richardson a copy of his memorandum of law which he quickly skimmed. "That looks pretty persuasive to me, but I'm not a lawyer. You think the judge will pay any attention to it?"

"Like I told you, Kevin, where the judge is weighing your right to discovery against Fox's fears, he's got to look at those suspicious deaths and worry about his public ass on the line if something happens to Fox. Imagine if you were the judge."

"So, basically what you're telling me is, even if I'm totally innocent, I'm still guilty."

"Kevin, this is just about discovery, not liability. If those witnesses of ours stand up in court the way they're standing up with those affidavits, Fox may not be all that persuasive. But I still have to wait and see what Gold comes back with in his rebuttal."

When the rebuttal came back with only a rehash, MacCallum called him with the good news, and Richardson didn't even need to pop a Quaalude. But then he saw the plaintiff's discovery identified Martens as a witness, and he felt his blood heating up. He couldn't allow Martens to come back after chasing him out of town. As important as chasing him away again was, still the key was getting rid of Fox as a witness.

No Nelda, no testimony.

CHAPTER TWENTY ONE

As they headed to the courthouse, Joe explained to Dad that he was still apprehensive about the plaintiff's motion to allow Nelda to remain cloistered and secreted. Joe had agreed to produce her for a deposition and identify friends and family who could discuss her background and limited personal history, but she insisted her present location and employment remain concealed. That wasn't good enough for MacCallum, who resisted the motion and also moved to disqualify the Gold Law Firm from the case. Joe knew this would be coming, and with a sigh, Dad accepted that. nothing was going to come easy. Joe and Mike researched and drafted what they thought was an ironclad response to MacCallum's motion, joined in by Zale for the hospital.

Ed Gold, a member of the board of Woodside, attended one board meeting, but since then he'd isolated himself from participation in the matter and turned it over to his son. Joe and Mike prepared to resist MacCallum's argument that the isolation wasn't enough while sharpening the crucial argument resisting MacCallum's motion. They decided to have Dad at the hearing in case the judge wanted to look him in the eye and measure his veracity.

Ed wore a sport coat and slacks to the courthouse, becoming accustomed to the more relaxed environment of the Gold Law Firm and to the 1960s. The change amused Joe. His dad, as a senior partner, never went to the Carpenter Gold office in anything less than a dark suit, power tie and white shirt. But one thing hadn't changed. Dad still exercised his button-down, prudent, caution and thoughtfulness, but as always, with confidence.

"You can handle it, Joe. However our motion comes out, you can be sure that Herb and the baby are taken care of. I have to be out of it, but the firm will make sure Nelda is safe. One way or another. I trust you."

"And what if Abelson kicks us off the case?"

"I understand I'm off the case, but if the firm is removed, you could take it straight to the Supreme Court. You could file a writ of certiorari, and it'll be granted. With the writ, you don't have to wait until the whole cases has ended to file an appeal. It's not my call, but you could take it straight up ASAP. With me out of it, there will be no excuse to bar the firm. The Supreme Court will tell Abelson to go ahead and try the case right now. Abelson will expect that, so he won't rule against the firm in the first place. That's my guess, but don't quote me." Ed, nevertheless kept telling himself he would stay out of it. Still, it was the biggest worry he had.

"Hope you're right, Dad." Ed, amused, patted his son on the head as if to say, "There, there, little boy."

When they walked into Judge Abelson's courtroom, Herb was already there, sitting in the front row. A couple courthouse buffs sat in the middle rows along with an old wino in jeans and a wine stained shirt, another derelict and, in the back, a little gray-haired lady with a circus clown hat, her glasses and her knitting. She idly stirred the grey yarn with the needles, producing some sort of a sweater or shawl, Joe supposed. When MacCallum and Zale walked in, they hung up their coats and laid their legal pads on the counsel table in front of them. They walked over and shook hands with Joe and his dad, and they all, with tongue in cheek, followed cordial, professional standards Richardson had seen before.

The mod-haired, mustachioed bailiff called out, "You guys ready?" After the nods in assent, he buzzed Judge Rudy Abelson, and the judge came out. Abelson was a tough looking, bespectacled old guy, bald with a white fringe, a scruffy looking brush of a beard and a tuft of mustache.

To Joe, he looked like the kind of guy you'd see hanging around a biker's bar. Joe had always regarded him as the stern sort of judge, not one to kid with, not the one Joe would have chosen. He thought another judge might be more likely to defer to Dad's reputation and trust him. Maybe somebody else would lean more to sympathy with Nelda. What the hell. You take the judge you're given. Luck of the draw. And anyway, who can predict the mood of the judge on any particular day?

The judge greeted the lawyers, and Joe introduced Herb to the judge. Herb stood up, said, "Good morning, your Honor" and sat down at the counsel table. The judge greeted him with a nod and then made a restrained show of hospitality upon seeing Dad. "Good morning, Mr. Gold. I'm glad to see you again, though this is an onerous occasion." Dad responded carefully, "I understand, and I thank you for your consideration." That little colloquy could not have been entertaining to the defense counsel. Finally, MacCallum made a stab at an introduction of Richardson and Zale introduced CEO Tobin. Abelson managed a smile and polite but restrained welcome.

First came the motion to bar the Gold Law Firm from the case. MacCallum started in with Ed's deposition and the "devastating admissions" of his family and his board of directors' activity that, according to MacCallum, disqualified Ed and the firm from the case. Abelson announced that he had read the deposition and let MacCallum talk for a while without asking questions. Then it was Zale's turn. Their point was that Ed Gold, a member of the hospital board, was the founder of the firm. His office was there. His two sons and daughter-in-law were partners in the firm, and there was no way he could be excluded from supervision and management of this major case. As Zale put it, "We shouldn't be required to accept on faith that Mr. Gold can be a member of the Woodside Hospital Board of Directors, privy to all the internal workings of the hospital and yet, somehow, his knowledge and contacts be excluded from use by his family's law firm. In fact, he has been involved in the case up to his eyebrows until now. He isn't suddenly going to become deaf and dumb."

The judge was ready to rule without Joe's oral argument. "I understand your arguments and your anxiety. Mr. Gold swears he'll recuse himself from both the board's and his office's activities affecting this case from now on. To bar the Gold Law Firm from this case, I'd have to believe there is a risk Mr. Gold would perjure himself in order to win this case. I'd be interested to hear whether either of you gentlemen for the defense is willing to swear you're aware of any instance of Ed Gold committing an unethical act. If you have something to base a distrust of Mr. Gold on, say it now. I didn't see it in your briefs."

He looked down at the two defense lawyers, waiting for either of them to say something. They didn't dare make an accusation and face the scorn that would produce in the Seattle legal community. Or maybe they didn't know anything they could mention.

"Based on the silence of Mr. MacCallum and Mr. Zale, I'll be denying that motion. On the other hand, if I am given any reason during pendency of this case to reevaluate my confidence in Mr. Gold, I won't hesitate. You won't give me reason to regret this ruling, will you?" He was looking at Dad.

"Your honor, I pledge that I will not betray your trust."

"Thank you, Mr. Gold. That disposes of our first issue. I'm signing the plaintiff's order. Let's move on to the question of Miss Fox."

Joe laid out the peculiarities involving the deaths of Myra Fletcher, Mickens and Hillibrand, the alterations of Myra's records and the pressure by Richardson to make those changes. Nelda's declaration showed her fear. She wanted to testify at the trial, but she feared what happened to Mickens and Hillibrand would happen to her. Joe argued that the discovery rules aren't absolute. Herb Fletcher shouldn't be in danger of losing a crucial witness as a result of her justifiable fear. Nelda's affidavit set forth what happened leading to Myra's death, the record alterations demanded by Richardson and the hospital exiling her and Lois to the psych ward. The affidavits of Tracy and the coroner explained the peculiarities of the death of Laura Mickens and Lois Hillibrand.

Joe summarized. "We don't have to prove guilt beyond a reasonable doubt for Miss Fox's fear to be justifiable. The defendants can have reasonable discovery as long as Miss Fox doesn't have to face intolerable fear. We'll make her available for depositions, and answer written interrogatories as long as they don't subject her to fear or danger. Her fear is entirely reasonable."

Mark Zale stood up to take his shot at the argument based on the "absolute right under the rules to production of the plaintiff's witnesses." Abelson made notes throughout the argument. Joe felt uneasy as Abelson seemed to be taking it all in. Once Zale finished, MacCallum put in his two cents and, at least on this argument, played the minnow and Zale the shark, chewing up Nelda's "baseless fears." When Joe got up for rebuttal, Abelson was ready to pounce.

"I read the argument and affidavits of the parties, and I want to tell you what my thinking is at this point. I'm not going to deprive anyone of his right to argue, but it seems to me, I can do a compromise. See what you think. The defense may engage in all the discovery available under the rules. Except, the plaintiff can hold back any discovery leading to the current place of employment and residence of Miss Fox commencing as of next week. All other discovery under the rules is available. The defense can have her background and history but not her then current location. If anything changes and there are new reasons to protect Miss Fox or remove protections, I'll be prepared to reconsider. Now, having said that, I'm happy to listen to anything you've got to change my mind."

This surprised Joe, and he had to improvise. "Your honor, that means the defense will have her current residence and place of employment. You understand that she is frightened, and this will force her to move. She isn't wealthy, and she doesn't dare work in any hospital. If she applies at a hospital, they'll contact Woodside, and Dr. Richardson will have the information. She'll have to depart from where she lives and where she works now. I request you extend the confidentiality to cover her present residence and employment."

Abelson looked at MacCallum, who gave it his best. "Your Honor, my primary consideration is that, if she reveals information to anyone or engages in conduct in her continuing employment that would affect her credibility, we wouldn't know it. This is extraordinary relief you're granting the plaintiff, and I don't think there's any precedent for it. The plaintiffs want to make it even tougher on the defense, concealing information that would've been available up until today."

Abelson sat back, with his hands in his lap with furrowed brow. "Mr. Gold, I'm willing to draw down the curtain for Miss Fox as of today, but I'll let the defense have her place of employment and residence up until today. If that means she has to move, I think that's still fair."

Joe prepared to rise again but felt a tug on his sleeve. He looked at the note his dad slipped in front of him. "Take it. Half a loaf." Judge Abelson waited briefly as Joe sat mute, then interlineated his changes and passed the order to the lawyers to review before he signed it. Abelson smiled benevolently at the lawyers. "Now, anyone have any remaining questions?" The judge had spoken and given the parties each something they wanted. He was happy. In his mind, as he signed the order, he'd been fair and even handed.

Joe and his dad packed up their briefcases as Zale and MacCallum went out the door without looking at them. One of the winos had left early and the remaining wrinkled, shabby old lady, with painful effort, extracted herself from the bench and got to her feet while the bailiff went back into the chambers with the judge. The gray-haired lady strode rapidly to the door, stuck her head out, looked around, peeked back in and, with a grin, waved to Joe and Herb, then skipped out. Joe and Ed looked at each other. Herb was embarrassed. "I didn't know Nelda was coming."

"Herb, we're trying to protect her, and she walks right into the courtroom. Was she the one who answered the phone last time I called you?"

"Yeah, she works at my office."

"I've been saying she's frightened, and that didn't look like it. She's at least, careless."

Ed Gold weighed whether he should open his mouth. He pledged to stay out of the case, so he went out in the hallway as the conversation between Joe and Fletcher continued. "If you understand the judge's order, it means Richardson will know where she's working if she stays there. Anyway, if my dad could participate in the case, he'd tell you to keep Nelda away from your office and away from you personally. Her value as a witness goes down the drain if you're involved with her in any way. Tell her to call me right away so I can talk to her about her situation. We can't appear to be bribing her, and you can't afford to look like you're seducing her. That's what my dad would say if he could talk to you."

"I'm not seducing her. I'm sorry. She called me. She was scared and was hiding out at her mother's house in Iowa. The only way I could get her back so she could be a witness and help out in the case was to find somewhere she could stay and somewhere she could work. I got her a job where I'm working, and my boss found an apartment for her. She's very scared, like she said, and the only kind of work she really knows is nursing, and she's afraid Richardson will find her if she works as a nurse. It turned out she has a knack for organizing an office, and my boss thinks she's terrific. How can I tell her to just go fend for herself?"

"Okay Herb, we'll figure something out, and I'll call you this afternoon. Meanwhile, tell Nelda to lay low. That stunt she pulled today was much too clever and much too risky. If she wants to be protected, she can't do that kind of stuff."

"Okay, Joe, I'll talk to her, and I'll be waiting to hear from you."

* * * * * *

Now, Joe recognized Nelda's voice for sure when he called that afternoon. "Nelda, I have to talk to you. Have Herb arrange some free time and call me back."

"He told me you aren't happy."

130

"Hell no, I'm not. I can't protect you when you just walk right into court like you did today. Don't you know how important you are to Herb?"

"I am?"

"I mean as a witness. But he cares about you too. He knows how much you sacrificed for Myra and now for the case and for Melissa."

"I'll do whatever I can, but I need some way to support myself. I heard what the judge decided, so I'm kind of scared again. What can you do? What can I do?"

"Nelda, I don't want you to answer the phone there. You have to leave. What if Zale called? And stay away from Herb. If you and he were involved, you'd lose credibility as an independent witness, and I think there's a good chance we'd lose the case."

"I didn't know. I'm sorry."

"And Herb didn't know either. I'll work on finding a way for you to take care of yourself. For now go to the downtown Seattle YWCA. I'll call to tell them you're coming, and I'll be sure there's a place for you. I think you'll qualify for unemployment compensation until we can find another job for you. Do you have any money to tide you over?"

"I have a little, but I'm going to need some kind of income pretty darn quick."

When Joe sought out his dad for suggestions, Ed said, "Go talk to your brother. I promised I wouldn't be involved and I won't. Everybody else in the family can discuss it with you, but not me."

At lunch that day, Joe and his brother, Mike, put their heads together. They sat in a back corner at the Bench and Bar, removed from the hearing of the other lawyers hanging out at their regular chow hall. Joe laid out for Mike what he discovered that day about Nelda's location and work. "I don't know what's going on between Herb and Nelda, but I suspect it could undermine her credibility. Just working with him is too close for comfort, and I fear it could be more than that."

Mike grinned. "What a clever girl she is. I can't believe she pulled a trick like that. Nobody recognized her until she left? Pretty funny. You think Herb and Nelda are fooling around? It seems kind of soon after Myra's death."

"I don't know if they are, but just think what it would look like in front of a jury, them just being close, him finding her a job at his business. I'll hate arguing that issue in front of the jury."

Mike thought out loud. "So your job is to find a place for Nelda to work and live while this case goes on. That's not Meach's job. I have an idea that might work. Suppose this: You call some of Dad's old friends. He doesn't have to be involved, and see if any of them could use a nurse for some elderly person and maybe live in their house until the case is completed. Or even if they just know someone who could use that kind of help. How does that sound? It's got to be better than just telling Nelda to go get a job."

Joe loved it. "Great idea, Mike. I think I can do it. I'll find a good place for Nelda away from Herb, and Dad isn't involved. I'll get on that this afternoon. I don't want to talk to Dad, but I can talk to Marie and maybe she can tell me who I can call." Joe finished his burger, and Mike finished his spaghetti except for the red stains on his white shirt.

That afternoon, Joe called Marie who said she'd make a list of people who might be possibles, and they could talk about it. Joe said to use an alias for her. "How about Linda?" Later, the phone rang, and it was Marie with some names and numbers. The first one that sounded likely was Rosa Thatcher, a wealthy and elderly widow who lived three lots south of his dad's home on the lakefront. She had trouble keeping a good nurse, and didn't want to be locked up in one of those healthcare institutions, one cracked rib away from the graveyard. She wanted to spend the rest of her years in her home, no matter what it took. Joe asked Marie to call her, and reluctantly, she did. Mrs. Thatcher wanted to know about this "Linda girl." Marie, carefully, tried to avoid being too effusive about her, but Mrs. Thatcher was anxious to see her as soon as possible. She'd tried to find someone and hadn't had much luck.

Early the next day, Herb dropped Nelda off at the Harbor Building, then Joe delivered her to Mrs. Thatcher's home for her interview. Rosa Thatcher and Nelda immediately took to each other. Mrs. Thatcher could see Nelda was exactly the open and warm person she needed to look after her. The close proximity of Mrs. Thatcher's home to the Gold residence reassured Nelda. Joe went three houses north to his dad's home and sat having coffee and a scone with Marie. Nobody in the Gold family knew that Rosa Thatcher was a second cousin to Cora Richardson. They had no reason to fear the elderly, frail lady could expose Nelda to the very hazard she was running from.

The loss of Nelda disappointed David and Saul Epstein. Costello Construction was running better than it ever had before she came. The brothers thanked her, and she apologized for leaving. "I hate to go. I'll miss you guys, but you've got good people here, and you'll be fine after I'm gone. I'd like to come back sometime and see you."

David and Saul thanked and hugged her and wished her the best. As she went out the door, Herb shook her hand. "I'll be seeing you." He winked at her, and she winked back.

CHAPTER TWENTY TWO

Kevin Richardson insisted MacCallum provide him a copy of all the pleadings connected with the motions. MacCallum thought it was simply idle curiosity, but as far as Richardson was concerned, he was a participant in the litigation and MacCallum's boss. The motions had turned out just about as he'd been warned. He had strategy to plan and was compelled to think it through out loud with Cora, to get her approval.

They sat together at the dinner table after Louisa served an apple torte dessert and withdrew to the kitchen to clean up. Louisa put the plates in the dishwasher after cleaning up the dinner table. Cora trusted she wouldn't eavesdrop from the kitchen.

Cora put the fork down and leaned across the table. "I don't care how hard the Golds try to hide Fox. Sooner or later our detective will track her down. She'll either disappear on her own, or you'll have to do something more. My dad always has a plan." Cora didn't need to spell out the "something more." They both knew it would be lethal. "Without Hillibrand behind her, I think she'll run if she gets a scare. She won't remember anything, and she won't be a threat. Didn't her affidavit say how scared she is? I bet she was telling the truth."

"Cora, I'm afraid you'll get me in more hot water. If anything happens to her, they'll know who had the motive, and everything is going to point to me. With the Gold family looking after her, it wouldn't surprise me if she stuck it out rather than run away. I thought you were worried about our precious reputations? Didn't you tell me you fear everybody in the medical community is spreading rumors, and everybody in Seattle society has heard them, too? Nobody says anything about the deaths in front of me, but there could be talk behind my back."

Cora wasn't impressed. "What they talk about is how angry you get. They think you're moody and overworked, and then you get sleepy. I'm sure they suspect you're taking something. They all know what a terrific doctor you are, so they give you some leeway. What else they say, I don't know, but my friends ask me how you're feeling. I know what that means. You'd think the doctors at the hospital would suspect you're on drugs, and it may be apparent to a lot of people."

"I don't worry about my reputation as much as I do about jail. You can't expect me to keep doing risky things, and your name will never come up. And I'm not much worried about my profession. They know I'm good. The Woodside staff is behind me, and that's all I need. They've kept me out of trouble more than once, but it hurts me when I have to do awful things. I don't want to take chances or hurt anyone anymore."

"Don't be stupid, Kevin. You have to shut up Fox or scare her off the way you scared Martens off. If not, you have to do something more. Is there anyone else once you get past those two?"

"I think just those two. The first thing I have to do is contact a detective in Denver. That's where Martens is now. It was nice of the Golds to help me out by giving us his curriculum vita. He's got an impressive background. Now he's at University Hospital in Aurora, Colorado. The detective can go visit him there. When he left, I promised I would leave him alone, but now he's listed as a possible witness for the Golds. I don't care about him giving his own Quaaludes history, but he better not make it look like I was an addict. He might claim I still use. I wonder if he told his family about his use of Quaaludes in the past. Maybe that's something the detective can remind him of."

"That's fine, Kevin, but your detective can't get our names in the papers. I don't care what he does if he doesn't say who hired him. People ask me questions. Last time we visited my aunt Claire, my cousin, Rosa Thatcher, was there. She's a neighbor of the Golds, and she's heard about your 'health' problem. Wherever I go, the Women's League, the DAR, charity things, I can't help wondering what people are saying behind my back, and it's very uncomfortable. There's never been a breath of scandal about my family until you started getting into trouble. Maybe it doesn't bother you, but it sure bothers me."

"Sure Cora, while I'm trying to hang onto my profession and my job, and never mind, keeping out of jail, I'm going to worry about your family's social standing? The real problem is what you and your dad have demanded of me. I think it's stupid for me to keep doing what you tell me and pretend there's no risk."

"And what about Cooper up in Vancouver? Isn't he a guy who could wreck your career?"

"Don't worry about Cooper. He needs me to be quiet the way I need him to be quiet." Richardson pushed his dishes away and said, "I guess that's enough coffee and pie for me. I'm going to head for the den and put my feet up. I'm tired, and it's been a long, hard day, and all this lawsuit headache doesn't make it any easier."

The conversation ended when Louisa came in to remove the tablecloth and replace the centerpiece, almost as if she had heard Richardson say he was finished. It gave Cora something to think about. After Richardson disappeared into the den, Louisa finished up, put down the scrubber and went back to the dining room, guessing what Cora was going to ask.

"Mrs. Richardson, I've appreciated everything you've done for me. Not seeing what I'm not supposed to see and not hearing what I'm not upposed to hear is part of my job. You and the doctor are never going to have to worry about me betraying all the trust you've given me, no matter what I hear."

Cora took her hands and looked into her eyes. "Louisa, I don't know that I've given enough thought to your feelings. I'm sorry. You've always been so loyal, and you're such a sweet girl. We'll look after you, and you can stay with us as long as you want to."

"I always want to stay with you. You know how I feel."

"Oh, Louisa, some young man is going to go crazy over you, and he'll want you all to himself, and I wouldn't want to keep you away from having real love and a family."

"I know, but I can have a family and still work for you. Any man who really loves me will know I can't give up working for you."

Cora was overcome by Louisa's love and loyalty and wondered how much greater it was than Kevin's. She took Louisa into her arms and had an impulse to kiss her again the way she did once before, but she didn't. Not this day, even if she hadn't always resisted the urge.

* * * * * *

Kevin Richardson did his homework. Discretion was imperative and the Better Business Bureau highly rated the AA Detective Agency on First Avenue in downtown Seattle. Woodside Hospital guard, Mike McKee, formerly a Seattle cop, confirmed that AA really was one of the best. In fact, he said Al Armour, the owner of AA, was absolutely the best. McKee's word was good enough for Richardson. AA operated in an unpretentious office in the decidedly unpretentious, old Hogue Building. Richardson observed the worn hardwood floor and a wooden desk in the reception area, a worn sofa and then two offices with frosted glass doors. The middle-aged, semi-blonde receptionist showed Richardson into Al Armour's office. Armour turned out to be an inoffensive, tall, square-jawed man in a worn, grey suit, wearing dark glasses. Richardson wasn't impressed by the man's drab appearance, but he could see how easily Armour could move into a crowd and get answers to his questions. He understood why Armour had a stellar reputation as an investigator. He was plain and easy to miss in a crowd of three.

"I need someone to contact a former colleague. He's at the University of Colorado Hospital in Aurora. I fear he's going to help the other side against me in a lawsuit. I'm afraid he'll claim I'm a drug user and that he used to take Quaaludes too, but he doesn't use them anymore. He'll claim

I made threats against him when he was at Woodside Hospital, and he had to go to another state, because he wasn't safe here."

"Is that true?"

"Well, for the sake of the discussion, let's assume that it's true."

Armour said, "Okay, I've got it. So what do you need me to do?"

"I want you to find out about his family, friends, any weaknesses, girlfriends, drugs, anything you can use against him. I need him scared off right away. I want you to encourage him not to testify against me, but I want you to be careful and don't tie me to any crime. Don't admit I hired you. Right?"

"Of course not. I've been around a while and I know how to get a job done without getting either me or the client in the crap. I know a guy in Denver with some contacts. I can tell him what we need. Before I do anything, I'm going to need some cash. This isn't something where I'm going to have a written contract and put it on the books. And if I were you I wouldn't discuss it with anyone either. But I will get you some results."

"Now you're talking."

CHAPTER TWENTY THREE

It took a week, but when the information came in from Armour, Richardson knew what he wanted. "I want your guy to talk to Martens' wife while he's at work. I don't want him to make any outright threats, just a hint, like 'We know where your little boy goes to school. Why don't you have your husband call up the head of Woodside Hospital and straighten some things out?' Have him tell the wife that her husband isn't being very nice to the Woodside doctors if he testifies in the Seattle case and, that isn't very smart."

Armour didn't make any promises, but he said he would see what he could do. After a couple days he said "I've talked to the guy in Denver, and he's going to talk to the wife. He's done some things for me in the past, and the only things I can promise you for sure is your name won't come up, and it isn't going to be cheap." It turned out he was right. Richardson waited to hear the result.

* * * * * *

His assistant told Eric Martens he had an urgent call from home. "Your wife says to call her right away." With a lump in his throat, Martens shut down the quality assurance meeting he was conducting. In Seattle it was called quality control, but it was quality assurance in Aurora. They'd have to wait to find out what he wanted to do with the two doctors who'd done the surgery on the patient's good knee. Family comes first.

It had to be a serious thing for his, wife, Anna, to call him away from a meeting in the middle of the afternoon. He guessed someone was hurt.

Danny, his son, was still in school at 2 p.m. Martens visualized him lying on a couch in the nurse's office while paramedics were treating the result of some schoolyard accident. Or maybe Anna was hurt. When he picked up the phone he consciously controlled his breathing. "What is it? You okay? Danny?"

"I had a visit from this big guy, a Michael Strauss. He says he's a detective, and that you're in a lot of trouble. He says you're listed as a witness in a case against Woodside Hospital. The scary thing was he kept mentioning Danny. This Strauss had a nasty look, big scar-faced fellow. He was mean. I'm telling you, Eric, this is scary. Can you come home?"

When Anna, sobbing, poured her fear all out, Martens had to wait for her to take a breath before he could answer. "Yes, I'll come home right now. Call the school. Tell them to keep Danny at the principal's office. I'll pick him up on my way home."

As he headed for the elementary school, his fear turned to anger. He knew Richardson was the one threatening his family. If he could, he would teach him a lesson he wouldn't forget, but his helplessness made him the angriest. He couldn't put Danny, his 11-year-old son or Anna at risk. Richardson should be in jail. He'd concluded, based on what he'd heard from Seattle, Richardson had committed two murders and got away with them. Martens hated admitting he just wasn't that brave. When he got Danny home, he still couldn't tell him what the emergency was. Strauss had disappeared, so Martens didn't know what he looked like. He could only visualize the man Anna described. He didn't remember Richardson's phone number after all those years, but when he called after getting it from Information, Richardson was tied up. Martens waited for the return call, old fears tormenting him as he waited.

When Richardson called back, he played dumb. "It must've been the hospital, Eric. I didn't send anyone. Michael Strauss? I've never heard the name. I'm not surprised you made some enemies. I did mention to someone that you endangered doctor trust here and weren't welcome anymore. I remember everybody agreed it's a good thing you left. We don't wreck the reputation of doctors so cavalierly around here, you know. I can't help you, but maybe if you tell the Seattle lawyer you aren't going to have anything to do with this phony lawsuit, your family will feel a little more secure. That would be my suggestion."

Martens never got a chance to ask him any pointed questions. When Richardson finished, he hung up. Martens had only a dial tone to talk to. Richardson's plan was working as designed. He felt that would do it. Martens wasn't so brave when his family was involved. When the word filtered down to Nelda, that would take care of her, too.

In response to Martens' call saying he couldn't help, Ed Gold explained to him Judge Abelson had ruled he had a conflict of interest, so Eric would have to talk to his son, Joe, not him. Ed debated whether he could alert Joe that a call was coming from Martens. On the whole, he concluded, the risk-reward ratio was no good. Joe could handle the call just as well whether or not Ed warned him it was coming. If Judge Abelson concluded Ed was still involving himself in the case, he might reverse his ruling and kick the Gold Law Firm out of it.

The threats to Martens' family stunned Joe. Martens told him some big cowboy named Strauss subtly threatened his family. Joe didn't have an answer. Martens wondered, "What are you going to do about it? I'm sure this Strauss guy was hired by Richardson. I looked him up. He's a private detective, and he's licensed in the state of Colorado. I know a retired cop who knew him on the Denver police force, and this Strauss doesn't have much of a reputation."

In the face of the threat, Joe started thinking. "I'm going to do something, I'm not sure what yet. I'm not going to let Richardson mess with you, I promise." His next move was to check his card file for the number of Detective Tracy of the Seattle PD. When he got Tracy on the line, the detective didn't try to conceal his anger.

"That bastard killed the Mickens girl and Hillibrand, and we can't prove it. He's just getting braver and braver. Give me Martens' number. I'm going to do something about this Strauss. If he's a private dick, and he's pushing things too far, maybe we can use him. Don't call Martens back, let me. I'll find a cop in Denver who can help us one way or another. I have an idea."

Before Joe could say another word, Tracy was gone. The very next day, Tracy was back on the line. "So you've got Martens listed as a primary witness?"

"Yes, he's pretty key."

"I want you to immediately take him off the list. Don't say anything to the other side. Just take him off and say Martens demanded it."

"I can't do that. If I take him off the list I can't call him at trial."

"First of all, Joe, if this goes well, you can add him back on. I checked with an attorney. He said if the defense can't show how they've been harmed by the temporary removal, you can add him back. Second, Martens says he'll totally clam up rather than endanger his family, so I suggest you follow my plan if you want to keep him. This is what you have to do." Tracy gave him the script to recite when he talked to MacCallum. Martens would back him up.

Joe, facing the pitiless pressure of reality, the direction from Tracy, and no alternative, sent a notice dropping Martens as a witness.

Then, as expected, came the call from Larry MacCallum. "How come you dropped Martens?"

"I don't know, Larry. I mean I don't know why Martens is refusing to testify. He just called up and said he was refusing to talk to me. He didn't want to give any kind of explanation. He just said he wasn't going to testify and hung up. I tried to call him back, but as soon as I said who I was, he just hung up on me. I didn't have a choice. Do you know anything?"

"No. As soon as I got your notice, I called Zale. We wondered why you dropped him, but it was one less witness for us to worry about. I don't think I'll be calling him."

"I've had one witness killed, one ran, and now Martens is refusing to testify. If he isn't scared stiff he should be. The Seattle police are going to be on this."

"Watch yourself, Joe, you're stepping into slander territory if you're not careful."

"I'm not going to walk into slander territory, but I think you should look out for the territory Richardson is walking in. Have a nice day"

When Joe called Martens, reciting what Tracy recommended, Martens thanked him for unlisting him and said, "When I feel comfortable, if you call me, I might be more helpful to you than I can be now." The "conspiracy of silence" was still operating. Joe wondered whether Tracy could do anything about it.

CHAPTER TWENTY FOUR

When the Gold Law Firm received the discovery responses from Richardson and the hospital, Joe, hoping for some help, had Jodi make a copy for every partner in the firm. They all had plenty to do, but with luck they might find something interesting and help move it along. With the discovery in hand, curiosity might just suck them in, and somebody might come up with a winning idea. Mike had completed his Army reserve obligation, but Joe had one more session. Joe wasn't going to have time to look at the file the next day, Saturday. His weekend Army Judge Advocate General duty coincided with clouds, gloom and drizzle over Seattle. He headed for Fort Lawton early. The appointments had been set up at 15 minute intervals. The officers got their own attorneys, so he just saw enlisted men. They snapped to attention and sat to wait their turn. Joe got their stories and gave his best, quick advice. Mostly it was the kind of thing young guys get into: bad car or furniture deals, shoplifting, abusing the wife or an impending Article 15 hearing for misconduct on the base.

At 3:00, after suggesting to a young Private he ought not to shoplift, Joe pulled free and joined the rest of the family at his dad's house where he, Mike and Diana met in the den. Sandra and Marie were intensely interested in the Fletcher case and wanted to hear, but confidentiality had to be protected, and they weren't lawyers in the firm. Ed, suddenly cautious and concerned about Judge Abelson's order, stayed out of the library. Gretchen brought in coffee and what the family called her "World Championship Apple Pie." Joe brought out Richardson's and the hospital's answers to interrogatories and a winnowed out copy of Myra's medical records. The records were most persuasive when he extracted just the ones dripping blood. "Dripping blood" was Joe's version of the old "smoking gun." He liked the blood analogy, more pointedly specific in the Fletcher case.

With Jodi's background as a nurse before becoming a legal assistant, Carpenter Gold relied on her for interpretation of medical records along with all her other duties. Jodi's memo pointed out the inconsistencies in the official record claimed by the hospital to be the "true" record: "Richardson blew it when he directed Hillibrand to write, 'I never called Dr. Richardson again though Ms. Fletcher continued to bleed.' The phrasing didn't sound like what an experienced nurse would write voluntarily. It sounded like a condemnation of her own failure to call a doctor in an emergency. If you just look at that one sentence, you know Richardson forced her to write it."

The records Jodi highlighted showed how the coagulants hadn't significantly reduced blood flow. Finding an expert witness for court ordinarily wouldn't be an easy task, but Jodi's pinpoint analysis made it a lot easier to recruit one. No local doc would risk sticking a thumb in the eye of Seattle's medical community. Joe had to go all the way to Houston to find an OB/GYN with the stature, integrity and intestinal fortitude to take on the insurance companies and the medical "old boys" network. Joe would be ready to send the records to the expert he picked the following Monday.

With Mike and Diana leaning forward and focusing themselves, Joe addressed himself to the next item on his agenda: the remaining key witnesses, Nelda and Martens. So far as Joe was aware, Nelda was protected. She was now an employee of the Home Care Corporation, a P.O. Box and a corporate resident agent. The resident agent acted on behalf of a number of corporations, fulfilling their state legal requirements. Joe bet Judge Abelson would be satisfied with the smattering of information Joe would supply. The corporation had one customer, Rosa Thatcher. If the corporate shield were penetrated, and the one specific customer were identified, Joe would have to find another customer. He didn't want Nelda tracked down to Mrs. Thatcher's home. That sounded reasonable to Mike and Diana.

Then came the question of Martens. Joe was waiting to hear from Detective Tracy. "I don't think we want to wait too long before re-listing Martens. The defense could complain their discovery was prejudiced if we delay too long, and Abelson could exclude him. But I don't want to get Tracy upset. He said he was doing 'something.'"

Mike gave Joe a pat on the back, saying it looked like the case was going to be on track as much as it could be. He wished he could be more help and was standing by if needed. Since they had covered the Fletcher case issues, Dad could come back in the library, and since he had finished his pie and still had some coffee left, he sent a smiling Gretchen off to even it up with another piece of pie for him. She expressed wonder that "He never seems to be able to get the pie and coffee to even out without a second piece." After dinner they gathered around the TV and watched Ed Sullivan except Sandra and Joe who went home right after dinner. She was feeling "a little tired." The very pregnant Sandra was entitled to be tired, if that's all it was. Diana put her hand on Mike's leg, which he took as an urgent request to get to their home and away from people who'd had plenty of romance in their lives. She could hardly wait to get the seatbelt off when they got to the house.

* * * * * *

Following a week to review the records, Dr. Hyman Berg, the Houston expert, called Joe. Directed by Jodi's highlighting and notes, he firmly concluded that the anticoagulants were like sticking chewing gum on a leaky gas tank and trying to keep the car running by continually pouring in more gas. "What he really needed to do for Myra was a dilatation and curettage, what we call a D&C, to find the source of the bleeding and tie off the bleeder to relieve it." Dr. Berg speculated that, most likely, there was some torn tissue to repair, but without a D&C or an autopsy, the most anyone could say was that, more probably than not, proper treatment would've stopped the bleeding. He was emphatic that Dr. Richardson failed to meet the standard of care of competent OB/GYNs in a number of respects. "He should have done a D&C long before the night of Myra's death, should have attended the patient when contacted by the nurses and should have performed a D&C on an emergency basis that night." Joe wondered that there had been no autopsy. Berg explained to Joe that Richardson had every reason to discourage the husband from seeking an autopsy. "But where was everybody else on the staff?"

Berg expressed confidence on cause of death. The record denoted a gradual decline in respiration, acceleration of pulse and a weakening of blood pressure progressively over an hour. He concluded these findings from the record were consistent with a continuous loss of blood, until finally the flow stopped, not as a result of any treatment or medication but exsanguination, the total loss of blood.

Joe wondered out loud, "Is there's anything that might have been missed? Is there any other possible cause of death?"

"Well, Joe, it's a little like asking if someone who was found dead in an airplane crash might have had a heart attack on the way down. There might be all kinds of possible things you could imagine, but when I go into court they ask me, 'Do you have an opinion on the cause of death based on reasonable medical certainty?' When I see a medical record like this, the only possible answer is loss of blood volume. I saw that Myra was hurt when she was helped to the bathroom by a nurse and then got back into bed. I suppose it's possible she could have torn some tissue on her way to the bathroom or back, but there is no evidence that happened. She had a slip and some pain, but I can't presume that was a new, independent injury causing death. She was already bleeding, so that doesn't affect my opinion on the cause of death with reasonable medical certainty. Does that answer your question?"

"I don't think I could've gotten a better answer." The doctor couldn't see Joe pumping his fist.

I smell a win coming here. It's all lining up.

"Doctor, there's one other thing. There's reason to believe that Dr. Richardson was addicted to Quaaludes and that's why he didn't come to

Mrs. Fletcher's bedside when she was bleeding. I'm wondering if there's some kind of test to prove that he's addicted to Quaaludes."

"Even if you can't prove addiction, you might prove Quaalude use by a blood test. That can show use within about a week. There are claims that the drug stays in hair for many months. So, you can test blood right away and that may prove current use. The hair test will essentially only prove use sometime in the past."

"Well that's not so hot. If I have to prove he's using drugs now, I'll have to file a motion and give him a week's notice. He could quit for a week and that would be no good, right?"

"It would be chancy. It might be all you would prove is he didn't use drugs within the last week. It's hard to tell how far back you can go with the hair test, and it's not all that precise anyway. Even if it worked, the hair test wouldn't be probative with the timeline of your case. You want my opinion? Don't do it."

That bastard slides by again.

CHAPTER TWENTY FIVE

For the next few days, Sandra kept complaining of headaches and blurred vision and Joe kept saying, "Call the doc." Sandra would wait a bit and think she was feeling better, and end up not calling. Joe eventually got too nervous, made an appointment for her anyway and went to bed knowing it was the right thing to do.

That night, Joe thought he was dreaming of an earthquake but realized Sandra was shaking him awake.

"It's worse, Joe. I'm scared. I'm getting dizzy, and I feel like I'm going to throw up."

He immediately leaped up, threw on the light and called her OB/ GYN. He reached Dr. Pederson's service immediately and held the phone with a shaky hand until the doctor came on the line. Joe told him what Sandra said.

"Can she get up?"

"I'll ask her. Sandra, the doctor wants to know if you can get up."

"It hurts."

Dr. Pederson heard her and promised to call an ambulance, stat. Joe shuddered as he threw on his clothes. Sandra, with a robe thrown over her nightgown, looked helpless, weak, in pain and frightened. They were overjoyed when they knew she was pregnant, and now she feared they'd lose the baby. Joe was frightened for both her and the baby.

When the two med techs arrived, an efficient, tall, black man and a sandy-haired, younger assistant, Sandra sat up with Joe's help. The black man was clearly in charge, directing the younger tech where to wheel the gurney and how to help lift Sandra onto it. They carried her with slow steps down the stairs and out to the ambulance. The head man turned to Joe.

"Dr. Pederson has us going to Woodside. You want to follow? We'll be taking her to Emergency, and you'll need to be there to check her in."

Joe suddenly had to confront the idea Richardson would be walking past Sandra's hospital room several times a day if she checked in. Right at that moment, her condition was emergent. Richardson was a problem he'd deal with. Joe followed the ambulance all the way from the Magnolia neighborhood in his Caddy. When the ambulance got to Woodside, Dr. Pederson had beaten it there and was ready for Sandra. She lay on the gurney behind a metal framed cloth screen. He wrote while talking to her. When Joe finally finished giving the Emergency desk staff his insurance information to their satisfaction, he hurried to his wife and heard Dr. Pederson's advice to her.

"You have a pretty serious case of preeclampsia, but I think we can handle it. Preeclampsia is a multi-system breakdown. Your BP is up, and we'll be looking for protein in your urine. That can lead to kidney problems and a stroke if untreated. So we'll treat it, and we can make it better. I can't understand why you let it go this long. Courage is a lousy substitute for caution when you're pregnant. I have some tests to do, and the nurses will need to keep watching the BP for a while, but this preeclampsia is something that can happen. We have to stay on top of it. Your baby can't look out for himself."

"Or herself."

Dr. Pederson had to laugh.

"Either way."

Sandra was checked into intensive care. Dr. Pederson reassured her that the baby was fine, but she was going to have to be very careful and follow his orders. She'd have to cut down on salt and lay on her left side to protect the baby. Joe sat by while Sandra completed tests ordered by Dr. Pederson and then walked along with the gurney on her way to bed. The nurses treated her like a fragile piece of china and at last moved her gently from the gurney to the bed.

Before Dr. Pederson left, Joe had to raise his concerns about Richardson. The doctor tried to laugh it off as just rumor and unfounded suspicions. "Dr. Richardson is a very able and responsible doctor. Some people have been put off by his occasional gruffness, but don't let him worry you."

Joe, not the least deterred, laid out the contentious battle between Richardson, the Gold firm and his client, and a quick summary of his fears if Richardson ever got near Sandra. Pederson promised to warn the nurses to monitor anyone going into her room. He would bar anyone from going in who hadn't been approved in advance. However, he made it clear he wouldn't specifically target Richardson. "But, it'll be okay. She isn't going to be here that long."

When Joe got home in the early morning, he realized there was a phone conference scheduled with Dr. Berg and wasn't sure what else was on his calendar. He called Jodi to fill him in on what happened to Sandra, and she was most concerned. Joe assured her that everything was under control, but whatever he'd scheduled for the day should be postponed.

* * * * * *

That day, Richardson went to the fourth floor Maternity ward to check on a patient. The grey, matronly nurse, Florence Wagner, was on duty at the desk. She smiled as was appropriate, whatever she thought of Richardson, and stood to the side as he checked on the list of patients on the ward. He observed his patient, Mrs. Lister, was in room 429, and a

Mrs. Sandra Gold was in 430. Richardson's reaction was apparent. He stiffened and took in a sharp breath.

"Is anything wrong?"

"No, I was just thinking about something I almost forgot."

If this was the wife of one of the young Gold lawyers, that could mean something to Cora. She'd want to know. The woman was pregnant and for some reason, at Woodside. He surreptitiously picked up her chart while pretending to get that of Mrs. Lister. The chart indicated Sandra Gold was Mrs. Joseph Gold, and her preeclampsia had produced an emergency. Seven months gone, and Dr. Pederson was her doc. Cora would expect him to tell her.

He wandered down the hallway toward Mrs. Gold's room as if aimlessly killing time. He thought about what the reaction would be if he spoke to her. He casually looked over his shoulder and saw Wagner observing quizzically. The risk was too great, no matter how great the temptation. Whatever Cora came up with, he couldn't do it with Wagner watching, not in the hospital, not with a vital signs monitor operating. He pondered what he might do without being observed. Sandra Gold might get an unwelcome visit within the next critical month. He hated himself for what he was thinking, but he was getting used to the feeling.

When he got home, Cora was in the living room reading a book by one of her favorite romance novelists. She was annoyed when he called her name. "What do you want now?"

"At the hospital, I discovered that Joe Gold's wife is in Maternity. She has preeclampsia. Maybe there's something we can do. You have any ideas?"

Now she smiled. "Maybe she'll be vulnerable, and maybe you can do something. I'll talk to my dad. I doubt you could do anything in the hospital. Everyone would know you did it."

She got on the phone, and Richardson heard only a lot of, "yes Dad" and, "okay" after she'd recited the situation as he'd told her. What a relief it was when she shook her head. "Dad agreed with me. He says we'll have to wait. In time we'll catch her home alone, unprotected. He's looking forward to it. Don't do anything obvious, he said."

Why do I have to do what she wants? Why do I have to obey Jerry Alden? Am I going crazy?

* * * * * *

After two days in the hospital, Sandra came back home but still was on bed rest. Molly, a nurse recommended by Dr. Pederson attended to Sandra's daily needs and checked her blood pressure every three hours. Dr. Pederson said she was doing better but warned Joe a Cesarean might be necessary if the tests didn't show the preeclampsia symptoms clearing up. He didn't want to do it at only seven months gestation. It was better to hold off at least another month, so the baby could fully develop.

"The baby is under stress, and Sandra still has an elevated blood pressure. She needs more protein, and you need to get her drinking more water, too. Okay? Sandra really has to be disciplined about this."

When Dr. Pederson left, the whole family gathered in the living room was allowed to come up and see Sandra. It was all a bit overwhelming for her, but she felt a certain guilty pleasure in the living proof of how much they all loved her and the baby. This would be Ed Gold's first grandbaby, and nothing could go wrong. He was accustomed to stress, but this was too much, and he had to turn away at last. Stress was yet another load for Joe, too. He couldn't stop worrying. Pederson had a good reputation and was recommended by some people Joe knew. Yet, he couldn't forget that Dr. Richardson also had a good reputation when he killed Myra Fletcher. The worries didn't go away. The health problems were enough, even if Joe didn't know of Dr. Richardson's interest in Sandra. That would be the greatest worry of them all.

CHAPTER TWENTY SIX

Doctor Kevin Richardson struggled through a busy day in his third-floor office at the North Seattle Professional Building with its clear view of the Woodside Hospital just across the street. There were still two patients to see before he could go home. One wanted to talk about a tubal ligation, and the other was ready to be scheduled for a Cesarean. Her baby was too big, and if she went into labor the baby would be pushing out feet first and might have the umbilical cord around his neck, a dangerous situation.

When his assistant, Maxine, told him Leo Cooper was on the line, Richardson would have been content to return the call when he was away from the office, not rushed and not at the end of another exhausting day.

But Maxine said, "He sounded really frantic, that it's an emergency, and it's finally happened, and you'd know what he meant."

Maxine, with eyebrows up, cast an inquiring look, but Richardson wasn't going to let on about his angst. He wouldn't let the sudden stabbing gut pain show on his face. With resignation and fear, he sank back in the cushiony leather recliner behind his oak desk.

It's finally happened! Oh Lord. Please no!

Cooper could put him in jail if Richardson let him. He picked up the phone and took the call.

"Leo, do you mean what I think?"

"Yes, Kevin, this is it. My lawyer wants me to make a statement at 8:30 tomorrow morning. He says they might charge me with violations of the drug laws."

"How'd it happen, Leo?"

"It was like this. Americanada wants to expand their U.S. drug markets, so they brought in a new American agent. That took the Washington State auditing out of my hands. I tried to sidetrack him and gave him some phony records. I thought we were going to be okay, but yesterday the sales manager called me up and said the province health department knew about it, and I needed to get a lawyer. They knew I was fooling with the drug records and they want the details."

"I didn't want to get you into trouble, but I had to disclose where the drugs were going. So they know the Quaaludes are going to somebody at Woodside. I wanted to warn you so you had time to explain where they went. The dangerous ones for you are the insulin and chloroform. The Vancouver PD aren't going to know about that Mickens girl that worked for you or about nurse Hillibrand either. I'm not going to say anything, but you better get ready in case somebody figures it out. You need to think of someone else that was getting those drugs. Martens has been gone a long time. I don't know how you explain the chloroform. If anybody asks me, I understood you were taking care of the drugs sent to your building."

Richardson felt his pulse picking up. "Leo, you don't know anything about those women, and you better not say anything to the Vancouver PD. You can't mention my name. That would be stupid. I trusted you to keep your mouth shut. You better leave me out of your records. Leave those shipments in Martens' name. If they have a problem with that, let them figure it out"

"I'm sorry, Kevin. I have the records in Martens' name, but the sales manager also receives inquiries about orders from quality control at a hospital in Aurora, Colorado. That's where Martens is, and they know he's there. Now the police have all my records, and the only way I can stay out of jail is to own up. I have to figure out what I can say and what I can't. And

I know more than you think I know. You aren't the only doctor I know at Woodside. Naturally, I didn't put any of that stuff about what you did with the drugs in my records. It wouldn't be part of my necessary knowledge. The provincial health department does inspections, you know. I have to let them see the records, but there's nothing in there that really names you."

"Leo, you're really making me nervous. I don't want you to talk to those people, so I'm glad we've had a chance to talk first."

"I'll be as careful as I can, but I'm in a mess. Kevin. It's bad enough without clamming up. If I refused to talk at all, I'd be going to jail, but it won't be that bad because I sent the stuff to a doctor. I can't say they're just samples, you know. It's a pretty tight situation for me, but as much as I can, I'll keep you out of it."

Richardson could see he wasn't going to be able to trust Cooper. "Don't be an idiot. They aren't going to send you to jail. If you're not careful, they'll have a way to connect my meds to those women. One of them wasn't even an insulin user, but if they test her they might find it. I'm warning you, Leo, if you get me charged with murder, I'm going to take you down with me. You better just shut up. I'll say you were part of it if I get charged. Whatever happens to me will happen to you, too. It's not just drug dealing you're in trouble for, Leo."

Richardson slammed down the phone hard enough and loud enough to bring Maxine to his door. "Patients are waiting."

"Maxine, I can't see those women. Have Tommy see them."

"But Doctor, these are your patients."

"I don't give a damn. I can't see them."

As he motioned Maxine away, Kevin Richardson felt his soul in dire pain clear down to his toes. He didn't know of an easy way to silence Cooper. He used insulin with Mickens and Hillibrand, but he had to find another way with Cooper. He was thinking of Cooper's 54th level condo on English Bay in Vancouver. The great view, the deck, his love of single malt scotch. It was taking shape in Richardson's mind and putting Cooper at more risk than he knew.

Richardson refused to call his father-in-law, Dr. Alden. It wasn't getting easier, but he could create a plan to shut up the witness as easily as Jerry Alden could. If he couldn't scare Cooper, he still had ideas. Richardson picked up the phone again. "We have to meet, Leo. Let's talk this over. You can't talk to the authorities tomorrow. I'm coming up." Cooper argued briefly, but just as Richardson expected, he didn't have the determination of Richardson.

Richardson prepared mentally with as much care as he had with Mickens and Hillibrand. He suffered huge pangs of conscience over the death of Mickens, and it got no easier with Hillibrand, even though she'd never been his lover. Now, Dr. Leo Cooper, with whom he had done business for years, had to be quieted, and a plan was taking shape.

Where would this end?

It was hard to remember who he was when he first started med school at the University of Washington. Nothing was more valuable than human life. Now, Cora's position in society and his in the medical profession had become more important to him. If he told Cora, she would again make him follow a plan her dad would concoct. He knew he was lost on a one-way highway, and he had not yet calculated where it would end.

In 1964 you could cross the border at Blaine, showing your driver's license and say you were a Washington state resident. There was no record you had crossed and no record you returned. His conscience was cursing him all the way up the freeway to Vancouver. With all the guilt, he still followed the path of least resistance, a path that didn't require a confrontation with Cora.

Can I do this? God, I hope so.

* * * * * *

Harbor Vista, a well-named condominium, enjoyed a spectacular, broad view of English Bay from the higher units. Richardson parked his red Corvette a block away, down a side street, just past a drugstore. Before he got out, he put on a wide brimmed hat and a pair of dark glasses. He ignored the local folk lapping up the cool, bright spring weather, an elderly man and teenage boy playing chess on the bench in front of the drugstore and the little groups of people walking back and forth between the beach and the condos.

Cooper emphasized the spaciousness of his unit with a beige carpet and stark white sofa and chair. He placed potted plants and a large, white armoire up against the wall near the sliding glass doors to the deck. The signed Lichtenstein and Klee prints on each side of the broad fireplace told the story of his wealth and sophistication. You could see that Cooper liked to spend sunny days out on the deck where he placed several reclining cedar chairs. On the cedar table sat a bottle of Scotch, an empty glass and a book lying open, face down. Cooper hadn't picked the book up since early the day before. However, he was emptying the bottle fast. He'd been proud of kicking the Quaaludes, but he started leaning more and more on Scotch to tame the nerves. Now the fear of Richardson kicked up the consumption. The more he drank, the more he worried, trapped in a vicious circle.

Cooper stood on alert, keeping in mind that Richardson had first chloroformed his assistant, Mickens, then injected her with insulin. And then, when nurse Hillibrand threatened him, he'd done the same with her. They both died of hypoglycemia, and without Cooper's help, the police would never prove he'd done anything. The only reason he agreed to meet Richardson was the threat Richardson could make him a defendant in a murder-conspiracy case. He planned to watch Richardson carefully. He thought, if he remained observant, the older man would never overpower him. Out on his deck, Cooper overlooked the front entrance to the condo. He couldn't miss the fire-engine red Corvette wrapping the corner and jerking to a halt in front of the drugstore. With this ostentatious lack of discretion, Cooper wondered how much judgment Richardson could have.

Since that last phone confrontation with Richardson, Cooper stressed out and needed more courage. That's what the Scotch was for. He poured two inches, looked at it and poured another two. When Richardson said he was coming, Cooper got the S&W .38 out of his car's glove compartment, brought it upstairs and concealed the pistol behind the cushion of his leather easy chair. Cooper planned to protect himself if Richardson had any strong-arm ideas in mind.

When Richardson arrived, he acted like a friend who wanted to get him over the crisis, now being helpful and understanding. Cooper, happily surprised, patted him on the back, showed him to the couch and quickly retreated to the leather easy chair next to it. Richardson smiled when he saw the Scotch bottle. Cooper poured a stiff one for Richardson, and to keep him company, poured himself another one. Cooper felt a little relief when Richardson took the glass and seemed to relax on the couch. He leaned back, legs crossed, savoring the 12-year-old liquor. They began an earnest conversation about ways Cooper could escape charges.

"Leo, I hope you now understand that you can't mention my name at any time or for any reason with the police. No matter how tough it gets, if you have to find someone else to blame, it can't be me."

"I'm with you Kevin. I'm not going to bring up your name unless I'm trapped. For all I know, the police have talked to Martens, and I'll be in hot water worse if I make up a story. It won't help you if I get caught in a lie."

"You worry too much, Leo. All you have to do is find a likely, dumb employee to blame. You had no idea he was smuggling packages of drugs to Woodside hospital. See, you don't even have to mention my name. Pick the dumbest employee you have and manufacture the evidence. In fact, have your lawyer feed that to the police. You don't even need to talk to them. You'll see. It'll work. So now, can I have another drop of Scotch?"

Just as Richardson expected, Cooper couldn't resist and poured another one for himself too. Despite his pretense of helping Cooper, Richardson still couldn't trust him. They chatted jovially while sipping, but Richardson drew him away from his glass and over to the window.

While Cooper pointed out the interesting life out on the street below, Richardson surreptitiously poured his own drink into a potted plant. He walked over to the stereo and turned on the light jazz Cooper had available for the young ladies he romanced. On his way back to the couch, with Cooper still focused on the street life, he dropped a couple crushed Quaaludes into Cooper's Scotch glass. With Cooper back to his drink, Richardson walked over to the deck door, then out. He pretended to be admiring the view while Cooper continued sipping Scotch and feeling a little safer, a little more relaxed.

Cooper joined him on the deck. Still a little cautious, he kept himself behind Richardson rather than near the railing. When he walked back inside, the Quaaludes had dissolved, and he didn't really notice any significant change in taste. As he leaned back on the couch and sipped, his senses numbed out. By the time he finished his third Scotch he wobbled and didn't focus. Richardson, pretending to be a little tipsy, visualized what he was about to do, felt an adrenaline rush and an inner turmoil. Cooper had trusted him, and he'd trusted Cooper.

How can I do this? There's no other way. I have to.

When Cooper was ready to be dropped over the railing, Richardson quickly scanned the nearby buildings for potential witnesses. Seeing none, he helped Cooper back out the door with only ineffectual resistance and complaint from Cooper. The railing wasn't too high, and Richardson didn't think it would take a supreme effort to get him over it. Richardson's adrenaline continued pumping, and with his heart beating like a high-power factory, he started edging Cooper toward the railing. But Cooper, suddenly alert and alarmed, began pushing back. Richardson was taller and well-conditioned, yet Cooper was younger and stronger. Richardson feared he couldn't achieve the easy victory he expected when he conceived his plan.

Cooper scuffled, grabbing and trying to swap positions so Richardson would be the one in danger. Cooper threw all his weight against Richardson, but in his dazed condition, his coordination failed. As he tried to push Richardson toward the railing, he missed and instead, with Richardson's help, threw himself over. He flailed futilely, grasping for Richardson, perhaps to save himself, perhaps to take Richardson with him. Pedestrians heard his scream as he dropped toward the pavement. Richardson jumped back out of view as the people jerked toward the sound as he hit. It was louder than Richardson expected. Running back inside, he forgot he had planned to wash his glass, put it away and wipe his fingerprints off the door handles and Scotch bottle. His heartbeat felt the way it had with Mickens and Hillibrand.

Face sweating, heart still pumping furiously and knees weak, Richardson took the elevator down and exited the building through the garage, putting on the cap and dark glasses he'd stuck in his jacket. He innocently joined the crowd out on the street looking at the result of a tragic accident. He stood behind a balding, elderly man discussing what happened. The man said, "I don't know. He was just lying there when we got here. The guy sure smells like alcohol, must have just fallen over the railing." A young boy standing next to him started whispering to the older man as Richardson walked away down the street. The boy, Percy Boykin, followed, keeping close to the building, slow and cautious, step by step. At a distance, young Percy locked on to the camouflaged, white-haired Richardson headed down toward the corner. In a moment, he saw him in the beautiful, bright, red Corvette, whipping away down the street.

Within a few minutes he'd witnessed two memorable events firmly joined in his mind. With his grandfather too stunned to hear him, Percy saved it till the police arrived. He'd seen a tall, white-haired guy leaning over a railing right after the impact. This suspicious looking man might have been the one. He looked guilty of something. Percy wished he could have read the complete license number, but he saw it was a Washington state plate on a spectacular, new looking Corvette. Constable Stokes seemed a kind, gentle officer, and when Percy was interviewed, he told the constable everything he remembered. The officer wrote it all down.

It was only while Richardson was on Interstate 5 headed south towards Seattle, that he wondered to himself whether he had wiped the glass, door handles and bottle. His stress level was increasing, so he took another Quaalude in order to make it all the way home. Then he remembered what the Quaaludes had done to his driving on prior occasions, but now calm about it, he hurtled down the road only 15 miles per hour over the limit and clearly at risk for a DWI.

Did that boy get a good look at me? Maybe the old man?

Chapter Twenty Seven

Within a couple weeks after Mrs. Rosa Thatcher hired Nelda, she had got used to answering to "Linda," and they established a warm relationship. Rosa no longer worried about going up and down the stairs. She didn't have to remember to take her pills, and "Linda" had her tea ready before she even asked. Though Nelda lived with Mrs. Thatcher, she could be contacted through the Home Care Corporation employing "Linda Wilson." Mrs. Thatcher never wondered why "Linda's" mail didn't come to the Thatcher residence. She was just grateful to Marie Gold for recommending her. Rosa found the girl every bit as nice, intelligent and capable as Marie said.

"Linda" always seemed to look around nervously when they went grocery shopping together, but she seemed relaxed and comfortable at home. Rosa didn't care much for entertaining, but her cousin, Cecile, said she was bringing to lunch a cousin on the other side, Cora Richardson, the prominent society lady married to the distinguished Dr. Kevin Richardson.

Rosa told "Linda" about Cecile, and that she and Cora Richardson were coming, when suddenly "Linda" appeared startled. She finished laying out the table and readying the croissant sandwiches and salad and then began complaining of some undefined pain. She had to leave before the company came and apologized abjectly. "I'm sorry, Rosa, I have to go right away. I've had this before, and I need to see the doctor as soon as possible. Rosa felt deep concern for "Linda," but it didn't even occur to her that her friend, companion and nurse might be leaving forever.

Nelda went into Rosa's office, shut the door and dialed the Gold Law Firm. The call caught Joe in the library, and Jodi switched the call there.

"Slow down, Nelda. It's not that bad. Mrs. Richardson has never seen you, and the name "Linda" wouldn't alert her or her husband either. I do agree it's not a safe situation, but maybe you can bluff it out through today. I suggest you just pretend everything's okay for now. I'll see what we do. Does that sound okay?"

"I'm sorry, Joe, but I can't serve croissants and salad to Mrs. Richardson. My hands are shaking, and I just can't handle it."

"Do what you need to do, Nelda, but if you can, try not to make it a big thing. That might not be good. Why don't you just make some kind of excuse, go over to my dad's house and put your car in their garage? They have an empty place, so no one will see it from the street. If you want, you could call Mrs. Thatcher later and tell her that you have to go away for a while. Would that work?"

When the ladies arrived Nelda put the tea, sandwiches and salad on the table and told Rosa, "I have to go now," and before Rosa could say anything, she headed to the door. Joe had let Marie know Nelda was coming. When Nelda arrived with hands shaking and red eyes, her fear had returned. She thought that by being a few driveways south of the Gold home and using an alias, she'd hide safely. No one could have imagined the nice, elderly Rosa Thatcher would invite terror back into Nelda's life. Jodi arrived with Joe, and after their reassurance, Nelda calmed down again. Joe put his hands on her shoulders. "I promise you, we will not let Dr. Richardson anywhere near you. You'll move in with me and Sandra."

The Gold family lawyers exchanged a series of phone calls that night and then met with Nelda at the firm's office the next day. Joe's brother, Mike, came up with the next big idea. Joe loved it. "That's it, Mike. Damn, we should have thought of that before. We'll have her testify to preserve her testimony. It'll be on the record, so, if anything happened to her, the testimony would still be there. That should take away Richardson's incentive to harm her and Nelda's fear of him."

Joe had previously warned Nelda that before trial, the defendants' lawyers would want to take her deposition. From the first, it sounded like an ordeal, but if she was going to testify in court for Herb and Melissa, she'd just have to face up to it. Now, Joe explained this deposition to preserve the testimony was different from the deposition he expected the defendants would take before trial.

"In their deposition, the defense attorneys can ask anything that might lead to discoverable evidence. They aren't limited to testimony admissible at trial. Many questions not permitted at trial are permitted in the deposition. The judge won't be there to rule, so I have to put an objection on the record to give the judge a basis at trial to bar improper questions. When you testify in their deposition, I can put in an objection and tell you to go ahead and answer. They can get the information, but your answer might not be admissible as evidence against us at trial.

"The deposition we'll do is different. You're a crucial witness, and you're afraid you have to hide out till the trial. Everywhere you go, Richardson could be around the next corner. He doesn't want you to testify. How about this? What if we have you give all your testimony in a deposition we schedule? The rules allow us to take your deposition to preserve your testimony, and you'll testify that we're doing it this way because you're afraid of Richardson. Abelson already understands Richardson was a suspect in the death of Hillibrand and the young woman named Mickens.

"If anything happened to you, Judge Abelson, sure as hell, would put the deposition testimony before the jury, just as if you'd testified in court. Richardson would almost be better off with you alive for the trial rather than dead and have your testimony go before the jury. He'd have to worry that the jury will hold him responsible for anything that happened to you." As he talked, the light bulb went on for Joe. He could protect Martens the same way he was going to protect Nelda.

While Nelda thought about it, Joe called Detective Tracy, explaining the plan to him. He wanted Tracy to establish contact with Martens in Aurora, Colorado. Tracy, at first, was annoyed that Joe asked him to convey messages as if he were a lackey of the law firm. On the other hand, he was getting something out of it and knew he owed a debt to the Gold Law Firm. As he thought about it, he was glad he could do something in return for the firm's assistance in building a case against the "conspiracy of silence" and a very dangerous doctor. When Tracy reached out for his contact in the Denver PD, he explained the Richardson problem and the guy promised to have Martens call him.

* * * * * *

Later that day, Nelda called Rosa Thatcher and apologized. The doctor told her she needed to take a rest. Otherwise, the condition she had would come back. Nelda avoided identifying the condition and Rosa wouldn't pry. Nelda would have somebody pick up her things for shipment to her family's home in Iowa. She felt badly about leaving Rosa and lying to her and immediately started thinking about finding another place to work and about living with Joe and his wife. She liked the idea she'd get her testimony on record and Richardson couldn't help himself by hurting her.

* * * * * *

As Tracy explained it, it seemed too simple to Martens, and he was dubious. But Martens called Joe as Tracy requested. When Joe explained the plan, it made sense. But he asked Joe to give him a couple days to think about it. Martens called his lawyer and explained the whole history. When it finally came down to the question of giving his deposition, the lawyer said, "Sure, I can't think of a better way to protect you than have your testimony put on record immediately. Then there's no motive to harm you or harass your family in any way." Martens didn't want to argue about it, but he suspected Richardson might do something awful, even if it made no sense at all. He had his own plan.

Joe received a call from Martens' attorney, Phil Shimkus, in Aurora Colorado. "Can you do the deposition here in Aurora, in my office? Just being cautious. It's an unusual solution to an unusual problem, but I'd have to say you came up with a damn good one."

166

"Thanks, I'd like to do the deposition down there for you, but I know I'll have a fight with the other side and, tell you what, I'll front the money for you and Martens to come up here and do the dep at my office."

After calling his client, Shimkus called back, saying "It's a deal. Have your secretary work the schedule and accommodations out with Sandy in my office. Send me the notice and plane tickets and so on, and we'll hop up there."

Joe re-identified Martens as a plaintiff's witness and decided to schedule his deposition. He sent out notices to MacCallum and Zale for the depositions of Martens and Nelda. The defense lawyers immediately tried to stall the depositions. Zale called, claiming he had to investigate before he could prepare his cross examinations. Joe pretended to be accommodating. "Take all the time you want to prepare your cross. If you even want to waive cross-examination, you can do that. But, if you want to delay the direct examination, that isn't going to happen."

"If any harm comes to Fox or Martens, don't think Richardson isn't going to be the prime suspect. First of all, Abelson will allow the full depositions to come into evidence even if you haven't done your cross and second, Detective Tracy of the Seattle PD is going to be talking to you." Zale was irate at the implication, as if he had never thought of it before. Just to undermine the argument he knew Zale would be making, Joe sent a response rejecting a two-week delay and setting forth the reasons he'd identified. Not surprisingly, Zale sent a proposal to do the two depositions at his office and delay them until he decided he was ready.

Joe turned down Zale's offer, saying, "Thanks, we'll do the depositions at our office like it says in the notices. When Zale's motion for a delay and to do the depositions at his office came to court, Judge Abelson wasn't persuaded by Joe's argument. Joe argued that Zale had already received the plaintiffs' answers to interrogatories and that Nelda and the Martens' were very concerned for their safety. Since there was no proof of any real threat to them, Abelson thought, Joe should have agreed to the two week extension. He warned MacCallum and Zale that if any harassment of Fox or the Martens' occurred, he would re-think everything he said. The depositions were going to wait. It was too bad Abelson couldn't hear how worrying his decision was to the two witnesses.

He would have cause to repent scoffing at the witnesses' fears.

Chapter Twenty Eight

Burnside, Iowa is a bedroom community just a few miles from Des Moines. Nelda had warned her mother she might get an unwelcome visitor. The family of Eric Martens, another witness, was harassed, so thought she had to be ready in case she got that kind of visit. Nelda's mother watched "As the World Turns" on a dull afternoon while knitting. A new pink cotton sweater would be nice with her black pants. She saw a gray Ford stop just across the street from her home. A big, bulky, baldheaded man in a dark suit a half size too small stepped out. As he came up the walk, Mrs. Fox got ready and headed for the door with her knitting basket still in her hand.

Chris Dugan, an experienced private eye came up the walk. No neighbors were observing his arrival, so far as he could tell. The well-kept, small, white rambler sat behind a low, white picket fence, pink chrysanthemums in front and white hydrangea behind the fence. From what Al Armour told him, Dugan envisioned a sweet, little, gray-haired lady who probably would welcome any visitor. Armour said, "Go in heavy." Dugan's detective license was suspended before and it cost him. He knew what Armour meant by "Go in heavy," and he wasn't going to do it.

When Mrs. Fox, exactly the woman Dugan envisioned, opened the door, he flashed his fake, friendly smile as though saying "cheese" for the camera. She looked at him expectantly, with eyebrows raised. "Hi, I'm Chris Dugan. You're Mrs. Marion Fox, right?"

"Yes, Mr. Dugan." She seemed bland, innocent, her eyes questioning.

"I've been sent to talk to you. I hate to alarm you, but you're in a spot, sort of. Your daughter, Nelda, is getting ready to testify in Seattle in a deposition, and there are people who might want to hurt her or you if she testifies a certain way." Now, he seemed earnest, almost imploring. "For your own safety and your daughter's, you should warn her of the danger that she's in. I know people have talked to her, and she hasn't listened to them. Maybe she'll listen to you."

Then Mrs. Fox showed him the Smith and Wesson .38 she hid in her knitting basket, now pointed at his groin.

"Come sit down with me, Mr. Dugan. I've been waiting for you. We need to talk, but not the way you had in mind." She showed him her insincere, friendly smile, and his look became more like a man who'd eaten a rotten fish instead of the chocolate ice cream he expected. He perched himself uneasily on the blue, mohair couch where he was directed. She had a ready lie to put him even more ill at ease.

"In the first place, I think you should know that the Mrs. Fox you wanted to talk to is my sister-in-law, not me. In the second place, take off your jacket. I want to see the gun in your shoulder holster."

Dugan started to deny he had a weapon and quickly stopped as Mrs. Fox's gun was extended further toward his crotch and her face turned angry, nostrils flaring, maybe a little crazy. "Don't make me do something I'm trying not to. You can't threaten me," she snarled.

Alarmed, he unbuttoned his jacket. "Now get the holster off, slowly, gently. Don't make me angry, okay?" His eyes told her he took her very seriously. She could be crazy or reckless. That she must have some experience with guns was apparent as she slowly and carefully took the gun out of the holster using a cloth to avoid dirtying the gun with her fingerprints. She ejected the cartridges, then, still holding the barrel in her left hand with the cloth, one finger through the trigger guard, she handed it toward him. She still maintained her aim and caution throughout the entire procedure.

"Lay your fingers very gently on the grip, just the grip."

"Why are you doing this?"

She was still snarling. "Do what I said, Mr. Dugan, or else."

"No, I'm not going to do that."

"Yes, you are, or you won't walk out of here." He saw her sudden glare of anger and her hand tensing in apparent preparation to fire, stopped arguing and spread his fingers on the grip. She quickly ripped it back and dropped it loudly on the carpeted floor. Dugan's wide eyes and suddenly dropped jaw showed his increasing fear. Mrs. Fox, smiled again, satisfied at the success of her surprise attack.

"Now, your wallet. Slowly." The brown leather wallet fell open on the coffee table. She quickly scanned his state issued private detective ID. She kept careful aim then and while she dialed the Burnside Police Department. She wasn't finished tormenting him. When the two policemen arrived, they restrained themselves from laughing out loud. Here was a little, gray-haired woman pointing a big, powerful pistol at a beefy private detective sitting in his underwear in her living room. She smiled and happily handed her revolver to one of the officers. They couldn't help laughing when they observed it was completely empty. She was too clever for poor Dugan, who couldn't see the empty chambers with the weapon aimed low.

She embellished her story a bit, claiming he pulled his gun first, and his protestations didn't impress the officers much. Mrs. Fox, previously advised by Nelda, only had to give them Detective Tracy's phone number in Seattle to get all the backup she needed.

Dugan, astutely enough, said someone in Al Armour's office, not Armour himself, called him. The investigating officer explained to Dugan, his threat was enough to justify the lady's actions in self-defense. "If she blew your nuts off, she'd win the good citizens award." The officer grinned with pleasure at his brilliant wit. "Mr. Dugan, would you like the suite near the torture room or one closer to the conjugal shower?" The officer clearly enjoyed his work.

Dugan didn't go down easily. "Look, what I'm telling you is the absolute truth, and she's the fake. You give me a lie detector test, and I'll prove it."

"Look Dugan, it'll cost us $350 to put you through a polygraph, and I'm not going to pay for it. You want to pay for it?"

"You're damn right, I'll pay for it. I've had my problems before, and I wasn't going to stick my neck out. There's no way I'd give up my license in order to threaten an old lady. Armour wasn't paying me enough for that, but I'll sure pay for the poly, then I'll sue her.."

The next day, when the polygraph report came in, wonder of wonders, he passed. Now they believed Dugan was telling the truth, including the new fact that Armour really had talked to him and told him to "Go in heavy." Instead of charging Dugan who'd done nothing he could be nailed for, Mrs. Fox got a misdemeanor citation for obstructing an officer and false reporting. The police judge, familiar with Dugan's dubious stature and unconcerned about the inadmissible polygraph result, dismissed the charge against Mrs. Fox, tersely announcing, "I have a reasonable doubt." The charging officer knew what he meant, and Dugan, while disappointed, wasn't surprised and didn't file suit.

* * * * * *

Nelda Fox felt the detachment from reality again. She was inspired by her mother's show of courage and grit and then just wilted. She wondered that there was something in her mother she hadn't yet found in herself. The episode with Rosa Thatcher and the loss of the job working with Herb for the Epstein Brothers and now hiding out at the Joe Gold residence brought back occasional episodes of agoraphobia. The world was a frightening place for her again. Waiting to face the defense attorneys in a deposition aroused dread. Every time she saw a car go by, her heart stopped, and she caught her breath.

Nelda carefully contemplated her testimony. She tried to keep a grip. Knowing that her mother was safe reassured her and freed her mind of at least one evil worry. Joe scheduled her preservation deposition as soon as he could. He didn't want to leave her in the fog of fear she was enduring and scheduled the deposition to preserve her testimony. He explained the process and took her through his direct questions and the anticipated cross. He studied the hospital records, and Joe pronounced her ready.

The direct testimony went slowly with MacCallum's harassing objections joined in by Zale. MacCallum didn't want Richardson there to hear her testimony laying out his negligence and her reasons for fear. She started with fists clenched, but as Joe took her through it, she ignored MacCallum's harassment and just focused. She recited the whole story of the night of Myra's death. Nelda had to hold herself together under the strain of the deposition, then she'd be free. Nelda was so determined, she waited for the lawyers to finish their argument and then rigorously answered the questions. Even when questioned about her relationship with Herb, she simulated calm. She cared for Myra and the baby, and she was determined that the doctor should face what he had done. She would do whatever it took the way her mother would.

"Myra didn't do anything wrong. That poor little child, Melissa, didn't do anything wrong. I can't say what the cause of death was. I'm not a doctor, but I do know that Dr. Richardson refused to come attend Myra when she was bleeding, and what he prescribed wasn't helping."

She testified the original medical records showing the racing pulse, the shallow breaths and declining blood pressure and finally the last drop of blood were the true records. She said she couldn't stand up to Dr. Richardson if Lois didn't. Signing off on the phony records was how Lois thought she would avoid a fight with him. She was the one who made the copies, so the truth would eventually come out. "Maybe if Lois had told him I had copies of the originals in another place, he wouldn't have killed her. Maybe if she'd told him I had a copy, he would've killed me too."

MacCallum objected and moved to strike from the record. It would be up to Abelson to decide how much of her ramblings would be admissible.

"And the fact that Mr. Fletcher found a job for you in his own office had nothing to do with it? And your relationship with him had nothing to do with it, right?"

Joe observed the compound question. "Mr. MacCallum, do you think you could ask one question at a time? I object."

MacCallum, unruffled, straightened out the objectionable procedure with a grin at the corner of his mouth. It was just a little ploy to throw Nelda off stride, but she was determined to fight off all his tactics.

"There's never been anything between me and Mr. Fletcher, no matter how much Dr. Richardson wishes there was. The only way I could come back from Iowa was to find a place where I could be safe. I'm grateful to the Epstein brothers for helping me hide from Dr. Richardson's detectives. I'm glad I wasn't there when they came calling on my mother."

MacCallum objected and again moved to strike the answer. Zale observed his tactics, knowing they wouldn't look pretty in front of a judge and jury, and the more mud MacCallum tried to throw, the easier it got to be for Nelda to handle it. She wasn't the little girl he expected. Zale had to ponder how he could put her on defense at the trial without riling the jury.

When MacCallum finished, Zale got his turn for cross examination, and Nelda, though at first she'd been terrified, got used to the process and no longer hesitated. From the first, Joe told her the truth was their secret weapon. He said to look the attorneys in the eye, so they could see how strong a witness she was and how honest she would appear to the jury.

Mark Zale re-plowed the same ground MacCallum had been over and forced her to look at her two contradictory medical records. "When you wrote the original records you copied and saved, you knew there was a true record in your writing, didn't you, the one that absolved Dr. Richardson? The hospital had been provided the correct one, right?"

"No, sir. The phony record Doctor Richardson wanted came second. Lois Hillibrand gave it to me after Richardson pressured her, and she said we'd keep a copy of the true record as proof. So I did. I don't know what happened to her copy. Maybe someone stole it from her house, maybe the same person who killed her."

"Objection, move to strike."

"You can object, Mr. Zale, but that's the way it was."

He moved to strike again, but Nelda actually continued smiling. She looked forward to getting Myra's day in court and briefly relished the payback.

* * * * * *

For several days, Cora couldn't get her mind off Kevin's problems. She was fully involved with her re-election campaign for the presidency of the Women's League. Her social standing was more important to her than her husband's personal freedom. She had a fine focus on her image at the apex of the Seattle aristocracy, a character trait she inherited from her mother, and it was her ultimate preoccupation in life. She and her husband often discussed what to do about his enemies, and she was satisfied that, with her guidance and despite all the suspicions he engendered, he'd slide past any potential criminal charges. Tracy talked to the doctors, and Franklin Tobin's wife, Irene, told Cora what her husband discussed with Detective Tracy. Now, discovering Kevin's careless failure to put insulin in Hillibrand's needle, she was forced to confront what was likely to happen if Tracy continued his investigation. Tracy's pressure was getting to the Woodside doctors, and the loose pact for secrecy Richardson relied on could end up slipping away. The threat couldn't be ignored, and Cora cast about for some way to resolve it that didn't require her to trust Kevin's skill and judgment.

Cora and her father, Dr. Alden, now fearing Nelda's testimony, kicked around the idea that she might be staying with Ed Gold and his wife. Armour's detectives reported they didn't see anything, so they wondered if Nelda could be at Joe's house. She might be even more vulnerable, if young, pregnant Mrs. Gold weren't there one day. Then there was the idea of getting to Joe Gold through threatening his pregnant wife. It would be the last desperate measure if all else failed. There was no moral objection to it, just a practical doubt that hurting her would provide any benefit.

Sitting in her lovely, grey, silk Hepplewhite chair in the living room, staring out the window at the maples, Cora was suddenly struck by a sharp bolt of mental lightning. She knew who she would call. Laura Newton, the mayor's wife, owed her a favor, and it was time to collect. Cora knew how to solve the Tracy problem. To those familiar with the family, Mayor Newton's jut-jawed image as a stern and upright protector of community values was just a little bit amusing. Laura was the brighter, steel spined one in that family, and he would do what Laura suggested. She knew Cora had such great ideas. Cora had organized the complete support of the wealthy members of the Women's League and their friends for Mayor Newton's re-election, and the dollar benefits Cora provided them were crucial. Cora had a plan, and when she told Dr. Richardson, he jumped up from the big easy chair in the living room, dumping the newspapers on the floor. Uncharacteristically, he went over to the couch and planted her a big kiss right on the mouth.

"Call right now. Cora, that's a fantastic idea."

Chapter Twenty Nine

Seattle Police Detective Tracy ran his hand wearily through his thinning gray hair as he read again the transcript of private detective Dugan's statement sent from Des Moines. He gave an unadorned, unabridged statement that he had not drawn his weapon on Mrs. Fox, and the polygraph supported him. The rest of it was all about shifting blame. Tracy thumbed to the part that interested him, where Seattle detective, Al Armour told Dugan to throw a scare into Mrs. Fox, so her daughter would be reluctant to testify in a Seattle case. Let's go right at Armour, Tracy was thinking.

Armour served other clients. He got back from a tour of the West Seattle bars, where he flashed around pictures of an insurance company claims department manager and a blonde. The insurance guy was negotiating something interesting with the blonde and the company, and Armour's client, a company VP, didn't like it. Armour had to get back to the serious stuff when he picked up the message from R. Leland Tracy, Detective, SPD. Armour's ever loyal secretary, Lucy, was waiting for him to tell her if he was in trouble. Having already known what Armour told Dugan, Lucy figured the answer would have to be "Oh, oh."

When Armour got him on the line, Tracy reeled him in slowly. "Hi, Al, how are you doing? I heard from your friend, Dugan, in Des Moines, Iowa. Still keeping busy?"

"Knock it off. After the thing with Martens in Aurora, I'm doubly careful. If Dugan misbehaved with Mrs. Fox it's on him, not me. He was just supposed to investigate, not threaten. I know what he told the cops, and it's crap. He's just trying to get himself off."

"That's pretty interesting, Al. I guess you know he passed a polygraph. One of you guys is a fool. And I'm guessing it's you. I hope Richardson gave you a lot of dough to pull this stunt. How much did he give you for this?"

"I can't answer your questions, Dick, there's too much at stake." Evidently Armour was aware that Seattle Police detectives close to R. Leland Tracy kiddingly called him Dick, but perhaps he hadn't heard that anyone else who called him that was stepping into hazardous territory. Tracy wasn't someone to get cute with, but he didn't snap this time.

"Al, I think you need to come down here, let's say, oh, about 3:00 today. Here's what you have hanging over you. You've got tampering with a witness and that's a felony. You've got the possibility that Judge Abelson might charge you with contempt. And for sure, you're going to get at least a detective license suspension. Now, I can see why you wouldn't want to have a little chat with me, and maybe you're more scared of Richardson than me, but I'm going to be looking for you at 3:00 today. If you're not here, you better be in the hospital having heart surgery."

Tracy wasn't completely sold that a polygraph was 100% reliable. The results aren't admissible in court, but for purposes of intimidating creeps like Armour, he'd rely on the poly. Somehow, Armour was able to find the time, and Tracy sat him in the cozy warmth of a windowless SPD interview room. Like the rest, it was painted institutional gray, windowless, equipped with gunmetal gray chairs, table and a tape recorder. "Can I get you a cup of coffee, Al?" Tracy was smiling, cordial, almost as if he were not trying to make Armour's life hell on earth.

"Just get it over with. What do you want?"

"I want Richardson. I'll settle for you if I have to, but I've already told you what you have at risk."

It was what Armour was expecting. Out of his suit pocket he pulled the pages of the yellow legal pad where he noted down his innocent interpretation of what Richardson was asking for. Armour was okay with the idea that Tracy wanted to corner Richardson and pull his teeth, one by one. If Richardson were in jail, Armour would be safer, but he didn't want the blame for Richardson getting taken down. He had plenty to fear from Tracy, but more from Richardson. When Tracy finished redrafting Armour's notes, a brand-new statement waited for Armour's signature. Tracy administered no additional arm twisting, no threats. It was just sitting there for Armour's interlineations and edits. After he twisted Tracy's work, what was left was Richardson's word against Dugan's words softened by Armour. Just like in Colorado, fear of Richardson prevailed. The weak statement included his attestation that he had been subjected to no threats or coercion.

Tracy added his signature and said, "I'm going to turn this over to the attorney general. I would have liked to include my comment that you've been most helpful and cooperative. I'm not going to be requesting any action against your license, but I expect it will happen. Sorry." Armour's tummy was grumbling on the way to SPD and wasn't feeling much more comfortable as he walked back to his Hoge Building office.

CHAPTER THIRTY

The day after Cooper's demise, the burly Constable Jeffrey Stokes of the Vancouver B.C. Police Department leaned across the cluttered desk of the black mustachioed Chief Constable, Roland Shirley. "Good damn job Stokes. I mean, you've got us a nice little mystery. If you hadn't been such a nosy copper, we wouldn't have ourselves any case at all. Really, good show Stokes, no kidding."

Stokes was not exactly a rookie, and Shirley had been grooming him from the time he first put on a badge. Shirley saw a future criminologist star in Stokes. He reminded him so much of himself at the same stage. A mentor brought Shirley along, and he enjoyed the pleasure of teaching Stokes everything he'd learned. Stokes, a willing student, had a bit of a whimsical side, but showed he was bright and aggressive, sometimes almost to the point of ferocity. If there was something he was missing, Shirley hadn't seen it.

Stokes took a statement from a graybeard, Andrew Wilhite, and his young grandson, Percy W. Boykin at the scene of Leo Cooper's high dive. Percy saw a suspicious looking fellow come out of the building and drive off in a bright red Corvette with Washington state plates. The man whizzed away after nosing around the crowd. As far as Stokes was concerned, that didn't prove a crime, but it did make his antennae twitch. He contacted the building superintendent, a grizzled man not much younger than Percy's grandpa.

When Stokes gained entrance to the condo, the building super walked away, leaving him with temptation too great to resist. Stokes started rummaging through the roll top desk after finding the key under the lamp base. Cooper left a file regarding his performance as agent of Americanada Ltd. Stokes found a letter beyond his understanding or his authority, but it piqued his manic curiosity. The letter suggested questionable drug transactions involving Americanada Ltd. and Doctors Kevin Richardson and Eric Martens. The company had raised drug peddling issues with Cooper. Both doctors were, apparently, connected with the Woodside Hospital near Seattle. It wasn't a huge surprise that a drug company would be sending drugs to doctors, but it could end up worth investigating. Stokes feared he would be tossed out when the super stuck his head back in and asked, "Hey, when are you going to be done, eh? I can't get to other things till this gets buttoned up."

Stokes stood up, gave him his best glare and said "I'll be done when I'm done, eh. Get it?" The superintendent, unaccustomed to telling police investigators where to get off, meekly withdrew. Stokes smiled with satisfaction as he got back into the papers on Cooper's desk. Without further conversation, he hauled the file to his office to inventory and analyze it. His notebook reflected his "permission" to take the papers. At headquarters, he found another officer had gotten a report of a struggle on one of the decks of the condo, and it sounded like it must have involved Cooper.

Sitting across the battle weary desk from his enterprising understudy, Chief Shirley found Stokes' account amusing, but Stokes had a question not involving humor. "So, Roland, have you got anything yet, to connect the Corvette chap with the struggle on Cooper's deck, eh?"

"No, Stokes, haven't gotten either the driver or the person in the struggle, and this fellow, Johansen, who saw a struggle from his building, said he was too far away to give any sort of identification. I'm sending a fingerprint crew up to Cooper's unit. We'll see what they get. Meanwhile, we're getting in touch with the drug company, whichamacallit, Americanada Ltd. and we'll find out what the deal was with their question about turning Cooper in for drug running. And maybe they'll give us some info on this Martens and Richardson."

"What kind of drugs was Cooper peddling?"

"You're the one who found the letter, Stokes. You know, eh?"

"Well, I saw what the letter said, but it doesn't make a lot of sense. Who peddles insulin and chloroform? The Quaaludes, I understand. The lab should tell us what Cooper had in him when he went over the side. Come to think of it, I've got a friend in the Seattle Police Department, fellow by the name of Tracy. I'll call him and ask if he can track down Richardson and Martens. Kind of looks like they might have had some motive, eh."

"Good, Stokes, that's your next job. Find them and get me their fingerprints and photographs. Find out where they were yesterday."

When Stokes called Tracy, the Seattle detective practically burst a blood vessel. "You're telling me you've got a death up in Vancouver where both Richardson and Martens are implicated? Let me tell you what I have here in Seattle where both these guys are involved." When Tracy finished, Stokes could not believe what he had heard, and he couldn't wait to ask the next question he had.

"Can you tell me whether either of those guys, Richardson or Martens has a red Corvette, eh?"

"Red Corvette? Damn right. Dr. Kevin Richardson is so proud of his red Corvette, I swear he must get it detailed about every other week. If you have a red Corvette tied to your case there, Richardson is the guy."

"Well, at this point, Dick, all we have is a guy in a red Corvette showing up after the death, but we haven't caught him red-handed or anything like that. Can you get me the fingerprints of Richardson and Martens so we can match them to the crime scene? How about pictures of them? And can you tell me how to get in touch with those guys?"

With the phone number supplied by Tracy, Stokes contacted Martens and followed up with the Aurora, Colorado police. It turned out that Martens spent the entire day before at a staff meeting, and it would have been impossible for him to have been in Vancouver. Martens, still in fear of Richardson, was afraid to be dragged into the investigation of Cooper's death. He was afraid to tell Stokes he was certain Richardson was the killer, and it couldn't have been an accident, but when Stokes asked if he knew what kind of car Richardson drove he quickly confirmed what Tracy had said. Martens instantly understood the significance of the Corvette. "Please don't mention to Richardson that you talked to me. I can't get involved."

Stokes reported back to Chief Shirley, whose coffee ran out. As he dribbled coffee across his papers while refilling, his focus was on Stokes, who was ready to report what he found. "I verified that Martens was busy all day yesterday in Aurora. It took me half the day, but BC Bell tells me Cooper called Richardson two days ago. The Seattle police will get me Richardson's fingerprints and photograph. Here's the big news: Richardson has a red Corvette. How do you want me to approach him, eh?"

With that news jarring him, Shirley spilled a little more coffee on his desk. He conscientiously mopped up his splotches, spreading the brown droplets on more and more papers while pondering Kevin Richardson's uncertain future. "If you can put Richardson inside the room, he's probably the chap grappling with Cooper. We've got to show Richardson's picture to that reluctant Johansen fellow who supposedly saw Cooper's struggle but can't identify anyone."

Stokes had the scent and could hardly wait for the Seattle PD to special deliver the picture and prints. They arrived the next day, and Richardson's prints perfectly matched those found on the coffee table, the sliding glass door to the deck and the front door handle. The Vancouver Police found an empty whiskey glass behind a leg of the couch. It had good prints matching Richardson. They found the whiskey bottle, and it had only smudged prints. Later that day, Johansen still drew a blank, but young Percy firmly picked Richardson out of a photo montage. The scent Chief Shirley smelled was Richardson's blood.

"I want this son of a bitch. He can't come up here and spread other people's brains around my streets. You go down to Seattle. Tracy will give you a little jurisdictional muscle down there. You can start by asking

Richardson if he knows Cooper. Don't put it in the past tense. Don't tell him Cooper's been murdered. See if he knows and ask how he knew. Tell him there's a drug case involving Cooper. Get him to say he's never been to the condo and he wasn't in Vancouver two days ago. You be real innocent. Ask him if he is aware of any drug dealings Cooper had. I want him to lie his ass off. Then you write a statement for him to sign. If you can get Tracy to go along with you, so much the better. If Richardson won't sign a statement at least you'd have Tracy to verify what you're hearing."

Stokes loved it. "So, I'm just to get Richardson verifying that anything that happened in Vancouver involving Cooper had nothing to do with him. He wasn't here. We'll see whether Richardson has any knowledge of Cooper getting killed."

"That's it. We'll let him walk into it and tell him what he walked into later."

As Stokes pushed back the chair and left, Shirley noticed the mess he'd made on his desk. The thought of having to dictate those letters over again dampened (with coffee) the joyful anticipation of Richardson's murder trial.

CHAPTER THIRTY ONE

After a three-hour drive, Stokes, in plain clothes, arrived at the Woodside Hospital parking lot in a sneaker car, a blue, Porsche Carrera roadster. Tracy, right on time, was suitably impressed with the wheels Stokes was driving. Stokes had a big grin. "This was a generous contribution to the Vancouver PD by an ex-drug dealer, eh."

"You Vancouver cops live right. When I get a forfeited car, it's usually a bright pink pickup truck with a jacked-up rear end. I wouldn't be caught dead in one of those piles of crap."

"It's my reward for a three-hour drive from Vancouver here, and then three hours back."

"Okay, Stokes, it's almost 1:00, and Richardson's office is in the North Seattle Professional Building, over there across the street. I want to get there on time. I don't want to give him an excuse for saying we missed our appointment. He warned me about his tight schedule."

When they entered Richardson's office, it was Stokes' turn to be impressed. He gawked at the antique carvings, contrasting modern paintings, oriental rugs under oak tables and a nicely decorative, blonde receptionist ushering them into Richardson's inner sanctum, which she referred to as an office.

"Come on in. I was wondering when you guys were going to get here."

Stokes, surprised by the remark, took charge. He was sure they weren't late.

"Why is that, eh?"

"Leo Cooper and I were friends for years. I was up in Vancouver, going to see him when I saw what happened."

Now, Stokes got the point but wanted Richardson to say it. "What do you mean?"

"I was going to meet him at his condo and got there right after the fall. It was pretty awful. He wanted me to come up and talk to him about some trouble he was in involving some drugs, and when I got there I saw a crowd out in the street. I had just parked my car a block away when I saw them, so I walked over and there he was. You could hardly recognize the guy, but I could still see the right side of his face. I've seen a lot of dead people in 31 years of medicine, but this was my friend. I was really shook. I couldn't take it and had to get out of there."

"So what did you do?"

"This wasn't a kind of health emergency I could do anything about. I was so stunned, I just walked back toward my car. I sat down until I could come to grips with it. I guess you could say I just mentally called it a day, sort of. I started driving and headed back down the freeway to Seattle. I had the picture of poor Leo Cooper in my mind. It wouldn't go away."

Tracy doubted him, and he didn't mind letting him know. "You drove three hours to get there and then just turned around and went back home, your friend dead in the street? Really? Tell me more about why you were going to Vancouver in the first place, eh?"

"It's true. This isn't easy. There was a time I had some stress, and I was taking prescribed Quaaludes. I was taking too many for a while, but I forced myself to cut it down to the point where it it wasn't a problem and then quit. I still have stress a little bit, but I've gotten it under control without Quaaludes. It was a struggle, you know, but it was worth it. Leo had some troubles, but he helped get me out of my drug problem. I couldn't turn him down when he asked for help. He was really depressed. I don't

186

know if he was drugged up or drunk and fell or if he jumped. When I saw him dead in the street, it was a shock."

"Your loyalty is admirable." After his wry remark, Stokes had another arrow in his quiver. "When you got up to Vancouver, did you manage to get into Cooper's unit at any time that day or before?"

"Not that day. I knew him for a long time. He came down to Seattle, and I went up to Vancouver for one thing or another. Maybe a week or so ago, I drove up there. I had a couple drinks with him when I was up there that day. It seemed he saw trouble coming. It just turned out to be worse than he thought. He told me he was expecting to get fired by Americanada and maybe charged with a crime. He'd started peddling drugs on the side, and he used some pills. Americanada checked up on his reports and could prove what he was doing. He feared he'd be going away for a long time, so he begged me to come up and discuss what I remembered. That's why I went up there on Wednesday. Afterward, I didn't want to think about it. I knew somebody was going to want to talk to me sooner or later."

Richardson showed more agility than Stokes or Shirley could have imagined. His story seemed plausible. Tracy marveled at his smoothness, ease, and imagination. If he hadn't known of the evasions in the Mickens and Hillibrand cases and what Richardson was setting Armour out to do, the Seattle Police and the Vancouver Police might well have been convinced by Richardson's contrivance. The ball was in Tracy's and Stokes' court, but Richardson didn't give them much to work with. Still, there were other avenues to pursue, and they didn't give up easily.

"That's interesting, Doctor. In fact, it was Quaaludes and alcohol, Scotch I suppose. How did you know?"

"I knew Cooper."

"Doctor, we've got fresh fingerprints several places in the condo. You may have been there a week earlier, but the prints we found were fresh."

Richardson didn't bite. He probably guessed they couldn't time-date fingerprints that finely. He must have figured it was a trick. Stokes wasn't going to mention the witness, Boykin from the street, until he got a full statement from him.

"May we look at your weekday calendar? If you have any patient names you want to cover up you can have your secretary make us a copy with those names covered. Otherwise we have to get a search warrant, and you really aren't a suspect at this point. Right now I just have to eliminate you as a suspect, eh."

"I've already told you I was there. What's the point of looking at my calendar?"

Stokes shrugged. "If you have a problem with that, fine. Just preserve it."

As they were going down the elevator, Tracy was incredulous. "Nice try on the fingerprints. The man is a real Fred Astaire when it comes to tap dancing around potential liability. I've seen some creative imaginations, but this guy is a real artist."

Tracy was feeling empty at first. There wasn't much left. "That's our whole case right there unless Johansen can ID Richardson. If he had said he was in Seattle all day on Saturday last week we'd prove he was a liar, and that would be evidence of guilt. If he said he'd never been to the apartment or if he said he wasn't in Vancouver that day, we could've crapped all over it. He admits he was there but not in the condo. Now there isn't much."

Stokes wasn't done. "But we still have something. Richardson is saying, when he got there he parked about a block away, walked over and saw Cooper in the street, but according to the kid witness I talked to, Richardson was in the building. He saw him looking down. Then Richardson walked out of the building and up to the scene. He didn't walk there from a block away. He was in the building before Cooper fell, and I think we've got him in a big lie. I'm glad I didn't mention anything to Richardson about the kid. I don't want to give him a chance to squeeze out of this."

As they parted, Tracy was grinning and shaking his head. "Sounds good. If they believe the kid, Richardson is going down on this one. Can you be sure to nail down the boy's statement, so there will never be any way out for Richardson. Can't we just keep this little contradiction under our hats? I'm not going to tell the lawyers down here what we know. We need to keep it under or hats."

Chapter Thirty Two

Richardson's tall and lanky, defense attorney, Larry MacCallum often represented Med-West Insurance clients and worked with their claims reps. They had a cautious relationship, constrained less by faith in the law and honesty and more by common sense self-interest. Neither lawyer nor rep was a virgin, but they knew the value of a reputation for reliability. They also liked to win but not at too high a cost. Claims representative and defense attorney had to walk a narrow path. A lie today could be very expensive tomorrow. The reps and MacCallum each knew to be careful what they said about the other. MacCallum could lose a big client and a rep could lose his job.

As they closed in on the final days of preparation for depositions, balding, old rep, Howard Stenzel, carried his briefcase over to Larry MacCallum's classy office in the Smith Tower. It was jammed with files, notes from telephone calls, half-done research, law books or an empty coffee cup. Stenzel smiled as MacCallum took two piles of law books off the couch to make room for him. More remained. Stenzel's amusement didn't offend MacCallum. Everyone laughed at his scrap pile. "Sorry, Howard."

MacCallum looked thoughtful. "There's something I've been thinking about, but I've been kind of reluctant to bring it up. We have a potential argument that maybe Fox, and she's a white nurse, and Fletcher, a black guy, could be fooling around together. I know it would have to be handled carefully, but we might have some people on the jury who'd be upset by an inter-racial relationship. What do you think?"

Stenzel visibly recoiled. "Oh shit, Larry, we can't get into anything like that. Yeah, we can raise an issue that maybe there's a credibility question if Fox is overly sympathetic to Fletcher. But if you mean, we go after racial questions, that could be a big blunder. We could just as easily have people on the jury who are upset by discrimination. If someone on the jury wants to discriminate against Fletcher, he will, whether we say anything or not. A biased witness is a legitimate issue. Race isn't. You can't touch it. And one more thing you better think about. Med-West is a public insurance company. Anything you do racially can affect them with the public. By that I mean it could get me fired. Got it?"

"Okay. I got it. I won't mention it again. My mistake. Forget it, okay? We need to talk about that 'conspiracy of silence' thing. You are going to have to think about that. I'll tell you, as far as I'm concerned, that's the real risky thing and maybe just a little bit stupid. I know some of the people back at your headquarters have the idea that all it takes to keep claims down is just keep quiet when somebody accidentally kills a patient. They think nobody at Woodside Hospital is going to spill the beans. So far, it's worked pretty well, but I'm seeing some changes of attitude."

MacCallum continued. "The silence thing has pretty well run its course. Halloran, for instance, sees himself as the conscience of the medical profession, and sooner or later he's going to let out the guilty secrets of other doctors and the hospital, too. There are others who're ready to go once anybody talks. It's not the old days. If you haven't already put it into your reports, you damn well better. One of these days, your guys are in for a very painful surprise, and you can say I told you so, but only if you tell them."

"I got you, Larry, but what shall I report on this case? You're usually pretty good on predicting an outcome, so what do I tell my VP?"

MacCallum furrowed his brow. "Let's think this through. We have some problems; Gold got a darn good expert from Houston. If you look at Berg's report, he's going to tell the jury that Richardson made three fundamental errors that could have caused Fletcher's death. First, there's the failure to do a Dilatation and Curettage after delivery to find the cause of the bleeding. Two, the failure to immediately come to the bedside on the night she bled to death. And three, the failure to do an emergency D&C that night. He's got authorities to support that position, but we'll find an expert and an issue too. The testimony that Richardson's failures 'could have' caused the death isn't sufficient. Berg's statement doesn't say 'more probably than not.' Therefore his testimony shouldn't be admissible on that point. And the point is crucial. Assuming they somehow get past that issue, Fox's testimony establishing which of Fletcher's records are the real ones is important. If the jury believes Richardson you're a winner, but that's a tough one."

Stenzel looked dubious. "So, leaving out the race issue, what about Fox's credibility versus Richardson? He's been a leader in the OB/GYN community in the Northwest for a lot of years. And what's she?"

MacCallum shook his head. If he were on the jury, Richardson would be dead meat. "So many of Richardson's tactics are questionable. We have to hope we'll keep out the death questions with Cooper and Mickens and Hillibrand and the harassment of Martens and Fox's mother. I can argue all of those are irrelevant to the issues in this case, but some of it could indicate consciousness of guilt. The alteration of medical records at his demand is pretty tough to swallow."

The rep still looked for hope. "Martens isn't sticking his neck out, and I'm not worried about Fox's mother back in Iowa. She pulled the gun on Dugan, not the other way around. Besides, Armour will say he didn't tell the detectives to intimidate anybody. They were just asked to get information."

MacCallum didn't buy it. "Dugan's lucky she didn't blow his head off. She was aware of Armour sending a detective to Martens' house. Even so, just sending detectives after the witnesses' families crosses the line. These detectives weren't going out to find out what the witnesses were going to say. They were making those little visits for the purpose of scaring witnesses off. The judge could say that stuff isn't relevant to the issues, but if it comes in, the jury is going to hold that against Richardson. If Armour testifies that these detectives went further than Richardson had wanted, the jury could believe it's a lie. That's bad enough, but if nurse Fox is believed, Richardson knew the real medical records prove negligence. Demanding a change destroys his credibility."

"So, what could save Richardson is if Berg's testimony doesn't come in, or there are holes in Fox's credibility, right?"

"That's right, Howard. We have Fox visiting Myra's husband, and there's the work connection at Costello Construction. Maybe I can convince the jury she's gone all weak and blubbery over the baby. She denied it when we took the deposition, but there might be something to work with anyway. No matter what else, there's one fact that can destroy Richardson: If somebody at the hospital admits they know Richardson was, and still is, a Quaalude addict. I hope you can explain that to your dim bulb VP. I don't think he's ever going to admit that the doctors cover for each other, but he better make sure nobody else says that. Be careful how you put that to witnesses. If your VP encourages perjury, that's subornation and it's punishable just like perjury."

MacCallum shook his head. "I don't envy you, Stenzel. I wouldn't want to have to deal with boss like that. I didn't say that, right? What I meant to say was, I'll do whatever the company wants, but I think anyone who knows what's going on in the hospital can't believe a word the doctors say, and your company shouldn't have to pay for that. Maybe Zale could have that little talk with CEO Tobin, and it's covered by attorney-client privilege and lets us off the hook. I'm not going to tell the doctors to stop lying. I doubt they'd appreciate it, but they can't pretend forever that they're blind. I'd rather have Zale say that than you or me. Well, tell your VP and good luck to your job, and what are the chances he's going to pay any attention?"

Insurance representative, Stenzel made a zero sign with his right thumb and forefinger, picked up the trial summary and walked out of the office, looking forward to a full afternoon reading it and facing off with the VP.

At the end of the afternoon, Stenzel finally tracked down his VP, a little button-down guy with glasses and a three-piece suit. "We've got to talk, Tony. I just spent about 45-minutes with Larry MacCallum. I think we're going to have to be really careful. Take a look at MacCallum's trial summary. He's got everything there except for one thing, and that's not a good thing. He conditioned his summary on an assumption that secrecy on Tobin's hospital staff will protect Richardson's current addiction from being disclosed at trial. Only MacCallum and I discussed the fact that it could fall apart at any time. So, I think we need to be realistic and recognize it could possibly blow up in the middle of trial."

The VP started going red in the face, first his ears then his cheeks and finally a red, satanic glow. "Like hell I'm going to face that kind of a fact. Our rates weren't set on the assumption that the doctors on Woodside's staff were going to sell each other out. We've got the best rates in the state, and if doctors start ratting on each other, we're not going to be the ones who take the loss. You think our board's going to stand for that? They'll blame me then they'll raise rates."

Stenzel was taken aback. "You know, MacCallum had a thought. There could be something going on between Fletcher and the nurse, Fox. It might be completely innocent, but Fletcher's Negro and Fox is white. The jury might not like that, and that's something we could use. I told MacCallum we wouldn't use it, but it's your decision."

"Howard, you were right in the first place. We have no idea whether the jury is going to get mad at them and maybe not trust Fox, or whether they're going to hate us and make some very nasty newspaper headlines. If I allow that, I don't only risk losing the case, I risk losing my job. If that's MacCallum's idea, tell him to get another idea, a better one. What we really can do is make sure the doctors stay on our side. They need to know big verdicts can raise their malpractice premiums."

"Okay Tony, I'll talk to Brad Hultgren of Hospital Providers Insurance. He can talk to Tobin out at the hospital. Tobin understands it affects him if there's bigger malpractice verdicts. He'll get it that our rates will go up if doctors rat on each other. And it'll raise their rates too. Tobin can talk to guys like Rosen, Halloran and Karel. Let them chew on possible rate increases for a while if they want to be the conscience of the doctors at

Woodside hospital. If they want to pay more for malpractice coverage, God bless them. It's their dough. I'll let Hultgren talk to them. That keeps us out of it."

* * * * * *

After talking to Stenzel, Hultgren made an appointment with Tobin. He wasn't going to give the message to the hospital CEO over the telephone, and he wasn't going to give him a clue to explain the urgent nature of their meeting. He didn't anticipate a cordial meeting, passing on his helpful advice. He hardly cared that Tobin had gotten a nice new desk, some drapes he'd always needed, some artwork and a new hardwood floor, but mentioning them would be a nice way to start the meeting.

"Nice decorations, Franklin, whose arm did you twist?"

"It's about time. I had the ugliest office any hospital CEO ever had. Now let's see if the other guys can match it." Tobin was looking so smug, Stenzel was waiting for him to light up a Havana cigar.

"Frank, the reason I'm here is to give you a little helpful information, gratis. We've got a lot of concern about these guys standing up for Richardson. I was sent out here to tell you how we evaluate the case against him, okay? No matter how young this Nelda Fox girl is, it's looking like she's more believable than Richardson for a number of reasons. I'm sure you know those reasons, and I'm sure the staff here does too. It may be they can keep the lid on it, but I'm not going to tell you to do that. We fear sooner or later, the lid is coming off, if not in this case, then maybe the next one."

He continued. "This isn't coming from me, you understand. When the lid comes off, and we start seeing the doctors and nurses telling what they saw, damages are going to be going up in med-mal cases and so will malpractice coverage premiums. So, it's not up to us at the insurance company, but we just want you to know who it is that's going to be paying. Med-West is on the hook for whatever harm Richardson caused, but you can't really separate his negligence from negligence of the hospital. If the doctors testify about Richardson having problems, no one on the jury will believe the hospital is clean. I'll assume you want us to keep rates down, so you decide what to do. I can't talk to the doctors, but you're close enough where you can give them a little advice, Halloran especially. Get it?"

Tobin got it. Nobody had to draw a picture for him. He figured it out for himself long ago. There was a nice little tight wire for him to negotiate. Tell the doctors to keep their mouths shut without laying himself open to a charge he suborned perjury. Still, he wasn't about to encourage doctors to support a malpractice claim and generate a big verdict. The board would fire him if he caused something like that to happen. He could discuss the handling of these problems with Karel and Rosen but certainly not Richardson or Halloran, no matter what Hultgren said. They were at the two extremes. Halloran would be happy to deliver Richardson's body to the morgue. As far as he was concerned, Richardson should be an ex-doctor. Neither was Tobin going to raise this at a board meeting where minutes would be taken, and he would have no control over the opinions and secrets that might get into the minutes, or whether they would be removed.

Hultgren sat watching the wheels go around in Tobin's mind, waiting for him to give a clue which way he was going to go. Tobin wasn't in a hurry, and Hultgren wasn't going to rush him. The CEO got up and looked out the window then turned back.

"I've known this was coming someday, and I can guarantee you there isn't any pleasure in it. I'm going to have to talk to some people. There's nothing really I have to tell you right now. You'll warn Med-West about their duty to indemnify the hospital if we're held liable for Richardson's malpractice, right? We don't want to sue Richardson."

Hultgren stood up. "You aren't going to do that, Frank. I just need to know what these guys are going to say on the witness stand. When I know, I'll deal with Med-West so we can decide our settlement posture. Just one more thing. If Richardson and Fox agreed that neither of them was at fault, and the death was just an unfortunate accident, both these companies might save a lot of money."

Tobin suppressed a smile. Fox and Richardson were never going to resolve the liability problem by agreeing the other wasn't at fault. "Brad, that will never happen. The best I can do is a little encouragement for the staff to be a little thoughtful when they talk about each other. I can explain to them the connection between their malpractice rates and their testimony. And I've got to be careful about that." As soon as Hultgren left, Tobin got on the phone to Elliott Karel, a man he could trust. Neither of them would call what they were doing a criminal conspiracy to suborn perjury. But that's what it was.

CHAPTER THIRTY THREE

Before Martens' deposition, McCallum filed a motion in limine, seeking to bar inquiry into Richardson's drug use, claiming it was unnecessary and unfairly prejudicial. MacCallum submitted the motion on briefs without the attorneys' presence in court. Joe was surprised that MacCallum conceded Richardson once used Quaaludes but nevertheless asserted his drug use was now under control by his own treating physician and didn't include Quaaludes. The only hole the treating physician left in the affidavit was the assumption Richardson didn't get drugs from any other source than his prescription. That was a big hole, because Cooper's Americanada Ltd. records showed no significant decline in Quaaludes deliveries when Martens moved to Colorado. Joe used that hole to persuade Judge Abelson the inquiry into Richardson's drug use was reasonable. Joe and Martens' lawyer, Shimkus, agreed the deposition could be done in Joe's office in Seattle, just a couple blocks from the King County courthouse, and MacCallum was out of arguments.

Joe laid out his notes in the Tobey conference room, graced by the large Mark Tobey oil painting. It was now getting to be a comfortable war room for the young lawyers of the firm. With the other lawyers in the firm too busy, Joe was on his own. The firm now generated so much business, the young lawyers hopped from one frying pan into the next and couldn't spare much time to help Joe. The business practice was exploding worldwide, and even with a fully staffed law office devoted to the business, they carried more load than he'd ever seen. Sandra dreamed fondly of Joe someday running that kind of powerhouse business practice, but Joe liked what he was doing.

MacCallum and Zale came in dressed in three-piece suits. Joe wore his favorite, black, Brooks Brothers pinstripe. Like his dad, he followed the traditional Seattle lawyers' dress code for formal proceedings, extending it even to depositions. Martens, stiff from the trip, dressed in casual slacks, stayed next to his lawyer and looked edgy. Joe had seen witnesses so intimidated by their coaching they couldn't think. He wondered if Martens' stiffness was intimidation or travel, but once they got going with his mundane professional history, the deer-in-headlights look went away briefly.

When Joe dug into Martens' history with Richardson, Martens' pain showed. He denied talking to Richardson about his testimony, but somebody had caused him to pull his punches. He now turned into the soul of wide-eyed innocence, looking right at Joe and denying that his wife had been in fear, denying he was in fear. It was just a misunderstanding. Michael Strauss hadn't threatened his wife, Anna, or his son, Danny. If Detective Tracy thought he said that, he was making a mistake. He certainly hadn't left Seattle because of any fear of Richardson. They once both used Quaaludes, but they both quit. He did deny any knowledge of Quaaludes currently going to Woodside Hospital or The North Seattle Professional Building. Otherwise, there was nothing in the deposition that Joe was going to be able to use to bolster the case. Joe didn't say anything to Martens about what he thought of his honesty. Joe chalked up as just another good example of the "conspiracy of silence."

* * * * * *

Joe couldn't find anything Martens had put on the record unaffected by his fear of Richardson's detectives. When the deposition was over, Martens escaped the office without apologizing to Joe for his cowardly, wishy-washy answers. Joe's eyes said he was mad as hops, but he understood Martens' fear for his family. So much for commitment to justice and professional duty. Who can say how they would have reacted in the same pressure situation? Martens refused to expose his wife and son to the very risk he'd run from in Seattle.

It galled Joe that Richardson could get away with chasing out Martens, killing Mickens and Hillibrand and finally, intimidating Martens. Without real proof, not supposition, the jury would never hear about it. And now Cooper.

Joe got the word from Vancouver detective, Stokes. The fellow who supposedly saw a struggle on a balcony couldn't even get the right balcony. Then they showed him Richardson's picture along with some others, and he couldn't pick him out of that either. But Stokes found it interesting that Richardson, amazingly, seemed to know that Cooper was taking Quaaludes and drinking Scotch before he went over the side of that balcony. And then they found Richardson's fingerprints on a Scotch glass under the coffee table, but he claimed it was a glass he'd used when he'd been there some time before. Joe was hoping he could get that one to the jury. It seemed like pretty good evidence he was inside the condo the day Cooper died. Stokes held back his knowledge of Percy Boykin. He didn't want him exposed to danger if Gold bandied his name around.

Joe was pondering all these coincidences where somebody dies, and everything tells you Richardson did it, but you can only prove suspicious circumstances. It could be a close call for Abelson to let him take any of it to the jury. He was imagining what MacCallum would say:

"Suspicion isn't evidence."

Joe took a little visit to his optimistic side. Stokes, up in Vancouver, was still digging. He seemed to think he could prove Richardson guilty of the Cooper death, but he was mysterious about it and couldn't give any specific reason for his optimism. Tracy, the Seattle cop, seemed to be influenced by Stokes' optimism and was telling Joe not to give up on that one. The Americanada records might connect the Quaaludes and Cooper, the supplier, to Richardson's drugged behavior leading to Myra's death. Abelson could base admissibility on that connection.

Tracy could still bring in some of the Woodside doctors and put the pressure on them. Joe wondered how the "conspiracy of silence" would stand up when Tracy warned the doctors about the consequences of making false statements to the police. Zale and MacCallum would have to discuss that with them. Joe would love to hear that conversation.

CHAPTER THIRTY FOUR

Nelda knew Joe would object if he knew where she was going, so she made sure to wait till Sandra took her nap. She left a note that she was going to the dentist. Herb had serious misgivings, but Nelda said she needed to see Melissa. Herb headed home early from the office, wondering how much of the attraction was Melissa and how much was the electricity between him and Nelda. Neither of them imagined that Richardson would have a detective putting a watch on Herb, but Al Armour's friend, the non-descript, sallow, gray, old guy in the Volkswagen trailed him, undiscovered, at a distance for weeks. Now, early in the afternoon, one block behind Herb, he figured Herb was going home. When Herb was two blocks away from the little, yellow rambler in Lake City, the detective made a fast right then a left and another right and parked half a block away and waited for Herb to get home. After Herb arrived, Nelda drove up in her rattly, old Ford. Concealed by a neighbor's laurel hedge alongside the driveway, the man's dogged pursuit was vindicated, and he snapped photographs as fast as his fingers allowed. After a warm hug, the pair went into the house, while the detective noted the time and wrote what he saw in his journal. He took the job on spec, and Armour would be paying off big on this one.

Melissa's blonde, teenage babysitter smiled broadly when told to take an early afternoon break and a couple bucks extra for a burger and shake. Armour's spy hadn't seen this sitter before and duly noted her license number and a description of the car and driver as she left.

Herb wrapped his arms around Nelda and was torn between duty and attraction. As they stood in the living room behind pulled drapes, he released her, though neither really wanted to let go. Nelda took a step back and looked up at Herb inquiringly, her feelings plain to him. Silently they agreed to respect their limits. Nelda smiled and sighed. "Let's go see Melissa." Then he led her to the baby's darkened bedroom.

There in the darkness, Melissa lay looking at Nelda, who couldn't resist her. She gurgled contentedly as Nelda gently picked her up. Nelda's heart overflowed with love, and her eyes were full of tears. Nelda was sure that the dark, cuddly child would not go through life without a mother. Melissa didn't have Myra anymore, but Nelda felt strong feelings of responsibility for her and Herb. "Let her sleep now." Herb took her from Nelda and laid her back down in the crib with her pink rattle in her hand. Melissa made cooing sounds as her eyes shut. Nelda and Herb watched her happily, together for a few minutes before they walked arm in arm to the living room. Nelda needed that kind of warmth to keep herself together. After the loss of Lois, she turned to Herb's strength and Melissa's soft need.

Herb resisted the easy way, was determined and understood it would have been all too damaging for them to fall into a vulgar romance while he was still mourning, to begin gently, to hug each other, to explore, to give in to their feelings. It was right to hold back, for once they began, the sure result would be the destruction of their decency and self-respect even without the lawsuit. And the lawsuit was no small thing. The jury wouldn't trust Nelda if she was having an affair with the plaintiff. It would cloud the jury's concern with Melissa's loss of her mother. The jury's focus on the loss wouldn't drive the case. Suspicion would. Herb worried that just this visit by Nelda to see Melissa could be misconstrued.

"Nelda, I think you need to go now. If you were seen here, people could jump to nasty conclusions."

"No, Herb. We haven't done anything wrong, and I had to see her. I can explain it even if we were being watched."

Still, the thought made her nervous, so Nelda left before the babysitter returned, being followed at a distance by Armour's man. Nelda anxiously looked in her rearview mirror and saw the Volkswagen matching her turn for turn, even when she made a circle around a block before she got to the freeway. She made one more turn and pulled into a driveway. She made a fast left turn out of the driveway as the Volkswagen approached from the left, and she lost him. She got a look at the man, but his face wasn't one she recognized. She couldn't make note of the license number, but after making another turn, pulled into an alley behind a neighborhood grocery store. She waited for fifteen minutes and didn't see the Volkswagen again though watching her rearview mirror all the way back to the Joe Gold residence. She couldn't face Sandra and crept back to her bedroom. She sat on the bed, legs curled up, gripping her knees. How could she tell Joe what she had done? The Gold family had trusted her, and she'd abused that trust. All she could say in her favor was that she and Herb hadn't done anything wrong, and she hadn't led the detective back to Joe's home.

After wrestling with her conscience, she felt obligated to call Joe at the office. He got there in 45 minutes, arriving as she sat nervously on the living room sofa with Sandra. "Nelda, how could you? Some guy followed you? He probably got pictures. Some people will assume you had sex with Herb. They'll assume you're lovers, and the race difference may upset some people. I'm not sure how I can take that suspicion away. I thought you understood."

"I'm sorry, Joe. I just had to see Melissa. That poor little girl hasn't got a mother because Richardson didn't care enough to save Myra's life" Nelda felt her burning eyes. "I'll tell the truth. The jury will believe me. If they want to crucify me they can, but I'll tell the truth anyway. Whatever happens, I will. We didn't have sex."

Joe admired her firmness and unyielding focus on his eyes. If the jury saw what Joe saw right then, they wouldn't doubt a word she said. Still, it wasn't going to be easy for them to trust her the way Joe did. Richardson finally had some ammunition of his own. The jury's trust in this young girl was crucial to the case and now it was endangered.

* * * * *

Armour called Richardson, and he called MacCallum. "What do we do about it? Save the pictures for trial or demand that Gold dismiss the case? We've got them now."

MacCallum thought it over, and Richardson waited patiently. "Well, finally. What's it going to be, Larry?" He drummed his restless fingers.

"I don't know. It's a nice little gift. I think I'd rather save it. Gold probably doesn't know about it, so why warn him we have it? I say we just tuck it away. In their answers to interrogatories, they said there was no personal relationship, just getting her the job, that's all. So we don't have to tell him we can prove it's a lie. It's their duty to say that their answers to interrogatories are now different."

MacCallum's deviousness delighted Richardson. They shared that style. It made good sense.

Richardson exulted. "I've been waiting for this. Finally we've got the black-white racial thing, and we can put it right front of the jury. Nelda having an affair with a Negro. Nobody's going to believe her after that. We don't have to warn them it's coming, just save it for the trial."

"Wait a minute, Kevin. We have to be careful how we handle this. I can't just come out and say you can't believe Nelda because she's having an affair with a Negro. There are people who'd be offended, and if they can see it themselves, we don't have to mention race. Some of them will hold it against the plaintiff without us hitting them over the head with it."

Kevin got the point and grudgingly agreed MacCallum was right. The 1960's were, to say the least, not tolerant.

Cora grinned with mendacious glee because they'd caught Nelda and Herb Fletcher sneaking around. What a disappointment three days later when an amendment to the interrogatory answers disclosed that Nelda and Herb had met, followed by the innocuous explanation that came with it. MacCallum now had something to work with and he'd tear into the "visiting Melissa" story. That would be good, but catching them in a concealment would have been better. Richardson still had a surprise coming for Cora.

CHAPTER THIRTY FIVE

Late Friday afternoon, Police Chief Thomas Craven sent out a press release announcing that he'd promoted Detective Tracy to Major and Tracy would lead the Fraud Division, a substantial promotion with a substantial raise. Tracy appreciated the recognition and advancement, figuring that would pay off the mortgage and both kids' first year of college. Craven moved Elvin Kurtz up to Detective while Tracy would bring him up to date on the pending cases. What Tracy wouldn't find out until later was that part of the deal was to drop any of the "rather fanciful" suspicions about Kevin Richardson. It wasn't a surprise to Cora Richardson who had merely made one call to an old friend.

Cora appreciated the favor and owed a call to the mayor's wife, Mrs. Laura Newton. "Hello, Laura, I just heard the news."

"Hi Cora, I was glad Chief Craven was able to get the promotions for Elvin Kurtz and Tracy. It took a little finagling and a little time, but I told you I could do it. You probably thought I was doing you a favor, but as it turned out, the mayor was able to make everybody happy. He convinced the chief it was all his decision. It wasn't any kind of a favor. You and Kevin were a lot of help in the last election, but the mayor explained to me, this wasn't a reward for anything. Understand?"

"Of course I understand. It's just an interesting coincidence that the man who who was causing my husband a lot of trouble isn't going to be in position to do it anymore. I love doing things to help you and the mayor. And I love those coincidences." They both laughed and agreed they needed to get together and have dinner "one of these days."

Cora got on the phone to Kevin, and he celebrated the good news he knew was coming. "Fantastic job, Cora. I knew you were smart, but that was amazing. I don't have to worry about the SPD anymore, I guess. Thanks, hon. I might be bringing something home you're going to like."

"What is it?"

"You'll see when I get home."

* * * * * *

Joe Gold didn't understand the game until he found that Tracy's replacement wasn't returning his calls and had filed away the deaths of Mickens and Hillibrand and the harassment of Martens and Mrs. Fox. Kurtz was too busy when he finally made contact.

"I looked at those files, and if Tracy couldn't do anything with them, neither can I. I'm running full bore just to catch up to where Tracy was. If I catch up someday, I'll try and see if I can do something with Richardson." The phone went dead and so did Tracy's investigation of Richardson.

Franklin Tobin quickly figured the significance of Tracy's promotion. He left messages for Dr. Karel and Dr. Rosen. "As to the last thing we talked about, don't worry, I'll talk to Halloran." Life had just gotten easier for Tobin and tougher for Halloran. Tobin explained to him that the police couldn't make a case against Richardson, and he should lay off. Hosp-Pro Insurance told him that a verdict against Richardson would affect the doctors' rates for their coverage. If the hospital lost too, Hosp-Pro would have to contribute along with Med-West and hold it against the doctors. Tobin laid the law down. He summoned Halloran to his office and required him to listen to a recitation of the consequences if he continued to insist there was such a thing as a "conspiracy of silence."

"Kelly, I suggest that you watch your mouth. I think having privileges at Woodside must be pretty important to you. Don't do anything to lose them."

"I don't want to lose my privileges, but I don't want to watch Woodside destroyed by tolerance of the kind of incompetence you've been putting up with."

"That's great, Kelly, I'm impressed. You make me think of a guy standing on a dock, all set to jump in, but he doesn't know how deep the water is. There you stand, pretending you're ready to jump in, but you and I both know you aren't going to. You aren't that dumb."

Halloran swallowed hard. He contemplated what his life would be like without the practice of medicine. His conscience was losing a nasty battle with his professional ambitions and his family's finances. Half of him wanted to dump Tobin's vase full of roses right in his lap, but his coward side knew it would accomplish nothing good, and he restrained his rage. Halloran got up from the silk brocade side chair, walked across the Persian carpet and out the door, maintaining his silence. He didn't know whether he'd ever dare tell the truth. He didn't dare jump, but maybe he could be pushed.

* * * * * *

When Kevin Richardson walked in smiling and shaking his wet raincoat, Cora didn't look at all happy. He said he'd be home by 6:00, and here it was, 6:20, and that ruined her evening. She'd been so pleased and now he'd upset her.

"Kevin, why do you say you're going to be home at a certain time, and then you're 20 minutes late? You don't call. Nothing. I told Louisa to serve at 6:00. Well, that's not going to work, is it?"

Kevin's face still showed his meaningless smile, and he tossed the wet raincoat onto Cora's Hepplewhite chair, next to the matching étagère. He gave little concern to the certainty this would further upset her. She'd figure he was goofed on some Quaaludes, and he didn't care about that either. Everything was good, and she'd be tickled when she heard his news. He just had to let her blow off a little steam.

"You done now, honey? I've got something to show you."

Cora arched her eyebrows and waited, skeptical of Kevin as ever.

"Remember I told you detective Armour caught Nelda Fox with Fletcher? Well, we got the pictures today."

Just then, Louisa came in with the duck l'orange on the great silver platter, so Kevin waited while she went back to the kitchen and came back with the fruit compote and a couple casserole items Kevin couldn't identify. It looked so good, and the aroma was so delicious Kevin was distracted. Cora had to wait for Louisa to finish the service and retreat to her station in the kitchen before Kevin could continue his tale.

"Okay Kevin, let's see what you brought home to me?"

"Like I asked, Armour put a guy on it and here's some lovely pictures. Look here."

These were pictures worth a thousand words. He took three blowups out of his briefcase, leaving a pile of photographs still there. There was Nelda Fox, arms outstretched to Herb, then one with Nelda in his arms and then one with them, arm in arm, walking toward Herb's house. You couldn't mistake them. It was Herb and Nelda together. Kevin showed Cora, on the back of each picture, the date, June 26, 1964 with an address on 30th Avenue Northeast near the Lake City neighborhood in Seattle, and there was an unreadable signature of the photographer.

For a few minutes, Cora forgot the wet raincoat and the Hepplewhite chair and the delicious aroma of the waiting dinner. She savored the big deal.

"So, you've got her. She's the only one attorney Zale said could nail you. And here we've got her sneaking over to Fletcher's house for a little playtime. I bet they enjoyed themselves when the wife was in the hospital. I don't care what kind of story they tell. I think the pictures are the only story we need. You're not the one who has to prove anything. She is. Today was a doubleheader. My, that duck l'orange smells lovely."

Chapter Thirty Six

Tracy called Jeffrey Stokes who passed the word on to Chief Constable Shirley of the Vancouver PD.

"They've taken the Seattle cop, Tracy, off Dr. Richardson, so I guess that leaves it to me. I don't know how I do it all from up here and with my other cases. I'm truly pissed. It's a cover-up in Seattle, eh."

Shirley seemed unconcerned, thinking about a million other things.

"Why do we need any more help from Seattle?"

"Because we can't complete the case against Richardson all by ourselves here. We can prove he lied about being at the scene, but I doubt we can prove guilt beyond a reasonable doubt. We're missing some motive and character proof, but we can help Seattle put him away. Richardson got the insulin and chloroform here he used to kill a couple women in Seattle. Besides, I want to prove his drug violations. You remember, after Martens left the hospital in Seattle, the drugs continued to go there to Richardson, eh?"

Shirley came back to the case at hand, looked out the window and idly fondled the speaker of his Dictaphone. Sending a letter making a record of his assistance to the Seattle police wouldn't be his kind of diplomacy. He didn't want his name even to be in the conversation, but he doubted Stokes could muster the horsepower necessary to dislodge the Seattle PD.

"Jeffrey, you go to work on something else right now. Let me think about it."

As soon as Stokes left, Shirley was on the phone to his boss, Vancouver Mayor, Ben McKay.

"Office of the Mayor."

"This is Shirley, can I speak with His Honor?"

"Yes, sir"

Shirley stayed with the mayor on the phone about 10 minutes before Mayor McKay caught on to what was going on and gave in. He understood Shirley's problem.

"Okay, I'll call Mayor Newton in Seattle, but I still don't know why you can't call the Seattle Chief of Police yourself."

"Trust me, Ben, I'd rather do it that way, but I don't think I have the power to move the Seattle PD. You can tell that bastard, Newton, we need his chief to cooperate on our investigation. Tell him the press wants to know what's going on and why we aren't moving on the Cooper killing. Tell Newton we don't want to cause trouble for him, but we really do have to be responsive to the press. I think all you have to do is say the word 'press,' and he's going to be your chum, eh. I'll call Tracy, he might be able to do a little pushing from the other end."

Shirley didn't expect it so soon, but the next morning, before he got off his galoshes and his heavy rain jacket, he saw the memo to call the mayor, who turned out to be in an unusually jovial mood. He sounded as if the effort to sidetrack Tracy's investigation never had a chance.

"You're going to like this, Roland. How we work this out is, Stokes is going to call the fellow in Seattle who just got kicked upstairs, this fellow, Tracy, and tell him we can help him with his case in return for some help with our Cooper case. It's kind of funny. The Seattle Mayor is in a bit of a political box. He can't contact us, but our pressure will allow Tracy to continue what he was doing with Richardson, even outside his regular authority. Don't you just love this foreign intrigue action?"

Mayor McKay almost giggled. To Shirley, he'd never sounded so much like a teenage hell raiser. Shirley didn't see quite where all the fun came in, but he liked seeing some progress. Stokes was equally tickled when Tracy called him to sit in on some witness interviews in Seattle. He loved that he got to take the Porsche to Seattle again, and Shirley told him he didn't need to ask, just go. Tracy had a bunch of doctors lined up the next day at Woodside Hospital, and Stokes was going right at them. As he put it, "This is going to be an energetic inquiry. I'm not going to let them slide by on that 'conspiracy of silence' bullshit. I'm going to warn them about lying to the police. That should generate a little cooperation."

Tracy wasn't as optimistic, having seen Seattle doctors struggle with their ethics before. Still, he hoped Halloran might be the key to loosening up the whole thing, so he was the first one in the box. Halloran hadn't come to grips with his dilemma. He wanted to tell the truth as best he knew it and not play the games the hospital staff expected of him. Still, he knew he could lose his privileges, so he had to be careful.

Halloran met with Stokes and Tracy in a hospital conference room. "I can't tell you whether Richardson committed malpractice or whether he was under the influence of drugs the night the Fletcher girl died. I know he's used prescribed Quaaludes in the past. In fact, he seems quite willing to admit that. I think he will say he wasn't under the influence that night Myra Fletcher passed away, but the nurse, Nelda Fox, should have some idea what he was like that night. I can tell you there really is a reluctance at the hospital to acknowledge negligence by anyone. And there are people who are reluctant to criticize Richardson, but I can't swear who that will be or whether anything might be covered up. There's a former doctor from Woodside, Eric Martens, who's in the Denver area now, who might help you. I wish I could do more."

Stokes and Tracy looked at each other as Halloran walked out the door. Undoubtedly Halloran thought he was being helpful, but he wasn't giving much information the police didn't already have. The two officers agreed that Halloran's testimony about "conspiracy of silence" could be useful at trial to defeat any supposition that hospital officials who didn't have anything to say about Richardson's condition would testify to it if they'd seen anything untoward.

Karel, the Quality Control Director, Rosen, the Emergency Room doctor, who was the last to treat Myra Fletcher and Tobin, the Woodside Hospital CEO, in their turn, each earnestly and uniformly agreed Richardson probably had once used prescribed Quaaludes, but so far as they knew, didn't have a problem anymore. The idea of a "conspiracy of silence," they said, was entirely contrary to the culture of Woodside, a fine hospital. Tracy and Stokes intimated in tactful words, they were dubious and had proof of the conspiracy, but the Woodside staff held the line. The officers didn't want to outright threaten a perjury charge. That would have had the odor of coercing testimony.

The hospital staffers, sweating and anxious when they left, ended up whispering together at the Seattle-First National Bank Building Coffee Shop, away from anyone who might be curious. Tobin calmed them down. "All you have to do is say "I've never seen anything like that. If Richardson was affected by drugs, I don't know it. He gets stressed, but most people consider him the top OB/GYN in the north end. I think that's good enough." The conspiracy was still in business and the conspirators thought there would be no price for their lies. That remained to be seen.

* * * * * *

Stokes and Tracy wanted to get Joe Gold's take on the phony interviews, and Joe stayed tough. He sat across the nice new desk from Tracy at the more expansive office two floors up from Tracy's former shoebox in the Public Safety Building. With Stokes looking on, he made it all very simple.

"If a jury believes Nelda Fox, that's the end of it. It's a little hard to believe that Richardson could be such a bastard he'd let Myra bleed to death, but you can't have any doubt after you listen to Nelda. We've got her mother and Martens' wife who could testify about intimidation, and the wait staff at Rix to testify about the Mickens girl and Lois dining with Richardson there, and we've got the changed medical records. I only have to prove my case by a preponderance of the evidence. I think, with Nelda I can do it, but I don't know if that gets you guys what you need for your murder case. If you could prove it, my case becomes a slam-dunk."

Tracy grumbled, "I'm missing the connection I need for my cases. What do you have on Cooper?"

He was looking at Stokes, who shrugged his shoulders. "I need for Richardson to make a mistake, but he's a clever rascal." Stokes was still holding back Percy Boykin, the witness who might convict Richardson of Cooper's murder.

Nelda wasn't an impressive sight when she walked in, not much older than Myra, winsome, small, dark-haired and a little intimidated by the police and their headquarters. Joe had warned them not to expect an overpowering performance. She smiled shyly and sat where she was told. The department's reporter sat next to her, fingers on the keys of the stenographic recorder. Tracy took her through the full history of the night when Myra died. He threw in a few misstatements to see if she could be led astray. Myra looked hard at him and refused the offer.

"Detective Tracy, you know that isn't true, I didn't walk out. I was there the whole time. I helped Myra to the bathroom, and I had to half-carry her back to bed. I refused to tell her that she was going to die. I was afraid, but I couldn't admit it, not to her, not to myself. I'm not sure she knew she was going to die, but she was afraid. What was most important to her was that Herb would be there to take care of Melissa."

Nelda went through the falsification of records, finding Hillibrand dead and her copies missing. She was angry at Richardson trying to force her to support a phony offer of a D&C to Myra by Richardson. She didn't waver an inch.

It wasn't so much the simple words Nelda was speaking, but her fierce grip on the facts and her emotions. Her eyes were so locked onto Tracy that she was in utter control of his consciousness. He could not raise a doubt in his mind if he tried. He believed every word she spoke, and after all his years on the force and in court, he was sure no jury would doubt a word she said. He felt his eyes watering as she described that terrible evening. He was amazed that could still happen to him after all he had seen and heard as a police officer. Under the table, so Nelda couldn't see it, Stokes clenched a fist. Tracy, mercifully, let her out of there as fast as he could.

After Nelda, the last witness finished, Tracy sat with his head in his hands, elbows on the table, looking at Stokes. You could see he was drained, exhausted. Stokes had played the interested bystander, and even he had been affected. Tracy's final words reverberated in Stokes' mind.

"I want that bastard. I want to nail him. Whatever it takes."

Stokes perked up, enjoying the ride back to Vancouver in the peppy little Porsche as much as he enjoyed the ride down. The miles melted away unnoticed. He felt a new focus and commitment and decided to talk to the young eyewitness, Percy W. Boykin, again. He wasn't sure he'd yet done his duty to the city and most of all to Cooper.

How do you do justice when the people all around a killer don't care?

CHAPTER THIRTY SEVEN

Joe knew the time had come. It was a few months before trial and the case couldn't go forward without deposing the defense witnesses. He wanted to do those depositions before the plaintiff's expert, Dr. Hyman Berg had to prepare his testimony. Berg needed to know the factual basis, not only for the plaintiff's case, but for the defense too. Joe had to prepare Berg by telephone because he lived in Houston, and he didn't want to go there to do it. It was an intense two weeks for Jodi. Scheduling the depositions of the hospital staff was a complicated process. She had to give an estimate of how long Joe would spend with each witness, a pure shot in the dark. And then she had to fit that into the schedules of those witnesses. The defense attorneys and the witnesses could throw a monkey wrench into the schedule just to be nasty or because it was fun. Jodi was smart and tough enough to pin down times for each witness, and no stalling. Then on top of that, she had to help Joe prepare for the depositions by clarifying the medical records for him, a task she'd practiced over the years at Carpenter Gold.

She sent out the deposition notices and filled up Joe's calendar. Then, Joe sat for hours roughing out the subjects he'd cover with each witness. It was mostly doctors and nurses, so their education and curriculum vitae would come first, subjects that would be long and boring. Also necessary.

Joe needed to discuss the deposition of Jim Schwinn MD, designated by McCallum as a D&C expert. Joe's background investigation disclosed the man's reputation as a DMW, what plaintiffs called a Defense Medical Whore. Schwinn's reputation was that he would say anything for a fee. As they discussed him in Joe's office, Mike and Diana pondered what he could possibly say for Richardson. Joe couldn't imagine. Diana could.

"I'll bet he'll say something like, doing a D&C is a judgment call for the doctor, or he might say, if Myra didn't want it, Richardson didn't have to do it."

Mike wasn't impressed. "Nelda will take care of that, 'Myra didn't want it' BS. And the texts you dug up will take care of the 'judgment call."

Joe and Diana agreed, and Joe showed them Schwinn's testimony in another case, where he'd said exactly the opposite of what MacCallum would need him to say. He'd testified that, with persistent bleeding following delivery, a D&C is mandatory. They concluded that Joe should inquire of Schwinn, of opinions he held about Richardson's care and their basis but not disclose Joe's counter ammunition. They didn't want MacCallum to go find another witness.

Martens had already been deposed. First would come Schwinn, then Steinman, the night supervising nurse, then Alex Rosen, the ER doc, then Elliott Karel, Quality Control, and Franklin Tobin, CEO and Chairman of the Board. Finally would come Richardson. Joe and Mike were reluctant to depose Halloran before trial. They weren't going to take a whack at the guy who might voluntarily unmask the "conspiracy of silence." You don't expose the guy who can help you by cross examining him.

When Schwinn appeared for his deposition, he was a solid looking, dark haired, well-dressed man in his mid-40s. He was a guy who would look good on the witness stand. Joe made quick work of the deposition, letting Schwinn testify to his knowledge of the Fletcher medical records and his opinions of Richardson's care. Joe didn't drop a single clue to his cross-examination at trial or what he knew about Schwinn.

All the hospital witnesses sang from the same hymnal: There's no conspiracy. Richardson is a top OB/GYN, even if he can be a little testy at times. There were rumors about him having stress issues but certainly no apparent drug problem anymore. On the night of Myra Fletcher's death,

Dr. Richardson should have been called, but Dr. Rosen did all anyone could have done. Joe felt like he was in a pillow fight. As hard as he swung, all he got was passive resistance. Joe assumed Zale and MacCallum had coordinated the defense testimony, probably just one inch on the safe side of perjury. Someday Halloran would have to step up. All he'd need would be a conscience.

Chapter Thirty Eight

Joe broke free at the line of scrimmage. He saw nothing but green in front of him, all the way to pay dirt. He secured the ball, but all of a sudden an arm snaked inside his and jerked the ball out. A little defensive back scooped it up and headed the other way, and no one else had a chance. He was faster than Joe, but he had to catch the defensive back no matter what. The crowd screamed silently. Through sheer willpower, Joe closed the gap and caught the nasty little runt. He ripped the ball loose, picked it up and started back the other way.

He sat up in bed, with Sandra still asleep. It was the most vivid, solidest, most real dream he'd ever had. Where had it come from? He hadn't thought seriously about football since many years ago when assistant coach Furman told him he wasn't fast enough to be that small or big enough to be that slow. In other words, "Empty your locker."

Something was connecting. Was he dropping the ball on the Fletcher case? That was too easy and trite. Maybe it was the truth anyway. He had to be as determined and aggressive in real life as in his dream. All that was running through his mind while he showered and shaved that morning. He tried to tell Sandra about the dream while he was eating oatmeal. Coming downstairs was too much for Sandra in her still weakened condition, so they had breakfast together on a tray in the bedroom. For Sandra, Herb Fletcher and Melissa didn't register. She had her own problems.

* * * * * *

Mike laughed at Joe's earnest dream review, but he admitted there might be something to it. Drinking the quick morning cup of coffee in the break room was usually a welcome pressure release for the young lawyers. This day, it wasn't. In a few minutes they would be in the Tobey conference room for Richardson's deposition, and it was full of file boxes. Mike helped Jodi to bring up exhibits they needed. Zale for the hospital and MacCallum for Richardson were there along with assistants.

Richardson, despite his bearing and stature, thick white hair and impeccable, dark blue suit, looked a bit diminished to Joe. Zale and then MacCallum sat to his right. Jodi sat to Joe's left. At the end of the table was the court reporter, E.E. Lescher, a stubby, balding, old elf with his steno pad on his lap and pen in hand, steadfastly refusing to use the new (to him) dictating machines. He administered the oath, and they were off. First, Joe inquired into the basis of Richardson's education and the nature of his practice. Joe breezed through Richardson's curriculum vita, detailing his impressive education and professional history.

Joe wanted to nail him on the Quaalude use. "Was there ever a time when you were addicted to Quaaludes?"

"No, there was a time I was taking Quaaludes under a doctor's prescription, but I determined that I didn't need them anymore and stopped their use. I didn't like the side effects, and stopped before I ever met Mrs. Fletcher."

Joe expected the evasion, and so he moved on. According to Hyman Berg there would be no point to file a motion for either examination of Richardson's blood or hair. He couldn't count on proving any more than what Richardson had just admitted.

Joe went for what he figured was the jugular, the deaths of Mickens, Hillibrand and Cooper and the intimidation of Martens and Nelda's mother. Richardson claimed he had no involvement in any of it, that he had only a professional relationship with Mickens and Hillibrand and wasn't in the Harbor Vista in Vancouver when Cooper had his unfortunate event. Yes, he had been there on other occasions, and it wouldn't be a surprise if his fingerprints were on a glass or two. He admitted he arrived for a meeting there just after Cooper had his fall, but he wasn't in the condo that day.

Joe had no trouble establishing who Cooper, Mickens, Hillibrand and Martens were. Richardson claimed he didn't know anything about Mrs. Fox. When Joe started digging deeper, MacCallum stepped on the brakes.

"That is unlikely to lead to discoverable evidence. There is no basis for these questions. They don't bear on any issue in this case, but I am not waiving Dr. Richardson's right against self-incrimination."

Throughout the deposition, MacCallum and Zale punctuated Joe's questions with objections for the record. It's the defense attorney's counterattack. Preserve your objections, make the plaintiff's lawyer wish he were doing something else and wear him down. Distract him. Make a mess of the record, so the judge will lose his way. Meanwhile, the defense attorney is paid by the hour for what purports to be a serious exercise. Joe expected it and knew he just had to keep slogging toward the goal line and not drop the ball.

In preparing for the deposition, MacCallum had carefully explained to Richardson that he couldn't take the Fifth if Judge Abelson allowed those death issues to come up for trial. He'd already waived his right to be silent. MacCallum figured the intimidation of Mrs. Martens and Mrs. Fox could be found to be illegal coercion, also a crime, and the intimidation of a legitimate witness in the case would be relevant evidence. If Richardson tried to take the Fifth Amendment, he would alienate the jury. Richardson decided he wouldn't take that risk. As to the deaths, he only knew what the public knew. If asked in the deposition, about intimidating witnesses, he would testify he'd just wanted Armour to have someone get information from Martens on his drug use and from Nelda's mom on Nelda's education. He would be "surprised" they would claim harassment. If it occurred, he would say, it wasn't his fault.

Joe recited for the court reporter's record the argument for relevance of the Cooper death case, having decided he would file a motion rather than try to get the judge on the phone during the deposition. As expected, Richardson admitted he'd been to Cooper's condo and was going to see him the day he died. Joe decided to go into the Quaalude issue a different way. Though Richardson admitted he once used Quaaludes and insisted he had stopped, he couldn't explain why the Quaalude deliveries stayed the same when Martens went to Colorado or who was getting the pills addressed to Martens.

Joe figured he could make the case Richardson had a motive to kill Cooper, not good enough for a criminal conviction, but maybe good enough for a civil case. It wasn't so much that Richardson and Cooper were good buddies, it was more that they were partners in crime. Richardson had a reason to shut up Cooper. Joe figured he could sell that to a jury.

Joe dug into the records alterations, comparing the copies of the originals with the altered records. Richardson wasn't surprised, but the nurses' duplicity angered him. Richardson, ready for it, claimed Hillibrand had wanted to correct the erroneous record. It wasn't his idea. He claimed never to have asked Nelda to slip into the record a notation that she witnessed Richardson suggesting a D&C to Myra. When asked about the "conspiracy of silence" he claimed he'd never heard of it. Joe explained to him what the conspiracy was, but Richardson assured him nobody at Woodside would ever cover up wrongdoing that way.

It was finally time for the lunch break, which was limited to a half hour. Joe and Mike walked out, solemn faced, along with Jodi. It wasn't until they hit the break room that Mike tried to cheer Joe up. He slapped him on the back and congratulated him on what little he'd dragged out of Richardson. It would be fun to see Richardson on the witness stand if independent witnesses eventually proved how much of what he had said was lies. That would tee him up nicely for Nelda's testimony.

Before they started again at 12:30, Zale, with a friendly smile said, "How long are you going to be? I have to pick up my wife at 3:30."

"Sorry Mark, you aren't going to be able to. With all the objections and at the rate we're going, we could take a couple days. I don't mind if you leave, but your client might be disappointed."

Then Mike announced to the court reporter "Back on the record," and away he went as if Zale's supposed predicament was no concern of his. He assumed it was a lie anyway. Mike restrained his grin as Joe opened up his binder again.

When Joe finished, MacCallum didn't ask any questions of his client, but Zale had to take the responsibility for the death of Myra off the hospital. He put the screws to Richardson, who acknowledged what a capable nurse Hillibrand was. She'd never falsified records before, and there never had been a complaint about her that he was aware of. She had never before failed to call the treating physician during an emergency. He admitted this was an obvious emergency. He didn't know anything about Fox but acknowledged that a trainee won't be held to the same degree of knowledge as Hillibrand. Joe understood the insurance companies for Richardson and for the hospital would be looking out for each other as best they could. Neither had accused the other of negligence; that would only help the plaintiff. Richardson couldn't come up with a persuasive explanation for having signed a bunch of blank prescriptions. All he said was "Convenience." Joe was determined to drag all the dirty linen into Abelson's courtroom. The more the jury saw the better for Nelda's credibility and the worse for Richardson. When Joe completed the deposition, he felt like Richardson was pretty well pinned down and Doctor Berg, plaintiff's expert, would be in a great position to show the contradictions and inconsistencies.

CHAPTER THIRTY NINE

Two weeks, later, MacCallum, Zale and Joe appeared in front of Judge Abelson. The extent of deposition testimony would come down to an appeal to the judge's discretion. Nobody had a simple law principle that dispensed with the judge's authority to decide as he saw fit. Relevance of the death cases would be a stretch. Joe submitted affidavits by Detective Tracy, Mrs. Fox, Dr. Hsu of the coroner's office, Nelda, Milo Mickens, husband of the late Laura and a waitress from Rix. Percy W. Boykin, the young man in Vancouver had finally been revealed by Constable Stokes, and Joe turned his information over to MacCallum and Zale. He had to if he wanted to use his testimony. The defense lawyers demanded access to the young man, and prepared a subpoena. Percy understood he had to testify. His grandfather was willing for he and Percy to take a paid vacation to Seattle.

To Judge Ableson, Joe argued there were too many coincidences to be explained away. The doctor shouldn't have that many people near him with convenient deaths. Dr. Richardson's claim that he had arrived in Vancouver after Cooper's death would be rebutted by the newly disclosed young witness who saw him coming out of the building immediately after the fall. Zale and MacCallum were angered by the late disclosure. After the lawyers ran out of words, Abelson was ready to pounce.

"These deaths are certainly peculiar, and Cooper's and Hillibrand's deaths are particularly troubling. They may be related to the issues in this case, and I'll allow discovery. There is no connection yet proven between Richardson and the death of Mickens. I will allow discovery on the harassment of Mrs. Fox and Dr. Martens, but we're not talking about admissibility for trial yet."

The judge did have a smile for Joe.

"I'm always willing to listen if something provides a little more connection."

Joe smiled back, as if to say "Thanks for nothing," and they all walked out. Mike later poked him in the chest and asked, "What more could you expect? That's a win."

* * * * * *

Al Armour never got a subpoena from Joe Gold, who didn't trust him to say one true word. Still, he was nervous. Ever since he'd first met Tracy, he knew his license was in danger, but Richardson was scarier. Martens was okay, but detective Dugan in Des Moines had sold Armour out. When the choice was either get himself in deep trouble or put the blame on Armour, it was easy for Dugan. Armour called Richardson who was too busy to talk to him, but then Armour received a call back from Dr. Jerry Alden. He explained that Richardson was his son-in-law. He wanted to meet Armour at the Pioneer Square pergola in one hour. It seemed a rather clandestine approach, and Armour wasn't a naïve teenager. He agreed to meet and came equipped with a receiver and tape recorder concealed in the briefcase he innocently carried.

Armour recognized the bulky and tall, white-haired man in a blue down jacket by the telephone description. The man was tossing breadcrumbs to the pigeons scratching around by the pergola. He sat on a bench under the old, gray cast-iron structure. The smiling man motioned him over across the cobblestones and Armour joined him. When Armour sat down, Alden handed over the bag, and Armour started feeding the pigeons, too. It was a cool, pleasant afternoon.

Alden sounded friendly and cheerful over the telephone and continued the charm when they met. Armour switched on the concealed receiver-recorder, but Alden wasn't a rookie either. Armour had to show that he wasn't concealing any kind of listening device before Alden would say anything of significance. Armour didn't think Alden would suspect the briefcase, now parked next to the bench or the pen in his shirt pocket, a transmitter. It turned out to be an object Alden couldn't miss. He grabbed the briefcase, flipped it open and ripped loose the tape. Still smiling, he grabbed the pen, laid it on the ground and crushed it under his foot.

Alden asked, "Thought I was a dummy? Listen to me. I can't have you accusing Kevin of coercion. If you say threatening Mrs. Fox was Dugan's mistake or you say you were careless you'll be okay. You can't say Kevin told you to threaten her or Martens. There's still money to be made here. We need you to keep tracking Nelda Fox. You don't need to approach her, no strong-arm or threats, just keep us informed. Are we okay now?"

Having rid Armour of his protective recording system, Alden felt safe giving Armour his orders. Armour was disappointed, but his blank expression didn't show it.

"I'm okay with still working for Richardson, but you know, I'm in danger of losing my license. I need to get more money, because if things go wrong, I'll be out of business. The police aren't very far from shutting me down."

"Just make sure you don't rat on Richardson. Don't say anything that gets him in trouble. In the first place, you'd get yourself in trouble. In the second place, don't get me in trouble. I'm not some street thug, and I didn't say I would do anything to you. You'll just exercise your good common sense and understand your position. We can talk money when you've produced. Nothing for me to worry about. Have a nice day."

Armour picked up his wrecked equipment and walked up the street to his office to ponder the lousy choices he was facing: Risk his life or risk his license. He sat in his office staring out the window, until he finally decided he would be worthless the rest of the day, until he made the decision. On the way home it came to him clearly, whatever else he might do, Tracy wouldn't kill him but Richardson might. He would never testify on oath that Richardson asked him to intimidate Martens or Mrs. Fox, and he'd keep doing the surveillance. And he decided he'd write out a history of everything Richardson and Alden demanded. It would be in his safe if any harm came to him.

Chapter Forty

Med-West had told MacCallum to negotiate with Joe through a mediator, but nothing worked. MacCallum told Kevin and Cora about their risks, but Joe Gold stood firm. Herb Fletcher refused to settle within the limits of coverage. If he won more than the coverage, the Richardsons could lose everything they had. Their reputations could be ruined if they went to trial. But, the real sticking point for settlement was the question of fault. Herb and Nelda insisted that the "truth" must come out, so the mediation had ended quickly. Herb's opening bottom line was $5 million, an end to the "conspiracy of silence" and a full confession by Richardson, who would never accept those terms.

Gold, Fletcher and the mediator had gone, and MacCallum ran dry. He stared out the window, nothing left to say. He turned and looked across the desk at Richardson, frozen in his rugged anger. Echoing in his mind were the last depressing words of MacCallum: "Frankly, we are really in deep shit. I've discussed it with my partners. That kid, Percy Boykin up in Vancouver, does you in. The judge is going to allow it in the end. It relates to your drug use, and you'll need to explain the Quaaludes and, especially, the insulin and chloroform."

"Everybody will believe you left the Harbor Vista after you dropped Cooper off the deck. The only good news is there's no proof beyond a reasonable doubt, so no criminal conviction, but in our civil case, it will be admissible, and your credibility against Nelda will disappear. There's a lot of bad stuff we've been able to keep out, but I fear it isn't going to continue. She'll probably be a convincing witness in front of the jury. I thought that episode of her and Fletcher would turn the case, but I can't really promise that now. She comes across as so sincere and honest."

Richardson sat looking at his hands. He didn't know what those hands were going to do and to whom. He did know he couldn't just let a catastrophe be his last hurrah.

* * * * * *

The Golds knew Nelda had been tracked to Joe's residence. There was either a red-headed detective in a Chevy van during the day or an old guy wearing sunglasses, sitting in a pickup truck at night. Whenever Nelda left the house, she looked over her shoulder. It was getting tougher to shake the detectives when she went in disguise to her home care jobs. Nothing relieved the stress. And just walking around the house, she was constantly looking out the window. She bit her fingernails, and the crinkled eyebrows gave away the anxiety and fear she was living with. Sandra asked her, "How much longer can this go on? The trial isn't for another couple months, and you aren't going to last that long. Do you mind if I ask Joe to find you another place where they won't be able to track you?"

Nelda shrugged her shoulders. "What difference will it make? They can follow me wherever I go. I can't stay locked in all the time. I thought I'd lost them after I went to see Herb and the baby, but now there they are. If they want to find me they will, no matter what I do."

"I'm going to talk to Joe. He'll think of something."

But that night, Nelda saw some hope for ending her misery when Joe called and told her about hearing from Zale.

"Hosp-Pro Insurance will have to contribute to Richardson's carrier for the loss if the jury finds against the hospital. The board wants us to meet with Richardson's lawyer again, MacCallum and with Zale. This isn't quite a mediation, but it might get us somewhere. I think they're getting desperate since the mediation failed. I don't think they'd waste their time if they weren't going to meet our terms. They know where you and Herb stand. Will you just listen to them?"

"If it helps Herb get the case settled, I'd like to cooperate, but somebody has to do something about all the covering up, and what are you going to do about Richardson? Will he be there? I don't want to do it if he's going to be there."

"If that's what you want, I'll make sure he's out of it."

Joe told her there was nothing to lose. "All we have to do is listen." Two days later, Nelda sat with Herb Fletcher in Franklin Tobin's executive office suite at Woodside Hospital, waiting for the lawyers to arrive. She felt like the target in an amusement park shooting gallery. She was uneasy on enemy turf, but there was no real risk. When Joe and Mike Gold and McCallum and Zale walked in, she could see that Richardson was in the outer office. This was what she had feared in the first place, but as long as he wasn't in Tobin's teak and leather, private office she decided she wouldn't say anything. Tobin opened up the door to his private conference room and seated everyone. Nelda had Herb on one side of her and Joe on the other. MacCallum and Zale were on the other side of the table looking straight at her. Even without Richardson there in the room, she still was in as much stress as if he had been.

Tobin began with an angelic smile on his face. "See, you don't have to meet with Richardson. We want to be reasonable and so should you. Listen to what we have to say, and then you can take some time to see whether you agree. Here's the deal. Nelda, you relax about any problem that you might have had that night with contacting Richardson, and your record will be clean, no blame either way. You did a fine job and, Woodside will give you a strong recommendation. Richardson will agree to that. You need that if you want to continue in nursing. Herb, both insurance companies are offering the max available for this type of loss, and Richardson will kick in $500,000 of his own money. You can't hope for more. It's all there is."

MacCallum brought out a single sheet laying out the disputed facts which were, according to his draft, nicely finessed so no one was at fault.

He passed a copy also to Herb and Joe." Can we get an agreement on these facts in connection with a full settlement?"

Joe looked up at MacCallum after reading it. "We need some time. Do you have another room where Herb and Nelda and I can meet in private?"

As soon as the door to the empty library was shut and Nelda read it, she said, "There's no way I'm going to agree to any of that. It's a complete lie. Richardson should not be practicing medicine, and I'm not going to agree to any more lies to cover up his incompetence."

They spent ten more minutes with Joe pointing out what was likely to happen and Nelda and Herb listening.

Joe was cautious. "If you don't agree to this, in all likelihood, they'll want revenge. They'll try to make you the villain. The hospital's reputation will be damaged. They want out, whatever happens to Richardson. You could have a tough time professionally. Herb, there's no guarantees. They're going to fight this, and who can guarantee what a jury will do. There's two policy max-outs and more on the line for Melissa's future. You can just reach out and take it."

When they walked back into Tobin's conference room, Nelda was shocked to see Richardson, but she remained calm until he stepped forward, smiling, as if a friend, to shake hands with her. Little Nelda, with Richardson towering over her, with her jaw jutted out, stood sternly, face to face in front of him.

At that moment she felt her rage rising, her fear evaporating, and Herb stood up next to her. Maybe they'd regret it on later reflection, but right at that moment, they were fiercely determined. Almost snarling, with curled lip and fiery eyes, Nelda spat out, "Doctor, you're a disgrace. You're a killer, and you shouldn't be walking around free, let alone treating patients."

Richardson exploded. Before he could do something intolerable, MacCallum and Zale grabbed him, and they ended up wrestling him up against the wall as if they were a bunch of teenagers. Herb and Nelda turned to walk out. Tobin yelled with all his strength and fury, "You're done in the profession, Nelda. Get out and don't ever come back here. You'll never put on a nurse's uniform again anywhere."

Nelda turned back to him and smiled defiantly. "Thank you, Mr. Tobin. That's okay. If I can get Richardson away from patients, that will be enough for me." Joe grabbed Herb's arm, not wanting him to walk out with Nelda. They had to remember, they weren't a couple.

Nelda went alone down the long, empty hallway, her heels clacking on the tile, certain Richardson was going to try tracking her down, suddenly realizing what she'd done.

My God, I have to go to trial with these people?

* * * * * *

Meanwhile, in Vancouver, Percy W. Boykin dropped in at Miller Drugs, as he often did after school. Old Mr. Miller was happy to see him, but Miller's nephew, Ralph, looked away. Uncle William was all the little kids' best buddy, and sometimes they got a free banana split. Ralph's work in the shop didn't earn him a banana split. Some kids got it just for a friendly word and a smile.

Percy was Mr. Miller's best pet, and Ralph smoldered every time Percy got a freebie.

"Hi Ralph."

Ralph gave Percy back a weak "Hi," without a smile. Before he left, Percy, as usual, browsed the magazines. This time Ralph was going to catch him. There it was. Percy slid a *Playboy* magazine inside his sweater and headed for the door. Ralph grabbed him by the back of his red school jacket and jerked him back in.

"Uncle Bill, I've got him! Look, he's the one who's been taking *Playboys*."

Mr. Miller was irate. Steam rose over his head.

"Percy, how could you?"

Percy squirmed, trying to shake Ralph's grip so he could run. The *Playboy* fell to the floor.

"Ralph, lock the door and turn over the 'Open' sign."

Mr. Miller called, and the policeman walked in five minutes later. The normally cheerful Percy stood there looking at his shoes. It took a few days, but Constable Stokes reached Detective Tracy in Seattle.

"We're dropping charges against Richardson. Our young witness, Percy Boykin, just got picked up for shoplifting. Do what you want on your case, but I'm not going after Richardson relying on Boykin."

"Oh, crap. You sure on that?"

"The kid admitted it. Sorry."

"Richardson leads a charmed life. Every time I think I got him, something goes sour."

When he heard about young Percy's arrest, Joe wanted to scream. Every promising backup for Nelda had fallen apart for one reason or another. Cooper and Hillibrand dead, Martens and Detective Armour intimidated, all the hospital employees, probably even Halloran, wobbly on the "conspiracy of silence." Percy, the last, best chance to tie Richardson to the murder of Cooper, goes rotten.

Was Nelda on her own? It seemed that way. How do we protect her?

* * * * * *

Armour couldn't have been clearer. "We've got a man at the Joe Gold residence, but he doesn't see much. We really aren't always sure if Fox is there. We think she's there, but I suspect Joe hides her in his car and drops her off at an office building every day, and she disappears. There's a pretty regular, private police patrol in the neighborhood, so our guy stands out like a sore thumb. One of our guys got out of the car one time, and a patrol car came by and stopped. In the evening, we think Joe's bringing her home, but he puts his car in the garage, so I can't prove it. The only thing I can think of is sneak somebody in, maybe in disguise as a salesman or something."

Richardson pondered the strategy. "That sounds tough. I'm wondering if you could stage a car accident to get the attention of the local cops. Maybe we draw them away, then we can get to her when she's alone."

"There is no 'we' in this. Anything you pull is strictly on you. All I'm providing is surveillance. I have no idea what you're going to do with the information I give you. Maybe you're right. A car accident would distract the protection. As long as you pay for my guys' time, we can try it. But that's just for surveillance. Right? I can give you names, but the rest of it is up to you."

"Fine, the rest of what?"

Chapter Forty One

Following the disastrous conference at the hospital, Nelda and Joe headed back home. On the way, they talked about fooling Richardson. Obviously, Richardson's detectives were watching the house. Nelda assumed Richardson knew she was there and wished they could end it somehow. He intended to intimidate her, but he'd deny committing a crime or even any connection with the strange cars in the neighborhood.

Joe needed an answer. "I think I have an idea how we can get you out from under those damned spies."

When he told her, despite all her anxiety, Nelda couldn't help laughing. And when they got home and told Sandra, she was tickled and knew the taxi driver to call. Nelda was ready when the taxi arrived. It went right up the long driveway to the Golds' garage. As the garage door opened, Nelda walked out carrying her suitcase and a garment bag. The driver stowed them in his trunk. Sandra walked out and gave Nelda a big hug. As the taxi drove off, Sandra waved a friendly goodbye and Nelda waved back. Sandra walked back in and the garage door shut. Armour's detectives followed the taxi all the way to the Olympic Hotel where the hotel porter brought in the luggage.

Armour figured he was done. If Nelda were really moving into the Olympic until the trial was over, Richardson wouldn't be reaching her there. Armour harbored some suspicion, but he didn't care whether it was real or a fake. He wanted out. The money was good, but spending a good chunk of his life in a penitentiary wouldn't be. Richardson had been lucky so far, but if he got unlucky, Armour could go down with him.

He explained to Richardson. "It could be a scam, and Nelda could come sneaking back to the house. If it's a scam, they'll assume we're fooled, so she'll be off guard. Whatever you do, I don't want to be involved. I'm out."

"What do you mean, you're quitting?"

"Hell yes, I'm quitting. If anything happens to Nelda the police will know who did it. You can't expect to get away with anything that hurts her. If you continue, they'll fry your butt, and I'm not joining you."

Cora wouldn't let Richardson give up just because Armour was bailing out. Armour told his top spy to call Richardson and make his own deal. If he wanted the money, the risk was up to him. He told the man it was stupid.

Still, "Bobby" called Richardson and they met at the Blue Moon Tavern in the University District. "Bobby," a short, bearded, muscle-bound street-fighter in a sleeveless sweatshirt and jeans, said he'd help. The deal called for him to spy on Joe's home. He understood any information he provided might be put to a bad use, but he wouldn't be involved in whatever Richardson did with it. He took on a couple helpers and pursued a stealthier surveillance of Joe's home. One guy played a mailman, and a woman pushed a baby carriage with a genuine, imitation baby, a doll. A house up the street was for sale. With the innocent help of a realtor, "Bobby" rented the house at an absurd price, and moved a couple friends in. They were there the day several ladies arrived for some sort of social event. One of the men suspected a small, slim woman with grey hair could be Nelda in disguise. He wasn't sure if she left with the others and reported the news to Richardson, who started thinking about his revenge. "Keep somebody on Joe Gold's house. Let me know if she leaves."

* * * * * *

When the word came out that Percy W. Boykin had been arrested in Vancouver, there was an explosion in Seattle. Larry MacCallum immediately got on the phone with Richardson, who erupted. "Fantastic, so all they have left is Nelda to help out her boyfriend. All the crap they wanted to throw against me is gone, right?"

"I don't think you're home free, Kevin, but maybe when I'm finished cross-examining her, the jurors won't be so sure. That's the best I can promise." Richardson, under the influence of his favorite drug, felt like he could do whatever he wanted, regardless of what MacCallum thought or what the police could do.

Unbelievable! All that planning, all that stress, for nothing. I can end this case right now!

* * * * * *

MacCallum couldn't wait to call Joe. He positively gloated on the phone. "Look, without Boykin, there's no support for Fox. You can't think she's going to look better than Richardson in front of a jury. If you agree with me, we ought to just work out a reasonable settlement and pay you for your time. Right? Cost of defense settlement? I think I can get the company to go for it."

"I don't think so, Larry. We've got harassment of Mrs. Fox and Martens and three murders. Juries can know about that kind of thing, and juries don't believe in coincidences. Everyone knows Richardson demanded the record forging."

"Nice try, Joe. Judge Abelson isn't going to allow proof of deaths not connected to Richardson. Forging? Is that what you call it? Bull. All you have is innuendo. It's too remote, and Abelson isn't going to let you build a case on that. And little Nelda vs. Richardson is no contest."

"Let's suppose you're right, Larry. Even if you are right, our expert, Dr. Berg, nails Richardson."

"Yeah, I know what he says, but what Dr. Berg doesn't know is what would have been the result if the D&C had been done. She still might've died, so you can't prove proximate cause. It's still Fox vs. Richardson, and Richardson wins that battle."

Despite his bravado, Joe wasn't all that certain the case couldn't slip away. MacCallum now glowed with confidence he would win, while Joe still faced the crucial question of what evidence of Richardson's suspect conduct Abelson would allow at trial. Joe believed he knew the answer to that one, but until the judge spoke, uncertainty remained. He knew MacCallum wanted to clear up the uncertainty as much as Joe.

"Tell you what, Larry, suppose we put that to Abelson again on a pretrial motion. Then we'll know."

"I don't know, Joe. I'll have to talk it over with the Med-West Insurance rep and see what he says."

Ten minutes later, MacCallum called back. "He says to take it to Abelson. I'll schedule it with his bailiff and your paralegal, Jodi, is that right?"

The battle was on. In Joe's mind, this could decide the case. He rolled up his sleeves and went to work. Mike put his own clients aside and joined Joe in the law library. Two lawyers pounding away at the same time produced piles of law books on the conference table and a lot of traffic in their library. Each worked different aspects of the evidentiary issues. In between, they checked with Stokes in Vancouver and Tracy in the Seattle SPD. Young Percy Boykin's grandfather, who looked after him, was sympathetic but didn't want the boy subjected to the additional abuse he'd get in the civil case while facing the juvenile charge. It looked like Joe couldn't even keep a damaged Boykin in the case.

When the day for the pre-trial motion came, Joe was as ready as he could be. The crowd in the courtroom stunned him. Both Richardsons were there. Herb Fletcher, naturally. Ed and Mike came to observe as spectators. MacCallum and Zale were arranging their yellow legal pads and their piles of briefs when Joe arrived. Then, add in the insurance reps, members of the Woodside Hospital, Board of Directors and a couple writers from the *Seattle Times* and *PI*. In the back of the room, still trying to be unnoticed in the mob, was a young woman disguised as a man with glasses and a blonde wig, Nelda Fox. Joe wasn't fooled.

Joe, stepping to the lectern, led off, quickly summarizing "a pattern of events any one of which," he argued, "might not be admissible. Collectively, they are overwhelming evidence of a pattern of criminal conduct by Richardson. The jury is entitled to judge his credibility in the light of this evidence of a guilty conscience."

MacCallum scoffed. "One hundred rumors of acts by Dr. Richardson are no better evidence than one rumor. The plaintiff can't connect any one of these events to the doctor. As far as the law is concerned, it's just as likely that someone is trying to frame him as it is that he committed the acts. The jury can't be allowed a coin flip basis for decision. That's all they have."

Judge Abelson had spent hours on the briefs and affidavits and was ready to rule. That Percy Boykin had disappeared from the case was crucial. "There's a lot riding on this, I know. I've never seen a crowd like this for a pre-trial motion. I know the importance of the case to the parties and the medical community, and I can see the case may be decided on this motion, so I've given it a lot of thought."

To Nelda, the judge's voice betrayed a tinge of sadness that reached all the way to the back of the room. She sensed what the decision was going to be and felt disappointment and fear of what the ruling would mean for Herb's case. There would be no support for Nelda's testimony. It would be her against Richardson, and he threatened her life. She felt a little safer after the Olympic Hotel scam. A little.

Abelson concluded, "The circumstances are unique. I have to agree with the defense. None of these peculiar or tragic events can be positively tied directly to Dr. Richardson based on the evidence submitted. I can't let the jury consider them. I know the press is here, and I am directing counsel and their clients to refrain from discussing this motion and ruling with the media."

* * * * * *

Richardson left the courthouse pleased but not yet satisfied. Part of him wanted to deal a blow to Nelda. His conscience struggled with it. He sat in the living room and tossed it around in his mind then called "Bobby" with a little deception. "I don't think we're going to worry about Fox anymore. Abelson ruled in our favor, so all that stuff they're saying about me is gone from the case. All they have is Fox, and she can't beat me by myself. I don't really care where she is now, just mildly curious. I don't need you anymore."

"Well, just so you know, I did my job. I'm still pretty sure she's at Joe Gold's house. They must figure their trick fooled you. There's no guards anymore. If I'm done, I'm moving out. Pay me what you owe, and I'm deaf and dumb. I'll be by your office today. You can just leave an envelope. Cash, okay? $2500?"

Richardson felt edgy and told Cora about his conversation with Armour and "Bobby." "We're almost there. I still can go after Nelda if we need to." Cora didn't trust him and checked with MacCallum. He reminded her how crucial a witness Nelda still was. Despite her recorded deposition testimony, she could make a powerful face-to-face impression on the jury essential to her power as a witness. Cora decided that the girl wouldn't testify. She knew, if anyone asked Armour, he would say Kevin had abandoned any idea of harassing Nelda. "Bobby" didn't exist. She focused on both the revenge and the relief she was waiting for. Cora and her dad met at the house. They mixed anger and fear and the anticipation made Alden's stomach do cartwheels.

He confronted Richardson in the living room. "We're going after Fox tomorrow. Here's my plan." He then outlined a scheme that would free them from any fear of Nelda ever drawing forth a jury's trust and sympathy, from her ever being a threat again.

Richardson's nerves cracked. His face went blank, and he fell back, helpless on the couch, looking straight up at the ceiling. "I can't do it. No more."

Alden's face reflected his disgust. "Kevin, just as I always thought. You're gutless when it counts. Shit. You drive. I'll do it."

One of Armour's thugs stole the car they needed a month earlier, and Alden stashed it in a rented garage. That next day, before Joe got home, Richardson, contemplating fearfully what Alden was about to do, parked the nondescript, old, junker Chevy up the street from the Golds' home. Richardson, with his dyspepsia carving up his stomach, sat in the car. It would be up to Alden, who confidently smiled as he slipped quickly out, then between the trees and shrubs in the park like grove adjoining the old mansion.

Nelda saw the man's shadow through the antique dormer window as it appeared from behind one tree and then disappeared behind the next. With just a brief glimpse, she couldn't tell if he was one she'd seen before, as he was dressed for concealment. He wore jeans, an oversized dark coat, a slouchy hat and, ominously, a beard and dark glasses. He tucked his right hand inside the jacket, holding something. She was sure this man wore a disguise if she'd ever seen one. Nelda ran upstairs and told Sandra to get into the closet. She got out the shotgun Joe had put there "just in case." Nelda told Sandra to lie down and pile some clothes on top of her. Then she called SPD, excitedly whispering, "There's a burglar in my house and he's got a gun." She figured the slight exaggeration would get their attention and action.

Nelda's hands sweated, and her heart thumped while, rather than melting under the fear, her spine stiffened. The thought she could be forced to kill a man nauseated her, but if she had to, she would. Sandra was going to have her baby, and Nelda would be there to hold it. When the front doorbell rang, Nelda hid in the hall closet, grasped the shotgun and nervously fumbled two shells into it, the closet door left open just a crack. She could see just a sliver view of the man as he gave up waiting, turned and ran towards the back of the house.

Who is the man? Why is he here? Why is there something familiar about him?
It's not Richardson.

He disappeared from view, and Nelda headed for the breakfast nook where she could surreptitiously spy on the backdoor. She could see and hear the man scratching with some tools at the door lock. Then he appeared to give up. Nelda saw him raise a pistol and swing it, breaking the backdoor window. He used a rag to muffle the crashing sound, but Nelda was close enough to hear it anyway. She gripped the shotgun with shaking hands. Off in the distance a siren sounded. The man paused, looking in the direction of the siren. Abruptly, he took off running while the sound got closer. Nelda went to the front entry hall and saw him dive into the passenger side of the old car. It then instantly screeched down the winding street and was gone just before the two police cars, lights flashing and sirens howling, pulled in.

When three officers arrived with guns drawn, Nelda, still trembling, described the car, and the police immediately called it in. As she started to get a grip and could, she gave a calm and complete description of the burglar, given the clumsy but effective disguise. Nelda told the policemen, "I think he grabbed the back door knob." They called Seattle downtown headquarters to get the technicians to dust for fingerprints from the knob. Nelda sat looking at the shotgun, then unloaded it, grateful her life didn't depend on her gun prowess that day.

* * * * * *

Richardson drove as fast as he could, pulling rights and lefts, avoiding well-traveled streets as much as possible. Alden, not so confident anymore, sweat coming from every pore, looked both ways and behind the car, expecting to see flashing lights any moment. After the wild, backstreet escape, Richardson, completely drained, stopped at the rented garage and leaned back in his seat. Beads of perspiration formed on his forehead, and his shirt was wet.

Alden's predatory urge, once aroused was unsatisfied, and he only withdrew reluctantly. When they got back to the Richardson home, he proposed wilder and crazier, alternate plans while his eyes lit up with enthusiasm again. Richardson's depression deepened, and he badly needed his meds.

"Leave me alone, Jerry. I can't handle this. I'd rather just let whatever happens in court happen than go through this sort of shit again. Just forget it. Why do I have to go through this?"

Richardson took the little metal container out of his pocket and swallowed one of the Quaaludes. Then Alden went back to the rented garage. There was no sign of interest from any police, and he wiped the car clean. Later that day he dumped the gun off the Fremont Bridge. Richardson called the wrecking yard thug he'd lined up to crush the car. He put down the phone, lay back on the silk couch at his own home and reported to Cora, "We're clean, nothing to worry about." Despite the clean escape and the meds, Richardson's depression became deeper. He took another Quaalude and just faded for a couple hours. Cora watched his collapse with a sense of hopelessness. She wondered what he might do as she watched him losing touch.

The police stayed at Joe and Sandra's home until Joe could get there. By then, the security patrol Joe hired had returned, and the house was guarded like a castle. If they couldn't prove that Richardson was the perpetrator, whoever it was would never have access to that house again. Sandra was shaking, but Nelda's anger overcame any fear she had of Richardson or his goons. "If he thought he could scare me off, he's going to find out different in court. Someday, we're going to see him marched off to the state pen."

CHAPTER FORTY TWO

Joe knew the press would get on him sooner or later. As he sat back in the desk chair in his office, feet up on the end table, underlining the key parts of the Richardson deposition he'd use for cross examination, Jodi buzzed him, with an excited catch in her voice. "Joe, it's Albert Setser on the phone. He wants to talk about the Fletcher case, what else."

Setser of the *Seattle Times,* the reporter who'd made the Gold Law Firm shining heroes over the Perini case wanted in on Fletcher. When Joe first met him, Setser was a sloppy looking, little, four-eyed reporter, basically just a cub starting out. Now, every time Joe saw him, he wore a sharp suit and didn't look like the same guy at all, suddenly a professional. With his new image came a little insight, and he figured he could call Joe in return for the boost he gave the Gold Firm. Joe expected Setser to gobble up all the scuttlebutt he could from bailiffs and court reporters. But, with the trial coming, Joe had to censor what he let out into the press.

"Oh shit, Jodi. Sorry, okay. I guess I have to talk to him." Joe kicked himself for never having prepared for this moment. The family hadn't discussed what to say if Setser, who'd written the glowing paeans over their work in the Perini case, or some other newsy wanted a story on Fletcher. What to say?

Setser tempted him. "Hey, Joe, you guys are at it again. With all that ink on Perini you must be busting at the seams with new clients and cases."

"We're grateful for those kind words you printed about us, Al. Seriously, we are busy. I'd really like it if I didn't have to take my time answering questions for the press right now. I'm really loaded up. We're almost at trial and there's no time to spare."

"Well, I got a look at the court file. Richardson seemed to want to keep it secret. Looking at the deposition excerpts in the file, I can see why."

"Al, please tread lightly. Newspaper headlines could complicate our job. Judge Abelson isn't going to like it if he thinks I was trying to dynamite the defense by making my case in the press."

"Don't be so nervous. I just have a few questions, and if you'd like, I won't quote you."

"Okay, but I might not be answering your questions anyway. It depends."

"Okay, first question. Can you prove that Richardson murdered Cooper or Mickens or Hillibrand?"

"Nice first question, Al. What's your second question?"

Setser laughed. "I thought that one might be a little nasty. Well then, how about this one? Isn't it a little tough doing a case like this without your dad involved? If you want, I'll keep this just for background, and I won't print your answer. I'm really just curious."

"Al, let's do this. After the case is over, however it comes out, I'll give you the whole story if you do your job straight until then. No puffing stuff or slamming the defense. The judge could get pissed. Okay?"

Setser paused only briefly. "Sounds good to me. I got a nice pat on the back and a bump in the wallet for the Perini story. This one looks even better. You know I'm not going to hurt you. You guys have done me a lot of good."

"Al, I'll give you first shot when we're done."

Setser laughed again. "Joe, if you don't, I'll be cleaning out toilets for the paper. Thanks. Talk to you later. I've got enough for now, but I want the real deal after." When Setser finished his in-depth analysis, he came out with a pretty good, plain vanilla story setting up the readers for a fascinating trial and the blockbuster he planned for after Joe's victory.

CHAPTER FORTY THREE

The night before trial, Herb was wearing down after a long session of trial prep in Joe's office. Herb, a strong young man, looking fit as an Olympic decathlete, sat mentally exhausted, leaning back in the dark walnut side chair in front of Joe's broad, leather-topped desk. His head flopped back and Joe had used up all his young energy too.

"I've had it, Joe. Can we take a break?"

"Sure, Herb. Hell, let's call it a day. You're as prepped as you're going to be. One more thing. Remember MacCallum and Zale want you to say something negative about Myra, anything at all, or just unfeeling. Don't hold back on your love for her, and don't let them put words in your mouth. I don't care how tired you get, you know what the plain truth is, so stick to that. Don't accept their wording of a question if there's a bite to it. If you say yes, be sure that isn't a trick. Okay, now go home, take a nice, hot bath, and I'll see you at 9:00 in Judge Abelson's court tomorrow."

Herb didn't move and still needed to talk. He had so many anxieties batting back and forth in his head, he couldn't express them. It was his moral duty to win this for Melissa and for Myra and to end Richardson's murderous professional career. But most of all, the damned "conspiracy of silence" had to be exposed for the sake of every hospital patient. If Richardson got away with it this time, nobody was safe.

"Are we going to win?"

"Wish I could say, but we have so much on Richardson we can't use. Right now, it really is mostly up to Nelda. I don't know if she'll handle the pressure of trial. Sometimes she seems tough and then sometimes not. That attempted break-in or whatever it was seems to have stiffened her spine, but there are no guarantees."

"I've experienced cases where there were loose ends. I remember one where a new witness showed up at trial. I raised hell, claiming it wasn't fair, the new witness hadn't been revealed. I didn't have a chance to depose him, so I demanded a chance to talk to him before he testified. The judge didn't like the situation and said 'Oh, yeah, okay. You have an hour to talk to him.' The witness was evasive, and I didn't get much chance. I couldn't have prepared for that, but that's the kind of stuff that happens. You just deal with that as best you can when it comes up."

"Jesus, Joe. How'd it come out?"

"I shoved the guy around a bit till I figured his secret and then kicked his ass. You just use your head. Don't be scared. Be focused. I think we're focused, and we're set. Abelson isn't a dummy or a pushover, and I feel pretty good. I just want you to know there are no sure things."

"Thanks, Joe," he said with a wry smile, "Just what I wanted to hear." Herb finally dragged himself out.

When he got home, Joe checked in with Nelda. He needed to know her state of mind. She had pretty well shown at times she could be a toughie, but was she ready to face cross-examination in trial? They had talked about it before, and he saw a certain amount of bravado he wasn't sure was still there.

Nelda and Sandra were sitting over coffee in the family room. The first thing Joe noticed was something he'd seen before. Nelda was twisting her fingers nervously. "MacCallum will get nasty, won't he?"

"Sure he will, and you'll handle it the way you have up to now. Just let it roll off your back. He can't do anything to you. You listen to the words, and answer the questions. Never mind the tone of voice. He might want to get close and sort of loom over you, and if he does, I'll ask the judge to move him back. The jury will be your friend. Just don't worry, okay?"

Nelda knew what he wanted to see and forced the kind of confident smile Joe was looking for.

If I can convince Joe I'm okay, maybe I can convince me.

* * * * * *

Abelson presided over a courtroom jammed with jurors, lawyers and spectators. It was a spectacle the courthouse didn't see routinely. The bailiff, ex-cop, Rocky O'Brien, handed out passes. It was strictly first come, first serve, and the first two rows were prospective jurors. Witnesses were ordered to remain outside until called. Joe had Jodi with him, monitoring the exhibits, his brother and Herb Fletcher on either side. Before trial, the parties marked as admissible most of the exhibits, and the clerk, under the judge's direction, marked as rejected the documents related to the deaths other than Myra's. In chambers, Abelson ruled out exhibits relating to the harassment of Martens and Nelda's mother. Most admitted exhibits were in by agreement.

As usual, a lot of housewives and Boeing Aircraft employees, who got paid when they were on jury duty showed up on the jury panel. Joe wanted all the women he could get, hoping they'd identify with young Myra. The defense lawyers wanted every nitpicking engineer available and every wage slave who imagined his insurance expenses would somehow go up if Herb got a big award.

It took half a day to psychoanalyze the panel, winnow out the biased and the reluctant and satisfy the lawyers they couldn't get anyone better. It irked Joe that he had only two peremptory challenges, an objection to a witness for which he didn't have to state a reason, while each defendant had two, a total of four for the defense.

That's life.

248

After Abelson seated and swore in an intelligent sounding group of twelve, it was so close to the lunch hour it made no sense to start opening statements. Before he adjourned, he gave his first direction to the jurors. "You are to avoid any conversation about the case with anyone outside the jury room. Don't make a decision until all the evidence is in." He was adamant. "And you are directed not to watch any TV discussion or read any newspaper articles about the case. This rule continues till the case is over. Then there's one other thing. No one in the courtroom is permitted to have any kind of a weapon."

He didn't mention that he and the bailiff each had a pistol available. In all his years, he'd never had to think about using it, but it gave him a feeling of security. He then adjourned the court room and told everyone to be back by 1:30. As everyone walked out, MacCallum whispered to Richardson to take his briefcase to his car, pull out the pistol and leave it in the glove compartment. He took it for granted Richardson would do as he said. Richardson nodded his head.

Mike, Herb and Joe walked out and headed down the hall with Nelda in tow. They got a booth in the Gold Coast, a restaurant across the street from the courthouse. Herb understood having Nelda with them would demonstrate for any juror who saw them, her connection with the plaintiff's case. Defense counsel might notice and bring it up in cross examination. After all the other ties between Herb and Nelda, Joe didn't give it much thought. When they were seated, Herb asked Joe what he thought of the jury panel. Joe was satisfied.

"They looked pretty good to me, but I could do without the Boeing engineer. I've had my experiences. B must follow A, and C must follow B. They're so damn technical. But I like the number of women we have. They'll empathize with you, and they'll love Nelda."

Mike agreed and Herb was happy to hear it. "You ready to kick some butt?"

"I'm ready and you better be ready too, Herb."

At 1:30, Abelson turned Joe loose to give his opening statement, step one in the ancient trial trilogy: 1. Tell them what you're going to tell them (opening statement) 2. Tell them (the evidence) and 3. Tell them what you told them (closing argument). Joe painted a picture of the young, innocent victim, the loving husband and trust in the eminent Dr. Kevin Richardson. Even when Richardson failed her, Myra refused to question his ability or devotion.

"How could she know he was addicted to Quaaludes, a mood altering drug that rendered him unfit?"

With that, MacCallum leapt to his feet, objecting to any mention of this "unsupported slander." MacCallum was frothing blood and anger, his eyes flaming. Before Joe could say a word, Judge Abelson, with a calm gentleness, responded.

"No, I think it's permissible in this opening statement. You'll have your chance."

Joe, ready to strike back, returned to his argument, and his pulse returned to a calmer beat. He expected his next point to rouse MacCallum again. Joe needed Dr. Berg's testimony. Joe explained that the failure to do a dilatation and curettage was negligent. He admitted Dr. Berg had testified in deposition, an autopsy was necessary to be certain of the cause of death. "But," he said, "defense counsel, Zale and MacCallum didn't inquire further during the deposition. If they had, Dr. Berg would have said that, more probably than not, the loss of blood was the cause of death, a competent D&C would have found the bleeder and that surgery would have stopped the blood loss. That will be his testimony here."

MacCallum and Zale looked at each other. That testimony would be enough to take probable cause to the jury. When Joe briefly summarized Berg's opinion testimony, McCallum and Zale were frozen into silence. They realized their lapse. Other than the obviously malleable Schwinn, they'd never found anyone to rebut Berg. They couldn't fight the uniformity of literature supporting Berg's opinion. He put the steel in Joe's spine that supported him when MacCallum told him he should settle cheap. Wishful thinking isn't a defense. Zale sat there telling himself he should have known better and maybe MacCallum did too.

Joe took on Richardson's best argument right from the start in his opening statement. He couldn't let the closeness of Herb and Nelda come first from the defense.

"You need to know about Myra Fletcher. She trusted Lois Hillibrand, her nurse, and Nelda Fox a young student nurse. They formed a close emotional bond during the extended stay in the Maternity Ward. This was more than the ordinary relationship of the patient and nurse who provided day-to-day care. Herb Fletcher, Myra's husband, shared that bond and was grateful. He is still grateful, and that bond still exists. Nurse Hillibrand has died, but Nelda Fox is still here to testify to what happened on that terrible evening when Myra Fletcher bled out her last drop of blood and what Dr. Richardson did to protect himself against the truth. Though the defense may suggest otherwise, Miss Fox and Mr. Fletcher are friends, tied by the memory of Myra Fletcher and concern for Myra and Herb's baby, Melissa. They are not lovers and their testimony isn't affected by any impropriety. Nelda Fox visited Herb once to see the baby, there is no affair and there never was."

"Nurse Fox has had to hide from Dr. Richardson for fear of what he might do to her. She is a crucial witness who fears Dr. Richardson. Herb Fletcher has helped her find employment and safety."

Joe hoped for an objection to the statement that Nelda was in fear. The objection would open the door to testimony explaining the reason for her fear. In would come all of the testimony previously excluded by Judge Abelson. Nelda's mother, Jeffry Stokes and the Americanada Ltd. secretary all had airline tickets and had accepted subpoenas. Richardson would go from sleazy to scary. MacCallum wasn't dumb enough to object and invite Joe's response.

Oh well.

"Dr. Richardson suffered from a condition which led him to take Quaaludes long before Myra Fletcher was under his care. He cannot explain why his supplier continued delivering those drugs after he claims he was cured of the need. And he can't explain why emergency room doctors had to come to Myra's bedside on the night of her death, while he was resting in the doctor's lounge. He will claim that he wasn't called, and nurse Hillibrand is not here to rebut that claim but Nurse Fox is. Dr. Richardson will tell you the medical records were changed after Myra Fletcher's death because the nurses had made mistakes in creating the records. He was very angry when he discovered they had copied the original records which were truthful and accurate after he had demanded they make changes absolving him of responsibility. It will be his word against Miss Fox. She will be telling the truth. He can't. The truth condemns him."

* * * * * *

Nelda came to the courthouse in the backseat of Joe's Caddy. She'd lain down under a jacket on the floor, and nobody bothered her. Joe made sure he wasn't followed. Now, she sat fidgeting on a bench in the hallway with the other witnesses, wishing she could hear what Joe was saying to the jury. She wondered how he was handling it. Better than her, she hoped. Nelda didn't know what to do with her hands. Her mind went back to a sort of guilt she felt that she had not kept Myra safe. In her mind, she owed it to Melissa, Myra's sweet baby and Herb, to help them get justice when the forces of the hospital system were focused on denying it.

When Joe sat down, Larry MacCallum, ignoring Joe, rose to address the jury. He was proud, erect, imposing, and scornful of the young lawyer and his little entourage. Uncharacteristically for MacCallum, his argument started cautiously, narrowed down to Richardson's experience, knowledge and reputation, as opposed to the green, untested, semi-educated student nurse. MacCallum didn't want a careful examination of Richardson's behavior. He was sure he'd lose that battle. That was his thinking before the adrenaline started flowing.

"Miss Fox was obviously captivated by Mr. Fletcher, the handsome widower. Whatever their relationship, even if it wasn't an affair, was clearly outside the professional norms of a hospital. It was an act of revolt. Miss

252

Fox couldn't face up to her responsibility. After examining the conduct of the nurses, the hospital administration has kept Dr. Richardson on staff and Nurse Fox, apparently, remains unemployed and unwanted by any healthcare institution. The hospital did not dare keep her on its staff, certainly not in the Maternity area. She was in a less demanding position for a short time, and even there couldn't perform adequately."

MacCallum stole a look out of the corner of his eye after inviting a valid objection. His conclusions were a far stretch from the facts. Joe hoped the jury understood the difference between argument and evidence and would withhold its judgment until hearing the case. Cleverly, Zale reserved his opening statement, so he could make it after the plaintiff presented his case. The jury would understand his argument better after they heard the plaintiff's testimony. He wanted to start out fresh and be able to paper over anything presented in the plaintiff's case.

It was time for the main event. Joe put Richardson on the witness stand first, reasoning that he wanted to rough the doctor up as much as he could before his own attorney painted him with gold leaf in front of the jury and turned him into a Greek God. It wasn't an unusual tactic. Attorneys often preferred to weaken the opposition before they can present their case. MacCallum had warned Richardson, and he was ready. He'd had enough Quaaludes to keep his temper under control but not enough to dull his mind. Richardson under control was a powerful presence in a hospital and, presumably, in the courtroom too.

Joe headed straight for the jugular and quizzed Richardson on his treatment of Myra and his knowledge of when a D&C is necessary. Richardson explained he'd done them on many occasions, that it's a decision of the individual OB/GYN, whatever the literature says. He testified, "There's a bond between the doctor and patient you can't find in books." Joe didn't move to strike the testimony, which was contrary to the standard of the profession. He had a better strategy. Over MacCallum's objections, he forced Richardson, reluctantly, to admit there is literature relied on by other doctors that might have required him to do a D&C. The bleeding often couldn't be stopped without finding the bleeder. Again, over MacCallum's objection, Joe brought out the books which Richardson tried to deny represented the standard of the practice. Then Joe cornered him with his own prior words and read for the jury the language which established Myra should have had a D&C. As he found his case slipping a bit, Richardson struggled to maintain his composure, and the jury watched his face redden. He managed to keep going without another "lude."

Next, Joe dug into the records alterations. Richardson admitted he'd taken Hillibrand to a very nice steak restaurant, helped her "correct" her medical record entries, and then she died a couple days later. He claimed not to have known at the time, she'd made copies of the originals and of the blank prescription forms he'd signed. Since her copies disappeared from her home, he didn't want to open the possibility he took them on the morning of her death. That was a trap he and MacCallum had discussed. MacCallum was careful to avoid suggesting he commit perjury, but Richardson got the point. If he didn't know about the copies, they weren't a reason to go to her house.

Both sets of Myra Fletcher's hospital records had already been marked and admitted by stipulation. Joe walked Richardson through the differences between the two records, the "original" and the "altered" set. He forced Richardson to admit that the altered set was directly consistent with his handwritten demand submitted to Hillibrand at Rix.

Richardson had already admitted in deposition, a past dependence on Quaaludes, which he claimed he'd overcome. There was no evidence he entered any program. It was only his "strength of will" that ended it. Joe asked the defense to finally stipulate to the admissibility of the Americanada records they'd resisted up to then. The last thing MacCallum and Zale wanted to do was emphasize the importance of those records. They were aware the Americanada Ltd. representative who had been subpoenaed could be there the very next day, so they stipulated and waved off the records as if they were nothing. Joe confronted him with the records. Richardson tap danced.

"I realized that, even though the drug was a prescribed medication and that I kept it under control, there was always the potential for harm, so I simply ended it. I understand the manufacturer's records indicate some drugs being sent to the building, but I never received them after I quit. That was a couple years before Ms. Fletcher was my patient. I know there was another doctor in the hospital who used them, and I suppose they must have been sent on to him even after he left."

Joe started to address his objection to Judge Abelson, but before he could finish, the judge turned to the jurors. "Ladies and gentlemen of the jury, I'm sustaining the objection to that last supposition by the witness and instructing you to disregard it entirely." He turned to MacCallum. "Mr. MacCallum, please explain to your client the need to respond based on knowledge, not supposition and explain my ruling when you get a chance."

"Sorry your honor, I'll explain the problem to the witness."

In his examination, Joe didn't come near questioning the suspicious deaths of Mickens, Cooper and Hillibrand and risk a mistrial.

MacCallum gave Richardson the opportunity to explain how disappointed he was with Hillibrand and Fox's care of Myra Fletcher and their inaccurate record keeping. He explained that he gave Hillibrand and Fox an opportunity to clear up their errors on the record and that it wasn't for his benefit.

After Richardson finished, rehabilitated to a degree, Joe put on Karel, Quality Control and Rosen, Emergency Room. Rosen concisely laid out the medical events leading up to the death of Myra Fletcher and Karel admitted his meeting with Richardson after the Fletcher death.. Though the doctors tried to avoid emotion in their testimony, it was impossible, even for the stoic Rosen, to conceal the painful impact of his experience culminating in the death of Myra. He looked down rather than face the red eyed jurors as he recited the story. Karel denied suggesting Richardson clean up the "inaccurate" record.

Then Joe called the plaintiff's expert, Dr. Hyman Berg, a short, balding man in a dark blue blazer with gray slacks, a man with as much gravitas as Richardson, but much smaller. His experience included teaching at Johns

Hopkins, lecturing at national AMA conventions and writing extensively on D&C, his special area of expertise.

It was striking, the close and logical connection between Karel's and Rosen's factual observations and the conclusions of Berg. He analyzed the medical records, both the original, actual records and the phonies dictated by Richardson. Berg explained in detail what a D&C is and why it was necessary. He explained why the changes in the records were important, and in the process, destroyed Richardson's testimony. He connected his testimony to the authoritative literature already before the court and left little room to quibble.

"Any competent OB/GYN would have understood the patient can't be allowed to bleed indefinitely. Dr. Richardson violated the recognized standard of care in the profession. There was a significant blood loss, and the source of the bleeding is ordinarily discoverable. Surgery was essential to discover and end it. Dr. Richardson's procedure allowed the bleeding to go on day after day. More probably than not, based on reasonable medical certainty, Myra Fletcher would be alive today if Dr. Richardson had done what was required. The real medical records show the progressive decline resulting from the loss of blood and consistent with the loss. Dr. Richardson's substituted records are inconsistent with the course of Myra Fletcher's decline and death."

MacCallum went after Berg with innuendo, sarcasm and insults Joe had never seen before. It seemed the harder MacCallum tried, the calmer and firmer Berg became. MacCallum elicited Berg's process of deciding which cases to take as an expert witness. He explained he would testify for either a plaintiff patient or defendant doctor if called upon. But he frequently wasn't hired to testify when his opinion was contrary to the party who hired him. MacCallum's cross-examination was the whipped cream and cherry on top of the direct. Through his efforts, McCallum established that Berg was a fair and unbiased professional. Zale whispered something to MacCallum who decided to stop abruptly.

"Thank you Doctor. That should be enough."

After Zale saw what Berg did to MacCallum, he asked to adjourn a few minutes early. He suspected any further cross examination would only augment Berg's stature and opinions. Berg seemed such a steady, calm and thoughtful man, attacking him appeared vain and abusive. Berg had obviously heard it all before and was ready. All Zale's prep work reading Berg's testimony in other cases had warned him. Now he saw it live. The man was good.

CHAPTER FORTY FOUR

Joe let Nelda know he'd put her first on the stand for the second day of trial. When the bailiff seated the jury, and the judge was ready, Joe sent Mike out to get her. He saw her nervously twisting her fingers out on the bench in the hallway, but she walked in as focused as any experienced witness. She knew her job and exuded confidence she would do it. Head held high, she grew in stature as she approached the witness stand. After the bailiff swore Nelda in, and as she started answering questions, she addressed herself to the jury. Anyone in the courtroom could see the connection she was making. She seemed to speak from the heart and connected her facts to the records. As she spoke of Myra, the baby and Herb, she was determined not to cry and yet showed her emotional depth, open and believable. Before trial, Joe considered a risk the jurors would believe she slanted her testimony in favor of the plaintiff, but he opted for ease and honesty as a better approach than a false sort of control. He hoped the jurors were within range of her emotional strength. Because Joe had seen her in action before trial, he counted on it.

She testified simply to the horrible night Myra died. Then she explained Lois' precautions to save the original hospital record from extinction by making copies. She avoided the objectionable reason for the precautions. Rather than talk about the "conspiracy," Nelda only said she wanted to be sure the original could be proven in court. With a firm and dominant voice, she testified to Richardson's demand that she support his fictional offer to do a D&C, right at that moment looking directly at Richardson himself. The jury turned to see him sitting frozen and staring angrily at his hands. Then Joe went into her observations of Myra's pain and suffering, both physical and emotional. The jury was in her hands. It was as though they were in the hospital, seeing the pain through their own eyes. Joe knew that was the perfect time to pass the witness to MacCallum.

He had damaged himself trying to carve up Berg, and now MacCallum, applying the same technique on Nelda, continued falling short as a trial lawyer. She didn't overdo the anger. She simply focused it. She answered on target and swatted away his spears and broadswords. MacCallum's frustration showed, and Joe, with satisfaction, watched Richardson now trying to redirect MacCallum's questions, whispering in his ear and writing notes. MacCallum tried to ignore him while Richardson reddened. Zale leaned over toward MacCallum and whispered something. MacCallum nodded, then asked to approach the judge. He requested a "short recess." Joe knew it would be granted. It dawned on him that Abelson might need to create a record showing the Court of Appeals how he bent over backwards to be fair to the defense. If the case went up on appeal, Joe would need that record for ammunition. Abelson directed the recess and the two defense attorneys walked out.

In a few minutes, they walked back in, and after Abelson reconvened, MacCallum announced he had no more questions. He hadn't finished the examination, but he understood he had to end anyway. It was obvious Zale had told him during the recess, he was alienating the jury. Zale stepped up to take his turn, avoiding MacCallum's style of cross-examination. He wondered why anyone thought MacCallum was a clever trial lawyer. His cross examination did more harm to the defense than Gold's direct. Zale didn't care whether he taught MacCallum how to cross examine, but he certainly saw what wasn't working. Zale walked up respectfully close to Nelda, not so close as to raise an objection.

"Miss Fox, I wanted to ask how you felt about the baby, Melissa. Am I correct, you felt some grief that she'd lost her mother?"

"Yes, that was terribly sad."

"You have no children?"

"No."

"Any time you were in the presence of this little girl, your arms wanted to pick her up?

"Yes, that's true. She was so small and helpless. I think babies need to be held, and I'm a nurse."

"You're a nurse because you care for people who are hurt?"

"Yes."

"You have feelings for these people?"

"Yes."

"You sympathized with Mr. Fletcher because he lost his wife?"

"That's true."

"Could you see him suffering grief?"

"Yes."

"And he needed comforting?"

"Yes, I'm sure he did, but not in the same way as the baby. He wasn't a helpless child."

"No, he had grown-up male needs?"

"You mean romance? That would be horrible. If you think he wanted that kind of thing when Myra died, you couldn't be further from reality. I didn't get the least sense he wanted any kind of romance at all. The most I could give was a shoulder to cry on. He was devastated beyond my capability."

"You gave him your shoulder, sort of the grown-up version of the comfort you gave the baby?"

"Sort of."

"So now, here we are in a court, and you're a witness. You still want to comfort Mr. Fletcher?"

"You mean as a witness? That I want to help him with my testimony? Yes, absolutely. I came here to tell what happened. I wanted to be sure the jury knew the truth, not to help Mr. Fletcher, but because it's the truth. If he needed lies to help him, I wouldn't want to help him."

Later on, Zale would marvel at what a great witness Nelda was. Right at that moment, he needed something better to end on. He had a nice picture of Nelda and Herb Fletcher hugging in front of the Fletcher house. When Zale and MacCallum obtained the picture, they figured they had the stick to beat Nelda with. He planned to ease into it and throw it in front of her face when he had her all set up.

"Do you ever imagine yourself married to Mr. Fletcher, raising Melissa as your own?"

"No, I shut my eyes and imagine Mr. Fletcher married to Myra, raising Melissa. That would be so beautiful. But, it can't happen, and it breaks my heart, so I try not to think about it."

She couldn't help it. Despite her efforts, little droplets spilled out of the corners of her eyes. Zale would have liked the judge to chastise Nelda for her decent display of human emotion, but then the sober, dignified judge was looking a little misty himself. And some members of the jury were fighting back their own tears. Zale wanted so badly to introduce the photograph of Nelda with Fletcher, but his senses told him, if he tried to make use of it the way he intended, the jury would hate him forever. He jammed the photograph down to the bottom of his briefcase. The most he could do for his case now was to get Nelda off the witness stand as fast as possible. He was kicking himself for doing, if anything, worse than MacCallum.

Boy, I sure taught MacCallum how to do it. I'm fried.

Joe, feeling good about Nelda's performance, called Nadine LeDoux, Myra's mother, a bespectacled, slender, black woman in a neat gray suit, and she stepped forward leaning slightly on a cane. A retired school teacher, she had the aura of an elderly, professional woman, with her neat, dark, conservative dress, her horn rimmed glasses and gray hair. MacCallum felt a hormonal instinct to get tough, make an issue of her black son-in-law having an affair with the young white nurse her daughter had trusted. Earlier, MacCallum mentioned to Zale that when his turn came, he thought he could drive a wedge between her and Nelda that way. Zale had been as firm and pointed as he could be. He reminded MacCallum, they had rejected that. Now he quietly, under his breath, gave his final warning to MacCallum.

"You come at that bereaved woman who's lost her daughter, and the jury will kill you if I don't do it first. You've had a reputation for common sense, but I don't see it. If that's your idea, you drop it or you'll be finished. They'll fire you and you'll deserve it."

"Lay off. I understand. I'd like to go after her, but I won't."

"Honestly, MacCallum, you scare me. I can guarantee somebody, someday on a jury is going to hate you and bury you by burying your client."

Mrs. LeDoux, still on direct, ignored Zale's whispered rancor, but the jury could see something was going on. At Joe's prompting, she recited her child's accomplishments. Joe was aware, but hearing it recited in court was still as overwhelming for Joe as it was for the jury: Senior Ball Queen, high school straight As, National Merit Scholar, high school graduation a year early, charity work, student mentoring, field hockey, interscholastic debate. There were letters of appreciation from the Red Cross and the YWCA. It was incomprehensible the young girl could have done as much as she had. She could have made anything of her life she wanted, but first came love and family. She and Herb agreed she'd get her college degree as fast as parental duties allowed.

Zale didn't intend questioning any of it. Joe had pre-marked certified school records, and without objection Abelson pre-admitted them. Only a fool of a defense lawyer would spotlight them in front of the jury. Mrs.

LeDoux refused to break down in court. She held her handkerchief tightly, ready to wipe away the tears if she couldn't fight them back. She struggled in full view of the jury, and she was winning until the end.

"There is so much Myra could have done if she'd survived Dr. Richardson's treatment. I can't ask for anything for myself, but Herb and my little granddaughter, Melissa, have lost a wonderful wife and mother. And Seattle has lost a wonderful future community leader." Suddenly Mrs. LeDoux's control broke and her tears flowed freely until the handkerchief dammed them up.

Zale observed the jury, even the Boeing engineer, gripped in Mrs. LeDoux's understandable agony. MacCallum wanted to make some objection but feared Zale would knock him flat right there in court. He wisely kept his silence as Mrs. LeDoux struggled with her pain. Herb jumped up and helped her away as soon as the defense waived their cross-examination.

Joe saw Dr. Halloran come in during the recess. He had a notepad and was writing as Joe approached him. When he saw Joe coming he waved Joe off.

"Sorry, I can't talk to you now, maybe later."

Joe wanted to ask why, but Halloran looked away firmly. Halloran apparently didn't want to display any kinship with a plaintiff's attorney in front of his Woodside colleagues. When he walked away, Herb asked Joe how they were doing. Joe didn't want to raise expectations which could turn out to be overoptimistic vanity and misleading, after defense witnesses testified.

"Like I told you, the Americanada Ltd. records, Dr. Berg's testimony and Nelda's testimony might be enough to win the case, but the defense hasn't put on its case yet. I don't want you to be declaring victory. I'm counting on you to make Myra a real person to the jury. And I'm really counting on you to destroy any suggestion that there was something going on between you and Nelda. Just be honest and be yourself."

Chapter Forty Five

Because mid-afternoon was too early for Abelson to end the case for the day, and MacCallum and Zale needed to confer to rebuild their collapsing case, they asked Joe to join them and talk to the judge. Joe only agreed to meet in chambers, and Abelson agreed to talk. He fundamentally opposed sending a jury home early, but the plaintiff was moving faster than anyone could have expected. The defense attorneys pressed Abelson with the notion they had sped it up by waiving a lot of cross examination. The judge restrained the impulse to tell them the speed was a result of their cross examination causing more harm than good to the defense. Joe urged the judge to keep the case moving.

"Your Honor, I only have a couple more witnesses, and then the defense will have all the time they need to present their case. The defense has had ample time to prepare, and the strain on Ms. Fox and Mr. Fletcher is enormous. The jury doesn't know what they've had to put up with. You don't have to decide that Dr. Richardson did what we suspect. You just have to understand the fear Fox and Fletcher are suffering every day, and especially, every night."

"I understand, counsel, but the defense has had a rough day, and I should give them a chance to regroup. We'll come back tomorrow. You present your witnesses, and then it's the defense's turn." Joe silently wondered why the defense deserved an extraordinary break. Because they were screwing up?

While Joe explained Abelson's decision to Herb, Zale whispered to the hospital CEO, Tobin, that they needed to settle as fast as possible, and

MacCallum tried to tell Richardson substantially the same thing. Zale led Tobin and Brad Hultgren of Hosp-Pro Insurance into a conference room in the King County Library on the sixth floor.

"We're not doing real well. Honestly, every one of the plaintiff's witnesses has come across strong. My cross examination just makes them sound better. The best Richardson can do is just dig his hole deeper. I'd like to sound the plaintiff out for settlement again. Come to think of it, we need to sound Med-West out too. Their hole is deeper than ours."

Tobin wanted to salvage something. "Whatever the amount is, it should be paid by Med- West. It was Richardson, not us."

"Sure, but you guys ignored Richardson's addiction and covered up for him. The jury could give as big an award against you as it does against him."

Tobin huffed and snorted.

"That's their argument, but they don't have proof. Just saying it doesn't prove it."

"Franklin, they've had testimony, and I wouldn't be surprised if the plaintiff finished with a big attack on the 'conspiracy of silence.' We can argue about it with MacCallum and Med-West but good luck."

Kevin and Cora Richardson and Howard Stenzel, Rep of Med-West, met with MacCallum in the conference room at McCallum's office in the Smith Tower on the 30th floor and ignored the street life view of Pioneer Square. This meeting was the flip side of Zale's conference. They discussed how to drag some money out of Hosp-Pro. Cora, who saw the disastrous cross examination, showed her contempt for MacCallum.

"How many times do we have to go through this? We aren't going to settle. If you lose the case, you should pay the judgment. Little Nelda isn't as innocent as she plays it. The jury can see through her act. She'll marry Fletcher just as soon as he collects. It's obvious."

Stenzel, not wanting to make an enemy for Med-West, restrained the impulse to say what he thought to Cora.

Your husband is a lying, cheating scum, and we never should have insured him. And I can see where he gets his moral guidance.

Instead, he narrowed the argument down to dollars and cents.

"We initially figured this case could settle at $1,000,000, but you've seen it double in value throughout the trial. If we could settle for $1,500,000, I'd grab it. We should get a half million from Hosp-Pro on top of our $1,000,000. I can try to get more from them, but our bargaining position stinks."

Richardson jumped at him. "What about that 'conspiracy of silence' stuff? Everything bad the hospital can say about me is their responsibility. The hospital says it's every doctor's partner and then they cover up everything that goes on there. They should cover the loss."

"Sorry, Kevin, you're in no position to make that argument. They didn't counterclaim against us, but the jury could dump the whole load on us anyway, and if the verdict exceeds the coverage it could bankrupt you. Then, there's no way we can force Gold to look to the hospital for even a penny of it. If we can settle, you won't have a jury decision that you were negligent. Doesn't that concern you? Your name will become a swear word. You worry so much about your 'good name', you should fear a verdict against you."

Before Richardson could answer, the phone rang. MacCallum went to his office to take the call. He came back looking somber.

"Zale talked to Gold already. His bottom line is now $2.5 million, and they still insist that no matter what, there will be no agreement for confidentiality."

Hearing that provoked Richardson to argue. "I remember when we first met, you promised that confidentiality would be an absolute demand.

266

We have to have that or we can't settle. There's no benefit to us. We'll be ruined. If the stuff we kept out goes to the press, my wife will kill me."

Cora seconded that. "Without confidentiality we won't be able to face our friends, and no one will allow us in their homes. You don't realize. We're somebody in this community. That's more important than your money. We've paid a fortune in premiums over the years. You can pay now, but don't you dare ruin us."

"Suit yourself. I fear what the next thing from Gold will be. If the jury awards anything over policy limits, that's on you. Just let me make some calls."

When the calls ended, the Richardsons got in the ornate, ancient Smith Tower elevator cage, and the uniformed operator took them down. The Richardsons marveled that two million dollars from the insurance companies and hospital might be available, but that money meant nothing to Fletcher.

Richardson's last words to Stenzel and MacCallum had been, "Without complete confidentiality, we don't settle."

The case would go on.

Chapter Forty Six

With the defense refusing to settle, Joe decided to finish the plaintiff's case with Herb. Joe got up from the counsel table, carefully pushed the chair back into place and approached the witness. When the bailiff asked if he swore to tell the truth, Herb looked directly at the jury and answered with a strong, "I do." First, Joe gave Herb a chance to describe his athletic career and the engineering degree he received at Louisiana State. While in college, he met and fell in love with Myra, who had just graduated high school early and with honors. He identified their scrapbook chronicling her triumphs and their wonderful times together. They got married while she was seventeen, and she immediately became pregnant. Herb testified to Myra's complete trust of Richardson, though Herb had told her his doubts. He finished his testimony by discussing how unprepared he was to raise a baby. "I don't know how to do it, but I'll do whatever it takes. One thing I won't do is get married just to provide a mother for the baby." He showed the jury the picture of Myra with the baby and described the loving scene they could all understand. Again he looked directly at the jury, and saw them wiping their eyes.

Herb expected a nasty cross-examination about his relationship with Nelda. He didn't know it, but Zale had demanded the reckless MacCallum leave that cross-examination to him. Zale, not wanting to inspire even more sympathy to the plaintiff, cautiously limited the inquiry. He politely went into a discussion of how helpful Herb had been to Nelda: the job at Costello Construction and the apartment at White Center. He chanced asking how devoted a nurse Nelda Fox was to Melissa. Herb admitted Nelda expressed a lot of affection for the baby and seemed to feel she owed

THE LAST DROP OF BLOOD

Melissa a lot just because she'd been on duty when Myra died. Zale ended by tiptoeing around the relationship between Herb and Nelda again and the word "love," but the jury must have gotten it. They could only draw one conclusion. Whatever you called it, there was something between Herb and Nelda. It was something Zale could argue. Joe couldn't see past the jurors' eyes to know if it affected Nelda's credibility. When Zale finished, the plaintiff rested and the court was about to take a break.

As soon as the jury went out, Zale addressed the Court: "Your Honor I'd like to make a motion to challenge the sufficiency of the evidence at this time."

Joe calmly assumed the defense would make its routine motion in the jury's absence. He doubted Zale expected to win on the motion, but he risked nothing by trying it. The motion is granted only if the plaintiff's evidence, if believed, does not present a sufficient case under the law. If the motion is justified, there is nothing for a jury to consider, and if it's granted the case ends. But, the motion, made in open court, might be reported in the press and could get to the jury despite the judge's instructions. Joe didn't have the nerve to ask that the motion be heard in chambers because that would be rejected and also could be reported.

Zale rose and stepped to the bar. He opened the argument by raving about Richardson's honors and distinctions then attacked Dr. Berg. "The witness, relying on Texas, not Washington practice, has no testimony that the jury can rely on to establish Dr. Richardson's duty under Washington law." He went on to assert that, "Miss Fox didn't have the authority to replace the actual hospital records with the drafts in her possession which had no official status. Fox isn't the hospital custodian of records. The claim of negligence has no basis, because there are no reliable records." He attacked the consumer protection claim, based on the failure to prove the reliability of the records and that, "there is no evidence the hospital agreed to any conspiracy or alteration of its records."

McCallum restrained his overheated impulses and mostly echoed Zale. But he added, "If Dr. Richardson had asked for a change in the records, it wouldn't be an unfair and deceptive business practice. It's only one case so doesn't establish a 'practice' and therefor a consumer protection issue. Furthermore, the hospital isn't his business. Changes in its records aren't a consumer protection breach by him."

Judge Abelson responded before Joe could rise: "These are points of argument to the jury, not to the Court. The motion will be denied."

The judge had made the routine denial of the routine motion. It forced MacCallum and Zale to put on a defense. The two insurance companies decided they had no choice. Richardson, the Woodside doctors and the hospital insisted there was no such a thing as a "conspiracy of silence." Herb demanded they admit it existed, a key settlement demand and one of the main obstacles to settlement. The other, Richardson's refusal to admit any fault.

MacCallum had lost his enthusiasm for putting Richardson on the witness stand. The two defense attorneys determined their last hope to win was to defeat Nelda. The last thing they wanted to do was put her on the witness stand again, but they just didn't have a choice. If MacCallum hoped to salvage his case, he had to try again to undermine her credibility without angering the jury.

Nelda knew the defense intended to target her. Joe made that absolutely clear. Though she nailed it in her direct testimony, she still nervously fidgeted, and they were wearing her down. She tried to stay away from Herb, and couldn't lean on him during the trial. And it wasn't easy. But she still forced herself to concentrate.

What can they ask that they haven't already asked? I have to talk to mom.

Before she went to the courthouse that morning, she picked up the phone, needing somebody's support. She called her mom. "Nelda, I'm having breakfast. If I could help you, I would, but I can't help you. Just relax, and do what you have to do. Like I've told you before, it's not your case. All you can do is tell the truth and hope for the best. They can't put you in jail for that."

When she put the phone back down, Nelda didn't feel any better. She lay staring at the ceiling and could see nothing but Myra lying in bed looking up at her. Exhaustion didn't help Nelda's stress level. She struggled through the previous day's combat. Now to do it again? When the clock finally told her it was okay to get up, she went through the mechanics of showering, dressing, breakfast and getting to the courthouse on the floor of Joe's car. She brought all that exhaustion and stress to court along with a fierce determination to do the best she could for Herb and the baby.

* * * * * *

Called as a defense witness, Nelda did well under attack from the beginning. On direct, she ignored the innuendo and returned to the facts calmly: the effort to get Richardson to the bedside, Myra's decline as her blood flowed out, the accelerated blood flow and Rosen's last desperate effort to save her. She gave a simple recital of the facts supported by the true medical records. MacCallum tried to paper over Richardson's mood swings attributed to his drug use. Nelda stayed firm. If he'd broken his addiction, his behavior didn't show it.

If MacCallum inquired into why she hid out and secretly went to work for Costello construction, he would be asking for trouble. Joe had explained to her why the evil deeds, even murders, weren't appropriate for her direct testimony in the plaintiff's case. The direct testimony was reserved for proving Richardson's malpractice and the resulting death. Joe was explicit. If the defense wanted to inquire about the reasons for her fear, she could tell it all, the whole story. The defense, if they knew what was good for them, shouldn't ask. If they opened the door, she was ready to step in, but Joe directed Nelda not to overstep.

The examination started low key, but gradually MacCallum moved closer and got a little more aggressive and louder. "You voluntarily prepared medical records you, yourself admit are untrue?"

"No, Lois Hillibrand said Dr. Richardson was demanding a change, and she said we couldn't refuse. I was working under Lois' direction, and

271

she gave me a copy of the true records and of the doctor's draft of the change he wanted. Then, as I said before, Dr. Richardson wanted me to falsify the records yet again, claiming I was present when he offered to do a quick surgery to stop the bleeding. But I'd never been present when he said anything like that to either Mrs. or Mr. Fletcher. And I didn't witness any refusal either. He got angry when I refused to lie."

MacCallum moved to strike what he called "the non-responsive part of the answer", but Abelson denied the objection. Zale understood the signal to MacCallum. Abelson would allow the answer to include some testimony that explained the answer to the question. After all, Joe could have brought out the additional information on cross so, the judge would reason, why waste time? MacCallum didn't need the judge to explain his ruling. He could see it coming, but it seemed everywhere he could put Nelda on defense ran the risk of giving her a free shot in the same way. He knew the box he was in but dared to take chances, even dumb ones.

Nelda got stronger until they got to the relationship with Herb again. She'd handled it once and could do it the way she did before. McCallum decided he had to chance it, no matter how angry Zale was going to be. "You've seen this photograph of you leaving Herb Fletcher's home?"

"Yes."

"Nobody there but you and Fletcher?"

"And the baby, Melissa."

"You went there often?"

"Just the one time."

"Did you have a nice time that day, you and Herb?"

"I came to visit the baby. I worried so much about her. She'd lost her mother, and I felt so awful I couldn't do anything for her."

"So you made up for it with Herb?"

"I don't understand your question. Herb let me pick up Melissa and hold her in my arms. She was looking up at me and cooing. All I could think of was, she would never know her mother. You think I did something bad with Herb? How can you?"

She fought back the anger, but heard her voice getting shrill and her eyes getting red and moist, and, the tears were ready to go. She was losing control. Joe leaped up, appealing to the judge. Abelson was ready for it. He pounded the gavel to quiet the courtroom.

"We'll take a recess. Counsel, we'll meet in chambers."

When they got in chambers the judge looked at Joe.

"You'll have to get your client together. I haven't heard an improper question yet. I know it's repetitious and ugly, but Mr. MacCallum can inquire again in his case. Next time she gets upset, I'm not going to grant a recess. If Mr. MacCallum crosses the line, I'll let him know it, but warn her. She'll have to get a grip. If she doesn't, I'll just let the questions and answers go on. I'm not going to bail her out next time, unless counsel oversteps."

Turning to MacCallum, he said, "You be careful you don't cross the line. If you do, I promise you'll pay for it, right?"

Before Nelda got back on the witness stand, Joe warned her to be ready for the nastiness and get control. She nodded her head somberly, her eyes still red. Now MacCallum, thinking he'd got to her, went after her with an aggressive, probing style, eliciting her admission that she considered herself part of the plaintiff's case. She volunteered she had feelings for Herb, not romantic feelings, sympathy for his loss and the burden of raising a baby by himself.

She admitted she'd hid in the home of Herb's attorney, and she'd discussed her expected testimony with him and how to answer. Richardson had a smug grin on his face, thinking that MacCallum had drawn blood, thinking a little grinning display on his part would help them with the jury. MacCallum noticed and whispered, "Cut that out." Despite his own questionable tactics, he chided his client that being obnoxious wasn't the way to win the jury. MacCallum questioned Nelda's honesty in using the alias "Linda" to get a job and then abandoning nursing. She admitted she'd been warned nobody would hire her if they knew her background.

Zale, more circumspect than MacCallum, only pretended he was cross examining. He dragged it out to the point of boredom. When he finally let her go, he hoped nobody would remember what she'd said an hour before. That was as much as he could hope for. From Zale's perspective, nobody would blame him for losing the case. He still had to be able to hold his head up after this train wreck had been hauled away. The profession and the public would blame MacCallum, if anyone.

When Zale ended, Joe drew out Nelda's reasons for hiding out without getting into specifics that would risk a mistrial. She only said she feared Richardson, but not why, only "some things she heard." The door had been slightly opened by MacCallum, but not enough. Joe reasoned, Herb was winning. Why risk a mistrial? Nelda had done well.

When Nelda got off the witness stand, Abelson adjourned for the day. Everyone else had left when Joe and Herb walked out. Halloran suddenly appeared from down the hall where no one would notice him, and he rapidly approached so as to catch Joe before he left.

"I've been thinking about what I'm going to say, and I'd like to call you tonight. I think I want you to put me on the witness stand tomorrow morning, okay?"

Joe looked at him quizzically. "But we've rested our case. Maybe I can call you for rebuttal, but I don't know what you're going to say."

"Give me your number, and I'll call you tonight." Joe nodded his head, wrote down the number and left with Herb and Mike.

* * * * * *

274

Kelly Halloran had been debating himself. On one hand, this was not his battle. He could stand by, innocently pretending he didn't know Richardson was still as addicted to Quaaludes as he'd ever been. He could forget that the doctors had met to discuss the benefit to them of remaining silent in the face of their guilty knowledge. He could maintain his successful practice and his reputation for integrity, exaggerated though it might be. Fletcher was going to win, as he should, but what about the future patients, like Myra, who might not even know what happened to them?

He hated facing the unforgiving mirror every day when he shaved. He raised his children to be honest and courageous. Someday they would find out what a phony their father was, and they would have to share an intolerable shame. He'd become aware, years ago, how Richardson escaped the consequences of so many of his personal failings. Truth became a fragile thing, and Halloran finally faced it. He had to discuss it over the dinner table with his wife, Lynn. The children had grown and moved out. It was just the two of them there, alone. Halloran always discussed his deepest problems with his wife. When he came to grips with a dilemma and needed her support, she could sense it. He had his favorite turkey and stuffing with gravy and yams sitting in front of him, untouched that night. He sat there with a fork in one hand and a knife in the other poised to attack the dinner, yet motionless. What would he tell Joe Gold?

"What is it, Kelly? I thought you decided. It's the trial isn't it? You know you're in the right, but now you're starting to worry about what those liars are going to say. Don't you dare come home and tell me that you chickened out for those characters. Those aren't the swell guys at the cocktail parties when one of them is cornered. Are you one of them? You need to hear it from me?"

He laughed nervously. "This is going to be good. They're so sure they're in charge, and they are so dumb about this stuff. I can't let this pass. I've been sitting on the fence for too long."

"You're right finally, but the others need to know what's coming. Make them line up with you. When Richardson loses and gets kicked out of the practice, you don't want to be pointed out as the one who did it to him. Explain to them this silence stuff is coming to an end sooner or later. If it continues at Woodside, maybe no outside doctor will refer patients to any of you there, and maybe you all could face discipline. I want you to stand tough, but I don't want you to be all alone. You need to talk to the other guys on the staff, warn them."

* * * * * *

Those were nasty dilemmas that Lynn posed him, and he hated to confront the people who could stand up with him. He got on the phone. Rosen and Karel agreed to meet him at Rix. Rosen looked up from an isolated corner table when Halloran arrived. Soon Karel showed up, but they sat quietly until a waitress finally came by. The two others wanted dinner, and without looking at the menu, ordered the sirloin. The delay proved they didn't have Richardson's clout. Halloran settled for a Rainier beer.

Rosen and Karel were preoccupied with the war they'd be facing if they said what they knew about Richardson and he were found to be negligent. Halloran's conscience was neither common in the profession nor welcome. Rosen earnestly fixed a glare on him and didn't make personal honesty his highest priority.

"If Richardson goes, it can happen to any of us. He's the most prominent M.D. at Woodside. The reputation of all of us depends on the outcome of this case."

"Really, Alex? I sure hope not. He's lucky he isn't facing homicide charges, don't you think?"

Karel and Rosen began heating up. Frowning, they looked at each other, and Karel couldn't contain himself.

"You don't know that, and you'd better shut up about it. You start talking like that and God knows what it can lead to."

Halloran still remained staunch. They hadn't salved his attack of personal integrity.

"It's no joke." Rosen was leaning across the table. "You better think this through. You're either with us or against us. We've been worrying that you'll start spouting that 'conspiracy of silence' stuff. Neither you nor I have anything we can say about Richardson. We all have to keep our mouths shut when all they have is supposition."

Halloran wasn't about to sit quietly and take it. Looking at Karel he said, "Elliott, I know how the records got changed after the Fletcher girl died." To Rosen it was, "I know what you saw that night. All three of us know Richardson is unfit to practice medicine, and he sure as hell hasn't recovered from the addiction. I don't care what he says. When the jurors look at the Americanada Ltd. records, they'll see that there was no reduction in Quaalude orders after Martens left for Colorado. So don't bullshit me. We can't save Richardson. If you want to go down when he does, go ahead. I'll decline the invitation."

Karel spluttered with indignation. "We've stood by Kevin, and you want to destroy him. You are a real bastard. But you know what? We'll keep our hospital privileges, and you're going to lose yours."

What upset Karel and Rosen most was Halloran remaining so calm and steady in the face of their mania. He sipped his beer, still waiting to hear a respectable reason to abandon his duty as he saw it. Their inability to justify their position strengthened his.

"Guys, don't waste your energy trying to sway me. It isn't going to happen. I'm sure you're saying what Richardson would want you to say, but the best thing for you is to back off right now. I don't want to hurt you, but I talked to a lawyer. I knew this was coming. If I took you seriously, I'd conclude you are guilty of conspiracy to commit perjury and aiding and abetting negligent homicide. If I were to lose my hospital privileges, I'd sure have to remember this little chat. I thought I could talk some sense into you, but if you think you're better off standing by Richardson, you may find out differently and soon."

Having tired of the steak, Rosen angrily slammed a wad of bills on the table and shoved himself away from it. Karel jumped up right behind him, glaring at Halloran, who showed no surprise or even any discomfort.

As they walked out, Halloran, under his breath, whispered, "Say hi, to Kevin for me."

* * * * * *

As soon as he returned from Rix, Halloran called Joe Gold at home.

"Put me on. Go into my emergency room background and the blood loss articles I wrote. Berg had it nailed, and I'll support him. Ask me about Richardson's mood swings and how they appeared. Ask if those mood swings changed over the years and if they changed when Richardson said he'd stopped taking Quaaludes. I won't disappoint you. Ask about the 'conspiracy of silence' at Woodside. I just got home from a little visit with Rosen and Karel. I warned them what was coming."

"Okay, Kelly, you'll be a rebuttal witness when the defense finishes."

Kelly Halloran decided he just didn't give a damn anymore. For years he'd let Woodside doctors take care of each other to the harm of patients, and now he had to atone. Joe, impressed with Halloran's courage, thanked him for standing up for the truth. "I appreciate that, Kelly, but what about the other guys, Karel and Rosen? Are they going to come around?"

"No, they will continue to lie their butts off. They threatened my hospital privileges, and I warned them they had a problem and not to try to mess with me. See you tomorrow"

The next morning was Richardson's last chance on the witness stand. MacCallum thought back to his youth when he worked in a carwash and as a grocery delivery boy. This wasn't better. He sometimes hated having to take the clients and cases handed to him, no matter how corrupt and evil. Richardson was his first witness that day. With great trepidation, he gave one more reminder to Richardson. "I don't know how much medication you've had, but whatever it was, this is your last chance to demonstrate you have enough self-control to be a doctor. Whatever else you do, don't lose your temper in front of the jury."

The background and personal history questions were easy. Richardson loved to talk about his high school valedictorian days, his brilliant, undergrad Baccalaureate career, the number one in Harvard med school and the Johns Hopkins internship and residency. There was no mystery why he became a commanding presence in Seattle. When he was young he would have commanded respect anywhere.

Unfortunately, MacCallum had to move on to the death of Myra Fletcher and Richardson's peculiar behavior. They'd already heard the plaintiff's side of the story. Now Richardson could tell his side.

"Doctor, what caused "Myra Fletcher's death?"

This was the opening door, and Richardson was primed. "It was awful when I found out. I knew that there'd been a little bleeding, and just to be on the safe side, I'd suggested a D&C. It's a fairly routine procedure, and I'd done hundreds over the years. Sometimes they're helpful and sometimes not. But the Fletchers were against it, so I couldn't do it. I suspected they were trying to save money. Still, Mrs. Fletcher did alright until that night. While I rested in the doctors' lounge after a busy day, Nurse Hillibrand contacted me for a prescription for Fletcher. The bleeding had bumped up a little, so I told her to keep me informed. Unfortunately, she left and her replacement had a car accident. I didn't know anything about it. Poor Mrs. Fletcher was left with a young nurse, Nelda Fox. She didn't call me and didn't call the ER until too late. Myra bled out while Nurse Fox was cleaning up the blood."

"Did anyone make corrections to the hospital records?"

"Yes, Nurse Hillibrand wanted the records corrected. I think she was a little embarrassed at Fox's record keeping and performance, and I okayed some corrections Lois requested."

"Now Doctor, some people have talked about a 'conspiracy of silence' at Woodside. Do you know what that is?"

"Well, I know what some people say, but it isn't true. Nobody wants to cover up bad medicine at Woodside. There isn't a conspiracy."

Joe looked at the judge, the jury and then over to Zale. Two jurors had their arms folded in front of their chests, a defensive gesture. A couple were looking around as if seeking a way out. Zale's head was bowed as if praying for deliverance. Joe admired Abelson's capacity for stoicism, rejecting any response at all, neither skeptic nor naïf, ready to rule in the event of any objection.

Joe let the defense testimony go on without objection. Richardson had a right to tell his story, even if contrary to common sense and all the other evidence. He demonstrated his calm, medicated behavior and avoided any tantrum. Joe hoped the jury saw the contrast from the unmedicated condition. Joe planned to give Halloran his chance right after lunch. As Richardson wound down, exonerating himself, Joe whispered to Mike, sitting next to him, and Mike agreed. He'd waive his cross examination. He'd already done all the damage he could, and further cross would be boring and redundant. A little before the noon hour hit, Mike reported to Joe that Karel and Tobin were waiting in the hall. Maybe Rosen had declined to testify and had an honest bone in his body. It looked like Halloran would have to wait to give his rebuttal.

MacCallum's last real hope before lunch, was that defense expert, Dr. Schwinn, could provide some help. He was a good-looking guy but so was Richardson. He testified as he had in the deposition, even though it wasn't believable, that the D&C was a judgment call of the OB/GYN. He walked himself right into the trap Joe had prepared for him. Joe had ready a certified transcript and had it marked by the clerk. When Joe confronted him with his own words in another case where he'd testified for the plaintiff, all he could say was, "Well, that was a totally different situation." He was left mumbling when Joe asked, "The difference was, who was paying you, right?" The jury had the lunch hour to digest that failed testimony.

When Abelson reconvened the court after lunch, Tobin stepped up next with his anticlimactic testimony. Tobin and Karel, in turn, denied the "conspiracy of silence." The defense was quick, perfunctory and pro-forma. Rosen never showed up. No need to cross. Halloran would deal out the truth in his rebuttal testimony.

The defense rested, and Joe started the rebuttal with Halloran's background and training, his emergency room experience and his professional writing. His testimony on blood loss nicely buttressed Dr. Berg, and he referenced Berg's observations, which he agreed with. Then came the question of his observations of Richardson.

"At the times Richardson admitted use of Quaaludes, his appearance was consistent with that use. He wasn't just calm but verging on sleepy. You could tell when he wasn't medicated. He couldn't control his temper. But after he claimed not to be using Quaaludes, even up to the present, the mood swings from anger to somnolence still continue, even up to the time of this trial. It is my medical opinion, based on observation and my years of training and practice, Dr. Richardson remains addicted to Quaaludes. His behavior on the evening Myra Fletcher died, as described by Miss Fox, was consistent with the effects of Quaaludes."

The jurors turned to look at Richardson, whose eyes were red, his fists visibly clenched, every muscle poised to charge away from his seat at the defense table. Anyone could see he was in turmoil, the perfect living exhibit illustrating Dr. Halloran's testimony. MacCallum grabbed his wrist, and Richardson forced himself back in the chair.

Having nailed Richardson on Quaaludes, Joe dared to ask Halloran about hospital meetings regarding Richardson's drug use. It was important that Richardson attended some of the meetings. They were evidence of his control of the other doctors. "Dr. Halloran, have you discussed 'the conspiracy of silence' with other doctors admitted to Woodside, in the presence of Dr. Richardson."

There came the explosion. MacCallum and Zale both leapt to their feet, objecting and demanding to discuss the objection in chambers. Abelson agreed and brought the court reporter. In chambers, the judge asked Joe to make his offer of proof to support the admissibility of the testimony.

"The witness will testify there were discussions in which Dr. Richardson was present, where it was agreed that the doctors would not disclose to anyone Dr. Richardson's addiction and its effects on his patient care and how it could have led to Mrs. Fletcher's death. The other doctors present will include CEO Tobin and Doctors Karel and Rosen. He will also discuss the 'conspiracy of silence' and state it is real and involved Richardson."

The defense attorneys tried to convince Judge Abelson they could provide overwhelming evidence to the contrary. Joe leaned forward and cleared his throat, prepared to respond, but the judge told him, "I don't need to hear any more. It comes in. He turned to the defense counsels. You can provide contrary testimony and argue the credibility and weight of it to the jury. Your objections don't go to admissibility, and you know it. I thought you had something significant. Don't waste the court's time."

When he got back on the witness stand, Halloran testified firmly. "At Woodside, the staff and I, including Dr. Tobin, Dr. Rosen, Dr. Karel and Dr. Richardson have, together, discussed Richardson's Quaalude addiction and the consequent need to all stick together any time his malpractice is asserted. We're supposed to be all one big, happy family. What hurts one doctor hurts all doctors and the hospital. We don't allow any of us to let on what we know about each other and in particular, Richardson. It's a 'conspiracy of silence', and it applies any time a doctor at Woodside is negligent, not just Richardson."

MacCallum, in his agitation, reflexively jumped up and called out "Objection." Judge Abelson calmly waited for a ground to be stated, and MacCallum took a stab. "That's a conclusion." Zale announced "I'll join that objection."

Judge Abelson addressed himself to the witness, "Denied. Continue."

Halloran, watching the judge as he spoke, now turned back to the jury. "The staff at Woodside talks openly among themselves about covering for each other. They try to justify it by saying the health care system requires that patients have trust and confidence. I have to admit that I've kept my mouth shut when I should have spoken up. Among ourselves, we discussed how to protect Dr. Richardson. He's refused to get help. He claims he's off the drugs, but it's obvious he's not."

"Did you agree with the other doctors?"

"In my heart I did not, but I went along with it. My conscience can't stand it anymore. We all have to be responsible for our failures and can't keep on covering up malpractice."

"Have you been threatened with punishment if you tell the truth?"

"Yes I've been warned by other doctors, I'd lose my hospital privileges."

"By whom?"

"By Franklin Tobin, Chairman of the Board and President, Quality Control Director, Elliot Karel and Emergency Room doc, Alex Rosen."

Richardson exploded, leaping up, walking rapidly out of the room in an undisguised rage. This was in full view of the jury with MacCallum and Zale unable to move. MacCallum had warned him to control himself, that his own behavior in court could prove the plaintiff's case. Here it was. Cross examination was futile after Richardson proved to the jury how unstable he was and, anyway, cross examination was curtailed by the clock. It was 4:00 PM, and MacCallum was grateful for that. He was thinking about Richardson's pistol and looked in his briefcase. It was still there. MacCallum couldn't think of any way to surreptitiously remove it and shut the case. Joe, watching Richardson's show with grim satisfaction, silently thanked him for making the blood and hair tests unnecessary.

With the court done for the day and the jury filing out, Judge Abelson asked the attorneys to step forward to the bench. Quietly, below the hearing of any others in the courtroom, the judge told MacCallum to get his client under control. "I'll warn you, I could censure him in view of the jury if he disrupts the court room. I don't want to, but I'm not going to allow a circus either."

MacCallum wasn't surprised. "Don't worry, your honor, I'll be sure he's on his best behavior, and he won't do anything stupid like that again. I apologize."

"Thank you, counsel. I'll rely on that."

When MacCallum got the fully medicated and calmed Richardson back to his office, he warned him that his display was certainly going to affect the case. "We really should settle, if we can settle anywhere near policy limits and save you from the potential of a really spectacular verdict."

Richardson smiled and said it would all be fine and that MacCallum shouldn't worry. He really didn't have anything more to say and decided he would just go home. The outburst and its aftermath brought home forcefully to MacCallum how violent the un-medicated Richardson could be and how irresponsible and lackadaisical the doctor was when he was medicated. This was why Myra Fletcher was dead. MacCallum felt a sick feeling in his gut and regretted representing this man. He hated that part of the profession but took one last stab before Richardson could leave.

"Doctor, if we can't settle this case it will only be worse. Some people will say you shouldn't be practicing medicine. If you don't voluntarily get treatment, I fear the state will take your license. Won't you listen to me?"

Richardson, as if he couldn't hear a word, grabbed the briefcase, the pistol still there, gave a cheery wave goodbye and was gone. Tobin and Karel waited outside in the reception area so MacCallum could speak freely and confidentially. Richardson was hardly out the door when they, ignoring him and uninvited, stormed in. Tobin, of course, was their leader.

"You have to put us on the stand. He's making us criminals."

"Richardson?"

"No, dammit, Halloran."

"You had your chance, and this isn't about you. Your problem is with the Washington State Health Department. What can you say that can help my case?"

Tobin didn't dare say what he was thinking. He would like to have said his reputation was what was important, but that would have ended the discussion. Their reputations were their problem. MacCallum ended it his way.

"Tell you what, if I can think of something you can say that isn't an obvious lie, I'll call you. Now let me work on it. Talk to you later, but thanks."

Chapter Forty Seven

With court done for the day, Mark Zale walked back to his office. Suffering his own apprehensions now, he couldn't care less what happened to Richardson, Tobin, Karel or even Rosen, who chickened out at the end. Zale's client was the hospital. But there was no way the hospital was going to win if the jury believed Richardson's addiction caused the death and Woodside was aware of the addiction. So, Zale knew it was over when the doctor displayed his illness in full view of the jury.

Furthermore, any chance of a reasonable settlement was long gone. Richardson had ended it forever. MacCallum's rough demeanor didn't help. Zale understood aggressiveness, and sometimes he used that strategy, but not when the plaintiffs are the surviving spouse of a young mother and the baby of the marriage. Herb Fletcher, clean, a likable and intelligent young man with a blameless infant, made a model plaintiff. You couldn't expect race prejudice would take the halo off him. You just don't go hard after a guy like that unless you've got him cold.

Then, on top of that, the key witness, Nelda Fox, stood up well to a nasty cross. Zale had to talk to MacCallum again. All he did was generate sympathy for the plaintiff. Back at his office, he called MacCallum, restraining the impulse to tell the younger attorney again what a rotten job he was doing. Zale pulled his punches for once.

"Look Larry, this isn't working. The tougher we get on the plaintiff's witnesses the better they look. This Gold kid has them nicely prepared. Christ, he anticipated everything. If I were Richardson, I'd bail out.

Realize what the jury could come in with. It can easily go way over policy limits, and he can be liable for any amount. He can end up in bankruptcy."

"I know, Mark, but what can I do? I reported it to the rep and Med-West warned Richardson about the coverage limits. Now he's completely blown any chance he ever had. They were already set to go to limits, but Richardson refused to settle, and there's no way to talk to him now. He's crazy, you know."

"So we're going to lose, and we're stuck with it?"

As soon as their little chat ended, Zale called Hultgren at Hosp-Pro Insurance. "Brad, I wish you could settle by yourself right now. If Fletcher would take it, even without Richardson, you could get out. Med-West would settle, but Richardson went nuts in court today. He really proved the plaintiff's case. You do what you want, but I'm telling you, I believe it's going over policy limits."

"Okay Mark, I'm sure you're right, but you know damn well they'd lose their claim against Richardson if they settled with us. They can't effectively settle with just one joint tortfeasor. I sat in for a little while today and saw how the plaintiff's witnesses handled cross examination, and I already heard how Richardson went crazy. But, we've already tried to settle. Woodside went over policy limits. The hospital is afraid of the Consumer Protection Act, and they have other big worries."

"Of course they do. Besides a possible loss going way over policy limits, they still think they have to protect negligent doctors. If the doctors' coverage goes up, they'll blame the hospital. This case is a real example of what a mistake it is to play dumb. The doctors think all they have to do is cover up for each other. I warned you, right?"

"Right, and they fear a front page verdict ruining the hospital's reputation."

When MacCallum hung up, his secretary ran in. She'd taken down in shorthand a message from Richardson. She was careful to write it out precisely as she knew MacCallum would demand. She didn't bother to knock, and her voice came out loud and shaky.

"He sounded like a crazy man. I told him to talk to you, but he refused to wait while I got you. This is really what he said, I mean word for word."

She showed him the frightening message she had taken down: "*You better get this straight. I'm only going to say it once. I can't stand what's happening. I'm not going to take it. I'm not going to let this go on. I know who's responsible. That someone is going to pay the price, understand? I'm going to do it, and no one can stop me. This is going to end on my terms. The way I want. I'm in charge.*"

MacCallum's frequent headaches, which started when he first met Richardson, had only gotten worse as the trial went on. They now hit the absolute limit. He wanted to lay his head down on the desk and forget everything, but he didn't have time to feel sorry for himself.

"All right. First call the police, then Cora Richardson. Tell her what Kevin said. It may be she was the 'responsible' person. He told me some things about her. Tell her to warn her father too. Richardson told me things about his father-in-law. Oh Jesus. Who else? Don't let me miss anyone I have to call."

He worked through the question he had to ask himself. Who did Richardson most hold responsible for his problems? He got on the phone to the Gold law firm, and the receptionist directed him to Diana, the only partner there at the time. She instantly recognized the emergency too and dropped the briefing she was doing. He read the message to her.

"He said what? He's going to do something to the person who was responsible? Responsible for what? He didn't say who he meant?"

"He didn't say. I didn't get a chance to talk to him. He just left the message with my secretary here. Tell your client. Oh my God. Call Nelda Fox. I don't know who else. Help me here. I really fear he'll do something awful."

The word traveled fast at the Gold Law Firm. Diana enlisted Jodi to call Nelda and track down Herb, Ed, Mike, Joe and Sandra. She instructed

Jodi to warn them that Richardson was threatening to do something to whomever he decided was responsible for his problems, and he didn't say who. Jodi was to warn them to get somewhere safe. It may be Richardson was out on the prowl.

Mike called Ed and Marie so Jodi didn't have to. Joe called Detective Tracy who was forced to ignore the fact that he was off the Richardson case. Immediately an APB was out on Richardson, and his red Corvette was soon on every patrol cop's mind. Diana, called an already terrified Sandra, who'd been unable to sleep since the failed home attack. They thought they'd drawn Richardson off and sent the guard away. But, that hadn't worked. Sandra cried at the thought that Richardson could still endanger her baby. Nelda took Sandra, left the house, got her into her car and drove with one eye on the rearview mirror. Sandra got some relief when Nelda, heading south on Aurora reported, "There's nobody behind us. "Still, Nelda was driving as though followed by ravenous dogs.

Ed didn't want to leave the house. He wanted to call the neighborhood guard service, but Marie told Gretchen facetiously, "You grab his arms and I'll take his legs. We're getting out of here." Ed took this as a clue to their reluctance to chance it with Richardson. They got into Ed's Jag sedan, and as they headed south on I-5, they looked right, left and behind them for the red Corvette. They planned to keep driving until they found a halfway decent motel. If Richardson was looking for them it would be a long time before he would figure they'd settle for one of those "no-tell motels" near the airport.

* * * * * *

When Herb got the word, he tried to reach Nelda at Sandra's home, but there was no answer. He was frightened and drove as fast as he dared to get there. Driving through the town the way you'd expect a man obsessed to drive, he didn't care if he was stopped by the police. He felt deeply how intolerable it would be to lose Nelda. He had not recovered from the loss of Myra, but now he was tied to Nelda in so many ways, her love for Melissa, her concern for Myra, her essential support for the lawsuit and something else he couldn't allow himself to think. It was there, but he couldn't think it. Now, as he raced through town, the thought of what he might find at Sandra and Joe's house hung in the air he breathed.

When he arrived, he was shocked at the sight of a Seattle PD prowl car in front of the house. His imagination conjured terrible images of harm to Nelda and Sandra.

Oh my God, no! What happened? Please, no!

He had barely stopped before the cop stepped out of the black and white and approached his car window. Herb rolled it down "Please, officer, is everything okay?"

The officer, instantly alert, challenged him. "Who are you?" The officer didn't know whether Herb was friend or foe and eyed Herb warily. Herb figured he better keep his hands in view as he explained who he was and why he was there. He felt relieved that the officer wasn't there because something terrible had happened, but to be sure it didn't. He'd knocked on the door and nobody was home, but his sergeant had instructed him to stay there in case they did come home.

Herb asked the cop to call "Detective" Tracy and find out if he had any information, forgetting the promotion. The cop, despite some reluctance, finally reached Tracy, who verified that Jodi had warned Nelda and Sandra that Richardson might be on the prowl, and they left. Tracy assured him there was no need to stay at the Joe Gold residence. Tracy's last words to the cop were, "Be sure Mr. Fletcher is safe. Have him call me direct if there's a problem."

Herb guessed Sandra and Nelda would head either south to Costello Construction or to Ed Gold's home. He hoped it would be Costello. The Epstein boys would find a place to protect them, and Richardson would have a struggle finding the Costello office to start with. That boosted Herb's confidence. He thanked the officer and headed back to his car when the officer grabbed his arm.

"No, you don't thank me. I'll thank you. My wife's pregnant, and she's going to be safer for what you're doing. One second. I'd like to get permission to follow you since nobody's home here."

At Herb's request, the officer called at Costello Construction and verified Sandra and Nelda were heading there, then called headquarters. With the officer following him at a distance, Herb headed, still a little nervous for the women, toward Harbor Island.

Seattle police were searching for Richardson's red Corvette, looking in parks, beaches, on the freeway, in town and in the neighborhoods. As night fell, every cop involved in the case swiveled his head wherever he went. Jerry Alden sat with a .45 in his lap at home. He didn't have any more trust in Richardson than anyone else. Cora would be sleeping in the guest bedroom that night. Trying to sleep, anyway. Alden, in his fear, remained on lookout and ready to shoot at the first glimpse of his son-in-law.

Al Armour wondered where he fit in Richardson's plans and if he was the target and then strapped on his shoulder holster holding a .38.

Kelly Halloran, more than any of the other Woodside doctors, had reason to fear. He put his family in the car and headed east on I-90 and figured he'd just keep driving till he decided where he'd go. Somebody must have called Eric Martens, back in Aurora, Colorado. He was keeping in touch and was glad he'd gotten out of reach. Nelda called her mother back in Des Moines to reassure her. Mrs. Fox wasn't reassured.

The press went gaga all over it. Radio stations warned the public to look out for a red Corvette with license DES 721. The story had been a sensation from the start, the trial a honey pot for the busy bees of Seattle news. With the implied threat of an imminent murder arising, everything else was crowded out of the news. People all over town were calling the police about this red Corvette or that. Red was a popular color for the car. The police ignored every call that reported the wrong license number or no license number at all.

Kevin Richardson arrived at Joe Gold's home, parked his red Corvette and walked up the steps. The S&W .38 and a steak knife remained in the glove compartment. He didn't know what he was going to do or what he was going to say. He visualized little Nelda and the very pregnant Sandra alone in the house, but somehow believed, once it came down to it, he couldn't bring himself to hurt them. He knocked on the door then twisted the handle of the old-fashioned doorbell. Despite the ringing, there still was no answer. He looked through the stained glass window of the front door and saw no movement inside. Nightmares churned in his head as he got back in the car. He realized he had to get somewhere isolated where he could think, undisturbed.

Richardson felt himself step into limitless space, no solid ground under him, no place safe, no air to breathe. He had that feeling as a youth when his parents sent him off to college before he was ready. He knew he was smarter than most everyone else, but until Cora found him, it was as if the ground was too soft to support him. He smiled at everyone, because he didn't know what else to do or say. A sophomore at the fraternity was friendly until Kevin pledged, and then the sophomore turned on him, paddling him mercilessly. He never trusted a smile after that. Now, all the world was his enemy, especially the police.

He visualized the police looking for him, all of them looking for a bright red Corvette, the one he was now driving. He knew where he would go, a place in the northwest corner of Seattle where he imagined no one would expect to find him. He headed up I-5 and onto side streets through Ballard. When he got to Golden Gardens Beach, he drove straight through the parking lot, bumping over the curb onto the furthest corner of the sand, just up from the beach.

* * * * * *

Kevin took the S&W .38 and the carving knife out of the glove compartment and laid them down on the passenger seat. He picked up a pen and note pad from the seat, sat back and pondered. Who was the person really responsible for the terrible things he had suffered? Every effort to fix blame weakened and fell apart. Cora and her dad were evil, but they hadn't killed Laura Mickens or Myra Fletcher or Cooper. He heard himself say, "I could have refused." But he answered back, "No, I couldn't. My life couldn't go on if I hadn't done what I did. It was self-defense. It wasn't me. It was the Quaaludes. I would've stopped if I could." Then came his rebuttal. "So, all you have to offer is more deaths? What happened to, "Do no harm?" The answer was inevitable. It was slow in coming, but finally, gratefully, Kevin found the answer and knew what he had to do. His heart was calm and quiet, satisfied at last.

* * * * * *

Officers Keller and Schnitzler went through the parking lot at Golden Gardens earlier in the evening, but it was a quiet night for everything but the Richardson runaway Corvette case. After making their rounds, they went through the park again. As they cruised along, Schnitzler suddenly yelled, "Stop!" and Keller almost threw him through the windshield.

"What?"

"The Corvette. Look, it's at the end of the beach for Chrissake!"

They bumped over the curb and drove up onto the sand, parked and called in, reporting they found the Corvette. They got permission to investigate and warily stepped out. Schnitzler went left and Keller right, guns drawn, running in a low crouch. They approached the Corvette from behind, hearts beating heavily, not daring to breathe. They didn't know if Richardson was armed, but they'd heard warnings for extreme caution. Rumors in the department said Richardson was a suspect in several suspicious cases involving deaths and threats. Both officers were experienced enough to assume the worst.

Felons had shot at Schnitzler before, and he wasn't anxious for someone else to be raising his children. The two cops had been together for a couple years, each trusting his life to the other. They used techniques established long ago, both in position, ready to move at Schnitzler's signal. He found a couple little rocks. They were as good as one big one. He got good hits on the driver's side window and ducked down.

Keller sprinted from the right with gun drawn and pressed it up against the passenger side window. He saw the man sitting inert in the driver's seat, slumped against the steering wheel. He couldn't see the left hand, but nothing was in the right. Keller yelled to Schnitzler, "It's okay." As they opened the doors they could see the man was dead, gray skin, blue lips, and unseeing eyes. Out of caution Schnitzler checked for a pulse. There wasn't one. The arms and upper body stiffness told him the man had been dead for some time.

The left wrist had a slight cut, rather than a slash. It must've taken many minutes for the blood to flow out, but the dry pools on the seat and floor looked like a body's entire supply. Schnitzler pondered the sight. The man had sat there watching his life dribble away, drop by drop. Schnitzler couldn't, even after all his years on the force, comprehend what he saw.

A steak knife with a little blood on it rested on the console. A note pad and a pen lay on the passenger seat. They saw some blood smears on the pad, but the note appeared to be carefully written and readable. Schnitzler knew not to touch anything inside the car once it was clear the man was beyond help. He knew the evidence they were looking at would be on front pages around the country tomorrow. Just the start of the note told them that.

"I want the world to know that whatever else I have to say about others, I take the full blame for everything I've been accused of. I didn't have to do what people told me to. I could have used my own judgment. I was the one responsible."

They shut the car door and called in what they saw. "There's a dead man in the Corvette. It must be Richardson. It looks like a suicide."

EPILOGUE

The next morning, Judge Abelson read, with distaste, the startling headlines in the morning *PI*. He feared, when *The Times* came out in the afternoon, it had to go hysterical because, after all, the *PI* got the morning scoop. No one could predict how the news might affect the jury. With trepidation, Joe and Mike went into chambers with MacCallum and Zale. Meanwhile, Diana calmed and consoled Nelda and Herb in the courtroom. Judge Abelson had carefully pondered his duty. He could declare a mistrial, but the lawyers might take him off the hook. He would be careful. Then the lawyers came out of chambers with the judge's little declaration he would read to the jury:

"Dr. Richardson has died. The news that came out this morning in the *PI* is not evidence in the case. You have all taken an oath to decide the case on the evidence admitted here and under the law as I give it to you. I previously warned you to ignore the media. If any of you are unable or unwilling to disregard this news, you should notify the bailiff immediately. You will step down and an alternate will take your place. If you don't understand any of this, let me know now. Because of the circumstances, we'll take two days off."

He appended a written note to the lawyers' copy of the declaration: "Mr. Gold, Mr. McCallum and Mr. Zale, if you need more time, let me know. We'll plan on coming back Friday morning. I will entertain your recommendations for how to proceed."

The jurors filed out after the judge read his declaration. Not a single juror so much as blinked. The foreman took them back into the jury room. Meanwhile, the red eyed Cora Richardson arrived, and MacCallum sat her down on a bench outside the courtroom, a hanky held up to her face, and he came back in.

When the judge left the bench, MacCallum and Zale stood up, and MacCallum, straight faced, handed Joe a letter. They waited while he read it. A slight smile slowly appeared. He showed Herb, with Nelda reading over his shoulder. Herb wasn't smiling. You could see the wheels turning, and he said, "Joe, we need to meet in private."

Mike, Joe, Herb and Diana walked down to the law library and took a small conference room.

Joe wondered, "Herb, do you have a problem with policy limits of both Pro-Hosp Insurance and Med-West? Now that Richardson's gone, we're in Never-Never Land. It's hard to say what can happen now. That's what they're offering, full policy limits. They could demand a new trial, and we might have to start all over again."

"I understand, but unless they agree they'll end their 'conspiracy of silence', we have to force the jury verdict. Sure, I need the money for Melissa, but we all need doctors and hospitals to be honest. Either they own up or I go all the way, even if I have to start over. That's how I feel, if you're still with me on that."

Joe looked straight into his eyes, seeing nothing but grim resolve. Joe, though impressed, shuddered at the thought of doing it all over.

Wow, that was a load. For a young guy like Herb to have that kind of guts! What have I let myself in for?

"Okay, Herb, if you demand, it I'm with you. But understand. For them to agree they'll stop the conspiracy they'll have to admit it exists. It wasn't just Richardson."

"I thought about this, Joe. From the time we started, I decided I'd take this to the end in order to make them be honest. Nothing will change my mind. In time, getting the truth out may mean more than the money."

It was a relief to Joe, when Woodside, Mrs. Richardson and the two insurance companies immediately accepted that proviso. The starch went out of Tobin, Karel and Rosen. Cora and Dr. Alden had nothing to say. They weren't going to fight on behalf of Kevin's ghost. The trial was over. *The Times* got its scoop and all's fair in love and the press.

* * * * * *

With the trial over, former detective Tracy, now Major Tracy, suggested the word "perjury" to the hospital conspirators, who thought they were impervious if they just stayed tough. He gave them a little time to evaluate their career choices, while Ed Gold was free to reassert himself on the Woodside Board. He went right to it and inquired into the ethical standards of Elliott Karel and whether he could be trusted as Quality Control Director. Karel didn't have the stomach for a fight with either Tracy or Ed and quickly resigned. Ed asked whether Franklin Tobin could preside over a hospital that didn't conceal negligence and recommended Kelly Halloran for president. Halloran's first reaction was "Hell no," followed by "Let me think about it." When he finally agreed, no one on the board, especially Tobin's friends, dared to stand up to Ed or Tracy. They could make life uncomfortable for Karel, Rosen and a few other doctors at the hospital. Ed had made his point. The story of Martens' duplicity got to Aurora, Colorado via Tracy, and he was out of a job. The insurance companies finally caught on to the possibility the "conspiracy of silence" might encourage more malpractice than it concealed. Eventually, based on a reduced loss experience, they lowered their rates.

Nelda exposed Alden's involvement in the house break-in when she recognized him at a coroner's hearing. There had been something familiar about the man who broke the backdoor window. When she made the connection, the police brought Alden in for questioning and took his fingerprints, which matched the doorknob prints. The prosecutor offered him the choice of going to trial on attempted murder or pleading to burglary. He took the lesser deal and went straight to jail with people he'd never talk to voluntarily. Cora disappeared from the State of Washington with her partner, Louisa, and was never seen again.

In *The Seattle Times,* Al Setser did a weeklong series on the case and his heroes, the courageous Nelda and Herb and the tireless Gold Law Firm, especially Joe. It wasn't as if the firm needed more press and more business. Even without it, the young lawyers found themselves expanding beyond anything the Carpenter Gold Law Firm ever had been. Setser put his cap on the story. *"In light of the Fletcher case, some of the hospital personnel, particularly CEO Franklin Tobin, and Elliott Karel, Quality-Control, have decided to seek employment elsewhere. The notion that hospital personnel may not disclose the failings of medical professionals seems dead in the State of Washington. But we must all stay vigilant lest the monster of a 'conspiracy of silence' appear again."*

Sandra loved the press, and Joe shrugged his shoulders. "You can't buy that kind of publicity. I guess we're going to have to add some more associates."

Sandra laughed, pointing at her bulging belly. "That's the plan." At the time, it seemed like an ironic thing for her to say. She hadn't seemed terribly thrilled with tort litigation as a career for her husband. You wouldn't think she had that in mind for her son.

The new administration at Woodside happily rehired the incorruptible Nelda, but Harry Meach, while later discussing her damage claim, shared a moment of satisfaction at a meeting with the reconstituted board. He informed them pretty soon she had to take time off for a honeymoon. Meanwhile, the Epstein brothers, cutting down their own business involvement, needed a new CEO for the burgeoning Costello Construction. They picked Herb Fletcher, the obvious choice. It was no surprise he had to take time off for the honeymoon too. It had to be short, because he and Nelda couldn't bear being away from little Melissa too long.

Life returned to normal in the Gold family and law firm. Sandra bore her baby without fear or stress, a big, bouncing baby boy. His name was Sandra's idea: Oliver Wendell Gold, not Lance as they'd thought. On a festive Family Saturday at the Ed and Marie Gold home, the family welcomed the surprising choice. Diana wondered out loud, "I thought you didn't think much of trial lawyers."

Sandra owned up. "I admit it. I wasn't a big fan at one time, but I am now. I'm pretty proud to be a member of this family. My boy is going to be a lawyer. After all, it would be a crime against nature for a Gold family child not to become a lawyer."

The End

Made in the USA
San Bernardino, CA
21 December 2015